I0735226

WHISKEY TWIST

EDDIE ROY

WORKBOOK PRESS LLC
187 E Warm Springs Rd,
Suite B285, Las Vegas, NV 89119, USA

Website: https://workbookpress.com/
Hotline: 1-888-818-4856
Email: admin@workbookpress.com

Ordering Information:
Quantity sales. Special discounts are available on quantity purchases by corporations, associations, and others.
For details, contact the publisher at the address above.

ISBN-13:   978-1-953839-72-5 (Paperback Version)
                978-1-953839-74-9 (Digital Version)

REV. DATE: 01/07/2022

Whiskey Twist

Eddie Roy

1: Birth of the Beast

At 2:12 am June 2nd 1873 the ground shook: The shaking was brief, but violent.

It shook on both sides of the California-Nevada border. In point-of-fact the shaking was worse on the California side; but only slightly. It was what people born to the area, or those who had lived there for any significant stretch of time had come to refer to as an earthquake. Plates and pottery crashed from shelves, and pictures fell from walls, leaving the shattered remains of useful household items, as well as treasured family heirlooms scattered about for alarmed people to step on while stumbling around, dazed and confused in the dark. Fright will do that. More than a few people, taken totally unaware while sound asleep, rolled from their beds like improperly secured logs tumbling from a lumber wagon. Of course, for anyone experiencing their first earthquake, trusting the floor to be a safe, stable refuge was a natural, though flawed, expectation. Under such circumstances, most people wouldn't be likely to take the time to consider that if the bed was shaking, the floor it sat on must also be shaking.

Though the center of the quake; the point that suffered its most violent impact, *was* on the California side of the border, it was, fortunately, nearly a hundred miles from any heavily populated area, or the damage would have been much more severe. That fact wasn't known by or wouldn't have been believed by anyone near enough to that point to feel its effects even a little bit; especially those for whom it was their first earthquake experience. Most anyone who had been shaken from a sound sleep would feel one hundred percent certain that the center of the quake was directly under their bed. Any parent who'd had the misfortune of being awake pacing the floor with a restless child at that moment would be hard-pressed not to believe just as strongly that it was directly beneath their feet. Still, on the California side of the border, the quake was primarily just an inconvenience.

At the same time as the ground shook beneath the beds of a handful of newly-transplanted easterners and many surprised Californians, it shook almost as violently less than a day's ride away in western Nevada where the Whiskey Creek split in two. The violent tremor caused the face of a high rock cliff that rose almost straight up alongside the north bank of the creek to shear off like a slice of beef being cleaved from a hind-quarter. Most of the rock fell on the bank; the majority of it loose rubble that took out a lot of dense woods and nearly a dozen Bleu family stills. The Bleus awoke to an unpleasant shock at sunrise.

One large chunk of gray stone roughly the size of a freight wagon and with a shape frighteningly like that of a rough-hewn tombstone landed right dead in the center of Whiskey Creek. From then on whenever the creek was at flood level and really roaring, immediately downstream from that huge gray chunk of rock where the two streams of water came back together after being split by that stone was a whirlpool that could only be called lethal. At its highest, the water could reach well above a tall man's shoulders. And it would snatch a strong man under as quick and sure as a fresh-water sea monster. By just an hour past sunup the morning after the ground shook, the vicious whirlpool had acquired its name. The water overflowed the banks on both sides of the creek. A tow-headed boy of five who was overly curious stepped on a slippery rock while trying to get a look at the new mystery of the splashing, rotating water in the middle of the creek and was sucked in. A brave man who was riding by at the time was alerted by the shrieks of the child's mother and saw the boy whirling around like a trapped leaf in the murky swirling water. He rode into the creek and managed to grab the boy by his shirt collar and fling him to the bank. While the boy was bruised but breathing, the brave man and his horse were the first victims of the newly named 'Whiskey Twist'. Being a relative newcomer to Whiskey Branch at that time, one of Pastor Windor's first services was presiding over the burial of an empty pine box while the brave man's wife and children stood by and cried. The pastor helped dig the grave and also planted the cross that went at the head-end of it. The brave man's horse washed up drowned, and with both forelegs broken on the bank downstream the next day, but the man's body was never seen again.

The Whiskey Twist became, overnight, the thing of nightmares for every parent, grandparent, aunt, uncle, or even anyone who occasionally babysat for someone who was a parent.

The whirlpool was shown an equal amount of respect by adults fearing for their own safety. The story of the man who had disappeared for good while rescuing the little boy on the morning of the Twist's creation was never far from anyone's mind. Any fishing that was done in Whiskey Creek was done downstream from The Twist, or far upstream. Even when the creek was running low people walked near it on tip-toes as if afraid of awakening it.

In the year 1876 Whiskey Branch, Nevada was not big enough to warrant a town hall or any sort of official law enforcement, but it did have a church with the grand name of Whiskey Branch Church of our Holy Savior. The name conjured images of a cathedral in Rome, but the services were, in fact, held in the same one-room log building that served as the school. Miss Agnes Waters, a brave, adventurous widow lady in her late-seventies who had joined the wagon train approximately mid-way through its trip across the growing nation took the front spot in the room six days of the week. As Pastor Windor was quick to point out at every opportunity the church was not the building but the people; the building being only a place to keep the rain off while worshiping. Because there was, as yet, no official government in Whiskey Branch Pastor Windor found himself, by sheer default; the one who did the stepping up when stepping up was required. Once, a handsome drummer who brought his wagon full of products to Whiskey Branch in hopes of selling housewares to the ladies of the little town had said about Whiskey Branch, "This place is in the middle of nowhere." Pastor Windor had answered defensively, "No it's not, but you can see the middle of nowhere from here."

Pastor Windor certainly wasn't responsible for, or involved in, the naming of the town. That was purely the doing of the Bleu family. The Bleus were an old French Canadian family who had no-telling how long before floated down the Snake River into Washington State. They then begged, borrowed, and mostly stole their way through Oregon and into the then still young state of Nevada where theyset up camp along what they eventually started calling Whiskey Creek. It flowed from east to west, toward California, and ultimately toward the Pacific like every stream or river on that side of the continental divide. If they had named it in the early spring, after a particularly heavy snow melt or during a long rainy spell when the water level swelled over the banks and the normally dry areas for a quarter mile on both sides were swamped; Whisky River it would have been. The Whiskey part of the name came about as a result of the Bleu's profession, so to speak. The Bleus were a very strange breed of people who were good at two things; making and drinking moonshine, and marrying members of their own family. Either one of those things can be problematic. The two taken together is flirting with disaster. The most common and saddest result is meanness without the smarts to control it. The Bleu family was living, breathing proof of that fact.

Two thousand yards downstream from Whiskey Branch the Whiskey Creek split in two. There was a north branch and a south branch. The town of Whiskey Branch had grown right along the south bank of the creek for the same reason the Bleus had put their string of stills upstream along the north side of the creek for years; because the creek's water was crystal clear and tasted like liquid heaven. That was Pastor Windor's analogy. And who would question a statement like that coming from a man of God? The point where the Whiskey Creek split in two and the town of Whiskey Branch sat was less than a half- day's ride from the California border.

Three of the families living in Whiskey Branch had originally moved on west when the majority of the group coming from the east had picked the spot for the town almost at random, from the vast acreage the Federal Government was offering to homesteaders. Even before those three families went their own way it had been a small group; almost too small to qualify as a wagon train. Eight wagons made for a pretty small train. Those three families had been determined to continue on to California. Those three had also originally come from back east leaving more advantaged family situations, and so weren't in such dire financial straits. It was less than four months later that they were awakened by the ground beneath their beds shaking in the dead of night. They were amazed to find that the neighbors living around them who had lived for some time in the area seemed to hardly take notice of the trembling at all. With two of those three families hailing from Philadelphia and the third from Baltimore, they took definite notice. They sold their new properties at a no small loss and headed back to Whiskey Branch, figuring life and limb were of more importance than the dollars lost.

By 1876 the still new state of Nevada was taxing legitimate whiskey sales, which meant the Bleus were in direct and constant violation of the law with their stills and the illegal whiskey they had begun hauling into the real towns by the wagon-load and pedaling to taverns and saloons. Napoleon Bleu, patriarch of the clan, his twin daughters Millie and Lillie, and his son Napoleon Junior, or Nappy for short, were making money hand over fist.

That was the year the state tax revenue agents began combing the woods on the far side of the creek north of Whisky Branch hoping to stumble across the Bleu family's stills. It was the only plan they could come up with. As plans go it was about as fruitless as combing the woods hoping to stumble across a particular squirrel's nest. Because the Bleus were just as good at hiding as squirrels and just as uninterested in being found.

On March twenty-fifth of 1877 Toby Dove turned sixteen. In the four years since the winter that his parents had both succumbed to the typhus Toby had become an unofficial member of just about every family in Whiskey Branch. In the late 1800s much of western Nevada was still a wilderness. At least the area the Dove family's group had chosen to put down stakes was. Twelve was an awfully young age to be on one's own. Had the situation not been so sad there would have been some irony in it as Toby's father was the one who'd seen the spot where the town was planted and proclaimed that it was the place. It just felt right. Luckily for Toby, the core of the town was the group who had arrived in the original eight wagons, and to them he was already family. It was indeed a fortunate thing.

When the Dove family left Harrisburg, Pennsylvania to meet up with the other families with whom they'd communicated by letter and telegraph, they were excited and impatient.

Captain William Dove: U.S. Navy retired, his wife Gladys, their boy Toby, and daughter Cynthia made up the Dove family. In his mid-seventies, and the survivor of multiple long, challenging battles during the War Between the States, the Captain, though having been separated from the service for better than twenty years and who would now be traveling alongside men who had fought on the other side of the conflict, was itching to get moving. He said the hurry-up-and-wait mode was too much like old times. As the last-minute checklists were run and the horses were watered one last time, Gladys, always the mother, was still worrying at The Captain, with good reason, concerning Cynthia's health. At only five Cindy had always been sickly, almost continually leaning toward a congested chest. Sometimes in the spring when the blossoms sprouted it got to the point she could hardly draw a breath. And she'd catch a cold or the croup at the first hint of a cool fall wind. Gladys had debated leaving Cindy with her Aunt Josie for safe keeping, rather than foolishly dragging her into the unknown wilderness of the American West.

At that point young Toby was just desperately anxious to see a cowboy, or an Indian, or a gunfight, or bank robbery, or a real saloon, or a coyote, or even a prairie dog. Having fallen under the spell of the dime novels that were so much a part of popular culture in the east, Toby was ready to see anything that was more wild west than Harrisburg, Pennsylvania. Gladys lived in constant fear of Cindy 'catching her death of cold' as the term went. In the end, that's exactly what happened to Cindy. And Toby saw all the Wild West he could ever want, and more.

Poor Cindy caught the bug her mother had dreaded before they had crossed half the country. Her passing was a terrible blow to the remaining members of the family, but especially hard on the Captain, as he felt solely at fault for not heeding more seriously his wife's anxieties about undertaking the trip.

They buried Cindy on a Sunday morning in the middle of a field of clover. Mister James Hodge, one of the older gentlemen traveling with the wagon train gave a heartfelt eulogy. The Captain was inconsolable. It was nightfall before Toby was able to convince his father to leave the graveside and accompany his mother and him back to their wagon.

Out of respect for the Doves, the remaining families in the wagon train postponed resuming their westward trek three more days until Toby and his parents again felt ready to travel. In truth, they were just as concerned about the Captain's readiness to be their guide. Of course he was never really their guide in the official sense of the word, but his military experience had imparted to him over the years an understanding of maps and figuring directions by observing the stars as well as his natural surroundings. Then, of course, there was his also his leadership skills to consider. Still, what person could go through the loss of a child without losing part of his or herself? The Captain was a fine man, and they wanted to give him time to grieve. So it was three more days before the remaining members of the Dove family pushed on westward, along with seven other wagons, carrying seven other families, but leaving Cindy behind in the field of sweet smelling clover.

In less than four weeks the eight wagons pulled up alongside

Whiskey Creek, where the water was crystal clear and tasted like liquid heaven, though it would still be a number of years before Pastor Windor made that proclamation.

Five of the eight wagons stayed right there, including the Dove Family's wagon, and planted the roots of what grew to be a town called Whiskey Branch. The other three belonged to the adventurous folks who wouldn't hear of anything except California. They had that adventurous spirit shaken right out of them a few months later, and Whiskey Branch grew again, this time by three families. At least they didn't have to get to know new neighbors who were complete strangers.

At first things went so well in Whisky Branch that the residents sometimes wondered if they might be having more than their fair share of good fortune. Or just plain good luck. The land along the creek was rich fertile soil, and just about anything they planted sprouted and grew just as though they were experienced farmers. Of course, the novice farmers didn't know of the Bleu family or that they also chose the land upstream but across the creek before where it branched to plant the corn from which they distilled their whiskey. And farther off the creek where the woods grew heavier, they hid their stills to evade discovery by the federal marshals.

The settlers from the little wagon train made their first mark on the south side of the creek when Toby was just three months short of twelve years old. It was hardly a month since he'd lost his little sister to a cold that turned into the pneumonia that took her coughing and choking in her bed in the back of the wagon, sweat soaked but trembling with chills. At one moment he would be nearly bursting with a child's excitement at finally living out the adventure he'd dreamed of. Then the next he would feel almost crushed with an adult's sadness that Cindy wouldn't be there to experience the adventure with his parents and him.

Later some of those first founders of Whiskey Branch, and also some of the more superstitious, wondered if they didn't bring misfortune down on themselves by questioning why things had been going so well for them at first. A little more than a year after the first houses went up a rash of typhus struck the settlement. Six people died in a two week period; all of them folks who were getting up in years and already infirm and unable to fight off the infection. Two of those were former Captain William Dove and his wife Gladys, leaving Toby an orphan at twelve years old. Toby knew that his father had started dying of a broken heart the day Cindy died. But those were things he spoke of to no one.

It was a sad period in the short history of Whiskey Branch when six new graves were added to the small fenced-off area where the empty coffin of the brave man who had saved the small boy from being sucked down into the Whiskey Twist was interred.

Left with no family and few others his age in the town, Toby was desperate for something to do with his time. He read and reread his father's Navy manuals till he could almost recite them from memory. One day while searching through an old trunk for more reading material he came across his father's Colt Navy service revolver. It was in its holster, with the gun belt wrapped around it. Then it was wrapped in a white cloth and tucked carefully in a corner of the trunk. Upon unwrapping it Toby could smell gun oil. When he touched the cylinder his fingers came away slightly wet with it. Digging deeper in the trunk, he found four cartons of cartridges for the gun. He actually knew nothing about what he had found except it was a gun, and it had been his father's.

The next morning at dawn, after spending the entire night feeling like he'd done something wrong by snooping in his late parent's trunk, he went to the edge of the woods and stepped far enough into the trees to be out of sight from any of the houses and strapped on the belt with the gun in the holster. He didn't know what he looked like, but he instantly felt ten feet tall. He wondered if his father had felt like that every day when he strapped on the gun while on board his ship. His father had retired from the service before Toby was born, but he suddenly felt closer to him than he ever had felt in his life. He wished he could know something about the gun, but had no idea how he might learn. If he'd guessed forever he would never have guessed right.

At dawn again the next morning Toby stood at the edge of the woods with the gun in the holster, facing an imaginary Indian hiding behind a particularly large oak tree about twenty yards away. Glancing around to see if anyone was nearby, he made a clumsy attempt to draw the gun. It turned into more of a grab than a draw, and he barely avoided dropping the gun to the dirt and leaves. Then a voice from close behind him said, "Careful, Toby, a 36 caliber Colt is a fine gun. It'd be a shame to see it on the ground." The voice so startled him that he again nearly dropped the gun. Toby turned around and saw Pastor Windor was standing behind him. Toby said, "It was my father's." It was all he could manage. Pastor Windor said sincerely, "Then that makes it more than just a fine gun. It's a sacred object."

"Do you know more about it?" Toby asked. The pastor nodded.

"Will you teach me?" he was nearly pleading.

"Why do you want to know?" Pastor Windor looked at him narrowly.

"Because it was his."

"Good answer."

The following afternoon Pastor Windor and Toby walked together to a long, narrow field a quarter mile from the main street of town and the pastor began showing Toby how to handle the revolver; beginning with the proper way to wear the gun-belt. The next day he taught him how to safely load the gun, and explained the basics of the weapon's operation. He said, "Toby, this particular Colt was called a Colt Navy. It's an excellent gun, but one of the most important things to remember about this model is that it uses what they call paper cartridges. That's because the wadding between the slug and the powder is paper. That means you can never let your bullets get wet. Once they're wet, they're useless. That's why naval officer's gun belts were designed to ride unusually high on the hip, to help prevent cartridge wetting if a ship's deck was awash in a storm.

The following day Pastor Windor walked to the far end of the field, bending down to pick up small sticks and palm-sized stones which he put in a pocket as he went. He lined them up on a fallen tree trunk then walked back to Toby, counting his steps as he walked. "That's about thirty yards." He looked back at the line of things he'd placed on the tree trunk. "Let me have the gun belt Toby."

"The gun, too?"

"Please." Toby took off the belt and handed it to Pastor Windor. He cinched it around his waist. It was a tight fit. It took some effort to buckle it. "Your father wasn't a big man?"

"He sure looked big to me."

"Of course he did." The pastor adjusted the belt, tied the leather thong at the bottom of the holster around his leg, then straightened up and faced the far end of the field. Then so fast Toby's eyes saw only a blur the gun was out of the holster and sent out a series of thunderclaps and the sticks were splinters flying through the air and the stones disintegrated into clouds of dust being carried away by the wind blowing from the direction of Whiskey Creek. A narrow thread of smoke drifted from the end of the gun barrel.

His ears ringing, Toby's mouth opened and closed, but all he could say was, "Wow." Then after a moment he managed, "That was amazing!"

"It was okay for a strange gun," Pastor Windor said. Toby could tell he wasn't being modest, simply stating fact.

"Can you teach me to do that?"

The pastor closed his eyes as though in thoughtful deliberation, or maybe prayer. "Let me think on it," he said after a long moment.

"When will you know?" Toby asked impatiently. Then, realizing he sounded like a child, said, "I'm sorry."

Pastor Windor said, "We'll talk in the morning." Then he calmly pulled the long coat he always wore over the gun belt, and turning, casually walked toward town. Toby followed. As they walked, Toby asked, "How did you learn to shoot like that?"

Without looking back, Pastor Windor said only, "I wasn't always a pastor."

By the day twelve-going-on thirteen-year-old Toby had happened upon his late father's Colt in the early autumn of 1873, Whiskey Branch had shown little change from the collection of families who first pulled their tiny wagon train into a row along Whiskey Creek. A handful of simple unpainted or whitewashed wooden buildings had sprouted up along the dirt path, now christened 'Creek Street' that ran between Whiskey Creek and where the original row of wagons had set. Some of the settlers had put in gardens, many fairly large, and were breaking their backs working at a pace that proved they were dead serious about it. They were in it for the long haul. At the one end of the unnamed street was the Dove family's wagon; though it was hardly recognizable. Toby's parents had died so soon after arriving at the settlement that they hadn't even started to build a house. They'd still been living out of their wagon. When they passed away, the neighbors immediately jumped in to help. In a matter of months they made the wagon into a regular home. Its wheels were taken off and set aside. It was up off the ground on carefully laid up stones. The canvas top had been replaced with board walls and a pitched roof. One of the ladies had even sewn up an entirely acceptable straw-filled mattress for Toby to sleep on. He had enough blankets and quilts to keep a small army warm through the winter. Some of the menfolk claimed they were jealous of the boy.

Within another year, at the opposite end of the dirt street from Toby's wagon-house was the log building that was Whiskey Branch's first, and by then only, place of business; Grayson's General Store. At that early stage in the town's history, the store was as much a hope as a paying concern. Ben and Katelin Grayson were one of the youngest couples in town. They hailed from Maryland. Ben had no idea of his heritage except that as far back as any family member he'd spoken to could recall they'd always been farmers working their fingers to the bone. Katelin, on the other hand, was second generation Irish and would be proud to inform anyone of the fact.

Still in their late twenties, they were full of youthful energy. They had cleared the spot for the building in what seemed like no time at all, and Ben scratched out the plan on the ground. After that it was more like an old fashioned barn-raising; everybody had a hand in it. Once it was up, it started out as sort of a town hall. Folks would come to share a meal and the latest news. Then people started bringing things to trade; crops they'd grown, clothing they'd made, or game they'd shot, and the like. The Grayson's name went on the front because it was their idea and because they were fortunate enough to have come west with a little more folding money than most. So; they were most able to bankroll a growing business. After a month or two Ben started making trips every couple weeks to Sweetwater, the nearest established town, about seven miles north. He began coming back with some actual stock for the shelves. It turned out he also had a knack for haggling. He met folks along the way and made some contacts on his trips to town, and soon he had a couple milk cows and even a pair of goats. Presently a sign showed up on the front of the store saying that fresh milk would be six cents a quart, except for families with babies; for them it would be three cents a quart. The sign didn't say that for families with babies but without the three cents the milk was free, but it happened more than once, mostly on the days Kaitlin was working. Ben also sometimes served as a very informal broker, more of a go-between, and found some farmers on the way to Sweetwater who remembered how hard it was to start out and could see their way clear to sell some seed and even a head or two of cattle and saddle horses at prices other people starting from scratch could manage. With the help of a few of the men of

Whiskey Branch he led what may have been the smallest cattle drive in the history of the American north-west. Thus some of the settlers of Whiskey Branch became cattle owners, with dreams of one day being real ranchers.

Less than eleven months later Luther Wilson put up his livery stable and dug a pit for a forge. Luther was the only black man in town. A powerfully built man made of solid muscle, Luther could pass for a small mountain if he stood still for any amount of time. His was the most interesting story of any resident of Whiskey Branch.

Luther was a former slave who had learned blacksmithing while he was still the possession of a wealthy landowner in Virginia. By sheer coincidence that stately southern gentleman and patriarch of the family passed to his great reward some five years before President Lincoln signed the papers declaring the portion of Virginia he lived in was officially part of the new state of West Virginia. But it was pure fact that the majority of the state's residents had made that decision for themselves during the war. The President the old man so despised had already signed papers saying slavery was at an end in the great country of The United States of America. That had been all the motivation required for the two daughters and son who were the old man's heirs and who had always been of an abolitionist way of thinking to send Luther and their father's other slaves on their way with their best wishes. It was a situation that would have had the old man spinning in his grave; had he known. Luther had grown up with and was a close friend of the son, and so was given a gift of the son's white stallion saddle horse Luther had always particularly admired, as well as a wagon and a hitch of good horses, and a grubstake to get him started. Though Luther was the size of a bear he was as pleasant and gentle as could be; unless angered. Once the stable was up and the forge was in good working order he started hammering out useful iron items and shoeing horses with the aid of a bellows Toby helped him put together using the staves and canvas from the wagon in which his family had crossed the country. It was all done by following drawings he found in one of his father's old Navy manuals. While chatting one Sunday afternoon when services were over, Luther told Pastor Windor, "That Toby is the smartest damn kid I ever seen. Pardon my French."

As Toby continued to grow and change, so did Whiskey Branch and the area around it.

Things were happening across the creek, over on the north side; things that didn't bode well for the town of Whiskey Branch. The state and county lawmen, backed up by Federal Marshalls were constantly pounding their way through the woods on that side of the creek searching for any sign of the Bleus or their stills. By applying pressure on some of the bootlegger's known customers and spreading some cash around they'd gotten a rough idea where to look. But so far, all they'd accomplished was to make the Bleus dig deeper into the woods, like a tick working its way deeper into a dog's fur to hide and do its damage out of sight.

At first it was only someone catching a brief glimpse of a figure moving around in the trees across the creek. Then one bright sunny morning Luther was dumping some ashes in a ditch behind the livery. He happened to look across the creek at just the right moment and caught a reflection from back deep in the space left where several pine trees had been uprooted in a recent windstorm. It really was pure chance that the sunlight was slanting over the horizon at exactly the right angle for him to spot a pinpoint of light bouncing off metal that had no earthly reason to be where it was. That could only mean one thing; the Bleus were moving closer.

Under the continued weight of the authorities constantly hounding them, the Bleu family was looking for a way to expand into safer, less conspicuous areas of operation.

Much to Toby's pleasure, as all these things were happening to Whiskey Branch; both the good and the bad, Pastor Windor, who had initially been reluctant to train Toby in the use of his father's gun, relented. So at fourteen, Toby was learning to use his father's six-gun. When Toby had asked Pastor Windor why he wouldn't teach him at first, he'd replied simply, "If you don't know how to use it, you won't use it." Then one day the pastor took Toby into his small room in the back of the building that did double duty as school and church and had a talk with him. He began with, "Toby, I have a bad feeling. The Bleus are closing in on Whiskey Branch. They want what we have."

"What's that?"

"Organization and respectability. The Marshals know that this is nothing more than a settlement of good God-fearing people who are simply trying to scratch out a life here. This would be a perfect place for the Bleus."

"For the Bleus to do what?"

"What they do best; create white-lightning out of sight of the authorities in the last place that they would be suspected."

"Here, in Whiskey Branch?" Toby asked incredulously. "Why here?"

"Well, as I said, the marshals wouldn't think of looking here. Plus we have the buildings."

"What good are the buildings to them?"

"A still will work just as well indoors as out, as long as you're careful not to catch the building on fire. You leave a door or window open a little so the fire has enough air to burn. The smoke goes up the chimney just like a cooking fire's smoke, so nothing seems strange if the Marshals or state revenue agents do look this way. And it's October now. The leaves are already starting to turn. It won't be long till they're falling. Soon it will start getting cold fast. Then the smoke will be coming from the chimneys day and night anyway. It would all appear perfectly normal to a marshal or revenue agent looking on. And the Bleus could work indoors out of the cold and snow. Imagine the still that could sit on top of Luther Wilson's forge."

"But Mister Wilson's forge is not inside a building."

"No, not really," the pastor answered. "The forge part of the blacksmith's shop isn't. But it is under a roof. And a lot of smoke pouring out from under the roof of a blacksmith's shop with a forge isn't going to raise any eyebrows. And it'd be hard to distinguish anything under that roof when the smoke is rolling, unless you're right on top of it. There could be a big still-pot boiling away in there and nobody watching from a distance would have a clue. The Bleus really have multiple reasons for wanting the town. If they take over they have our buildings not just as places to make the whiskey, but also to store their corn after they harvest it. That way they can run their stills year-round. And they'd have a good place to hide their whiskey once it's made till they sell it."

Toby couldn't believe what he was hearing. "You really think they could take over our town, and keep it a secret from the law?"

"Only if we let them." Pastor Windor went to the cot he slept on. He paused to light the lamp that hung on the wall above the bed, and then bending down, pulled out a wooden box that was nearly hidden beneath the cot. He lifted the lid, and after moving aside a well-worn bible and some clothing and a pair of boots, he took out a revolver in a holster, with the gun belt wrapped around it, just as Toby had found his father's service revolver, except this gun looked much different; meaner, more severe, if that were possible. "I don't think we should let them, Toby. What do you think?" As he said the last, he flipped back his coattails and strapped on the gun belt. It fit him like a glove. There was no struggling like there had been when he'd put on Toby's father's gun.

Stunned into silence, Toby just shook his head and stared. Pastor Windor said calmly, "I wasn't always a pastor."

"Were you a gun fighter?"

"No. Not as a profession." The answer was short and sounded very final.

Toby was fascinated by the growing mystery surrounding the unassuming man. It seemed the more he learned about him the less he knew. And of course he was the only one to have these questions. No one else in Whiskey Branch had seen the pastor draw a gun so fast the movement was almost impossible for the eye to follow and destroy ridiculously small targetsat the far end of a field.

"But I've been around my share of them," Pastor Windor said as an afterthought. "When you're around them enough you learn. It could be a matter of life and death."

Pastor Windor pulled his coat around the gun belt, and Toby took the motion to mean the subject was closed. But before leaving the little room that was his quarters he got another item from the box; a small brass telescoping spyglass about six inches long, and slipped it in a coat pocket.

That was a Friday evening. When they were done speaking Pastor Windor wrote a brief message on a piece of paper and asked Toby to deliver the message to a select few of the men in the town. He then patted Toby on the shoulder and urged him to keep practicing his draw, but said their actual shooting practice might be late tomorrow. As it had turned out, the boy was a natural. Getting the gun out of the holster in one smooth fast motion had come to him with shocking ease, the pastor thought. Getting the hammer back as part of that same action would be next. But though the next morning was Saturday, Toby's lesson would have to be put off till the afternoon if all went as he hoped it would in the morning.

The following morning, Saturday, the people Pastor Windor had asked Toby to take messages to were gathered in the back of Grayson's store. Ben and Kate were, of course there, Ben as one of those who had received the message, and Kate to provide them with a hearty breakfast; she would have it no other way. In choosing who to call together, Pastor Windor had tried to choose wisely. Knowing that he was in effect gathering a fighting force; though he prayed a fight was only a last resort, he tried to find men with military experience, but if possible, without families to be responsible for. Ben was the exception, first because his devotion to the town was obvious, and had been shown in his actions innumerable times. But also because his store was a perfect fallback position should the battle that he hoped to avoid come to be.

Once they were there, the pastor began speaking, trying to sound like a friend, not like someone sermonizing to them. There were only a few people there; but he was pleased to see that all those he had reached out to had shown up. In addition to Ben and Kate, there was Toby, whose astounding skill with his father's weapon the pastor now wished had never come to light. The boy had already lost a sister, and then both parents. If he saw the town of Whiskey Branch; his extended family, threatened you'd have to hog-tie him to keep him out of it. There'd be no way he'd just stand back and watch. Also there was Jess Ivy. Jess was a man who had managed to turn a goodly patch of acreage along Whiskey Creek into an enviable farm. It had come at a price. He'd spent most of the summer after the group arrived limping around on a crutchafter a tree he was felling came down crooked and rolled up on his left ankle. He took it in stride. He had to ask for help unloading the plow from his wagon, but in less than three weeks he was out learning to farm. He still walked with a noticeable limp, favoring his somewhat bent left leg. But he wasn't one to complain.

Pastor Windor asked him, "Jess, were you in the war?"

Jess saluted sharply and answered, "Yes sir, I wore gray, and I wore it proudly. I was with General Pope at Bull Run."

"And you're a single man?"

Jess dropped his head and whispered softly, "Yes sir. When Grant's troops came through Richmond they shot anything that moved, including my wife. I found out when I got back after the war. My wife was killed and my home burned."

I'm deeply sorry for your loss Jess," the pastor said.

"I neither expect nor ask for any apologies. It was war." Jess said.

"War or not, that doesn't make the hurt any less real. It was a time of dreadful loss, for so many. I just needed to ask the question. And, there's no need to salute, Jess.

"Yes sir, it just felt right. The salute I mean."

Luke Parker, the other man the pastor had asked to attend spoke up, "I agree sir."

Luke was a carpenter. He had helped build the majority of the houses in Whiskey Branch and done work for most of the families there. He said his greatest claim to fame was having constructed most every privy in Whiskey Branch. Everyone in town knew he was a confirmed bachelor. He often joked that he'd like to play the field, but there was no field to play in Whiskey Branch and being the town's only carpenter kept him too busy to travel. The one thing he never joked about was that he had the sad job of building all of Whiskey Branch's coffins.

"And you Luke?"

"Union Army sir," Luke said stiffly, nearly losing a difficult struggle with his right hand to keep it at his side. "New York Irish Brigade, under Major General Richardson at Antietam."

Then Luke asked him in return, "And you, sir?"

Pastor Windor dropped his hands to his sides and took a deep breath like a man trying either to relax or to forget "Well, I wasn't always a pastor."

Luke looked at Toby and lifted an eyebrow. Toby shrugged and said, "Get used to it."

"So," the pastor said looking back and forth from Luke to Jess. "I'm afraid Whiskey Branch may be facing a bad situation. I hope we can keep it small, or maybe even head it off altogether. What I need to know is whether you men can fight alongside each other instead of against each other if it comes to it. It's as simple as that."

The two men looked at each other; the farmer and the carpenter. Men who once stood on opposite sides of an invisible line that divided a nation, now deciding if they could stand together for the little town they helped carve from the wilderness.

Luke waited, saying nothing, unable to imagine what Jess had felt at discovering the senseless loss of his wife upon making it home after surviving the war.

After a few moments Jess nodded at Luke and then Luke looked at Pastor Windor and said, "What are your orders, Captain?"

"Well first of all call me Pastor."

"Yes sir." Luke snapped a salute.

"And stop saluting."

"Sorry, sir."

"And the sir isn't necessary either, just Pastor will be fine. We're all in this together. No one's in command. I may make suggestions, but they won't be orders. Okay?"

Jess was the first to manage it. "Okay Pastor, do you have any suggestions?"

"Just some questions," Pastor Windor answered Jess.

"I know you're a hunter. And from what I've heard you're a very good shot with a rifle. I hear you never miss. Have I heard right?"

Jess said, "Pastor, if you want some venison steaks, all you have to do is come out and ask."

Pastor Windor chuckled despite the seriousness of the situation, glad for the brief distraction. "No Jess. I wish it were that simple. Then he asked, "But really, how good are you? No false modesty. This isn't the time for it."

"I'm an excellent shot," Jess answered awkwardly.

Walter spoke up, "He's better than excellent, Pastor. Jess can shoot the stink off a skunk at a hundred yards."

The pastor asked Luke the same question.

"I'm good with a rifle, but I wouldn't go so far as to say excellent," he answered. But I'm good with a pistol. And when I had to be I was good at close up fighting; hand-to-hand, knife or bayonet. I hated it, but when I had to do it, I did my duty."

"That's good to know. There's no telling what may be necessary." The pastor still prayed he could keep Toby out of any upcoming confrontation. The skills the boy had worked to hone daily were untested in battle. So far the only moving targets he'd fired at were a few rabbits and squirrels, never anything that fired back. He had hoped Toby's interest in his father's pistol would lead to nothing more than a hobby. Still, he knew that there was no way Toby would stand back and watch while the Bleus and their band of moonshiners moved in and took over. The boy would have to do something about it. So for better or worse, he may have no choice but to fire at a moving target, and most likely one that was firing back. But no matter what, he intended to continue schooling the boy.

Finally the pastor turned to Luke and asked, "Luke, do you have any experience at being a spy?"

Luke looked at him like he thought he must be joking. "A spy?" he said disbelievingly. "You can't be serious."

"I'm dead serious. I don't have a doubt that the Bleus have been keeping an eye on what's happening in Whiskey Branch. It's what I'd be doing if I were them. It's true the Bleus are no good. They're trash, in fact. They're worthless, they're vile, and they're many other things, but they're not stupid. Whatever they're going to do, they're going to have a plan. And if we can find out what that plan is it could make all the difference."

"But why me? How am I going to find out what they have in mind? They're family. How will I find out anything?" Luke was baffled.

"They can't all be family," Pastor Windor explained. "I've been keeping an eye out for a while and I've spotted smoke coming up in at least eight different places along the creek upstream on the other side over the last six months or so. That's a lot of stills. Unless the Bleus are a really big family they probably have to hire on some local jack-legs to do a lot of the heavy lifting. Moonshining is pretty hard work." He paused, and then before anyone could ask added, "I wasn't always a pastor." Then he said, "Luke, the reason I think you're the man for the job, is that you've been in the military, so you can take care of yourself. And even though neither you or Jess sound like you're from west of the Mississippi, New York east is going to sound better than Richmond east when you open your mouth to ask for work. At least New York is closer to Canada. And the Bleus will pick up on that and it will matter to them."

Luke asked, "Why don't you do it? You sound like you were born here."

Pastor Windor looked uncomfortable. It was a look Toby had never seen on him and it didn't look right. The pastor had always just looked right. Toby thought back to the day that the pastor arrived in Whiskey Branch. When he'd first ridden into town on a chilly Saturday nobody had given him a second look when he climbed off his horse and went into Ben and Kate's store. Kate was the first to meet him. She had related the story in detail many times. She said later that meeting Pastor Windor was second in her memory only to her wedding day to Ben. Once in the store he'd looked around, smiled pleasantly at Kate and said, "That coffee smells like just what a body needs on a day like this. I'd be more than happy to pay for a cup. At the time Kate couldn't think of the right word to describe him, but later it came to her; he was charming. And the most unusual thing wasn't that he was charming, but that he didn't seem to be trying to be charming; he just was. She'd gone through the door into the kitchen behind the store and in a moment come back with a steaming cup of coffee which she sat on the counter and said, "No charge." Then she said, "Sorry, we don't serve food. Ben and I, Ben; that's my husband, we've been thinking about maybe putting in a little café. Just a few tables and chairs; nothing fancy," She'd added. Maybe even a saloon, some day. No gambling or saloon girls; just a place where a man can get a drink and relax. Someday maybe… when the town's grown enough to make one go."

"Don't give it a second thought. The coffee will do just fine." Then he'd leaned on the counter and started sipping his coffee.

Kate had decided she couldn't have that after the way she'd been rambling on, and dragged a chair from behind the counter. He had nodded his thanks, and then said, "Pardon me for a moment." He'd gone out and quickly returned carrying saddlebags which he hung over the back of the chair.

Kate had looked him over again then. Whiskey Branch didn't see many strangers. When one rode in, it was worth getting all the information there was to get. Gossip was one of the little town's most popular forms of recreation. But if Kate had needed to describe him to someone, she wouldn't have known where to begin. Except for his long black coat and light tan colored hat; probably made of deer hide, with an odd rattlesnake-skin band, even his clothing was nothing particularly unique. He was just an average looking man; average in height, weight, and every other obvious category. Not especially handsome, but certainly not homely, there was nothing especially noticeable about him at all. Then he'd unbuttoned the long coat and taken it off prior to sitting down. That's when he'd stopped being average; when she'd seen the white collar he wore and the pewter cross that hung around his neck.

Kate was shaken from her reverie when Ben said, "You seem to know a lot about the Bleus, Pastor. Do you know them? Or is it that they might know you?" Then he smiled, but it was a little forced. "Don't get me wrong, I'm just curious, what with you not always being a pastor and all."

"Can I say a word or two?" Kate asked. It was the first sound she had uttered since asking if everyone's breakfast was all right.

"Of course," Pastor Windor said. Everybody mumbled agreement.

"You showed up here not long after the typhus struck." Kate's voice trembled as she spoke. "We hadn't been here long. I don't mean just Ben and me, the whole bunch of us. None of us knew what we were doing. Not a one of us. We were scared to death *before* the typhus. We were easterners in a new place wondering what we'd gotten ourselves into. Then we started losing people that were like family to us; people we crossed damn near the whole country with. And poor little Toby." She paused, then went on, "Course he ain't so little now, he did lose family, all the family he had left. And right on top 'a' losing his little sister on the trip." She walked over and hugged Toby. It wouldn't be long till he was as tall as she was. "Now understand, I'm not saying all this to drag out the bad memories. I'm just saying that you came along at just the right time to keep this settlement going. You may have kept it alive. I recall you showed up on a Saturday, introduced yourself, and visited the people who were sick and dying and prayed over them, then held a church service the next morning." Kate paused and wiped her eyes. "What I'm meaning to say is, short of barbecuing small children and selling them to the Indians I don't care what you did before you were a pastor."

"Well Katelin, I can assure you I didn't make meals out of people, young or old. But I get your meaning, and I thank you for it."

Jess said, "Pastor, though I feel pretty sure Kate's exaggeratin' a whole lot with her example, I think when it comes to her meaning' I believe it's safe to say she speaks for all of us."

Luke said, "Yep. Okay Pastor, sir. Sorry, that sir just slipped out. Well what is it you suggest that I should do? How do I go about getting in with the Bleus?"

"Well, I suggest the next time Ben goes to Sweetwater for supplies and stock for the store you go along. Sweetwater Crossing is a good ways downstream, so if you hunker down under the tarp in case any of the Bleu clan is out hunting or just loafing around town you should be okay. But you don't want to let any of them see you till you show up looking for work. You want it to look like you came across them by accident. We don't want them to think that you are from the Federal Marshals or even worse, from here. Of course it won't be very comfortable traveling."

"That's no problem. I've been uncomfortable before. It don't bother be none."

"Good. Then you hop out before you get to Sweetwater and work your way back to their territory, just a regular guy, nobody out of the ordinary. A typical out of work bum, more or less. You think you can play the part?"

"To a T," Luke answered. "I just have to remember back to when I was young."

"Good. I like a man with experience. Stay off the road. Keep as deep in the woods as you need to. It'll be close to a half a day's walk so take a pocket full of jerky or a couple apples or something like that with you. I'm afraid you'll have to make due with whatever water you can find. Make sure you come out upstream, in the area of their stills. We don't know where the family calls home, but we do know roughly where they produce their product. Oh, and dress like a drifter, like somebody who doesn't know where his next meal's coming from."

"In other words, someone whose willing to do anything for some grub, legal or not," Luke said.

"Exactly, and, be aware that you're far more likely to walk up on one of the hired flunkies I talked about than one of the family. If so, don't talk too much. Just say you've been on the road a long time, and that you're hungry and looking for work. Hopefully they'll take you to the one who does what passes for the thinking. Then if we're lucky you'll get a chance to hear what they have in mind, and you can slip back across the creek and let us know so we can prepare and head them off. Hopefully we'll have time to clue the marshals in. If it does come down to a fight they have way more firepower than we do."

"So when do you suggest I should get on with this plan, Pastor?"

Pastor Windor looked at Ben. Ben said, "I'm getting low on a few things. I could make a trip in the morning." Then he turned to Luke. "What do you think?"

"Would you normally go on a Sunday?"

Ben said, "Probably not, but I thought we'd want to get a jump on things. You know, find out all we can, as fast as we can."

Pastor Windor said, "We do, but we're sending Luke into the lion's den. We don't want to risk getting the Bleu's wind up by changing your regular routine. They may be more familiar with what's happening on our side of the creek than we know. They may even recognize him. It depends on how close a watch they've been keeping on what's been going on over here. We're up to better than sixty people here now, even not counting the kids. That means there's only a one in sixty chance that they've taken notice of Luke before. Those don't sound like bad odds. Still, I don't think we should press our luck." He paused and nodded at Luke. "Rather, your luck. I think Monday would be soon enough.

Sounds like a plan to me," Luke said. Then he asked, "Come to think of it, why don't I just ride into one of their camps on horseback? Why should I walk in? Won't that make it seem like I came from somewhere close, like here?"

"Hopefully nobody will ask. But if someone does, being on foot may be to your advantage. Again, keep it simple. The less detail you have to recall, the less likely you are to slip up. If you're asked, you were riding a stolen horse, and were being chased by the man you stole it from and a sheriff. You got down on a patch of rocky ground a few miles north of Sweetwater and slapped the horse to lead them off with a false trail. You've been on foot ever since. That puts you on the wrong side of the law, just like them. That's a good way to start a relationship. It can't hurt your chances of being accepted." Pastor Windor stopped speaking as if putting a period at the end of a sentence. Then he said, "What do you think?"

"I think you're pretty good at this."

Pastor Windor looked at Kate, who was sitting silently, with her hands clenched in her lap. Her lips were squeezed tightly together and the color had drained from her face.

"Are you okay Kaitlin?" he asked gently. She nodded, but the look on her face said something different. Finally she said, "I'm feelin' like we're sendin' them *both* into the lion's den! Kate's Irish background showed itself most when she was angry or stressed as she was at that moment. Ben had often said it was her distinctive Irish brogue that had first caught his attention. It was something she had picked up from spending so much time with her Irish-born grandparents while growing up. Ben took her hand and said, "It's okay Katie darlin' we'll just do some extra knocking." Kate actually managed a strained smile, and then explained, "My Da said when he was a lad in Dublin folks would knock on wood after some good fortune came along to thank the little people for bringing them good luck."

"The leprechauns," Ben added to clarify. "After a while, people started knocking *before* taking on something hard, or *dangerous* as a way of askin' in advance for good luck," Kate finished.

Jess said, "Don't worry Katie. There won't be an undented piece of wood in Whiskey Branch till they get back." Pastor Windor said, "With all that knocking and some kneeling, I'm sure they'll be okay."

That afternoon the pastor and Toby went to the field where they normally would have been at dawn. Before starting, he said, "Toby, it hasn't been long since hundreds, maybe thousands of boys not much older than you were forced to go off to war and fight like men. It's not right that a situation like this should be looming over this town. I'll do what I can, but it may not be enough." He closed his eyes and raised his head, as if looking upward through their lids. Then he wiped his hands on his pants and got down to business. "Toby, so far you've had the luxury of pre-cocking your gun before holstering it. That was so you could get used to drawing it and shooting fast. That was nice for practicing. And you've gotten fast at drawing and hitting what you're aiming at. But in the real world; the world you should try to walk away from if you can, pre-cocking your gun and holstering it just isn't going to work. It can even be dangerous if you happen to drop the gun, unless you keep the hammer on an empty chamber. I've even known of a pre-cocked gun going off in a man's holster when a curious small boy decided to grab at it." A dark cloud seemed to pass over the pastor's face when he said the last. "So you're not going to be walking around with your gun in your holster cocked. That means because your father's gun is single action you always have to pull the hammer back before the first shot, as you're drawing. That rotates the cylinder and puts a cartridge under the hammer. I'll teach you how. And Toby, you'll have to practice till that hammer-cock and draw move is as natural as breathing."

He paused and sighed deeply. "I've got a real bad feeling Toby. There's no telling what the Bleus will pull, or how far they're willing to go. If you ever come up against a real gunman, he'll most likely have a double action gun. All he'll have to do is draw and pull the trigger.

"Is your gun double action?"

"Yes."

"But you said you weren't a gun fighter."

Professional gunfighters aren't the only ones with double action pistols. They're common enough, and they can make Napoleon Bleu's hired thugs all the more dangerous. If he's been able to get them, that is. The Federal Marshals have probably been keeping a close eye on gun movement in the area. Still if he wants them bad enough he'll find them. They say 'where there's a will there's a way'. So it's important to be prepared.Some of the fastest guns ever have used single actions like yours. The best way to survive a gun fight is to avoid it. But if you can't do that, and you have no choice, you must be ready." The dread in the pastor's voice was genuine. After the pastor showed him how, Toby practiced his draw and cock move till dusk.

Two mornings later; Monday morning, as a rooster crowed somewhere in the distance Ben drew a tarp taut over the back of his wagon. Kate came from the store's door and kissed him and said goodbye. She looked terrified. As the rooster crowed again Pastor Windor walked up and said earnestly, "Get going before that cock crows a third time." Ben climbed up and flicked the reins as quickly as he could. The wagon pulled out for Sweetwater with Luke lying belly-down beneath the worn, dusty tarp tied across the wobbly plank sides. There were a dozen strips of dried deer jerky in one hip pocket and a small but full and tightly capped flask of legitimately purchased sour mash whiskey in the other. The whiskey was one of the items Ben sometimes returned with on his buying trips, and may, in fact, be restocking on today's trip. As always, Ben had a full canteen of water beneath his seat. But on this trip he also had a second which he would pass to Luke before he exited the wagon to take off on his mission. Ben wished he hadn't heard the tremble in Kaitlin's voice as she said goodbye. Until then he hadn't really felt much anxiety about the plan till he realized how scared she was for him.

In the back, Luke held a bandana over his mouth and nose in an attempt to filter out the dirt that was stirred up as the wagon was jostled over the rough road. He made a mental note to remind Ben to sweep his wagon out more thoroughly between trips. Then again, after his last inventory run Ben had no idea he would soon be hauling a spy. He remembered that Ben sometimes hauled fertilizer, and that was a recollection he could have done without. He wondered if they'd run into the Bleus or any of their gang once they crossed Whiskey Creek at Sweetwater Crossing. It would put them on the north side of the creek; the Bleu's side, at least a good five miles downstream from where they'd seen signs of their stills. But there was no telling how spread out they might really be. Luke longed to have his six-gun on his hip where he was used to it being but he knew he wouldn't have been able to stand having it jammed against his body as he was tossed around helplessly as the wagon bounced along the badly rutted road. Also, allowing the gun to be fouled by the dirt he was lying in would be unwise. Instead his gun was in its holster, and wrapped in its belt under Ben's seat, where he could quickly hand it off when Luke hopped out. As the wagon rolled along he patted the bulge in his pocket that was the small telescope Pastor Windor had given him. It wasn't his Colt, but it made him feel good. No matter what the man had been before he was a pastor, Luke had faith in him.He hoped that was a good sign; having faith before the real trouble started, if there was going to be any trouble that was. Luke remembered when he was small that his mother used to say, somewhat sadly; "Faith seems to come only when we have no other choice."

When the wagon was nearly out of sight Pastor Windor turned to walk toward the center of town and found that Toby was standing beside him watching it fade into the distance in the morning sun, its shape gradually growing less distinct behind the cloud of dust hanging in its wake. Toby lifted a hand and waved though there was no chance of it being seen with Ben concentrating on driving the horses and Luke hiding beneath the tarp. Pastor Windor saw the gesture and thought it seemed very sad and he felt certain he recognized anxiety in it that a boy of Toby's age shouldn't have to be experiencing. Especially after all the losses the boy had already suffered in his young life. It made a level of anger well up in him that he hadn't felt in a long time. He flipped the tail of his coat back and checked his gun belt to be sure it was right. Then he and Toby started to their field to practice.

But before they were a half-dozen yards from the store they heard what sounded like a shriek of pain combined with a loud grunt of effort. The sound came from the direction of the center of town and before it had faded away it was overlaid by the slapping of running feet on dry ground and the panting of labored breathing and Walter Denborough came charging up the dirt street toward them. Alerted by the uncommon shriek that had shattered the morning quiet Kate rushed from the store just as Walter reached Toby and the pastor. Toby was the unfortunate one he got to first. Walter was a big labor-hardened lumber-man. He lifted Toby bodily and shouted at him, "It's Mildred, she's come due!"

Toby stared wide-eyed at Pastor Windor with his arms hanging at his sides and his feet off the ground.

Pastor Windor looked at him and explained, "Missus Denborough is having a baby."

"Oh, "Toby said, hanging helplessly in mid-air.

Kate said, "Walter if you put Toby down the boy could go and get Doc Forrest. He's sure not doing Mildred a speck of good hanging there. And calm down for God's sake."

"Yes'm." Walter lowered Toby gently to the ground and said, "Sorry Toby."

"No harm done."

Toby took off like his feet had wings to the small log house of Doctor Clayton Forrest.

Doc Forrest lived in a house that set dead in the center of town. When he'd first pulled into Whiskey Branch about three years after the original eight wagons called dib's on their patch of ground along Whiskey Creek and introduced himself to the residents he was immediately welcomed with open arms. That was before Pastor Windor had joined what would eventually become his flock, so when asked whom he should first speak to he was directed to Ben Grayson who was taken totally by surprise and assumed he'd received the honor because his store room was large enough to hold some sort of town meeting. Then he had to decide if he should call one. After discussing the situation with Kaitlin and having a long talk with Doctor Forrest, he did precisely that. The next evening everyone who wished to meet Doctor Forest was there.

Originally from Connecticut, Doctor Clayton Forrest had served in the Union Army as a medic for nearly the full duration of the war, leaving a successful practice as a surgeon and general M.D. to enlist while in his mid-thirties.

Doctor Forrest was unmarried, and had no family at home in Connecticut when the war finally ended. The doctor had bought a two-horse and wagon rig and started traveling to the towns and areas that were decimated during the terrible conflict trying to bring some relief from the misery and suffering of those who had fought on either side. Once while traveling he saw a snake-oil salesman in one town selling dollar bottles of miracle elixir that he said would cure anything. He knew that the elixir was nothing more than grain alcohol with some cloves or mint mixed in to take the edge off. He wondered if he should paint Doc Forrest's Traveling Medicine Show on his wagon. But he knew that he had no medicine to cure the ills and horrors inflicted by the war just past. Only God could do that, and sometimes it seemed God had taken a few years off. And he didn't think any amount of even that phony's magic elixir would make him forget the things he'd seen in the battlefield hospitals. So he traveled, mending up Union and Confederate soldiers alike, doing as President Lincoln ordered; "Binding up the nation's wounds."

He eventually ended up in Kansas. Kansas was a border state during the war. He found that emotions still ran high in Kansas. He was welcome as long as he was treating the southern men and boys who had returned home shot up. But he had once received an enthusiastic beating for treating a young man with lingering gangrene in his left foot when it was found out the man had moved from up north and had once been a drummer for the Union Army. The doc had also on one occasion barely avoided being tarred and feathered. Thanks to the intervention of a grizzled old sheriff who took to heart his oath to protect and serve, he'd escaped that fate.

That close call precipitated Doctor Forrest's decision to return to private practice. While no genius, he was smart enough to know that a dead doctor can heal no one.

So after a great many miles, and more than a few close calls, Doctor Forrest and his third pair of horses rolled into Whiskey Branch, Nevada, a middle-aged man, gray before his time, worn and aged by the years of misery and suffering he'd seen and experienced, as well as the pain he'd endured for trying to help alleviate the suffering of others. He was looking for a place to put down roots and hopefully treat patients who were simply ill, not ruined in battle. From the moment he pulled his medical school diploma from his bag and Ben read it before the gathered residents of Whiskey Branch, Doc Forrest knew he was home. Afterwards, his hand was shaken till his shoulder hurt. By the time the gathering had broken up Luke Parker had already promised to meetwith him about putting up a house for him once he'd picked out a spot, and he also said he knew a couple of good places that might be worth a look. One was right plumb in the center of town; just the spot for a doc's office. And there were a dozen people with mysterious aches and pains that needing looking at. And it sure felt grand.

In the year since the evening of that hastily called meeting in Ben's store Doc Forrest had set a sizable number of broken bones; not at all surprising in a town where most everybody is a farmer or a lumber-man. He also helped a lot of people through colds and the flu, and brought ten babies into the world, an equal number of boys and girls; not including the one Mildred Denborough was on the verge of delivering. Hers would be the tie breaker. So in the previous year he'd assisted in increasing the population of Whiskey Branch by ten souls, soon to be eleven; based on the way Mildred sounded. The lady did have quite a set of pipes on her. Doc grabbed his bag.

As Doc was hurrying out the door, Toby rushed up on his porch. The Doctor nearly bowled him over in his rush out of the house. Startled, Toby thrust his hands out before him, knocking Doc off balance and nearly causing him to tumble over backwards into his own front door. Reflexively, Doc reached out and grasped Toby's shoulders to catch his balance, unintentionally lifting Toby's feet off the boards. Toby shook his head and said, "Doc, Missus Denborough is having her baby." Then he added, "I don't remember people ever picking me up when babies were born before.I hope it's not going to be happening every time."

"Thanks Toby. I thought that was her. That's just the way she sounded before the last one. This will be two I've delivered for her in the year I've been here; the first only a week after I rode into town. And she had a two year old and a four year old when I moved here; both girls. Apparently Walter is resolute in his desire to have a son, and won't give up. I don't know where the lady finds the time to care for them." He shook his head as he started down the steps.

"Well," Toby said, "I'd say Mister Denborough should find time to help. It sure sounds like he finds time before hand."

"That's an excellent point, Toby. You're a young man wise beyond your years. That will serve you well, if you don't grow out of it. Please try not to."

As Toby bounced down the steps much more quickly and easily than the doctor had he said, "Okay Doc, I'll try not to." He started to follow the doctor, who looked over his shoulder and said, "That's okay Toby, I believe I can handle this one on my own."

As it turned out the Denboroughs had twins, a boy and a girl; the first twins ever born in Whiskey Branch. It did nothing for breaking Doc's tie but it made the Denboroughs happy. Walter could look forward to the time he would have a son to help him with his lumber business, and even sooner Mildred would have another girl to help sweep up and dispose of the remarkable amount of sawdust and wood shavings Walter managed to carry in with him every evening.

Though the birth of the Denborough twins did nothing to break Doc Forrest's tie, it did bring about another very positive result, in an unusual and roundabout way. And even in that Pastor Windor had a hand.

The morning before the twin's christening Walter and Pastor Windor were talking over a cup of coffee. Walter said, "I hope Mildred will be a little calmer with the twins."

"What do you mean?" Pastor Windor asked.

"Well, fact is, she yells at the older girls something awful. She never mistreats them; she'd die first. I mean, she gives them an occasional swat on the butt when they need it; but only when they really need it. I only wish she could hold her temper when it comes to the yellin'. Bout drives me crazy. But it does make the girls listen, and they love her to death, in spite of all of her yellin.'Yep, they worship the ground she walks on. Follow her around like a couple little pups, they do."

Pastor Windor said, "Mother is the name for God on the lips and hearts of little children."

Walter closed his eyes and sipped his coffee. When he opened them again they were brimming with tears. He said, "You sure have a way with words Pastor. Was that from The Bible?"

"No, that was said by a British writer named William Makepeace Thackeray. You should read his works."

Walter shrugged, and peering shamefacedly into his cup said, "Can't read. I just cut the trees and saw the boards. Mildred does the paperwork. It's always been that way."

"Pastor Windor said, "Well Walter, maybe we'll talk to Miss Agnes and see if she would be willing to take you on as a student. It's never too late, you know. If that's something you're interested in doing, of course. Nobody else would have to know, if you prefer it that way. It would be totally up to you. Possibly in the evenings after her regular class lets out and you're done at the mill. There's a whole world out there just waiting to be seen and explored in books."

And so; because of the birth of the twins, their father learned to read.

On the North side of Whiskey Creek:

As the air began to take on more of an autumn chill and the days grew shorter the leaves turned first a golden color, and then brown before beginning to fall, rapidly covering the forest floor with a thick mat of what was at first a moist spongy residue. As the fallen leaves began to dry up the men tending the nine stills the Bleus had operating along the north bank of Whiskey Creek had begun carrying extra buckets of water up from the creek, in addition to the water they needed to make the product. They couldn't chance a spark or a stray ember from one of their distilling fires setting off a blaze in the leaves. If that happened and a flame touched off the hundreds of gallons of grain alcohol the Bleus had stored up, all nine of the stills and all of the men working them would be gone just like in the nitro explosions that sometimes happened in the mines down in California. There wouldn't be anything left behind but a big scorched patch of earth. So there was always a large tub of water kept full to the brim within quick bucket-brigade reach of the still. And it wouldn't be many weeks before one of the men would have to keep a watch on the tub and be ready to break up a crust of ice if one formed on top of the water. Working the stills was a miserable way to keep your belly full, and the Bleus paid as close to nothing as they could manage and they treated the men like that was just what they were worth. Most everybody who broke their backs carrying corn from the lean-tos back in the woods and carrying the moonshine in the opposite direction was a drifter or cow-poke who had heard about the Bleu's family business while hoping to hit it big playing poker in Sweetwater, or while pausing for a conversation somewhere on the road and then deciding to take a shot at putting together a grubstake by building fires or carrying jugs. Each of them was simply biding his time, using up a piece of his life doing something he hated, each and every one of them just like the other, including the new guy, Luke.

He was just like the other twenty-two men; all of them worked like the slaves had not too many years ago, before the war. Luke slept wrapped in a U. S. Army blanket the Bleus supplied, under a tent stenciled with the Confederate stars and bars. Luke had no clue with which side the Bleus had sympathized during the war, if either. But they obviously didn't care from whom they bought shelter for their worker drones, now that the war had ended. The other men who shared the makeshift work camps weren't big on small-talk. But Luke did get a feel of what the Bleu family was all about from some of the old-timers when somebody's lips got loosened up by a dose of hundred proof liquid-warmth. The general consensus was that Napoleon would buy threadbare flea infested horse blankets if it was the cheapest way to keep them alive long enough to produce the winter's yield. The tents were pitched close enough to the stills for the cooking fires to do the double duty of distilling the mash and keeping the men in the tents from freezing to death. That also kept the men near enough to the stills to assure that the stills and the product didn't go untended. The Bleus were far more concerned about their whiskey than the men who made it. Luke was glad it was just mid-October and the real cold hadn't set in yet. Plus, a fluke string of sunny days had knocked down the chill a little bit. Even so, he wouldn't be the least bit disappointed if he could find out what he needed to know right soon and slip back across the Whiskey Creek some evening not long after sunset, before the night had a chance to leech all the day's warmth from the water. Though he intended to try, he didn't think he'd be able to come up with a solid excuse for walking to one of the real crossings, like Sweetwater Crossing, so it looked like going home would probably mean wading across the creek or stealing a horse. And he had to stay well away from The Twist. Ending up somewhere a quarter mile downstream drowned like a rat wouldn't do Whiskey Branch a scrap-a-good, as his Ma' used to say. One thing that was working in his favor so far was that even on a bad day, and without trying hard, he was a gem of a worker compared to the majority of the ne'er-do-wells who made up most of Napoleon Bleu's workforce. That hadn't gotten him any closer to Napoleon himself. It seemed 'The Old Man', as everyone referred to him, at least in private, lived in a real house back in the woods. But

Luke's reputation as a strong and dependable worker had gotten him an unrequested but fortunate introduction to the twins; Lillie and Millie.

One sunny, fairly warm morning Luke was bent over stoking the fire under the still he'd been left to keep watch over while Jacob, the old reprobate he was forced to share a tent with, hauled the previous day's yield to a lean-too back up in the woods. He was suddenly startled to hear someone moving in the dry leaves behind him. Jerking to an upright position and spinning around, his hand went to the gun on his hip. He had expected to see Jacob or another of the men who worked the stills. Instead there were two women standing motionless at the edge of the woods. They stood side-by-side. They were obviously twins, and though they appeared to be in their early to mid-forties they were dressed alike in calico dresses and had their ratty looking, gray-laced dark hair twisted up in nearly identical pigtails. The result was that they were equally unpleasant to look at. Luke immediately knew they must be the Bleu sisters he'd heard about. He'd heard only that Napoleon Bleu had twin daughters, not that they looked like a pair of creepy, middle-aged china dolls. Of course it was totally possible that the intoxicated man who'd told him of their existence hadn't known that himself. Or had at one time known but had forgotten. Facts and memories tended to change frequently and quickly in the moonshiner's camp, sometimes as quick as the blink of an eye or a swig from a jug.

The sisters said nothing at first, only stood and stared at him in the nearly complete morning quiet; the only sounds the babbling of the creek a short way off and the honking of a few geese far overhead.

"Don't shoot us Luke," one of the strange women said at last, and Luke realized his hand was resting on the grip of his Colt. He'd totally forgotten he'd reached for it as a reflex action when they surprised him. He stood frozen, still startled by their sudden appearance. Then he was doubly surprised as the realization hit him that the woman had called him by name.

"You know my name?"

"Of course I know your name. You work for me." The one who spoke had a sprinkle of freckles across the bridge of her nose that the other didn't. At a glance it was the only difference Luke could see between them. He had no desire to explore farther.

"You work for *us*." The other sister corrected in a far less pleasant tone of voice.

"*Of course, you work for both of us,*" the sister with the freckled nose said in a cowed voice. Then, she yammered on. It was as though she rarely got to carry on a conversation with someone who wasn't quick to bite back at her every word like they were stones she had thrown. She said, "Your name is Luke, and you're the best worker we have. Everybody says so. *Daddy* even knows. I told him."

As she said the last, the corners of her mouth curled up in a petite smile.

"That's enough Millie! There's no need to share too much information with the help."

Over the years Luke had spent a sizeable amount of time talking with Luther at his blacksmith's shop. But even after hours of hearing tales of his life as a slave he knew he could never understand what the man had been through. That was a given fact. Still, right then, simply by the way she had referred to him as the help, by the inflection in her voice, he knew she looked upon him just as the slave owners had looked upon the Negros they bought, sold, and beat like mules before President Lincoln put a stop to it. Well, he supposed news traveled slowly out here.

"Yes Lillie," Millie, the freckle-faced sister said in a whipped-dog tone of voice. She made a show of looking at the ground obediently, but as soon as Lillie glanced away she looked up slyly at Luke and winked. At that moment Luke was unsure which of the Bleu sisters frightened him most. Lillie was obviously the strong one, the one in control. And for whatever reason, she didn't seem to like him much and that scared him, *she* scared him. But Millie frightened him almost as much; there was something disturbing about that smile and that wink that made him long for the south side of Whiskey Creek. And what was most unnerving of all was that he knew the sister's wildly different response to him may turn out to be useful, but that meant he would be forced to get close to Millie. And that would require feigning interest in her. He wasn't at all sure he was that good of an actor. Also, there was no way to predict what reaction it might draw from Lillie. Starting a feud between the sisters might do more harm than good. Lillie hadn't responded well when Millie said the word Daddy like honey was dripping from her lips. Plus there was the brother he'd heard about. He was the unknown wild-card in the deck. If Luke started playing the sisters against each other and the brother got into the mix, there was no way of knowing who he'd side with. All he'd come over here for was information. On the ride up from Whiskey Branch, while being jostled around under the tarp in the dusty confines of Ben's freight wagon he'd had no clue what to expect. All he'd known was that there was a family of moonshiners by the name of Bleu, and that they were a danger to Whiskey Branch. He'd heard those things from Pastor Windor. And coming from the pastor, Luke took them to be as sound as any gospel he spoke on Sunday mornings. The little he'd heard of the sisters he'd heard since actually being their employee.

Now Luke recalled something his mother whispered in his ear as she saw him off to war: Sometimes discretion is the greater part of valor."

Luke said politely, "Pleased to meet you ladies." being careful not to look at one of them more than the other.

Millie, the one with the freckles across the bridge of her nose practically glowed, but remained silent. Luke wondered how long it had been since she had received a kind word from anyone, especially her twin, let alone from a strange man.

In contrast, Lillie literally snarled. "If you don't get your hand off that gun you're a dead man, no matter how good a worker you are. All I have to do is raise my hand and a man with a rifle who's watching from the woods will drop you where you stand."

At first when they'd crept up on him, Luke's hand had gone to his gun out of reflex, but after Lillie's first few words aimed in his direction he'd seen the need to defend himself as a very real possibility, and had left it there. But now he had little doubt that her verbal threat was also very real. He decided to chance a look at Millie, not trying to hide the move from Lillie. He felt it might be a good way to see just how firm Lillie's control over her mouse of a sister really was. He hoped it would help him sense how far he could go without making it obvioushe was trying to play them against each other. He said, "I believe you." and he removed his hand from his gun. Then in what he prayed wasn't an excessive show of confidence he said, "Well I better get back to work before this fire burns low." He turned as casually as he could while expecting a bullet in the back, and started feeding wood to the fire under the still.

"We'll talk later," Lillie snapped at his back, her voice fading as he heard her footsteps trailing off through the dry, dead leaves. Then "Come on Millie!"

Finally she added a parting shot toward Luke, "I'll be keeping an eye on you."

He considered answering, but decided letting her have the last word was probably the wisest move.

He heard Millie run off after her sister, and felt a brief moment of pity for the peculiar woman.

In Whiskey Branch

The sun was lowering in the west, almost gone behind the hills. It was a cool evening outside. Possibly the coolest so far this fall, and the night promised to be the coldest. It was hard to believe that less than two weeks ago children were running around shirtless and in short pants. Once again Pastor Windor was in the front of the room. This time he wasn't standing in the front of the schoolhouse behind the podium Luke had built for him; which he always carried from his room in the back on Sunday mornings. Now he was in the stockroom in the back of Ben and Kaitlin's store. The podium *was* there, along with three rows of chairs borrowed from the schoolhouse. Pastor Windor, along with the original few who had decided on a course of action regarding the Bleu family, currently minus Luke had, after some discussion, decided it was time to explain the situation to the rest of the town. They deserved to know what they were up against. Ben, Kaitlin, Jess Ivy, and, of course Toby were sitting in a loose cluster against the wall behind him.

The stockroom wasn't large, but it was big enough to accommodate at least one member of most of the families of Whisky Branch. In the majority of the cases that was the husband, who was in many cases also the father. Even though the details of the situation hadn't yet been made public knowledge word had gotten out that a fight might be brewing, so the men wanted to know what they were facing and what would be required of them to protect their families. Many were veterans of the terrible war that was so recent in the past, and was burned into their memories forever. None wanted another battle, but were ready if needed. The typhus epidemic as well as a few cases of the flu during a particularly hard winter since, along with the unavoidable accidents that come with frontier life had left a small number of widows who were in attendance, several of whom had children. As the situation was explained, they were assured by those around them that they had nothing to fear; that they were not alone, they were family

Pastor Windor explained the situation briefly, but succinctly; not wanting to panic the residents of the town, but at the same time trying to impress upon them the reality of their position. It was the total unpredictability of the Bleus that made things especially bad. So little was known about who was running things on that side of the creek. And on top of that, they may have any number of hired guns on the payroll; all the way from whiskey fueled cow-punchers to professional gun-hands. The citizens of Whiskey Branch were up against a situation unlike anything they had faced in their small town's brief history. After speaking for only twenty minutes, but relating enough information to place the townsfolk on their guard, hopefully without putting them in a total panic, he opened the meeting up to questions. There were many; most of which he didn't have sure answers for. He told people what he knew, keeping his answers brief, intentionally avoiding expounding on his answers and bringing up more questions than he answered. It was just the sort of circumstance that would invite that kind of thing. The one thing he didn't relate was sending Luke Parker north to spy on the Bleus. He was afraid that letting them know he was concerned enough to resort to spying might push them over the edge into panic. He was glad soon he'd kept that secret.

Within minutes the meeting nearly turned into a mob scene, with people shouting out both questions and demands about how things should be handled. Pastor Windor, after trying fruitlessly to quiet the roughly two dozen unruly people in the room, slapped the flat-of-his-hand on the podium, making a whip-cracking sound and shouted, "Quiet!"

The room was instantly so silent you could have counted the number of individual breaths being drawn. Toby looked out across the room at the crowd of shocked, upturned faces; a roomful of people displaying more rapt attention than he had ever seen on a Sunday morning. And that was saying something; as Pastor Windor generally brought out the best in folks and had them hanging on every word. It was his unquestioned sincerity that did it. Toby had heard his mother use the phrase, 'you could have heard a pin drop.' Toby had wished his mother was alive every day since her death. Now he wished she was alive to see that that kind of quiet really could exist.

A full three minutes later Luther Wilson rose up and stood at his full height.

The only black man in the room; the only black man in the town, in fact.

He was a man whose life of hardships, if written out on paper, would make most of the other Whiskey Branch residents cringe. Even those who had struggled across the country in a wagon train, and survived the town's birth pains, would shrink with shame for feeling put-upon. He stood in the middle of the back row of chairs, his hands folded before him. After a long moment of silence, except for a few throats being cleared and the scraping of a chair on the floor as someone moved nervously, Luther said, his voice a deep bass rumble, "I'm sure everyone would like you to know how much they want to help, Pastor Windor. They're just a'feared. Fact it I'm sorta' a'feared m'self. Only difference is I spent my whole life bein' a'feared. I learnt long ago time ago it ain't somethin' you ever get to likin', or even get used to; but you either got to beat it or it'll beat you. And it won't just beat you till you're on your knees. If you let it, it'll beat you plum into the ground. And the only thing worse than bein' beat on is bein' walked on. And once you been beat into the ground, you're right down there just ready and waitin' to be walked on."

In the shadows behind Pastor Windor Ben elbowed Kaitlin lightly and whispered," You must've been communicating with the leprechauns. Because it appears that in addition to a spiritual leader we now have an inspirational leader. And one who's a powerful speaker at that."

Kaitlin shook her head, and said, "No, I'm thinkin' in truth that this time the wee folk had little to do with it. It seems to me that having one man around might of brought the other? Or maybe brought out what was inside too long and needed to be shared." She shrugged. "Maybe he just needed the right reason to share it; or the right time. There might be a lot more in there. My Da used to say, "Beware the man who is slow to anger." The way Kaitlin said 'Da' when referring to her father so that it rhymed with the way most other people said Pa when referring to theirs was one of her small mannerisms Ben found endearing no matter how many times he heard her say it.

"Your Da used to say a lot of things, didn't he?"

Kaitlin nodded.

"Ben whispered, "Which man are you referring to, Luther or Pastor Windor?"

Just then Pastor Windor said to the crowd, "That's all for this evening. Everybody please go home and build up your fires. It's going to be a cold one. I promise we're keeping a watch on what's going on across the creek and we'll keep you updated on anything important that happens just as soon as possible. You have my word. Now, please bow your heads." He lowered his own. "May the Lord watch over you and protect you till we meet again. Amen."

The crowd murmured their 'Amens' in response and started to shuffle toward the door. As the group of people milled around, Pastor Windor motioned across the room for Toby to come to where he stood. When Toby reached him, he nodded in Luther Wilson's direction and said, "Toby, would you see if you can catch up with Luther before he gets away. Ask him to come over here for a few minutes, please. Walter Denborough and Doc Forrest too if you can track them down."

"Sure Pastor. What's up?"

"It's time for a little brainstorming. And a few more brains can't hurt. Those brains in particular, I think. If you don't catch them before they get home knock on their doors. It's still early. I don't think Mildred will have put the twins down yet. Doc may still be seeing patients. Walter may have stopped by the sawmill. If he's not at home, look for him there. He's about the workingest man I ever saw. Find them if you can Toby." He lowered his head but peered up at Toby through raised eyes.

Toby got the message, and knew this seemingly minor errand could be far more.

"Will do, Pastor." Toby headed out the door to try to round up the men Pastor Windor wanted to see.

As the last of the townspeople squeezed out the door into the store and toward the door that faced the dirt street out front Toby headed after them. As it turned out it was He caught up to Doc Forrest before he reached the bottom of the steps and asked him to come back. He wasn't as lucky with Walter or Luther. He had to fetch the both of them and ask them back. They both came willingly enough, despite having put in long day's work; Luther over his forge and anvil, and Walter in his mill. They were back in the store's back room in minutes; curious and concerned. They joined Toby, Jess, Ben, Kaitlin, and of course, the pastor.

Pastor Windor began speaking, just as he had before sending Luke on the spy mission.

"Doc, Walter, and Luther, first let me explain a few things. Saturday a week ago a small group of us met here to talk about the problem of the Bleu family, and what, if anything, we should do about it.

I asked for Jess's help because I heard rumors that he's a pretty fair shot with a Winchester."

Walter spoke up, and in a voice that made it clear he wasn't kidding, "Those ain't rumors, their facts. Except they don't go near far enough. He's way more than a pretty fair shot. I saw him drop an elk that I could barely see at over a hundred yards. It was not long after he busted his leg. He was sittin' on a stump along the edge of the woods when he shot it and took it down with a single shot. That buck didn't move two steps. Dropped like a stone. I know how far off it was 'cause he wanted to go in with his leg still tied up in splints. I almost had to tie his ass to the stump to make him stay put. If he'd gone in after it I'd'a had ta' drug him an' the buck out." That thing had to weigh at least a hundred pounds. I know 'cause I got to know it real well during that trip outta' the woods. There was one silver-dollar sized hole from his 44/40 slug right through that buck's heart. I doubt it felt a thing. Went to sleep and never woke up. But he sure tasted good. Pastor Windor, if you were lookin' for a top-notch sharpshooter, you hit the jackpot with my friend Jess."

"Good! That's what I was hoping to hear." Here Pastor Windor paused reflectively. "We did make one other important decision at our first get-together that I didn't mention at tonight's meeting. It was my idea, and I'm really hoping it wasn't a bad one. We sent Luke Parker north into the Bleu camps to do some spying. More than a week has passed and I had really expected to hear something back from him by now. It's a pretty sure bet that in a camp full of moonshiners everybody stays drunk most of the time. And it's like an old saying they use a lot in the Navy. Toby may have heard his father say it. 'Loose lips sink ships.' Drunks like to talk. I'd have figured by now Luke would've heard every story the thugs over there have to tell, and found a way to slip back over here. But, right now I'm far more concerned for his wellbeing than I am about knowledge of the Bleu's activities. It's my fault he's over there, and I damn well want to see him home in one piece."

Luther asked, "So how can I help, Pastor?"

"You already helped Luther, more than you realize. When I finished talking to those people they were scared; scared stiff. When you finished talking, they were still scared, but they knew there was something that could be worse than fear. And that as terrible as fear is it's something that can be survived, something that can be overcome. You're proof of that; living breathing proof. And you have no idea how much that was just the right thing at the right time. You are truly a blessing to this community.

Then the pastor turned his attention to Walter Denborough. "Walter, I must say I've been second guessing myself when it comes to dragging you into this mess. You have a large family to be worried about, and seemingly getting larger all the time."

Walter nodded "Yep four girls; and one boy, finally. But that only gives me a bigger stake in this all the time. And my kids are gonna' have a decent place to grow up; the boy and the girls. Ain't nobody gonna' take that 'way from 'em. Not while I'm drawin' breath."

Jess walked up beside the big man and put his hand on his shoulder. He almost had to reach up to do so. "That's what the pastor's worried about Walter," he said. "He wants to be sure you keep drawing breath long enough for all those kids to take care of you when you're an old man."

"I know, but I want to do my part. This is my town too. I've been here from the start."

Toby said, "That's the truth; Mister and Missus Denborough's wagon was right behind ours on the trip out."

"Don't worry Pastor Windor, I'll watch out for him," Jess said, smiling broadly, then added, "After all, he did drag my buck out."

"Well Walter," Pastor Windor said, "Knowing how you feel, I wouldn't think of cutting you out of the action. As you said; it's your town, too. It's way more your town than mine. It was your town before I was anywhere close to Whiskey Branch, and before any of you knew me from Adam. I'll try to be of help when I can, where I can, but if I get in the way, please say so and I'll just drift on."

Ben surprised everyone by speaking up, quite emphatically, "I'll be damned!"

Everyone stared, stunned. He repeated himself, just as loud and clear, "I'll be damned if we'll let the glue that's holding this town together just drift on because we're too foolish to make it clear just how not-in-the-way he is." Then he paused and took a breath to calm himself. After a moment he turned to his wife "Katie Darlin' how about brewin' up a pot of your wonderful coffee. We may be here a while. And bring out the bottle for anyone who might want to add a touch and have theirs Irish style."

He glanced at Toby. "Anyone who's at least as old as the bottle was when your Da came from Dublin."

Once the pot was on the small woodstove in the back of the storeroom and the smell of coffee brewing filled the room, Kaitlin brought out a wooden tray with a half dozen tin cups and a bottle of Irish whiskey. As she set it down she said, "Anyone who hasn't tried Irish coffee doesn't know what you're missing. Once you've reached the bottom of your cup I'm guaranteeing you'll be knocking on wood to thank the wee folks for the experience."

Then she brought the coffee pot and began filling cups all around.

Just then there came an urgent pounding at the locked front door of the closed store.

Along with the pounding, and so loud and excited that it almost drowned it out was a babble of voices. The group in the stockroom jumped up, drinks forgotten, both coffee and whiskey, and charged through the store, led by Ben, running to see what the turmoil was about. When Ben pushed the door open the first person who was calm enough to make any sense at all was Miss Agnes Waters, the school teacher. He let her in. Pastor Windor nodded at the knot of people on the front porch and said, "Luther will you do what you can to calm them down?" Luther squeezed his considerable bulk out the door into the crowd. Miss Waters glanced past Ben and saw Doc Forrest. "Oh, Doctor Forrest, thank God! I was hoping you were here." Her knees failed her and she nearly crumpled to the floor. Ben and Pastor Windor caught her and lifted her up, then eased her into a chair. "They've taken him to your place," she finally was able to continue. "I hope it was the right thing to do. We didn't know where you were. When you weren't home they actually broke the lock and took him into your exam room so he'd be in there if we found you in time." Miss Waters again burst into tears and could say no more. Ben stepped up behind her, afraid she might tumble from the chair. Pastor Windor looked at Kate and said "Kaitlin, would you please bring Miss Waters just a small sip of your Da's coffee spice?"

Outside, Luther had done a respectable job of calming a crowd of people who were very excited about something that was still a mystery to those inside.

Then, a softer rapping came at the door and Luther entered followed by Mildred Denborough. "Missus Denborough has news; and it's not good." Luther sounded nothing like the cool, inspiring person he had been at the town meeting. He looked at Doc Forrest and said, "Come on Doc. You need to go to your office! Right now!" The two men rushed out, with Luther practically dragging Doc behind him.

Walter put his big grizzly-bear arm around his wife and asked, "What is it, hon?"

Mildred Denborough looked like she either had forgotten how to speak or what she had to say was simply too terrible to be said. She finally managed to produce, in a miserable blur of words; "Dale Birmingham was fishing in the calms upstream from The Twist and he found Luke Parker floating in Whiskey Creek."

Beyond that, her words dissolved into sobs, as Miss Waters' words had.

"Christ 'A-Mighty," Jess yelled. Then he threw the tin coffee mug he'd forgotten he was still holding across the storeroom. As the clatter of the mug faded Walter shook his wife; firmly but gently and asked, "Is he alive? Mildred, Is Luke Alive?"

With what was clearly no small amount of effort Mildred sniffed back her tears and nodded. "Of course he's alive. She said it as if saying it aloud made it a certain thing. He's not dead, but I'd say it wasn't for a lack of trying on somebody's part. She paused and drew a gasping breath. At least the last I saw him he wasn't dead. He was stretched out on Doc's exam table. But he's beat up somethin' awful. She rubbed the back of a hand across her eyes. Fresh tears almost immediately took the place of those she wiped away.

Pastor Windor had heard all he could take. He headed out the door.

By that time the sun was just a smear of orange from above the tree line to the west, and his breath made clear plumes in the rapidly chilling air. As Pastor Windor headed for Doc Forrest's place, he struggled to keep his pace somewhat short of an all-out run to prevent himself from bowling over any citizen who might inadvertently step in his way. The excited cluster of people that had gathered outside the Grayson's store had dispersed, he knew not because they'd lost interest, but primarily because the evening's rapidly growing chill had gotten the best of them. He had heard children's voices among those outside and despite all that was happening, he was happy that parents were showing the good sense to have taken their kids in from a night that would surely see the first hard frost of the season. There were still more than the usual number of people standing in front of their homes, or in pairs or small groups where the few cross streets intersected Creek Street braving the cold to worry together rather than alone. There were a lot of windows lit in Whiskey Branch that night. More than he could remember in all of his time in the small town. He wondered how many of the people huddled around those lamps were praying at that moment. He supposed that might depend on how good he'd been at his job.

Luther heard Pastor Windor coming up Doc Forrest's front steps and opened the front door as he approached.

Eight Hours Earlier - on The North side of Whiskey Creek

Luke made his best effort to put on an aw-shucks expression. He didn't know how good he was at play-acting. But he plastered a big grin on his face and said "Yep" when Millie asked, Wouldn't it be just the funniest thing in the big ol' world if we snuck up to the house and I introduced you to Daddy and Lillie didn't know a thing about it?" Millie said it like it was the simplest, most harmless little prank in the big ol' world. When she said it she didn't sound like the same scared, whipped-dog case she had when he'd first met her.

Maybe it was the prospect of getting the best of her sister, even in the slightest of ways that brightened her outlook, Luke thought. The idea of putting something over on her sister had apparently, at least for the moment, gotten the better of any fear of repercussions she might hold.

Luke looked at his feet for a moment, shuffling them nervously, putting on a show of indecision, hoping to feed her sense of excitement. With her help he may actually get a foot in the door that he'd thought he was going to have to sneak into, or possibly even break into. He'd been willing to do whatever it took. But the easy way wouldn't upset him. Of course, if Lillie found out, things would stop being easy real quick. He reached out and took Millie's hand. Her face reddened in such a furious blush the freckles across her nose merged so she suddenly appeared almost as though she was sunburned. But the smile that spread across her face was actually quite pretty.

They stood at the edge of the woods; at the end of a trail she'd led him along for the better part of an hour. Again, she'd snuck up on him, alone this time, while he was tending the still he'd been ordered to care for. But instead of hearing her in the dry leaves, she'd walked silently up behind him and laid her hand on his shoulder and said, "Surprise". Thank God she had said it softly, almost a whisper, or his heart might have stopped. As it was, he'd nearly jumped out of his boots, but kept his hand from going to his gun. Instead he'd smiled and said "Good morning, Millie is it?"

"That's right, Luke, Millie!" She had fairly beamed at him recalling her name.

Luke had glanced around the area behind her. "Your sister's not with you today?"

Millie's expression had changed instantly. "No, she's off doing important stuff." She sounded furious.

Then just as quickly she was happy again. "But that's okay. I get to do what I want for a little while; without her bossing me around."

Luke had decided to take advantage of her good mood, however fleeting it might be; strike while the iron was hot, so to speak.

"So," he said, giving her hand a little squeeze. "Maybe you *should* introduce me to your daddy while Lillie's off doing important stuff? That would be an important thing to do. *Real* important. That's what I think." Then he asked, "What is it Lillie's off doing?" He didn't really expect an answer, at least not a lucid one. He was wondering more all the time about the woman's mental faculties. The brief look of enthusiasm and the broad smile she'd shown when planning to pull a prank on her sister had been replaced by a look of near boredom as though she had trained herself not to think about her sister at all. Luke gave her hand a shake and said, Millie!" She blinked as though waking up, but she answered, proving that she really had heard him. "Lillie went to Sweetwater to arrange for the deliveries. She does all the bid'ness stuff since Daddy got sick. And Nappy makes sure the men do their jobs, and the stills get runned right, so the gin comes out good. He's good at that. They're all afraid of him. And they should be. I would be if I was them. But I take care of Daddy. He needs somebody to take care of him." Then, very softly, conspiratorially she'd said, "I'm his favorite."

And then she'd led him into the trees and along the path through the woods, clutching his hand tightly the entire way. The trail wound along for at least a quarter-mile by Luke's estimation, with him becoming more concerned all the way. He hoped that whatever he might find out at the end of the hike was worth it, and that if it was that he'd get a chance to report it back to Pastor Windor and not just become crow or wolf bait out here in the woods.

Finally the trail had broken on a large clearing in the woods. Luke was stunned by what he saw. Before he'd realized she'd moved, Millie had dropped his hand and walked behind him. She'd circled his waist with a firm hug and laid her head against his back and said, "Ain't it pretty?"

Luke could do nothing but nod and say, "Yes, it sure is."

In the center of the clearing sat a trim little yellow two story house with dark green shutters. A porch ran across the front. Flower boxes painted to match the shutters sat on the porch railings and several rocking chairs sat on the porch. Seeing it in the center of the thick woods dotted with moonshiner camps had the same effect as would suddenly stumbling across a rose in the center of an acre of poison oak and thistles. Millie had still been practically hanging on Luke's waist.

He'd turned to face her, gently prying her hands open, and smiling, asked, "Is this your house?"

"Yes, mine and Daddy's." Then, her face clouding over, "And Lillie's."

Then as a total afterthought she'd added, "Nappy's too, I guess." She'd said that as though the words were squeezing around or through a terrible taste in her mouth; possibly a dose of some unpleasant medicine or a sip of cider gone sour.

"Daddy makes sure it stays just like Mama liked it to be when she was alive." When she mentioned her Mama the sour face disappeared, replaced by a sweet smile. Then, just as quickly the smile became a sneer. "Nappy's mother hated it. And I hated her."

"Nappy's mother wasn't your mother?" Luke was fishing; but was aware he may be fishing in dangerous waters.

"No, Daddy married her after our mama died. He replaced mama with her. Except for the house, he threw Mama away." Millie grew deeper and deeper in her anger the more she talked about the family.

Luke's concern was growing into fear. Back during the war he'd heard stories of people who had actually been two people inside; in their heads. He'd always figured they were only made up tales like the ghost stories told in tents or around the fires by men trying to get over the shock they had suffered in battles they'd fought or the fear they were trying to distract themselves and each other from when they knew a battle was coming. But now he decided he actually had met two people in one. And the topper was that the angry one of the two had decided she wanted to use him to get at her sister. But the nice one seemed to be attracted to him, or at least attracted to having someone, anyone, who said pleasant things to her. And even stranger still was that he'd found himself kind of attracted to her; or at least the Millie who didn't act like she could happily strangle her sister. Maybe it was because after only meeting Lillie once he thought he could also happily strangle her.

Having come that far, and not knowing how much time there would be before Lillie returned from doing her *important* stuff in Sweetwater, Luke looked up at the sun which had moved far enough across the sky to give him a rough idea of the time. When Millie had first sprung up behind him and surprised him the sun was almost directly overhead, so he'd known it was right around noon. He'd left his pocket watch, a gift from his father, at home before crossing the creek on his mission for fear of someone stealing it. By then he'd figured it to be half-past. Lillie could make the trip from Sweetwater to Whiskey Branch easily in a half hour. So Luke had put his arm around Millie's shoulders and whispered in her ear, "Don't you want to introduce me to your Daddy before Lillie gets back?" He'd said it hoping it would be the right Millie's ear he was whispering in; the Millie who would relish a chance to pull a trick on her sister more than a chance to slit her throat. It seemed that she'd read the thoughts in his head almost before he'd finished thinking them. She'd smiled up at him and said, "Let's go up to the house and surprise Lillie when she gets home."

She'd taken his hand and led him across the clearing toward the house like they were strolling home for a Sunday dinner. She didn't seem at all concerned about whether Lillie might be there waiting for them. As they went Luke asked, "Would you know if Lillie had come home yet?"

"Nope, there's a wagon trail that comes up to the house from the woods on the other side of the clearing. It loops way 'round and ties into Sweetwater Road. But Lillie doesn't take a wagon anyways. She rides her horse. That way there ain't all that wagon rattlin' to bother Daddy since he got sick. She could come in from over there and you'd never see her from the way we come.

Then she tugged on his hand, hurrying him along. "C'mon. Les' git a move on!" Before long they were practically running across the open ground between the woods and the house. Luke was afraid that even if they weren't spotted the sound of their footfalls slapping on the dry, dying fall grass would be heard by someone in the house. When they reached the steps leading up to the porch Millie stopped and put her index finger to her lips, signaling silence, though Luke hadn't made a sound since they'd broken from the cover of the woods.

Luke nodded and made a gesture miming turning a key to lock and seal his own lips, and then he allowed himself to be led up the steps onto the porch. They crept down the porch till they were a few feet from an open window, where a breeze blew curtains that were far finer than those in any of the windows in Whiskey Branch. Millie bent close and whispered in his ear", This is Daddy's room. I wanna' listen for a while to make sure Lillie's not back yet. And if she ain't, maybe see when she's comin."

Two people in one head notwithstanding, Luke had to admit to himself that Millie had turned out to be a lot better spy than he. So as she stood with her back against the wall, with her head cocked and an ear directed toward the window he did the same. He immediately heard two voices, both male.

He and Millie stood there listening for quite a while before something that felt like a Union Cavalry canon came down on the back of Luke's head. Everything turned black. But the things he'd heard from inside the window before the blackness enveloped everything could mean everything.

"Don't kill him, Nappy, please!" It was Millie's pitiful voice Luke heard, but it came to him from a hundred miles off, as a frightening dream gave way to an even more frightening reality. He blinked, and blinked again, trying to blink away a lingering grayness that hung around the edges of his vision like a blurry frame around a painting. When his vision finally cleared a little, what he saw wasn't much to his liking.

He was on his back, on the board floor of the porch, staring up into the gun barrel of the man he'd spent many hours watching from far off. And now that Napoleon Bleu Junior was less than two feet away and separated from him by what looked like a huge revolver; a 44 at least, Luke liked his looks even less. And he hadn't liked him a bit from a distance. When Luke tried to blink to clear his vision his left eye felt like it was glued shut. He realized that he was seeing primarily with his right eye, and even that eye was seeing everything through a red tinged haze. What he did see was a splatter of bright red on the toe of Nappy's boot. That explained the pain in his throbbing in his forehead and the blood in his eyes in addition to the dull throbbing from the clout on the back of his head. Apparently Nappy had no compunction about kicking a man when he was down.

"He was spying, God damn it! What do you think I should do? I've got to kill him!" Nappy was shouting at Millie. "What will the old man think if I don't?" Nappy fell silent in mid-sentence, the incomplete thought hanging in the air between them almost like something visible.

Luke's head had been clearing enough to follow the conversation but he'd thought it wise to again close his eyes since Nappy hadn't yet noticed he'd awakened.

Then Millie spoke in a way, and showed a side that was totally different from the sweet-as-pie or mean-as hell characters she'd shown Luke up till then. It was like a cross between the two. It had a wheedling, whining tone. But it was apparently something Nappy had seen before, and was more than a little bit scared of. She said. "Nappy, I *really* like Luke. If you kill Luke I'll tell Daddy. I'll tell Daddy that I really liked Luke. And then Daddy will be unhappy with you. Luke's mind flashed back to Millie telling him that she was Daddy's favorite.She went on, "And when Daddy is unhappy he makes sure Lillie's unhappy. And you know that when she gets unhappy she's mad at everybody!"

Then Nappy began whining, "But if I don't kill him Lillie will be 'specially pissed at *me*."

Millie stomped her foot like a child throwing a tantrum. "I don't care. I don't want you to kill him!"

"Well, okay, I've got an idea. It's something just as good. Even through his still-clouded vision Luke could see the grin on Nappy's face, and he knew it didn't bode well for him. His expectations were immediately proven accurate. "I can make *damn* sure he doesn't tell anybody anything." As he said it, Nappy had hauled off and delivered a kick to Luke's ribs that drove the breath from his body in a loud woof and very nearly turned his still-gray vision black again. Millie dropped to her knees beside him and gently lifted his head from the wood and cradled it in her arms, while Nappy stood over them and laughed, while twirling his gun around his trigger finger.

Just then, almost as if her arrival had been timed to cast the deciding vote regarding Luke's sentence of life or death, Lillie reined her horse up to a sliding halt at the base of the steps, throwing a cloud of dirt in the air and said, "What the hell's he doing here?"

She was looking back and forth from Millie to Nappy with seemingly equal fury burning in her gaze.

Millie said, "He was just visiting. I brought him to meet Daddy, and Nappy hit him." All the while she was still holding Luke's head, his blood staining her arms in trails as it dribbled to the boards.

"He was spying," Nappy had practically spat out, anxious to sway the story of the situation his way.

"Lillie looked at the gun hanging in Nappy's hand. "Then, why is he still breathing?"

Nappy nodded toward Millie, and said, "It's her; always her. If it wasn't for her he *wouldn't* be breathin.'

Lillie had glared daggers at Millie, but said nothing. After the silence stretched for a few moments Millie said, "He's nice; and he was nice to me. Nobody's ever nice to me, 'cept Daddy. I like him, and I don't want Nappy to kill him." Tears had been streaming from her eyes; so many tears they ran down the length of her face and dripped from her chin. In the midst of fearing for his own life Luke had again felt sorry for the woman. And he sincerely hoped that she'd been right about being Daddy's favorite. Right enough, at least, for Nappy to be more afraid of Napoleon Senior than of Lillie; at that moment, at least.

Lillie's gaze shifted from her sister to her half-brother. "Get rid of him!"

Then, looking back at Millie, she said, with her mouth curled in a sneer, "I don't care how." She was still speaking to Nappy, but speaking to make a clear point *to* Millie; the point being; she was boss.

There had been no foot stomping or tantrum throwing then. Millie had cried like a four-year old; her voice so tear-choked it was barely understandable. "Nappy, please don't." She could go no farther.

"Aw, stop snivellin'. I won't kill your boyfriend." There was no trace of sympathy or understanding in his voice, only ridicule. "I got a better chance of a lightnin' bolt knockin' my off'n my horse than you got of finding another one," he'd said, then delivered a kick to Luke's thigh that numbed his leg from there down to his toes.

"Now get up!" Nappy had grabbed Millie's arm and dragged her to her feet, causing Luke's head to drop to the porch floor. That was when things had turned black for him a second time.

In Doc Forrest's Office -

By the time Pastor Windor reached Doc Forrest's office Doc and Luther had pulled tables up on both sides of the exam table where Luke lay. Lamps sat on both, their wicks turned up to throw as much light as possible where Doc needed it. Combined with the ones that hung from the rafters they had given a smoky, close feel to the air in the room. At Doc's request Miss Agnes Waters had opened the windows just enough to let the smoke out so it didn't cloud his vision, but not enough to let in more cold air than Luke could tolerate. Though the elderly teacher was trembling, she was doing a commendable job of serving as the doctor's assistant. Doc actually insisted at one point that she pause long enough to take a drink of water so she didn't become dehydrated from all the tears she was shedding. She didn't understand what he meant, but that didn't matter. She did what he said. She was in the process of carrying her second pan of water from the kitchen. He'd used the first to clean Luke's wounds, and the second pan; less hot, to warm his feet and hands.

The first thing Pastor Windor said was, "He's alive?"

Doc nodded, "It wasn't for lack of trying on somebody's part, but he's alive."

"Praise God." Pastor Windor walked to the head of the table and looked down at Luke from his right side, lying there bruised and battered. He lay there naked, with a towel covering his private parts. His eyes were closed. He was unconscious, or sleeping, hopefully the latter. Either would be better than dead, which was how he looked. At first glance it appeared that whatever parts of his body weren't an open wound were deep purple bruises or differing shades of red from the cold. Pastor Windor reached for Luke's hand, but Doc shook his head and stopped him before he could pick it up. Then the pastor noticed that though most of Luke's body was gradually regaining its normal color, his fingers and toes were almost the color of blueberries.

"As if the beating wasn't enough, he was dumped in the creek. This time of year, late in the day, once the sun has gone over the mountains a few hours in that water would kill most men. When Dale found him he was in the calms about an eighth of a mile upstream from the twist, and there was no telling how long he'd been in there. He said Luke's right leg was tangled up in some oak tree roots and he could see Luke must have tried to grab for some of the other growth hanging over the water, because his hands were all torn up. Pastor Windor looked down without touching Luke's hands and could see raw bloody patches where nails were missing from fingers on both. Dale said it took a while to get him loose. He got him up on the bank and wrapped him up in his own coat and his horse blanket, and built a fire. It was exactly the right thing to do. I just hope it wasn't too late. He knew he couldn't get him back to town on his horse in the shape he's in so he rode back here and borrowed a wagon. They said when he came into town he was going like a bat straight outa' Hell, and yelling like a banshee. He went to Luther's shop hoping to get a wagon, not knowing Luther was still at the store, and pounded on the door till Wilber Moss heard him and told him to take his buckboard. As soon as we had Luke taken care of here I sent Dale home. I told him to sit in front of a fire and get warm. He was soaked to the skin and about frozen to the bone from pulling Luke out of the creek. He was shivering so bad he could hardly speak. He's definitely done his good deed for the day. It might not sound like much but it was a very brave and very dangerous thing he did. I prescribed some hot soup and a shot of whiskey every hour for the next twelve hours. Specifically the legal stuff Ben sells, not the rot-gut that finds its way across the creek"

"What do you think?" Pastor Windor asked, looking down at Luke. "Will he make it?"

Doc said, "I just don't know. He took a hell of a beating. I'd love nothing more than to tell you that I'm sure he'll be fine, but I can't do that." Doc stared at his shoes for a long moment before continuing. "It's pretty obvious that whoever did this to him didn't mean for him to survive."

"No," was all Pastor Windor could say, just one word and it came out in a whisper, but with a bite to it all the same; a kind of severity Doc Forrest had never heard in his voice. That it was so clear even in a whisper made it frightening, and Doc was glad he wasn't the one the pastor was thinking about when he said that word. He looked at Doc after a moment and said, "This was a message Doc. You're right. They wanted him to die. But they wanted him to die from the beating, or from the cold. That's why they threw him in upstream, in the calms. If they were only trying to get rid of him, they'd have tossed him in where he'd have been sure to go down in the twist. Yes, this was a message. They want us to know they're on to us. And that they're in control. They want us to know they could have killed him easy if they wanted to, but didn't. They're playing with us." If they just wanted him dead a bullet would have done the trick. Somebody went to the trouble of hauling him down to the creek and dumping him. And dumping him in the one spot where he was just as likely to be found alive as dead. And even if he did die and float downstream to the twist, he'd have to float practically through town. His body would surely be seen, and the same message would be sent; "Here's what happens to anybody who sticks their nose in Bleu family business." "No, this was for our benefit," Pastor Windor said through gritted teeth, his voice bordering on a snarl, something so uncharacteristic from the man that everyone in the room took an involuntary step back. It's a move in a game being played out between us and them. They want to see how we'll react; what *our* next move will be. Unfortunately Luke got caught in the middle and became a pawn. And it's my fault." The outraged tone remained in his voice, but had changed somehow; and the people in the room; Doc, Luther, and Miss Agnes Waters could sense that the anger he was now feeling was focused inward; on himself, and would not be shared.

Pastor Windor looked at Doc and asked, point blank; "is he going to make it?"

"I wish I could give you a definite answer, but I can't. He's a strong man. Most people would have been dead already. I'd say if he makes it till morning he's got a good chance. That's the best I can do."

"Okay Doc, I know you'll do your best. You always do." He paused, his voice choked with tears. "Please pull him through." Then he said something rather mysterious, "I've been responsible for the death of more than one man, but only when it was necessary to prevent my own. And only then when I felt it was the way to ultimately do the right thing. But I've never caused a man's death by sending him into the lion's den." He rolled his eyes upward. "He has to pull through."

Then, his voice halting and hoarse, but surprisingly strong under the circumstances, Luke unexpectedly said, "See you in the morning pastor. I've got a lot of stuff to tell you. Important stuff."

The few people in the room gasped as one, and then the room went deathly silent, everyone waiting. The pastor again reflexively reached to take Luke's hand, but stopped before doing so, and looked at Doc Forrest. Doc looked pensive for a moment, considering it seriously before nodding, and then said, "Gently."

Pastor Windor took Luke's right hand as though preparing to shake it, and said to Luke, "You got it, buddy. I'll be here before the cock crows in the morning. When I hear that bird I'll be ready. I'm looking forward to hearing whatever you have to tell me. Big news or small; if you think it's important, it's important. I don't just want hear it, I *have* to hear it." Pastor Windor's voice faltered, failing him for a second, and he started over; "I *can't* feel I got you beaten half to death for nothing." Then he did shake Luke's hand, once up and then back down, very gently. It took no more than three seconds and during those few seconds he was afraid he would hear a cracking sound like a breaking twig and find he would be holding one of Luke's frozen fingers in his hand when he let go of the handshake. Or even worse; that one or more stiff digits would fall to the floor and shatter like icicles.

But none of that happened and Luke said, "Then I'll see you

tomorrow soon after the cock crows, okay Captain?" Then he snapped a crisp salute and managed a weak smile. It was clear that it took all he had in him.

Pastor Windor let it ride. He returned the salute. Being Called Captainwasn't something he expected or desired, but if it was what Luke wanted to call him after what he'd been through; and if Luke still felt he was the man to plan strategy, then that's the way it would be. Luke deserved that. But the truth was that he was scared, not for himself, he supposed anything he got he deserved; his penance, so to speak. He was scared for the people of Whiskey Branch. He was okay being their pastor. It had taken him no time at all to come to love them. But being their pastor was a very different thing from being their savior. He laid Luke's hand down gently on the examination table beside him and then stood by his side till the even steady sound of his breathing showed he had fallen asleep. Pastor Windor whispered to Doc Forrest, "I'll be here before sunup."

Doc nodded, and Pastor Windor eased out the door into the cold night, and sent a prayer of thanks heavenward that Luke hadn't been in the freezing water any longer than he had.

The next morning Doc Forrest's exam room was the most crowded it had been since Luke built the combination house and office for him soon after his arrival in town. Doc had pulled a few chairs in from his kitchen. Miss Waters had gone home just before sunrise. Though she wanted to stay, Doc insisted on it. She'd been up too long and been working too hard for a lady of her advanced age. Pastor Windor carried a lantern and walked the short way with her and made sure she was safely home before returning to Doc's. Along the way he met first Toby, then Jess, then Walter Denborough, and finally Ben and Kate, all headed for Doc's office, where Luther had insisted on spending the night. As they walked they were set upon by a very strong and extremely frigid wind.

Putting a hand on top of his head to keep his hat from blowing away, Jess said, "I believe fall turned to winter overnight while nobody was looking."

Pastor Windor turned the collar of his long black coat up and said, "I hope I'm wrong, but it feels like we may be in for a norther."

"What in the world is a norther?" Ben asked.

"An ice storm that sometimes blows down from Canada this time of year"

Walter said, "We're a pretty long way from Canada."

"Not so far, as the crow flies. And storms fly just as straight as crows, only a lot faster, and they don't care a damn about miles. Pardon my French."

A short time later Pastor Windor looked around the exam room and realized that the whole gang he'd had Toby deliver his message to only a couple weeks ago was now there. The only difference was now one of the gang was lying on a table while the rest of them were in a circle around him waiting to see if he'd ever open his eyes again.

Then he was instantly ashamed. Who should be strong, if not him? Just the previous night he had been saying a prayer of thanks for Luke surviving the freezing water. Inside he knew his mixed emotions wouldn't be so mixed had it not been his idea for Luke to go north across the creek. Now he felt it was something he should have done himself. That only would have worked if he could have been certain he could just blend in with some of the hired help. Of course there had been no way to be sure of that. And had he come face to face with Napoleon Bleu things could have gone very wrong very fast. So sending Luke had seemed to be the best option at the time. Now he hoped Luke survived, because if not, he wasn't sure he could live with himself.

A rooster crowed in the distance not five minutes after they arrived. It made the pastor recall his promise to be there before the cock crowed. The promise had seemed like an unimportant thing at the time, almost frivolous, in fact. But now he was glad he'd kept it.

Luke surprised them by saying in a strong whisper, quiet but easily understandable "That would be Nate Newton's Rooster. Damn thing gets me up at the crack of dawn every morning. I haven't had a chance to sleep in in years." Then he directed at Pastor Windor; "Pardon my French."

"Not a problem"

Doc said, "Luke, I think I can speak for everybody when I say I'm really glad Nate's rooster woke you up this morning."

Luke smiled. Then he asked, "What day is this?"

"It's Sunday, why?"

Luke's smile disappeared like it was never there. He looked at Pastor Windor and his eyes got so wide they looked like they might bulge clear out of his head. He looked like a man who was scared to the verge of death. "You have to listen! Right now! We've got to get ready! I got lucky." Here Luke paused and clenched and unclenched both hands as to see if they still worked. The right one responded, but the left barely moved. He shrugged and said, "Could be worse I guess. I suppose I was only half lucky." Then he continued, "You were right; The Bleus have been watching us; watching us close, and planning. I should have known sooner. But I thought that crazy bastard Nappy was only interested in you; you and Toby too. I don't know which one bothered him most."

"What do you mean by that" Pastor Windor leaned close, listening intently.

"Well first off, the whole family's crazy as far as I can tell, in one way or another. To listen to the old man I couldn't tell if he was crazy just from age; like some people get, or if he was drunk almost to death, or both. Nappy is crazy with hate. He makes a circuit of the 'shine camps every night about dusk and threatens the men if he thinks they're slackin' off on their yield. Or even if they're not. He wants to keep them scared enough to be sure they don't. Lillie runs the business end of things since the old man's so out of touch with what's going on. So Nappy hates Lillie for that. I guess it's cause the old man gave her the job instead of him. And Millie told me several times how she's their Daddy's favorite. So Nappy hates Millie for that. And it must be true, she really must be daddy's favorite or I'd have gotten a bullet in the head instead of an ice cold bath in the creek. She threw a fit like a little kid and Nappy let me live even though Lillie was standing there telling him to shoot me. I think he even hates himself. If he looked at himself in the creek; he'd probably cuss his reflection."

"Why's that? Pastor Windor asked.

"He's small. Can't be more'n five-five. That's why the men call him 'the kid' behind his back. He knows it, and it makes him furious, and he takes it out on everybody. But he hates you more than anybody."

"Why me?"

"Every time I got the chance I watched him with your spyglass. He climbs to the top of the cliff that big chunk of rock broke off of and landed in the creek and made the twist. From there he can see the whole town. I didn't realize he was paying so much attention to the regular goings-on over here till I overheard him shooting off his mouth in one of the camps one night. Before that I thought he'd only been watching you and Toby."

"What do you mean, watching me and Toby?" Pastor Windor asked.

"Nappy fancies himself a gunfighter. And he's damn certain he can outdraw you." Luke stopped speaking."This time it wasn't from fatigue. He was waiting to see how Pastor Windor would respond. Of course, only Toby knew what he was talking about. After a long awkward silence Toby shrugged and said, "He wasn't always a Pastor."

Jess looked at his feet for a moment, confused, and then when it appeared the pastor was going to offer no explanation; he said, to break the unbearable quiet, "You wouldn't have any coffee on, would you Doc?"

"Nope, sorry Jess. Then Jess stood looking at the pastor, not knowing what to say or do.

Finally after several minutes of everybody trying to think of something to say and finding nothing, Kate said, "I hope you don't mind my asking; do you have some talent we're not aware of Pastor?"

"I've been many places, and seen many things before I came to Whiskey Branch. Along the way I picked up some particular skills and habits. Among those was becoming good with a six-gun."

Toby spoke up, "Real good!"

Pastor Windor asked Toby, "Toby, would you mind keeping Luke company while the rest of us step into Doc's kitchen for a few minutes? I promise we won't be long, and I'll bring you up to speed on anything we discuss. Okay?" Looking a little dejected, Toby nonetheless relented, and said, "Okay."

Once in the kitchen the pastor continued, "Some of those habits and skills I practice every day, and at every opportunity; those involving my chosen profession." Others I hoped to never practice again; God willing, especially the gun skills. Then a while back Toby came across his father's Colt service revolver and was fumbling with it rather dangerously. I felt that in the interest of safety I should give him some instruction in its proper care and use. Also it seemed like it would be a valued connection to his lost father. That's how it started. Then it progressed to drawing and shooting. Then it started feeling good. I started practicing again, for the first time in …well in forever. It's that simple; it started feeling good. I gave in to temptation because it started feeling good. Just like alcohol gets ahold of some men who give in to temptation because it feels good. And Toby became sort of my apprentice; and I his mentor I suppose. I justified it to myself by saying that Toby's ability to shoot might be crucial if we're forced into a war with the Bleus. That much is true, though it's a sad day when a teenaged boy needs to take up arms to defend his home against the sort of thieves and cutthroats who would do what they did to Luke. And Toby took to it like a duck takes to water. In time he could be one of the best; and I've seen some of the best."

"Well, Pastor," Walter said "Better he know how than not know how if we do go to war."

Pastor Windor said, "Thank you for giving me the benefit of the doubt, Walter."

Ben said, "You'd do it for any of us."

When they went back to the exam room the first thing Doc asked Luke was, "Do you feel like trying to sit up" "I'd love to, if you think it's okay?" Doc put his hands under Luke's armpits and gently helped him rise to a seated position on the table.

"You're the only one who knows what you're up to doing," Doc told him. "I did put coffee on. I thought you might like a cup. And it's about time for some pain pills. If you'd like some, that is."

"Absolutely!"

Then I'll heat up some soup broth. It's not exactly what you'd think of as a hearty meal; but it would be a good idea to have something in your stomach before the pills hit it."

"Okay, you're the doctor. And I've got more to tell you, some of it's pretty urgent. I tried to keep an eye on Nappy whenever I could without him catching on." Luke paused and whistled through his teeth, before suffering a coughing fit that had him grabbing at his side. Doc put his stethoscope to Luke's chest and listened for a moment and then said, "Luke, this may hurt. But I need to check you for broken ribs I'm fairly sure you've got a couple on the left side. I'm sorry if it pains you."

"Luke said, "Doc I think you're a pretty smart guy, but I don't think you could find a place to touch me that it wouldn't pain me. But please don't go searching. I feel like somebody put the boot to me while I was down."

"I believe that's a correct diagnosis," Doc replied, feeling over Luke's side as gently as possible.

Pastor Windor felt an old and frightening sort of anger building in him. "Who?" he asked through clenched teeth.

"Nappy, after he clouted me on the back of the head. I don't know what he hit me with, but itfelt like the whole yellow house fellon top of my head right there on the porch, green shutters and all."

"What?" Pastor Windor looked from Luke to Doc Forrest, and then around the room at the others gathered there wondering if he had heard correctly. It, of course, made no sense to him, or to anyone else.

Luke managed a smile, and then said, "It's kind of a long story. I'll tell you all about it some time. The important thing to know is. "I lucked into a chance to stand outside of a window and eavesdrop on Napoleon Bleu Senior and Napoleon Junior finalizing plans for an attack on Whiskey Branch. I was out there for damn near a half hour before Nappy came up behind me. I also found out the old man is someone you'd want to stand upwind of even on a day there's no breeze blowin'. The smell comin' out of that window was the smell of death. I've smelled that smell before. He's either very old or very sick, or possibly both. He and Nappy talked over plans about an attack; an attack on us."

Luke fell silent, his wind failing him, and Pastor Windor looked at Doc. Doc said, "Give him a moment."

Everyone in the room stood waiting. And they were all praying, not just Pastor Windor, but everyone, including Walter Denborough, whose considerable bulk, despite his wife's pleading, hadn't darkened the doors of a church in many years. He was a good man; he was simply too busy to give up a whole hour every week, when he could be out cutting trees or sawing them into lumber. He figured God would appreciate the time he spent providing roofs and walls for the good people of Whisky Branch. And it should count for something when He was putting check marks in His book. At least Walter had always hoped so. Now he found he had absolutely no trouble at all praying for Luke's recovery, of course, but even more urgently that he would wake up long enough to tell them what else he'd heard of the Bleu's plans.

Suddenly Luke pulled in a gasp, like it had required a great effort and started to speak, "Well, once I got over there it didn't take me long to see the Bleu's have got a lot of men working for them. Only a handful of them have been with them for any length of time. Most are drifters; or maybe cow-pokes or ex-Army down on their luck. Not the kind that usually stay at a job long. Most of them aren't the kind that you'd expect to be very loyal when the going gets tough. But the Bleus have been keeping them warm and fed. And that beats the hell out of cold and hungry any day. And even drifters don't forget that. So we should prepare like they're soldiers who remember where their last meal came from."

Pastor Windor said, "Very well put." Then he asked, "Luke, are you sure you're up to this?"

Luke nodded, then said, "What time is it"

Ben checked his pocket watch. "Just before six am."

"Then we only have five hours!"

"Five hours for what?" Pastor Windor asked.

"Five hours till they attack."

"Please go on," Pastor Windor urged him gently.

"Before Napoléon Senior and Nappy had a chance to go at each other's throats, they found something bad to discuss; something really bad for us, at least. But them not knowing that we know; that could change the outcome completely. If we have time to get ready, that is. Not knowing what we're setting up to greet them, their plan's not really complete."

"They don't have time to get ready either." Walter blurted out arrogantly, stretching his suspenders. Then he tried to limber up by touching his toes, and could hardly bend. "What the shit!" he yelled, before looking down and seeing the bottom of his pant legs caught tightly in the tops of his work boots. He could hardly believe it when he looked again and realized he also that had his boots reversed; left on right and vice-versa. "Damn! Of all the times! I guess I wasn't payin' enough attention this morning. All I could think about was Luke, and what that bastard Nappy done to him."

Pastor Windor gently laid a hand on his shoulder and quietly said, "It's time for slow and calm, Walter. That's the ticket. We have things to accomplish. And we don't even know what those things are yet. Before we start running around in a panic we need to find out all Luke can tell us."

"Walter immediately was calm. The two went back to Luke's side. Pastor Windor said, "Tell us more about the upcoming attack, Luke. Everything you can remember; think hard; every detail. Leave nothing out."

Luke blinked his eyes to clear his vision, then said, "Doc, give me another slug of that mud you call coffee. Those pills are drowsing me and I've got to stay awake till I'm done talking."

Doc told Toby, "Toby, bring in some cups and the rest of the pot. It ought to still be half full."

While Luke was gulping down a cup, Pastor Windor said, "Ready when you are Luke.

Luke shook his hands as he had earlier and was pleased to see they both responded well. Then he proceeded to slap himself on both cheeks to wake himself up.

"Hey Buddy, you want me to dip your head in the nice cool creek to wake you up?" It was Jess who was trying for a joke.

"No thanks Jess," Luke shut him down. "My last dip in the nice cool creek just about put my lamps out permanently."

Then he began; "Well, before Nappy discovered me spying I overheard him and his father going over their plans for an attack on Whiskey Branch, and it's going to be a big one and it's going to happen today at eleven am!"

"Oh my God!" Ben said, stunned. "That was what you meant by having less than five hours to get ready!"

Luke said, "Yeah. Nappy laughed about hitting us with everybody being in church listening to the gun slinging preacher. So we won't know what hit us."

For a moment Pastor Windor was speechless; but only for a moment. Then he asked, "Did you hear any details of their attack plan?"

"Yeah, and if the situation was different I'd have to be impressed. It's very smart from a military standpoint. They intend to attack on two fronts at once. They're going to send a wagon-load of armed men right up Creek Street from the direction of Sweetwater. They don't expect to run into any resistance at eleven on Sunday morning. Still, they'll have two men on horses riding out in front with sticks of dynamite to throw ahead of them to clear the way if they need to; but only if they really need to. They don't want to blow holes in the street to drive the wagon through if they don't have to. At the same time a dozen heavily armed men will ford the creek and fan out into town. There's an old man that just goes by Hoss that was a Confederate bugler. He'll blow charge to signal the attack." Luke paused for a breath and a rest before continuing;

"Ben, they've watched us enough to know that your store is a natural meeting place, and that we've used it for that. So we better expect them to try to overrun it quick. That was about all the planning I heard before the conversation turned into an argument; a serious one." Luke looked at Pastor Windor. "About you."

"What?"

"It seems that when the old man heard about you, you must have struck a chord with him. And you scared him."

"Scared him how?"

"Well I don't know if he'd heard of you before or what, but it seems he isn't nearly as confident that Nappy can handle you as Nappy is. So he sent out word, and hired a professional gunfighter. My guess is that Lillie actually found him. That infuriated Nappy something awful. That's when he stomped out of the room. But I didn't hear him coming up behind me and he really let me have it on the back of the head. And like I said, if not for Millie, I'd be a dead man right now. I guess Nappy figured dumping me in the creek was as sure as a bullet. He figured I'd either freeze to death or get sucked down in the twist. Nappy not putting a bullet in me calmed Millie down right at that moment. So whatever happens, take it easy on her, okay?"

Pastor Windor nodded, "Done; at least as far as I can control it."

Then Luke added, "And remember; Nappy is totally crazy, and he's obsessed with killing you. You're all he talks about. When he did his circle of the camps each night he was often as drunk as the guys who were working the stills. Then his bragging always came out loud enough for everyone close by to hear. I heard him yell in one of the camps that he'd kill the kid if that was what it took to get the preacher to fight. And there's no question who he was talking about. You're all he thinks about. That's why he got so furious about Avey."

"Avey?" Pastor Windor's eyebrows rose questioningly.

"Yeah, Avey; that's the gunfighter's name; the one the old man hired. I heard it loud and clear through that window. Does it mean something to you?"

"It might, Pastor Windor answered. "Did you hear a first name?"

"I'm not sure. When Nappy said it, he only said Avey, and he almost spit it out, like it was a curse word. But I think the old man might have said it; Lance maybe."

"Vance, "Pastor Windor said. "Vance Avey."

"So you've heard of him? You know anything about him?"

"I know of him. And I heard he was in the area. I only saw him fight once."

"Is he fast?" It was Jess who asked.

"He's a killer." Pastor Windor answered simply.

"Toby asked hesitantly, "Are you faster?"

"I don't know," he said. When he saw the disappointment in the boy's eyes, he added, "I'm sorry Toby, I just don't know. There's only one way I would know that. And if I'd ever had the chance to find out one of us would be dead; either him or me. But he's been faster than a lot of other men; too many other men." Then he called Toby over to stand beside him and said to everyone else in the room, "If Nappy hurts Toby, I swear to you that I'll personally throw the first shovelful of dirt on Nappy's face."

Doc said "Pastor, we're seeing a whole new side of you."

Pastor Windor shrugged and said, "Well it's his own fault the first shovelful hits his face. He put our coffin builder out of commission himself. And that's another reason he deserves a hole in the ground." When Pastor Windor stopped talking nobody else knew quite what to say.

Finally Ben looked at his pocket watch and said, "It's nearly six-thirty. Aren't we wasting time? I think we've got a hell of a lot of getting ready to do if they're planning to hit us at eleven?"

And Jess said, "Hell yes we do! We aren't gonna' let them roll in and take whatever they want are we?

""Yes we are." Pastor Windor said solemnly."

Everyone simply stared at him, dumbfounded.

"*We are wasting time!*" Pastor Windor said. The tone of his voice was very firm, resolute, and had taken on an edge of enthusiasm, and the sort of excitement that Jess hadn't heard in a voice since being around men preparing for battle back during the war. He wasn't shouting; it was as though his normal voice; the one that always left no doubt that he was a man to be taken seriously was still there. But now the fire and brimstone that always simmered just below the surface on Sunday mornings was bubbling higher, and trying to force its way out and boil over and he was barely keeping it under control. Each word was clipped, and he looked back and forth from Luke to Toby as he talked. They could tell he was thinking of the beating Nappy had inflicted on Luke and the threats he'd aimed at Toby. The thought that Walter had as he waited and watched was; 'If Nappy is stupid enough to face off with him that crazy son-of-a-bitch better have his affairs in order.' And Walter couldn't help but smile as he thought it.

Pastor Windor said, "Kaitlin, I'd like you to help Doc get prepared for a fight. I'm sure he'll tell you how you can help."

"Absolutely!" Doc interjected. "Maybe you can get some of the other ladies to help you gather up clean white linen to cut up for bandages. From what Luke said this could turn into something really nasty. And I'm afraid I might not have enough bandages on hand for something like this. Better to have them and not need them than need them and not have them. Also, ask around town and see if anyone has any alcohol; the disinfecting kind, not the drinking kind. If you find any, bring it here. I may need it. Also chloroform or laudanum or any other pain killer."

"Chloroform? Laudanum? Who would have chloroform or laudanum just lying around?" Kate asked.

"Many Army medics took it home with them after the war. A lot of men carried substantial pain home with them. I've seen that first hand. And a lot of people could have other pain medications; even veterinarians give out pain medicine. Check with Shepherd Sloan, if you can find him, He would have other things we may need, too; bandages and splints and, so forth." Kate nodded. "No sooner said than done.

Luther said, Best of luck with that."

As Kate started toward the door she said, "Don't you worry. I'll find him!"

The pastor said, "I don't doubt it a bit."

Shepherd Sloan was the town veterinarian, who, sadly, doubled as the town drunk. He seemed by far to be more devoted to the town drunk duties.

Before finding his way to Whiskey Branch from first New Orleans, Louisiana, where Sloan had made his living as a professional gambler, filling in with his veterinary duties when he took a rare break between day-long and night-long games. Once in Whiskey Branch he'd found that the farmers and small-time ranchers usually worked from dawn till dusk then spent most of the night repairing and preparing for the next day of more of the same. They didn't have time to spare for tales of his conquests in the gambling halls in Phoenix. The majority of the ladies in the town and a many of the men wouldn't socialize with Shepherd because of his former profession as a gambler. Still, to a person, all of the populace had nothing but respect for his being a vet. Farmers and loggers alike knew the importance of someone who could keep their workhorses healthy and on the job, and their family dog perky and spry into old age. As far as Pastor Windor was aware, Sloan had never gambled for more than spare change or occasionally as a way to let someone off the hook for a vet bill they couldn't pay since arriving in Whiskey Branch. He'd once confided to the pastor that he hadn't really wished to become a vet, but had done so to satisfy his father, who was a rather wealthy veterinarian back in Illinois. The old man would only pay for Shepherd's schooling if he followed in his footsteps. Then, his medical training had served him well, after all, when he became an Army medic and treated men during the war. Bleeding flesh was bleeding flesh, he'd said, rather sadly. One battlefield technique he'd learned under fire that worked only on human patients was the art of cauterizing a wound with gunpowder. Sometimes sutures and the time to apply them were an unavailable luxury. If that was attempted on an animal, the patient's fur would catch fire. He had once asked Pastor Windor why people here hated gamblers so much. The pastor had answered, "Possibly it's because you're among a different sort of people here than you were used to in in the big city. Not better or worse; just different. A big part of them are church goers. They might recall reading that the soldiers gambled for Christ's garments after he was crucified."

When Kate had gone out the door the pastor turned to Ben.

"Ben, Your store probably has the biggest dug cellar in town doesn't it?"

"Yep. I started digging it as soon as I scratched out the plan on the ground. I figured if I had a big cold storage cellar from the start it would keep me from getting lazy, andwould make me work that much harder to make a go of the store sittin' on top of it. It stays cool day and night this time of year. Not to mention it's a storm cellar that's big enough for almost everybody in the whole damn town if we need it. Pardon my French. The stairs are under the storeroom floor, and the cellar's a good eight feet deep."

"Good, this is a big storm that's brewing. I don't mean the cold blowing down from the north, though that won't make things any easier. I'm talking about the Bleus. When Kaitlin is done making her rounds collecting bandages please have her tell the families with children to gather at your store by ten am at the latest; sooner if possible. We want to get them secured in your cellar by eleven at the very latest. Their husbands, those who are able bodied, should come along and bring any guns they have; pistols or rifles. Then the men who really feel they need to stay there close to their people and protect them can do just that, they'd be useless elsewhere anyway; unable to think about anything but those they left behind in the care of others. Ben, I want you to arrange them in a perimeter around the store to defend it in case of attack. And if you can find one, post a good man at the top of the cellar steps with a shotgun as a last line of defense in case the store is overrun?"

Ben saluted, and said; "Yes sir. Sounds like just the damn spot for me." And then he immediately dropped his hand to his side and said, "Sorry Pastor, for the salute and the French."

"That's all right. We don't have time for apologies right now. And I wish everyone would stop apologizing for every 'damn' they let slip. I lived in Canada for a while; French doesn't bother me in the least. " As he said the last, Pastor Windor smiled slightly.

Luke surprised them all again; something he'd done more than once that morning, by saying, "It's a damn good thing. Now would somebody get me off this table? We got a lot of getting ready to do."

Doc said, "Luke, it grieves me to say, but I'm afraid that for the next few days at least, you are going to have to be limited to serving in an advisory capacity." Before Doc could get another syllable out, Luke swung a leg off of the exam table and shouted, "I'll be damned! I'll not lay here and let somebody else put a bullet in that bastard Nappy. That's a right I've reserved for myself. I deserve it."

Jess stepped up to the table and put a hand on Luke's shoulder and said, "I know it's not the way you want it to be, and it's not the way any of us want it to be, for you. I hope you know that there's not a one of us that wouldn't do anything in the world to change how this turned out. But what you went through could save the town. And the last thing anybody wants is for you to kill yourself by not listening to what Doc tells you. Nappy couldn't kill you; so don't you do what that crazy ass-hole couldn't.

"Walter said, "You know what Luke? It's kinda' my fault; what happened to you. When you weren't back after a few days I should'a gone in the woods where Ben dropped you off and started trackin' you."

Jess chuckled and said, "Walter you couldn't track an elephant in the snow. Plus, Bleu's men woulda' heard you comin' a mile away. The only reason you could sneak up on my bull elk that time was cause it was a'ready dead, and you saw it drop or you couldn't'a found it."

Walter grinned at Jess and said, "Like you coulda' done better. With that gimpy leg of yours, you'd still'a been'a been pickin' your ass up out'a the leaves at Christmas.

Doc said, "Come now, children. If you two can't get along, I'll have to separate you.

"No, Walter if it was anybody's fault, it was mine," Pastor Windor stated bluntly. "The whole spy idea was mine."

Then, for the first time since he'd being brought back from the brink of death Luke became angry. "Stop it! Stop it all of you! What happened to me wasn't anybody's fault but Napoleon Bleu Junior's. Save your rage and your energy for him, and his family and friends. All you're doing is wasting time. And Pastor, don't forget, Nappy wants you, wants you bad, and he'll go through Toby if that's what it takes."

"Pastor Windor said, "You're right Luke, we don't have a lot of time to waste."

"True Pastor, what do you want us to do?" Jess asked, and indicated himself and Walter. You told Ben and Katie what you want them to do, and it's pretty clear what Doc's job will be. I'm just hopin' he doesn't get worked hard at all. But there's got to be something for Walter and me to do!"

"Me too," Luther said, his voice its typical quiet, but firm and impossible to ignore rumble.

"And you damn-well better not forget me!" Toby added, his voice showing a strength and maturity well beyond his sixteen years. "My little piece of this town cost me my whole family. I'll not lose it to the likes of the Bleus." He didn't bother to ask a pardon for his French.

Pastor Windor stood with his eyes squeezed closed for a moment, his fists clenching and unclenching at his sides before again opening his eyes and saying, "I don't intend for anybody to lose anything to the Bleus." There was a hard edge in his voice that seemed totally foreign coming from him. It was like something no one in the room had ever heard from him. His eyes had narrowed and taken on a flinty spark that made Walter take an involuntary step backwards. Then the orders began coming rapid fire; and there was no question that they were orders, not suggestions;

"Okay, first of all, anything Luke says is gospel! Gospel, understood? He nearly died going into that den of beasts. And he's the only one among us who understands what those beasts are truly like."

"Except for you, apparently," Doc said.

"Yes except for me. And that's why I won't underestimate what they're capable of. Especially this Avey they've brought in. He's the wildest wild card of all in this game."

So you do know him? Doc asked.

"Not personally, but I know of him."

"Does he frighten you?"

"The way he confuses this whole situation frightens me. Having Nappy to watch out for was worry enough without having Avey to watch out for, too. Nappy thinks he's a fast gun, and he may be. I don't know. I've never seen him draw. Have you, Luke?"

Luke rubbed his eyes thoughtfully. "Only when he was showing off against the men in the moonshine camps. And then it was clear that they weren't allowed to outdraw him. He never said it right out, but they knew it. And they knew nobody was going to pull a trigger. So it always came out with him lookin' fastest. But that doesn't really tell you much."

"So there you go," Pastor Windor went on. "I don't just have Nappy; who might, or might not be fast, to deal with. Now there's Avey; who's definitely fast, and also a known back-shooter on top of it. So of course the situation frightens me. I'd be a fool if it didn't. It frightens me because I don't know which direction to expect the trouble to come from. But that's my worry. Here's what I want from you men:

Then, no matter what he had said before, there was no doubting that when he began talking, the things he was saying were orders, not suggestions;

First, Walter, I know almost every time I see your wagon it's loaded; either with logs or boards. Is it loaded now?"

"Yep. Sure is! Got seven real big birch logs on there, all tied down good'n snug. I was plannin' on startin' to saw them up s'afternoon after Sunday service and lunch."

"Good. Walter, I hope it doesn't come to it, but if it does come to it would you be willing to sacrifice those logs to help stop the Bleus?"

Walter puffed out his chest, squared his shoulders, and said, "Pastor, I ain't no great shakes when it comes to fightin.' I was cavalry, but I was too big to sit a horse in combat, so they had me rigging wagons and loadin' cannons. I've never been especially smart, I can't move around quick, and I'm not the shot that Jess is, or anything like that. So if my wagon and those logs will help stop the Bleus, you consider'm yours. Hell, they grow'm on trees." Pardon my… Never mind. You just consider it done. I was afraid there might not be a way I could do my part. All you have to do is tell me what you have in mind."

"Excellent, I knew I could count on you, Walter."

Pastor Windor turned to Jess. "Okay, Jess, My question for you is; with that bum leg, can you climb a ladder?"

"You bet your ass! What do you have in mind?"

"Well, it seems like all I hear about is what a great shot you are with a Winchester. So it seems only logical to put you at the highest point there is in Whiskey Branch. Maybe this would be a good time for Luke to be the advisor that Doc said he should be for now. Luke, you had a hand in putting up most every building in town. What's the highest point in town that we could put a sharpshooter to give him a clear shot across the creek?"

Luke massaged his temples with his fingertips, as if trying to squeeze out the answer. He sat motionless like that on the exam table long enough for Doc to become concerned. He picked up Luke's wrist and felt his pulse. "Luke shook his hand free, and said, "I'm okay Doc; just a little fuzzy-headed. Maybe my brain's still froze up. Don't go treating me like an old lady. Then he said, "Pastor, in answer to what you were asking; the roof of the schoolhouse. That's the highest place in Whiskey Branch. And with the trees almost completely bare of leaves like they are now, a body would have a real good view of most of the north bank of the creek from up there. I'm guessing that's why you were asking if Jess could climb a ladder. Well, just so you know, my ladder is in the shed behind my house, and the lock's been busted for over a year, so getting to it won't be a problem. Then he told Jess, "Just be careful on that roof. Even late in the morning there will still be some dew-frost up there till the sun's been on it for a while. You don't want to end up with two bum legs."

"So true," Jess answered. If I'd known being a farmer could give me *one* I may have stayed in Baltimore and I'd still be a gunsmith. Some mornings I feel like somebody took my ankle bones out, dipped'em in mud and put' em back in."

Pastor Windor said, "So, that's how you got to be such a good shot."

"Yeah; you fix them, you have to test fire them. You do that a hundred times; you get good. And then there was the war." Jess said no more.

Luke said, "Doc, do you still have my pants?"

"Sure do. They're in the kitchen. Miss Waters hung them over a chair by the stove to dry last night. Do you think you're ready for them?"

"Well yes, actually I am. This towel does the job in a roomful of men, but I wouldn't mind having my pants on before Kate or Miss Waters come back in. Plus, I was wondering if Pastor Windor's spyglass is still in the left hip pocket. That's where I last recall it being. That's the pocket I always carried it in when I went out to watch Nappy watching you and Toby from the top of that rock cliff, Pastor. He was always using binoculars. He has the really good brass kind I used to see the officers using back during the war." As far as I know, I had the spyglass in my pocket when he clouted me on the head. That doesn't mean it didn't fall out while he was dragging me to the creek. You know the more I think about it, the more I remember. I think he drug me behind his horse. I guess he wasn't bothered about bruising me up under the circumstances. Or the bastard might have taken it just for spite. Well anyway, I was thinking it might be useful for Jess when he's up on that roof."

Doc said, "I'll go check your pants for it right now, Luke. Either way, I'm sure you're ready to get back into them, though I wouldn't feel too awful modest about Miss Waters seeing you without them on. The old sweetheart was the one who peeled them off of you when you were soaking wet and half frozen. She turned out to be a darned good nurse in a pinch." Doc went to the kitchen, and in a moment came back with the small spyglass. He slid it in and out a couple times to be sure it still functioned, and then gave it to Jess, who slipped it into his own pocket and said, "Thanks, I better get movin'. I got some things to do. I've got a ladder and a rifle to collect and load. And I think I'm going to put on my heavy wool coat. The wind's gonna' be whistlin' up on that schoolhouse roof." He took out his pocket-watch and checked it. "Eight-forty-five a'ready. Yep, I best get a move on."

'Pastor Windor said, "Give me fifteen minutes Jess, and I'll try to catch up to you at your house."

"That would be good. I'd like to know what you've got in mind for me up on that schoolhouse roof. But if you get held up, it's okay; I'll eat a couple eggs and swallow some more coffee. I got a feeling I'm going to need it. I'll go ahead and take the ladder to the schoolhouse. The back of my barn is only a few places up from the school. I'll just stay put till you get there. As long as you get to my house in time to let me in on your plan I'm good."

Jess nodded a goodbye, pulled his coat collar up around his neck and headed out the door into the cold northern wind.

Pastor Windor turned his attention to Luther.

"Luther, I think that after hearing your moving speech at the town meeting regarding how much you care about our little town and its people you would be the perfect welcoming committee to surprise the uninvited visitors who will soon be coming up our main street."

"You just tell me what you want me to do, Pastor."

Instead, Pastor Windor said, "Doc why don't you put on another pot of coffee? Then, before I head for Jess' house, we five can put together our plan of action. And we'll be doing it with something warm in our bellies. It always helps me think better on cold days. Then when Ben and Katelin have accomplished their missions, we should be fairly well prepared. I only wish I had told Katelin to bring Shepherd Sloan back here with her if she managed to locate him."

What in the world do you want him for?" Walter asked. She'll probably find him too drunk to stand up, if she finds him at all."

"But, Lord willing, she'll find him sober," Pastor Windor answered.

"And even if he is suffering a hangover from last night, we still have a couple hours. If we keep him from getting any more liquor and pour enough of Doc's coffee in him he might turn out to be valuable. He *was* an army medic. He might surprise you. I think there's more to him than you realize. Or maybe even more than he realizes. I think he has a good soul."

"Well now; that's more in your line than mine. I just hope you're not wastin' the little time we have."

"I know where to find him," Toby spoke up, surprising them all.

"What…? How…? Pastor Windor stammered. "

"I can see his back steps from my back yard. Sometimes when I go out early in the morning to look at the sunrise over the mountains I see him sitting out there on his back steps. Sometimes he's just sitting with his head in his hands; sometimes he's throwing up. Most times he's throwing up. But even when he sounds like his insides are about to come up he always waves if he sees me. If Kate knocked on his door and he was out back being sick he didn't hear her. I bet he's there right now. You want me to go see? If she didn't find him she never got to ask him about the things Doc needs!" Toby was barely able to control his eagerness to be a part of the action.

"Okay, Toby," Pastor Windor said after a moment's deliberation. "But you go straight to Shepherd Sloan's home and see if he's there. If he is there, explain the situation to him as quickly and in as few words as possible. Tell him that *I* asked if he would *please* come to Doc Forrest's. Tell him it's very important. And try to get a feel for what kind of condition he's in. Make it clear that time is short, so if he's not right he'd better get right. Also, find out if Kate's been there. If she has, ask him if he was able to help her with what she needed. If she hasn't been there, tell to bring the things with him if he has them. You know what Doc asked for, I believe."

He put a hand on Toby's shoulder. "Do you think you've got all that?"

Toby nodded vigorously. "Yes sir. You can count on me. And I don't know Mister Sloan very well, but I think I can talk him into coming. I heard what you told Mister Denborough, and if you think he's good inside that's good enough for me."

"Okay, that's perfect Toby," Pastor Windor told him." There's just one more thing. After you go to Shepherd Sloan's, go to your home and strap on your gun and get a full box of cartridges. Then return here as quickly as possible. "

"Yes sir!" Toby was instantly as excited and jumpy as a boy ready to dig into a pile of birthday gifts, or who had put away too much lemonade at a picnic and can't get his fly open. Pastor Windor was sorry to see him so eager about the prospect of strapping on a gun and doing harm. But in reality it was what he'd been training him for. There was no way around it. The facts had just caught up to him and seemed to be running away with him. He stopped Toby before he could head out the door and said, "If you see Kate tell her what's going on."

"Will do!" Then Toby was out the door and gone on his mission.

Walter looked at Doc and said, "I wish I had that kind of energy."

Doc said, "You probably did when you were his age."

Luke had finished struggling into his pants and was sitting on the exam table sipping coffee. He said, "That boy's really turned out good. He coulda' really soured after losing his parents when he was so young *and* his little sister when she was no really no more than a baby and he'd just turned eleven himself. I remember when she died. I was in the wagon train with the Doves. And you know, when I was across the creek I heard one of the men in the moonshine camps say that old-man Bleu is over ninety years old. Now you tell me Pastor; why does a faultless five-year old die from pneumonia while a worthless criminal like him lives all those years?"

"Pastor Windor said." That's a hell of a tough question Luke, pardon my French. I do know I've seen it written; The good die young that they may avoid corruption, the evil live long that they may repent."

"Walter asked, "Is that from The Bible?"

"No," Pastor Windor said. "It's from a Jewish text called The Zohar. Wisdom can be found in many places; and I look for it whenever and wherever I get the opportunity." Then he added, "I'm sorry, I know it doesn't seem like much of an answer, but I'm afraid it's the best I've got."

Luke said, "Well, I think it's pretty good under the circumstances; you do have an awful lot on your mind right now."

Pastor Windor said, "You're right about that, and I've got to start unloading some of it before it starts running out of my ears. Walter, what I want you to do, first off is be sure that Mildred and all of your brood is tucked in safe and sound at Ben and Kate's store. Their safety is your number one priority. Then hitch up your team and make sure those logs are roped down good and tight. And then please drive your rig to the east end of town where you'll be able to see the Bleu's wagon coming from the direction of Sweetwater. When you're there, pull it into the clearing behind the stand of pines on the south side of the road. Do you know where I mean?"

"Sure do. And what you're lookin' to do is hide my rig from the Bleus when they come tearin' up Sweetwater Road towards town, right?"

"Right as rain."

"What about me Pastor?" Luther asked. "You're not planning on leaving me out of the fun are you?"

"Not a chance! I want you in the trees on the north side of the road right across from where Walter's wagon is concealed. I've got a surprise in mind for them when they spring their surprise attack."

"You want me to bring my rifle?" Luther asked.

"No. I have a weapon in mind more befitting a man of your nearly biblical strength. Let me explain.”

“But what about the men coming across the creek?” Luke asked before the pastor could go on. “We can't forget about them! It was pure dumb luck that we know what they're planning, and we better be ready for them too!”

“You needn't worry about that Luke. I know it's hard to believe from where you are right now, but I'm feeling every one of your pains right along with you. I feel responsible, and I intend to make the Bleus pay. I'm truly sorry if others have to suffer, but I think that excepting for poor Millie; who you told us about, the Bleu family are due for some fire and brimstone, all the more for the way they've treated her, and I believe I know just the way to provide it for them.”

Behind a small unassuming frame house, bordering on shabby, that sat on the east end of Creek Street Toby found Shepherd Sloan seated on the steps with his head in his hands. He was sound asleep; exactly where Toby had expected to find him. He was snoring noisily, the ragged growl hitching occasionally, as though he was having trouble catching his breath. Toby shook him awake immediately, aware there was no time to waste. “Doctor Sloan!” he said, hopefully loudly enough to cut through the fog he knew Sloan would be experiencing. Finally Sloan shook his head, clearly confused, groaned, and then looked up, blinking. “Oh, it's you Toby.”

Toby asked “Doctor Sloan, are you okay?”

“You called me Doctor. And what, you mean is, am I drunk, right?” Sloan said

“Yes, I called you doctor. That's what you are.

“Nobody calls me doctor, Toby. The nice ones say, “Hey vet.” But most times I'm just the gambler, or the drunk. But Toby, you called me doctor, even though I'm only a veterinarian. You know what; Toby? I'm a damn good veterinarian. And during the war I was a damn good medic! Toby, I *was* drunk, last night, but I'm a lot better now.”

"You better be, because we need you!" Toby grabbed his shoulder and shook him and then gave him Pastor Windor's message, word for word.

Sunday Morning: Final Planning

10:10 am:

The door of Doc Forrest's office opened, allowing entrance to a bitter wind before Toby managed to get a better grip on the knob that had at first slipped from his grip due to the slight crust of frost that covered everything exposed to the cold. A light mist of rain had conspired with the frigid temperatures to ice everything over.

"Walter said, "You want me to give you a hand, Toby?"

"That's all right, I'll get it." Shepherd Sloan stepped around Toby and grabbed the doorknob. His eyes were red and watery, and the expression on his face showed that he practically expected the insults to start flying his way at any second. He stepped fully into the room, propping his hip against the door, bracing it against the wind. He nodded at Luke, and then turning to Pastor Windor, said, "'Morning Pastor. This is a strange place for you to be on a Sunday morning, isn't it?"

Toby was carrying a canvas bag over his shoulder and Shepherd Sloan was carrying the ubiquitous black leather bag which was universal to doctors and apparently also to veterinarians.

"Well, Shepherd, I've always believed I should go wherever the job leads me

"Funny," Shepherd Sloan said. That's kind of what Toby explained to me. Except the job didn't lead me; a teenaged kid led me. Or dragged me, was more like it. That kid's damn persuasive. Please pardon my French."

Luke and Doc looked at each other and Luke covered his mouth with his hand, but finally couldn't hold in the laughter.

Shepherd Sloan looked at the men grinning at each other like fools and asked, "What's so funny?"

Then all traces of good humor disappeared like smoke when Walter said to Sloan "Just what kind of help do you think *you* can be?"

Shepherd Sloan looked at Toby and said, "He's one of the ones I was telling you about."

Then Sloan said to Walter, "The same as you, whatever kind of help I *can* be."

Toby, who had been standing with the bag over his shoulder, said, "Doc, there's some of the stuff you were wanting in here; Bandages and stuff like that; things Doctor Sloan had at his house."

Shepherd Sloan, who had done his best to shake off Walter's remark said, "Doctor Forrest, I have to say I was shocked and appalled nearly to the point of disbelief when Toby told me what looks to be coming Whiskey Branch's way. My first response was to assume that he was trying to pull a mean trick on the local sot. But then I changed my mind about that."

Really, why was that?"

"He called me Doctor. A little respect can work wonders for someone who has nearly forgotten what it feels like. And, Doctor Forrest, I've got some items in my bag that may prove useful in the upcoming hours. As you know, animal medications and drugs can be very effective in treating humans. I have a horse and ass sedative that would be suitable for a very large person in an emergency situation."

Luke covered his mouth to hide his grin, but looked at Walter over his hand and said, "Boy, do I wish Jess could have been here for that."

Doc Forrest said sincerely, "Thank you Doctor Sloan. If I become overwhelmed with patients during the upcoming conflict, I'm sure *any* of our townspeople who become injured will be very glad you are around to care for them.”

“Oh, yeah!” Toby spoke up. “Pastor, we ran into Kate as we were leaving Doctor Sloan’s house. She spread the word about everybody gathering their families up at their store. And she had a whole row of ladies behind her carrying petticoats and dresses and things. They’re coming by here to drop them off before they head to the store. They should be here any time. So Doc, you’re going to have all the bandages you need.”

Pastor Windor said, “Okay, our time’s about up. When Toby and Shepherd came in the door the wind was at their back, from the north. That’s good for us, *very* good. When the Bleu’s bugler blows charge from the north side of the creek, the wind will help carry the sound our way. We’re going to use their attack signal to signal our counter-attack. We should know they’re coming almost before some of their own men do.”

“And then what?” Luther asked. “I still don’t know exactly what you have in mind for me to do.”

“Same here,” Walter said. “I know you want me to take my wagon out on the east end of town and stash it along the south side of the road where them Bleu bastards won’t see it when they come chargin’ in. So far, that’s all I know.”

“And I’ll be hiding across the road from where he’s got his wagon hidden, right?” Luther asked.

Pastor Windor said, “Well, I’ll tell you what I have in mind. You give it a listen and tell me what you think. You too, Luke; especially you. You’re the expert on the enemy.”

Then Pastor Windor explained his plan and their parts in it.

Luke’s reaction was immediate and enthusiastic; “Hot-damn! Get me out of this room. It’s pay-back time. I’ve gotta’ see this.”

Pastor Windor said, "I think you should see what Doc thinks about that first, don't you?"

Luke looked at Doc Forrest and folded his hands pleadingly, "What do ya' think Doc?"

Doc Forrest said, "You're a big boy Luke. You don't need my permission, though I suppose it *would* be too much to ask you to take it easy for a while? You guys seem determined to make this old man's job harder. First it's Jess, going up on a roof with that bad leg of his, and now you, determined to climb out of bed after being beaten half to death. What will be next?" Then he held his hand up and said, "No; don't tell me; I don't want to know. But don't get me wrong; I'm not saying I'm not proud of you. I'm not saying that at all. I'm just not looking forward to patching any of you men you up when this is over. Of course, the only thing that would be worse is being told I'm too late to patch any of you up."

Shepherd Sloan said, "You can count on me to help in any way I can Doctor Forrest."

Luke grinned at Doc. "Come on Doc Forrest. You act like I drug myself behind a horse, and threw myself in a cold creek just to make work for you."

Then Pastor Windor asked Walter and Luther, "Okay, do you two have any questions about what I suggested?" When neither of the men offered any, he said, "Good, what's more important, do you think it will work?"

Well, speakin' just for me, I think it's a crackerjack plan!" Walter exclaimed; practically giddy with excitement. "Don't you think so Luther?" Walter reached out and slapped Luther on the back. It was like a white mountain slapping a black mountain on the back.

"Yeah, crackerjack," Luther rumbled, as calm as ever, but with a broad smile.

"Yeah, but what about me? Am I supposed to stand around and watch all this stuff happening, while my friends might be gettin' shot up?" Toby asked, clearly more than a little angry at the prospect.

"No, Toby, not at all." Pastor Windor said. I see you're strapped up." referring to the fact that Toby had put on his Father's gun belt as instructed. Did you bring the box of cartridges like I said to?"

"Yes sir. It's in that canvas bag of stuff from Doctor Sloan's place."

"Good deal," Pastor Windor said, making Toby's smile grow so wide it looked like the upper half of his head might fall off.

"Right now," the pastor went on, "What I want you to do is make sure you're loaded with fresh, dry cartridges, and then fill all the cartridge loops on your belt with fresh shells. When you've done that, come outside. You and I will talk for a few minutes." Pastor Windor walked out the door.

Toby looked at Luke, who said, "It's gonna' be right cold out there."

Toby nodded. "But, you know what? When I'm talking to him, I hardly even notice things like the temperature. They just don't seem important"

Luke said, "Funny how that is, ain't it?"

"Hey Toby," Walter said, "If you get a chance will you get a message to my wife to put my old double-barrel under the seat on my big wagon?"

"Sure will. I'll either get somebody to give her the message or I'll go tell her myself."

"Good deal" Walter said. "That baby gives me a real feeling of comfort sometimes."

Then Toby said, "Excuse me," and went into the kitchen, where he went about doing as Pastor Windor had instructed. He wanted to be alone and undistracted. He knew it was very important that it be done exactly right; it wasn't practice anymore. When he had finished, he met Kate and her parade of garment-bearing ladies as he went out the door. He ushered them in out of the cold, where Doc Forrest set them up in the kitchen ripping the clothing into strips suitable for bandages he hoped wouldn't be needed.

Toby stepped onto the porch, shivering, and cupped his hands in front of his face, blowing into them.

Pastor Windor said "It might be hard to believe right now, but the closer it gets to noon, and the higher the sun climbs over the mountains, the warmer it'll get. Plus, I think the wind's going to let up."

"What makes you think so?'"

"It's just a feeling. The mist that was falling earlier and slickening everything up has stopped. That's a good sign; don't you think? At least we can walk around and stay on our feet.

"You can read the weather, too?" Toby asked.

"I pay attention, that's all. I'm just observant"

Toby pushed his hat up against the wind that threatened to steal it away, and said, Well, I hope you don't get to observe a snowstorm. "

The pastor glanced at the clouds overhead. "No, not today, tomorrow maybe; the storm we can expect today is coming from across Whiskey Creek."

Toby said, "Well, you still haven't told me where I'm going to fit into your battle plan." His eyes flashed with anger at the thought of being left out; of not having the chance to play his part in the town's defense. "Whiskey Branch is my town too, you know! Luke is my friend too! Do you think you're the only one who felt bad looking at him beat up in there? He was one of the first ones that jumped in and turned my parent's wagon into a home for me. I'd like the chance to put a bullet in the monster that beat him and threw him in the creek to die. Do you think you're the only one that feels that way? Why did you teach me?"

Pastor Windor took a rare, sad moment for reflection, and all he came up with was a mental question for himself; 'yes, why did I?'

But a moment was all he could allow himself.

10:30am:

"Toby, what I want you to do; your part in my plan, is as important a part as there can be in a battle like the one we're facing. What I want you to do is walk to Luther's shop (which was within sight of where they stood) and get his mare and buckboard. I don't think Luther will mind you borrowing them under the circumstances. Then go through town and begin pounding on doors and gathering up any and all guns you can locate, and haul them to the schoolhouse. The school will serve as our armory during this mess. It will be well protected with Jess on the roof. While you're at it, let anyone you see who Kate missed know that there is a fortress of sorts at the store, and urge them to go there till this is over. And make sure someone gets the word to Ben that we're storing up weapons at the school."

"Do you really think it will be bad?"

"I don't know, Toby. It just might be."

"Have you been through anything like this before?"

Toby could hardly wait for Pastor Windor's answer. In all the excitement he'd sort of forgotten till just then what a total unknown the man was. He wouldn't have thought that would be possible for a thing like that to slip his mind.

After he'd discovered the man he'd listened to sermons from on Sundays could handle a six-gun like the gunslingers he'd only read about and dreamed of seeing; how in the world could that thought be anything but the one very first in his mind?

The pastor took a moment before saying only, "A long time ago, but not long enough." That was all he said, and Toby didn't ask him any more about it; he got a clear feeling he shouldn't. After giving him a minute, Toby did ask, "What should I do after I get the guns collected at the school? And where will you be?"

"After that, you come back here and see if you can do anything to help the two doctors. I didn't make it to Jess's house early like I wanted to. I wanted him to take it slow and easy going up that ladder to the schoolhouse roof so he wouldn't break a leg, or worse. Also, I wanted him to have a chance to look things over on the other side of the creek with the spyglass. That didn't work out, so I've got to get over to his place and let him know where he fits in the plan before things start to get frantic. Because I believe when things start to happen they're going to happen fast. He's a very important part of the plan. It's only fair to let him know what the plan is, and what his part of it is, don't you think?"

Toby nodded. "It's only fair. Everybody else knows what they're supposed to do now; even me. Then what will you do?"

Pastor Windor closed his eyes for a long moment, his lips moving silently, and then said, "I suppose I'll come back here and wait to see what happens at eleven o'clock, like everybody else. I just pray that whatever happens, we're ready for it. Now, let's get to it! He put his hand on Toby's shoulder, and then they left the porch in different directions; Toby in the direction of Luther Wilson's shop, and the pastor toward Jess's home and the schoolhouse, before heading back to Doc's.

10:35am:

Pastor Windor knocked on Jess's door.

Jess answered on the third knock, yawning as if fighting sleep, and said, "Oh, I thought you forgot about me. Do you want a cup of coffee?"

Pastor Windor looked at his pocket watch, shook his head, and said, "I'm sorry Jess, I meant to be here a long time ago. The fact is,

I had a whole string of ideas, and yours is the one that's going to set things in motion; light the fuse, so to speak. I knew what I had in mind for you from the minute Luke described the Bleu's plans. What took time was lining up what will come next, and after that, and so on and so on, and …well, you get the idea. That's what took me so long; trying to get all the pieces in place. I'm sorry I'm so late."

"Don't worry about it. I wasn't pa'ticully anxious to get on that roof. I've still got goin' on a half an hour before eleven o'clock, but if you just tell me what you have in mind I'll head on over there now."

Pastor Windor said, "Jess, I think I'll walk over there with you. That way I can explain on the way, and then I can hold the ladder for you too, in case things are still slick."

"That sounds good to me. We can sit down and have a cup of coffee when this is all over."

"I'm ready to go whenever you are, Jess."

"Okay Pastor, let's go." They left for the short walk to the school.

10:45am:

Pastor Windor had barely made it back into Doc Forrest's house and closed the door behind him when he heard the sound of running footsteps pounding the ground, growing louder as they rapidly came closer. He moved to open the door, but heard shouting from the center of town even before he could take the few steps to reach it. The door burst open and Toby said, "Pastor, something's going on!" Then he hesitated, as though he'd thought better of it.

"What, Toby? What is it?"

Luke, who had heard the shouting clearly when Toby opened the door, said, "It sounds like Nappy has gotten impatient, Pastor."

Pastor Windor looked at Toby and said, "Toby, I want to know what's happening out there, and I want to know now!"

Toby said, "Nappy's standing up on top of the cliff the slab that made the twist broke off of, and he's dead drunk. He's calling you out."

Luke said, "That's where I was telling you about him going to watch you and Toby practicing, because it's right across the creek and you can see the whole town from up there.

All the while they could hear Nappy's loud, but unintelligible voice; baying over the sound of the wind and through the door that Toby had given only a half-hearted tug closed.

"Pastor Windor said, "I guess I better go see what he wants."

Before he could move toward the door Shepherd Sloan stepped up next to him and said, "Pastor, I'm about your size. Why don't you let me put on your coat and hat and go out there? He might just be drunk enough and crazy enough not to know the difference.

Pastor Windor asked, "Are you willing to take that gamble?"

Shepherd Sloan said, "I'm a gambler, it's what I do. Besides, from what Luke said, that man's pure-D crazy. I saw a crazy man accuse the most honest dealer in New Orleans of cheating. He bluffed the dealer into folding and took the biggest pot in the saloon's history. The next night the same crazy man got himself shot dead trying to bluff another dealer 'cause he thought he was too smart to lose. The crazy man across the creek thinks he's too smart to lose. Anybody can be bluffed. And you know Pastor; you don't stay alive for many years as a gambler without being in a few scrapes. I might just come out of things better than you expect, even if it does come to a showdown. I'm probably not the slowest gun west of the Rockies. I might take him. And if I don't, it's okay by me because you're the best friend I've got in this town. And, you know what, you're probably the best friend anybody's got in this town. That's why I should go out there. I'm a good value, as my grandfather; that crooked old horse-trader would have said. If he does get me, I'm a cheap trade to keep you alive."

"No Shepherd, it doesn't work that way. The Bleu family may be the town's unfair curse, but for some reason Nappy has decided that he should be my own personal curse, and I don't intend to push him off on someone else.

All the while Nappy kept raving; louder and less sensibly as he went.

Then during a momentary break in the wind they heard him bellow, "If you're too much of a coward to face me Preacher, send out the kid; your *pup*, and I'll show *him* who's the fastest.

Shepherd spoke up again over the noise with advice, "I've been around my share of roaring drunks, and I can practically guarantee *that* one is taking a pull from a bottle of courage between just about every second word. So he's getting drunker and more dangerous every time."

"But he's also getting more out of breath each time. You can't chug from a bottle and inhale at the same time, especially if you're already roaring drunk. So he's balanced on the edge of a cliff in the cold, and out of breath in wind that is bitter enough to take away what little breath he has."

"Pastor, you've just about got me ready to cry sad tears for the poor boy."

Pastor Windor said, "Don't do that; I'm just figuring the odds. I was looking for my advantages and how to use them. If I go out there one of us is likely to die, and I would rather it not be me."

He paused to listen. Nappy was again screaming threats aimed at Toby. How many bullets he could put in the whelp before the punk got his gun out of his holster…on and on he went.

Finally Pastor Windor had heard all he could stand. He walked to the door and pushed it open enough to look out and see if there were people on the street. He could hear Nappy raving and roaring, showing no sign of tiring out, as he had hoped he might. In fact, almost as if Nappy had read his thoughts, he shouted, "Hey Preacher! Since you're such a chicken, I think I'll punish someone else for your cowardice. I see noses sticking outta' a lot of windows an' doors; people wanting to see if their preacher is brave or not, I s'ppose. If you don't come out here and face me I'm going to start taking some target practice at those noses. It might be fun.

Pastor Windor adjusted his belt and holster. Then he pushed out the door into the lessening wind. He had predicted it correctly when he and Toby were talking. While still strong, the wind had eased and the steadily rising sun had warmed the air considerably. All things considered; not the worst day for a gunfight.

He walked the short distance that put him directly across Whiskey Creek from where Nappy stood looking down. Pastor Windor's first impression upon looking up at him was that Luke's description was accurate; he was small; and according to Luke not only in stature, but also emotionally. Nappy's position atop the stone cliff put him about twenty feet above him and twenty yards across the Whisky Twist, which right at that time was pretty calm; the creek level running low as a result of a Fall that had been short on rain.

Nappy had quieted considerably now that the target of his ridicule was there face to face and clearly not afraid of him instead of out of sight and perceived to be hiding in fear.

"Well?" Pastor Windor said. "Here I am. What will it be, *Kid?*"

Pastor Windor flipped his coat tail back, making his gun visible, and as Nappy watched, he removed the small leather loop over the hammer to free it from the holster and clear it for drawing. "Well *Kid*. What's the matter? Are you getting a little shaky up there in the cold? That wind has got to be making your hand tremble by now. You've been up there shooting your mouth off so long your trigger finger might actually be getting a little numb."

While this exchange was happening Toby and the two doctors had moved from the Doc's house to a place on the edge of a stand of scrub pines.

"You called me *Kid!*" Nappy shrieked; apparently unable to focus on anything other than his single-minded need to one-up the pastor. Don't you call me *Kid!*" he screamed so loudly his voice broke. Then he drew his gun.

Before his gun was halfway out of its holster Pastor Windor drew and fired, just once. Nappy jumped and shrieked, his knees buckling, nearly falling face-first from his perch, and frantically patted his chest all over looking for blood or holes, but found none. Then he realized he wasn't shot but his hat was gone, and then he caught sight of it swirling around in the currently slow-moving Twist. Even from where he looked down the bullet hole in it was clear to see. Nappy shrieked, "You bastard!" He was again at full volume. Then he again screamed, "You called me *Kid*." He clearly had a one-track mind when it came to that subject. Pastor Windor fully expected him to draw again, but instead Nappy reached behind himself with both hands. He came out with two things he must have had in his hip pockets. In one hand was a match, in the other a stick of dynamite. He flicked the match alight with his thumbnail. The flame flickered in the wind, and then grew. He touched it to the fuse. When the fuse was hissing and spitting sparks he drew his arm back over his head and threw the dynamite in a looping arc in the direction of Pastor Windor and the main street of Whiskey Branch. As he let it go he yelled, "Call *me* kid, will ya'?" Then he stood laughing and shrieking like a loon.

Everyone watching on the town side of the creek cringed as they saw the dynamite leave Nappy's hand, trailing a stream of sparks behind it. But before the dynamite had flown a dozen feet from Nappy, Jess's Winchester spoke from the roof of the schoolhouse and the dynamite exploded in a fireball in midair. Suddenly; it was if

Nappy was punched in the chest by a huge invisible fist, and he did a big graceful backflip off of the rock cliff and disappeared from sight, with a high-pitched wail.

Pastor Windor turned to the group of men from Doc's office, which had moved closer after Nappy had gone out of sight, with the two doctors helping to support Luke on either side and asked, "Anybody know what's on the backside of that ledge?"

Every one of them shook his head and answered in the negative, claiming never having seen the need of exploring over there.

A pair of tall, old fir trees in fact stood side-by-side on the far side of the huge ledge of stone behind which Nappy had vanished. As he tumbled out of control he fell through the boughs of those trees, slowing his descent as he went, till he hit the ground on his back on a bed of evergreen needles with the wind knocked out of him, and a large number of bruises, but otherwise whole. After taking a couple of minutes he needed to catch his breath, he climbed to his feet, and after several attempts, managed to claw his way out of the thick mass of tree branches.

10:55am:

Luke looked at his watch and said, "Time's getting short. It's almost eleven. I hope everybody's ready. At least Nappy's out of the way."

Just then a voice that had become all too familiar rang out from across Whiskey Creek, "I'm not done with you preacher! Or your pet kid!

Toby had by then stepped up beside the pastor.

I can take you both!" Nappy stood directly across The Twist, looking scraped and battered, and with his shirt practically torn from his body, but for the most part he appeared uninjured. Then he yelled so loudly his voice again briefly broke, "I know! I'll take the *K… Kid* first! He accented the word '*Kid*' as Pastor Windor had when taunting him, and then he turned slightly to face Toby.

Pastor Windor said calmly, "What's the matter, you afraid of me, *Kid?*"

Nappy couldn't handle the challenge or the taunt and he pivoted back to again face Pastor Windor and then drew on him. Before Nappy's gun cleared his holster, Pastor Windor's gun was out and he fanned the heel of his left hand down across the hammer once, twice, and then a third time, and three holes appeared in Nappy's chest.

There was nothing graceful about the way Nappy fell that time. The force of the slugs slamming into him drove him over backwards, causing him to land in the wet, icy soil with a nauseating plop, but sparing him the fate that a forward fall into The Twist would have provided.

Luke leaned close to Pastor Windor and said, "I hesitate to repeat myself, but it looks like Nappy's out of the way. And this time I'd say it's a pretty definite thing."

Pastor Windor nodded and said, "I didn't want it that way."

"I know you didn't. He didn't give you a choice. The question now is what will happen next?"

"I don't have a clue. We don't know if they're watching over there. So how soon will they know across the creek that Nappy's dead? If they don't know he's dead, how soon will they realize he's missing? And if they do know, how will they respond? Will they call off the attack, or will things go on as planned? Or maybe they'll even hit harder in retaliation?"

Luke shrugged, and said, "I don't know Pastor, the thing that worries me most is that Luther and Walter can't see clear up here from where you told them to wait on the east end of town, so *they* don't even know Nappy's dead. And so'far's I know Jess only knows Nappy pitched backwards off that cliff. So he doesn't know it either. He might *think* he's dead, but he can't know it for sure. But it sure is a good thing that Jess had a clear view of Nappy when he heaved that stick of TNT. Even I didn't know Jess was that good; to take that thing out of the air like that. Still, he probably *doesn't* know Nappy's dead. Now I don't know what you set them others up to do when ol' Hoss blows his bugle over there. But I sure hope they're still listening for it if he does blow it when eleven o'clock comes 'round."

Pastor Windor said, "Luke, if the Bleus do go through with it, it won't matter if Luther and Walter don't hear the bugle, as long as Jess hears it."

"Why is that?"

Pastor Windor smiled a sly smile. Just trust me; it will be a surprise, for *everybody*. I hope this war comes to an end before it gets a good start."

On the North side of Whiskey Creek:

Millie ducked behind a crooked old birch tree and dropped to her knees. She put her hands over her eyes as if her not being able to see anything would make *her* invisible. After a moment, she could help herself no longer, and lowering one of her hands she covered her mouth to stifle her giggles in case anyone was close enough to hear her. What she really wanted to do was to laugh out loud; to laugh so loud the whole world would hear. And most of all she wanted to laugh at Lillie; laugh right in her face. Cause Nappy was dead! Nappy was dead, and she was the only one that knew it! That stupid fool went and got hisself shot dead right out there by the creek. That man in the long coat and buckskin hat filled him full o' lead. And Nappy thought he was so special. Thought he was special 'cause his mama replaced theirs. But Daddy had kept the house the way their

Mama liked it. Bright and clean, just like Mama liked it.

But Nappy was gone now. That will teach him to drag Luke off behind his horse. Luke was nice to her. Nobody was ever nice to her. She wished that man could'a killed Nappy twice.

It took less than three minutes for Millie to realize she could keep her secret no longer and she ran to the house and burst into her father's room, where she interrupted her father and Lillie discussing what to do with Nappy since he hadn't shown up at such a crucial time. Millie did just as she had dreamed of doing; she told Lillie all about the man in the long coat and buckskin hat leaving Nappy full of holes, and as she did she was laughing so hard she had trouble getting the words out.

Lillie said nothing to her; just slapped her so hard she reeled back against the wall, before sinking to the floor.

Then Lillie spun to face their father and spat, "That fool! Now what? Should we call it off?"

"Napoleon Bleu Senior, his always alcohol-slurred voice now choked with tears, said, "No, they took my son! I'll take their town. Hit them hard. Show no mercy!" He was getting louder as he went. "Kill anybody that gets in the way. If we can't take the town, burn it. And most of all; you make sure Avey gets that damned preacher that killed my boy. That damnable preacher! Always that preacher! I want him dead!" He grabbed Lillie's arm with a gnarled, arthritic hand, and squeezed with startling force. "You hear me? That damnable preacher thinks he knows me! He has no clue how many people I've put in the ground!" By then he was screaming.

He looked over her head at the clock on the wall and said, "It's time! Go do it!" Then he pushed her away dismissively; pushed her so hard she nearly stumbled and landed on top of Millie.

Lillie turned without another word and ran out of the house. Millie cringed on the floor in the corner of her father's room like a frightened child. Napoleon Bleu Senior lay back in his bed, his chest heaving, and his eyelids fluttering weakly.

11:00am:

The Battle of Whiskey Creek: The Creek Assault:

11:02 am: On the North Side of Whiskey Creek:

Lillie reined her horse to a halt and was on the ground before the dust of her arrival had settled. She'd had no trouble locating the whiskered old man in the dingy grey coat and baggy pants that were constantly stained with what might be whiskey or might be urine; more probably urine, as old Hoss was not likely to waste whiskey.

He sat on the ground amid leaves and pine needles, leaning against a tree, with an uncorked jug propped between his knees. There was a dented old bugle on a leather lanyard around his neck. He was snoring soundly, unaffected by the clatter of her horse skidding to a stop nearby.

Lillie grabbed him by the lapels of his coat and unceremoniously dragged him to his feet and shouted in his face, "Hey, you, do you have a watch?" Yes." The man known as old Hoss mumbled, and nodded.

"Can you tell time?"

Again old Hoss nodded.

Then why didn't you blow charge at eleven?" Without waiting for an answer Lillie shook him bodily.

Before old Hoss's head stopped flopping back and forth, he grabbed his bugle and blew charge better and louder than he ever did in his entire military career. And what's more; he did it with his bugle right in that bossy bitch's face.

On the South side of Whiskey Creek:

The question Luke and Pastor Windor were discussing was answered as the discussion was still proceeding.

Luke said, "Well, there it was. Do you think Jess heard it?"

Pastor Windor said, "We should know within seconds."

On the roof of the schoolhouse, Jess shifted his position for the hundredth time. He was glad the sun had fallen across the wood-shake shingles for several hours now and not just melted away the earlier morning's frozen drizzle but dried the wood till his boots had a good grip on the surface so he wasn't in danger of sliding off. It was far from comfortable, but was tolerable, and his patience had finally paid off.

The Pastor's spyglass had been put to good use since he'd climbed to the roof, checking out the lay of the land on the far side of the creek. He now knew where things were situated, and it certainly provided what the military referred to as a "target rich" environment. And now, according to his pocket watch, the bugle came right on the dot of eleven, just like Luke said. One more look through the spyglass, then it would be his time to shine; time to see if he really was as good as Walter kept bragging on him being.

Jess drew a deep breath and put the spyglass to his eye and sighted across the creek; just a little way up off the bank and a little beyond the tree line. And damned if they weren't right there, just like Luke had said they'd be. They were a rag-tag group; downright ratty looking when brought up close through the lens of the pastor's spyglass; but there was Napoleon Bleu's army, lined up in a row like a regular British picket line. Except, from what Jess recalled of his history lessons the British commanders would have hanged any of their men who were so drunk that they wobbled from side to side while in formation.

Ratty or not, when that bugle sounded they started heading toward the creek, not at a dead run, and not in an organized military charge, but moving fast, like they meant business. And something that Jess had learned a long time ago was that there was nothing worse than a mean drunk, except a whole crew of mean drunks. Especially drunks who were being *paid* to be mean.

Jess pulled in one more breath and held it, and then he centered the small metal peg at the end of his rifle barrel in the V shaped notch of the rear sight and aligned them with his target.

Well, it's Show Time! He thought, and then he squeezed the trigger.

When Jess's Winchester went off, up on the high roof of the schoolhouse everyone in Whiskey Branch heard it. A 44/40 was a sizeable round that made a sizeable noise, but the sound of the rifle shot was dwarfed by what came after.

Just as Pastor Windor had planned, and Jess had aimed to, his slug hit the boiler pot of the third in the line of the Bleu's stills that sat in a row roughly twenty yards apart beyond the tree-line up the north bank. There were nine stills in all, just as Luke had reported. Jess had seen them all clearly through the pastor's spyglass. The wisdom in hitting the third one instantly became clear. When Jess's slug hit the boiler pot, it burst. That dumped twenty gallons of grain alcohol directly on the fire beneath it. The explosion was deafening. Immediately the clearing around the still was splashed with burning liquid and flames shot thirty feet in the air.

Suddenly Napoleon Bleu's army saw a pillar of fire rising up in the direction of the creek, exactly where they were headed, and they shifted the path of their charge to go around it. Jess watched it all through the spyglass. It was all transpiring just as Pastor Windor had predicted. Jess again took aim and this time put a bullet in the fifth still in the row. That still also exploded, just as the third in the row had. But then, less than a minute later, as a result of the burning liquid being thrown everywhere and the immense heat, the still between the two that Jess had shot also exploded and burst into flames. Jess didn't expect that, but he wouldn't have been a bit surprised to find out that Pastor Windor had.

Napoleon's forces again shifted directions, faced with a growing conflagration of alcohol-fueled flames that seemed to grow ahead of them wherever they went. No more than another minute later the still that was the first one in the line from where Jess was looking at them exploded of its own accord, without him firing on it. The chain reaction kept growing outward in both directions. The phrase "All Hell breaks loose" hadn't been mentioned to Jess by Pastor Windor, but it came to Jess unbidden, looking at the wall of flames on the other side of Whiskey Creek. And regardless of the circumstances; he felt pity for Bleu's men who were facing it.

As this series of explosions was progressing, the well-protected people at Grayson's store were listening, and wondering what was happening. The women and children were safely holed up in thestorm cellar beneath the building, and the building itself was circled by a ring of very diligent armed men, ready and waiting for anyone who tried to assail the stronghold.

As he had promised, Ben sat on a chair by the top of the closed trap door with a rifle across his lap, and a loaded shotgun at the ready and within easy reach.

Just outside of town Walter shouted across the road at Luther, "My watch says it's eleven, but I sure didn't hear no bugle." He was yelling at the top of his lungs to be heard over the sounds of explosions in the distance. The noise was nearly deafening, and getting louder by the second. It was like being back in the war. "You think it started?" he continued, still at full voice.

Luther yelled back, "I'd say so. Pastor Windor said to 'Be ready when all Hell breaks loose.' Look at that." He pointed at the sky to the north. Flames were visible rising up over The Twist. "I think that qualifies."

Napoleon Bleu's troops; faced with fewer and fewer options for a safe, clear path to the creek bank were beginning to hesitate and break apart into smaller groups. Some were looking over their shoulders longingly at the cool shade beneath the trees behind them. A number of them had already thought better of the folly and retreated in the direction of that inviting shady coolness. The frigid morning temperatures they had found so miserable upon waking up in the thin canvas tents now seemed wonderful when compared to the blistering heat they faced up ahead.

Across the creek Pastor Windor and his group, who were now gathered into a small knot, stood spellbound by the happenings on the other creek-side. Suddenly they heard the crack of pistol shots and the wild screams of a woman's voice. Then, through the smoke and heat-shimmered air they saw Lillie Bleu on horseback, charging back and forth behind the fractured line of men. She was shouting like a demented banshee and firing a pistol into the air. They had no idea what threats or promises she was hurling at the men, but some of them were frightening enough or attractive enough to get a number of the men moving. A group of about a dozen men broke off and ran toward the end of the row where the unexploded stills sat. Their plan was to circle around that end and cross the creek while hoping the town's defenses were distracted by the flames shooting skyward. That was their plan. When they were still more than thirty feet from reaching that comparatively clear, safe route, Jess's Winchester spoke again, and another explosion rocked the ground and yet another pillar of flame rose into the air. With every one of Jess's shots another piece of the Bleu's moonshining empire went up in smoke. More men swiftly turned tail and ran for the woods, as the majority of the others had by then. Lillie shot at them as they went. Because of the smoke, the men on the Whiskey Branch side of the creek couldn't see if she hit any of them, but Pastor Windor said a prayer for them anyway.

The men watching from the Whiskey Branch bank of the creek were horrified to see that some of the men were either loyal enough to Napoleon Bleu or too drunk to care and tried to charge through the wall of flames. Some succumbed to the pain of their injuries and collapsed before reaching the creek bank, their clothing smoldering or actually in flames. Others made it into the water, but ran out of strength and life there and ended up floating lifelessly on top of the cold creek water. Luke said, "I'll be busy building coffins when this is over."

Shepherd Sloan said, "Better for theirs than ours."

"Better none at all," Pastor Windor answered. Then he added, "This could be a long way from over."

11:05am:

Lillie rode back and forth, surveying the mess that had resulted from the failed assault. She was angry; she was incredibly angry! She was angry for many reasons, and at many people! She was angry because the assault failed. Angry, in part at least, at herself for the failure; because this part of the plan was hers. She was angry at the men who were too cowardly to keep advancing when she ordered them to. She was especially angry at Millie for bringing the spy into their midst; angrier at her than she'd ever been before. If she'd had her way, she'd have told Nappy to throw Millie into Whiskey Creek along with the spy, since he hadn't just shot the bastard, but Lillie knew that if she told Nappy to do that her own life wouldn't have been worth a plug-nickel, because Millie really was their father's favorite. And most of all; she was furious at Nappy for getting himself dead so she couldn't figure a way to put the blame for this colossal failure on him. Well, the only hope remaining was if the charge in from Sweetwater Road worked. But damned if that part wasn't Nappy's idea. Lillie was confident she'd find a way to take the credit for it if it worked. Her father was too confused to know which way was up any more. He would accept whatever she said; if, that was; she could only get his full attention. She had total confidence she could make that happen. If need be, she would devise a plan to get Millie out of the way. Lillie knew she had always been the smart one; even *before* Nappy got his dumb ass plugged.

At the East end of town:

Luther shouted, "Well, Pastor Windor sure called it right. We heard Jess's rifle shot from up on top the schoolhouse, then all Hell broke loose."

"And here come our uninvited guests!" Walter shouted back, and pointed up the road in the direction of Sweetwater. They could see a big cloud of dust rising up off the road just around the next bend. At that point the trees lining the road at the curve still blocked the oncoming thugs from sight. "Best get ready!" He shouted and ran for his wagon behind the trees.

Reckon' so!" Luther yelled back, and picked up the weapon befitting his nearly biblical strength; as Pastor Windor had described it. He flexed his considerable muscles so he'd be ready. He didn't want to chance a cramp at just the wrong moment. The last thing he did was rock his head from side to side on his broad shoulders till he heard the satisfying crack and felt his neck muscles loosen up. Then he adjusted his grip on the weapon Pastor Windor had selected for him, wondering if the pastor had selected it for the irony involved. The word irony wasn't a word Luther knew, but he understood the concept; and it suited the situation. If there was one thing of which he was certain, it was that Pastor Windor was a wise man. So picking a weapon that Luther's people had been forced to live with for so many terrible generations couldn't possibly be only a coincidence. Luther's grandfather had read the story of Samson to him from the Bible when he was small, so if Pastor Windor wanted biblical, damned if that's not what he would get.

No more than four minutes after Walter and Luther heard the report of Jess's Winchester; which seemed to have signaled some serious destruction on the north side of Whiskey Creek, they heard the pounding of hooves and the rattle and racket of harness and wagon hardware rapidly approaching from the direction of Sweetwater. The gang that Luke had warned them would be coming was right on time. And they weren't making any effort to sneak up on the town; that was certain. As if the noise of the horses and rolling stock wasn't enough, the men in the wagon were whoopin' and hollerin' like they were a bunch of drovers on their first Saturday in town after a long cattle drive. Either they weren't smart enough to be careful, or they were so certain of their overwhelming numbers and strength they didn't see any need to be careful. Or maybe they just thought taking over somebody else's town was a bunch of fun.

Walter climbed up in the driver's seat of his wagon and grabbed the reins.

He drew a deep breath to settle his nerves, and without knowing it, he mimicked Luther's motion; rolling his head from side to side, to loosen up. He recalled telling Pastor Windor just that morning that he was never any great shakes when it comes to fighting. But damned if it wasn't all he could do to hold in a cheer as he sat there waiting to lay down Whiskey Branch's unofficial law to the bastards that beat his friend. He knew Luke was hurt real bad, so he was just itchin' to take it out on anyone who happened to come charging into town on some of Napoleon Bleu's rolling stock.

He flicked the reins to be certain they were free of tangles; but not enough to signal the team to move. It wouldn't take much. The sound of the oncoming horses was making his team jumpy and anxious. Horses were like that, and Walter was very aware of the fact; so he was careful to keep a tight hold on the reins as the invaders grew closer. He was not ready for that yet. The only advance planning He and Luther had done was a small flat stone that they had placed in the center of the road before the invading forces had rounded the bend and come into sight. They had decided that if there were two lead riders ahead of the wagon as Luke had said to expect, that when those riders reached that stone, it was time to move.

It didn't take long for the cloud of dust rolling down the road ahead of the gang to roll over the flat stone. It was time!

11:07am

As soon as the oncoming dust cloud reached the stone they had chosen as their marker, but before the dust could obscure their view of each other from across the road, Luther nodded at Walter, who gave him a thumbs-up signal in return.

They both knew their part in the plan; and they had to be quick about it.

Each of the lead riders had a cigar clenched in his teeth and was holding the reins in only one hand. In the other each man held two sticks of dynamite bound up with twine, and with their wicks twisted together to form one common one. And they were coming at a full gallop.

Luther suspected the men's cigars would double as their fuse lighters. He also recalled Luke saying that the lead riders were to only throw the dynamite if necessary.

At Pastor Windor's direction Ben had lined up a half-dozen of the town's men, well-armed, on each side of the road a hundred feet past Luther and Walter's location, in case the Bleu wagon made it past them. Those men were well back from the edge of the road, and could not have been seen by the lead riders, so there was no reason for the riders to feel they had to use the dynamite. At least that was the plan. Luther hoped the riders held off just a minute more so he could make his move before they might decide it was necessary.

Finally when he felt the time was right, Luther took two long strides into the road, swinging a fifteen-foot length of two-inch thick logging chain in a circle over his head like a lasso. Then, remembering his Grandfather's story about Samson, when he reached the proper point, he dropped to one knee and swung the full length of the chain out across the dirt road. It hit the forelegs of the two lead rider's horses a couple feet off the dirt. Both of them went down. Luther felt bad about that, but in war there were casualties; better the Bleu's horses than Whiskey Branch's people.

The rider on the left was thrown ten feet and got up shaking his head and spitting teeth. Then he spotted the chain lying on the ground. He pulled his gun and looked around desperately for someone to shoot. But he saw no one. Luther had by then stepped back into the trees. The other rider; the one on the right, was less lucky. His horse's left foreleg snapped and the horse fell on its side, trapping his leg beneath it. The horse lay there kicking and thrashing, and whinnying in pain, grinding the rider's crushed leg against the dirt road with every movement.

After a moment Luther could stand no more. He stepped out of the trees and walked to the fallen horse and rider. The man had managed to muscle his gun from his holster. He aimed it at Luther. Luther could see the end of the man's shin-bone poking from the skin in a puddle of gushing blood. It was like red water flowing from a pump with someone working hard at the handle. The fallen rider shrieked, "Get me out of here, damn it!"

Luther glanced at the thrashing horse.

"Me, God damn-it!" the rider shrieked louder, and cocked his pistol. His shrieks drowned out the noise of the still-oncoming wagon. "I can't stand it!" The man's eyes were as wild as his voice. Then his voice turned into one long moan. "I can't stand it!" he screamed again. Luther aimed his rifle in the direction of the horse's head. "Yeah, kill the damn thing so it'll stop grindin' me up! Now git me out from under this horse or I'll blow your head off!" The rider's threat was a hollow one; he was so weak from shock and blood loss he could barely hold his gun up. Then he tried his last resort; begging, "Shoot me please! I can't stand the pain. Please kill me.

Luther looked down at the rider, and said, "Sorry, I only have one bullet left." Then he put the horse out of its misery.

When Wally; the driver of the Bleu's wagon realized something had gone terribly wrong up ahead he didn't know how to respond. An old war-horse with a faded leather eye patch over the empty socket that formerly held his left eye, Wally hadn't been chosen for his smarts.

Nappy had chosen him because he was a former stagecoach driver, and for no other reason. He'd managed to keep a stage on the trail for five years without totaling it or killing anybody, and to Nappy, that was qualification enough. So for an extra ten dollars and a jug of hooch he got the honor of risking his life sitting up front-and-center on the wagon that Nappy wanted driven full-tilt into a town he didn't give a Tinker's-damn about. But, Wally had said yes, all the same. That just went to show how much he valued his own life, he supposed, or how little. But, then again, there were some he knew who would have done it for just the jug, without the ten. Actually, although it was nothing Wally knew about, the original plan was to have Luke drive the wagon, because of all the good things Napoleon Senior had heard about him, until, that was, he turned out to be a damned spy.

At first, all Wally, the wagon-driver, could see up ahead was the dust thrown up by the falling horses. The two horses going down at full speed kicked up almost as much dust and airborne grit as the two of them had made going in the dirt road at full gallop ahead of the wagon. So it didn't take someone with an overstuffed brain-pan to figure out that one or both of them must have gone down. Then the next challenge was; what to do about it.

Forced into making a snap judgment, Wally looked left, and then right, quickly trying to choose which side of the road offered the clearest path he should aim at with his wagon full of drunk, wildly enthusiastic Bleu family employees, who were all spoiling for a fight. The road was blocked by the fallen lead riders and their horses. He couldn't give less of a damn about the riders; but the horses could get tangled up in his team and drag them down. Then all Hell would break loose. He wasn't aware that all Hell had already broken loose less than a quarter-mile away on the North side of Whiskey Creek and the fire and brimstone was of the Bleu's own making, or more accurately, their own distilling, just as Pastor Windor had foreseen it being. Though Wally wasn't long on smarts, he was good with a team, and he immediately saw that along the North side the trees grew right up against the road. He wasn't aware that; only a few moments before, a very large black man with an extremely heavy length of chain had stepped from those trees and literally started the downfall of this part of the invasion plan. That left only the South side of the road, where there was maybe a twenty or twenty-five foot gap before a grove of trees. It would be a tight squeeze at a sensible crawl; and he wasn't going anywhere close to what you would call sensible or a crawl. But, all he could figure, based on the way the yahoos in the bed of the wagon that was rockin' and rollin' around underneath of him were actin', there must be more than a little bit of cash, and hooch bein' spread around. So, if he tried to back out now, he was just as likely to get shot in the back as in the chest. And of course those idiots either didn't know, or didn't care how much harder their floggin' the wagon around would make it on him to hit that damn keyhole with this rollin wooden pile of scrap-wood. But through that space it had to be. Reaching under the seat for his personal jug, he took a long pull of whiskey, and then he sucked in a big breath of clean air; because he knew that in the next few moments the air around him would be getting even thicker with dust and road grit than it already was. Instead of pulling back to rein in his team as common sense would dictate, he flicked the reins and yelled out to them. He knew them, and they knew what was expected of them. They responded by instantly increasing their speed. Then he threw his body weight to one side and dragged the reins over and guided the team toward the southern shoulder of the road where he hoped there would be enough space for him to guide his charging team and wagon full of drunken half-crazed cowboys between the fallen riders and the grove of trees.

When he was Seventy-five yards from the fallen riders and a hundred and seventy-five from the first scruffy looking building in the town; the one they called Grayson's General Store, a team of draft horses hauling a wagon loaded down with the biggest damn logs he'd ever seen in his life came bustin' out through the stand of trees that he soon would be practically brushin' up against. It was movin' like a bat outa' Hell. The mystery wagon kept on rolling right across the road. The big man driving it was standing up, with one foot planted in front of him on the vertical floorboard like a man determined to stay the course. He was cracking the whip and cheering his team on in a loud voice that cut through the wagon noise like a fog horn. Wally couldn't hear the sound of his own rig over the racket of the logger's wagon and team. The man didn't stop till his lead horses were standing with their noses practically pressed against the trees on the opposite side of the road. When the horses finally stopped, the wagon sat broadside across the road; leaving Wally with two choices; pull up, or drive directly into the side of the wagon loaded with huge logs.

As under-burdened with brains as Wally was he realized that there was really only one choice. He planted his feet against his floorboard, pulled back on the brake lever till the old badly-worn wooden brake shoes smoked against the iron rim bands, and yanked back on his reins, trying desperately to pull up before plowing into the big logging wagon.

His horses did an impressive job of pulling back, digging in hard, with their thundering hooves plowing up deep, rough furrows in the half-frozen dirt surface of Sweetwater Road. They made sounds that were a horse's equivalent of screams as a result of the very substantial amount of speed the old brakes weren't up to scrubbing off of the forward motion of the heavy wagon. The wagon's tongue, harnesses, braces, and other gear tried to shove them forward violently. When Wally got his wagon stopped, no more than twenty yards separated the chests of his lead horses and the side of the log-laden wagon. Before the dust settled, the big man climbed from his seat on the logging wagon and walked to the side of it and stopped, just leaning there with a double-barreled shotgun propped on his shoulder and staring at Wally, saying nothing. The cold air was filled with a cloud of road-dust

It took Wally a full five minutes and a long pull from his jug to gather up the nerve to speak. The problem being that; even building up the nerve to speak didn't give him a clue what words they should be. So another drink was in order. He tried his best to keep his eyes on the big man as Wally propped the jug on his shoulder and tipped it to his lips. But he discovered it was impossible to keep him visible through the whole process. Wally expected a load of buckshot the whole time the big man was out of sight behind the jug as he drank. But the man only stood leaning on the wagon full of logs. All Wally could think about was that if he was drunker he might not feel the buckshot when it hit. So he drank as fast as he could, intending to immediately guzzle more. He figured the drunker the better. He should have been trying to figure a way out of his predicament, since under the circumstances, the big man wasn't likely planning to spend the rest of the cold early-winter day slouching against his wagon piled high with massive logs and staring at Wally.But prioritizing thoughts was another of Wally's shortcomings. When the drunks behind him got tired of Wally just sitting there like he was nailed to the seat they got to arguing about what to do and faced off into two groups; one of which felt they should turn back, the other wanting to charge the town. As such groups always do, each chose a leader. The leader of the latter gang; a big man and a trouble-maker back in the camps who was also falling-down drunk decided he was the smartest. So he decided to take over. The big trouble-maker got tired of waiting and nailed Wally on the side of the head with a bottle and pushed him off the wagon. The man was so drunk he jumped up into the seat, and grabbing the reins, attempted to drive the team around the back of Walters's lumber wagon, with the intent of mounting an attack on Whiskey Branch.

Though there was little chance of the man getting the wagon past the trees without crashing it, Walter reached under his seat and pulled out a machete. With one big swing he severed the ropes tied across his wagon and seven sixteen-foot-long birch logs rolled off, hitting the Bleu wagon broadside, flipping it and pitching close to a dozen drunken cowboys all across the cold, hard, and wheel-rutted dirt of Sweetwater Road. Most were fortunate; the ones who suffered relatively minor injuries; a lot of lost skin, or maybe a broken nose, or even a concussion was nothing compared to the man impaled through the gut by a splintered wheel spoke, or the one who was trapped beneath the wagon and whose back was broken. A lot of the others came up yelling curses, and promising to kill the son-of a-bitch who did this to them. One man who could barely stand was shaking his fist at Walter's wagon. (Not realizing Walter had slipped away into the trees on the North side of the road to confer with Luther, but was never out of sight of his wagon) The man shouted oaths to do hideous things to Walter's descendants for several generations.

Wally, who had taken a while to regain his feet and get his bearings about him, stood at the edge of the road staring at his overturned wagon and wondering what to do. He had a vague thought that, because he'd been in the driver's seat when the catastrophe happened, he was responsible, and so, might be in serious trouble with Napoleon Bleu; a frightening thought indeed. On the other hand, it might mean he was in charge; also a frightening thought, but one with a lot of "exciting" mixed in. Wally decided to take charge. It seemed less stupid than running, right at that moment. He yelled at the fallen cowboys, "Okay, you all listen up! You're going to break into two groups and go around those logs, and the wagon they came off of!" Wally pointed at the logs and Walter's wagon as he started shouting orders. You were so excited about taking over that town all the way here. Now you're turning into a bunch of cowards?" His one good eye looked like it was on fire. "Do you want to face Nappy and tell him you turned tail and ran?"(Wally, of course, wasn't aware Nappy was dead).

"I want those who have rifles, and two good legs to go around that way. But only if you're sober enough to walk straight." Wally pointed toward the north side of the road; the side on which Luther had stepped from the trees with his weapon of biblical power. Of course Wally knew nothing of that. He hadn't seen Luther or his huge chain. And then Wally looked around at the rest of the men and said, "Okay, you fools line up in rows of five. We're going to form up in some kind of military order and move around the south end of that wagon where there's the most space and move on that town like we were ordered to do. He pointed his rifle, which he'd kept a firm grip on through his fall from the wagon, at the men, waving it back and forth, and said, " Anybody who wants out, get out now! But if'n you do, I'll personal see that you don't get paid nothin' for doin' nothin' but ridin' out here an' landin' on your drunk, fool asses. If you wanna' get paid for' a job you damn well better finish that job."

Wally's newfound feeling of power must have been believed-in by what remained of the wagonload of Napoleon Bleu's fighting forces, because while they didn't exactly snap to attention, they at least headed in the right direction. Many of them staggered, because of injuries suffered in the wagon rollover, or from drunkenness not yet worn off. But some of them had regained their former bravado, and were cheering and shouting about what they were going to do to that lousy little town.

Wally lead the troops around the south end of the mountain of logs and Walter's wagon like a proud commander, not like someone who had just scraped the remaining few mobile men he had up off the ground. They slowed down considerably, and stopped cheering completely upon coming upon the tangled pile of the lead riders and their mounts. It took the wind right out of their sails.

The frightened leftovers, which were exactly what they were, who Wally had ordered around the north end of Walter's wagon, clambered over the hill of logs, and peeked cautiously around the wagon. As much as anything else, they were listening for any indication of the progress of the group on the other side of the road. All they heard was the creaking of the wood still settling, in their own overturned wagon, thirty feet away. They decided it was safe to move forward. As soon as they moved past the end of the big logging wagon, they could see the two fallen lead riders, and immediately across the road, the rest of their own group, who looked as unsure of what to do as they themselves were. They stood staring across at Wally, who found himself longing for the days of sitting in the driver's seat of an overland stage, where a long run or the possibility of a holdup by bandits were the worst things he had to worry about.

The old days when the idea of a battle with a whole town, or a gun-slinging preacher were right smack on the edge of impossible. Now, the chest-swelling rush that had come along with the feeling of power that Wally had experienced only minutes before evaporated in an instant.

"Well now what?" the man who had knocked Wally from the driver's seat of the wagon shouted from across the road. "Well, come on! Aren't you the man in charge?"

Wally put his hand to his temple where the bottle had struck him, and something felt all jagged and crooked inside there. His brain hurt, and thoughts didn't want to come to him at all.

At that moment Wally wished he could be anywhere but where he was, and doing anything but what he was doing. And he wished he was dead, stinking drunk. And most of all he wished with all his heart that he'd never heard of Napoleon Bleu. So his overwhelmed mind simply repeated the last word it had heard, and Wally shouted at the top of his lungs, "Charge!"

Most of the few remaining battered members of Bleu's gang of outlaws who attacked whiskey Branch on Sweetwater Road took a look at the fallen lead riders and gave up the attack for the lost cause that it was. Still on foot, some of them chose to beat a retreat toward Sweetwater, though the town was nearly five miles distant. A few others melted into the woods, for reasons known only to them; maybe they had a mountain or backwoods heritage that made them feel it was their best shot at hiding out and surviving. But ten men, all but two of them on the south side of the road, where Wally stood totally baffled about how to proceed, and all of the ten longtime Bleu employees, gave war-cries, and rifles held overhead, charged toward Whiskey Branch.

They were deadly serious, and had every intention of taking control of what Napoleon Junior had assured them was a pitifully under defended little town of sheep that would cringe and bow before the slightest show of force. With one possible exception, that was; the bible-thumper, of all people. Well, a bullet would send him to his great reward just as sure as it would anyone else.

So the ten of them charged ahead; eleven, including Wally, who had caught up after taking time to dig his jug from the overturned wagon. He was thrilled nearly to the point of giggling to find it half full (and Wally was normally a glass half-empty sort of guy). He lubricated his tonsils well and then yelled, "Let's go!"

Some of his whiskey-fueled enthusiasm sloshed over on the few wasted, staggering group of Bleu soldiers that remained from the Sweetwater Road assault on Whiskey Branch, and they forged ahead. But the charge stopped almost before it got started. And Wally was fairly damned certain that this time not even an entire barrel of high-grade shine would get it going again.

As if reacting to his shout of "Let's go," two figures stepped from the trees into the road ahead of them. On the south side of the road stood the huge man who had driven the big wagon across the road and dumped the load of logs which had overturned Wally's wagon. He stood looking at the oncoming men and silently shaking his head back and forth while patting the big double barreled shotgun propped on his shoulder. On the north side was an even more enormous black man who, despite the cold, stood shirtless with a heavy logging chain wrapped around his thick neck and the knotted muscles of his shoulders. He also stood silently shaking his head at Wally's confused, panicky men and wagging a finger back and forth as a parent would to warn a child off from doing something wrong.

Upending the jug that he'd held onto as desperately with his left hand as he had held his rifle with the right, Wally drained the last dregs from it and shouted, "Retreat!"

Unseen by Wally, while all his attention was focused forward toward the two remarkably large men blocking the road ahead, the big cowboy who had struck him with the bottle, by sheer chance, stumbled across a stick of dynamite dropped by one of the Bleu's two lead riders when his horse went down as a consequence of

Luther's chain-swinging attack. Though totally dazed by all that had happened up to that point, and despite stumbling along on a badly injured ankle, the man recognized what he'd found. He held the stick of dynamite overhead and cheered like a man who'd just drawn a royal flush at the poker table. Unbelievably, the other men cheered along, and again began to advance. Luther watched the ridiculous display. Then the man with the dynamite had to turn to three of his fellow outlaws before finding one who had a match. That pause proved to be his undoing. It gave Luther time to act. When the man triumphantly struck the match across the sole of his boot and lit the fuse, the other remaining Bleu men cheered him on.

Wally stood dumbfounded, unable to fathom everything that was happening around him. He had gone from simple wagon driver to the leader of a small fighting force practically in a matter of minutes. It was true that the force was mostly a bunch of drunks who were doing good to stay on their feet. But now that the man with the dynamite had his arm cocked back over his head, ready to throw it in the direction of Walter and Luther, who knew what might happen? Then Luther let go of the chain he'd been swinging in a circle over his head like a lasso. Wally could hear the air whistling through the chain as it flew. It hit the cowboy chest-high before he could let go of the hissing stick of dynamite. He dropped to the ground in the middle of the gang in a bloody heap; the dynamite he'd never had a chance to let go of still clutched in his hand. It exploded, blowing him and several of the other men to pieces, making short work of their last charge.

Wally dropped to his knees; totally used up. He was absentmindedly wiping his hands on the front of his shirt, before looking down and realizing that what he was trying to wipe off was the remains of some of the men who had been standing close to the man who'd fallen victim to the chain the huge black man had flung at them. Once Wally realized what he was wiping his hands through, he promptly threw up, adding the bacon and eggs he'd had for breakfast to the gore that covered him nearly from head to foot.

The remaining few of the Bleu thugs who had survived the debacle the attack had become either turned tail and ran back up the road toward Sweetwater or scattered into the woods on either side of the road.

Wally remained alone on his knees in the center of the road, continuously wiping his hands through the blood and bits of human remains that covered his clothing, as though trying to wipe them clean, while tears from his one eye cut a downward trail through the gore on his face, then around his mouth, and finally dripped from his chin. At that moment he would give anything for a drink; just one drink. He felt sure and certain that at that moment a big drink was the only thing that might prevent him from losing his mind completely; not that there was much of it left to lose at that point.

By the time Luther's chain nearly cut the outlaw on Sweetwater Road in half before he had the chance to hurl his stick of dynamite, the string of explosions and their accompanying wall of flames on the north side of Whiskey Creek had died down to primarily the large briskly burning trees and other foliage around the clearings where the stills had set. Those remaining fires alone would normally be enough to put a stop to most any attack mounted by an unstructured group like a bunch of whiskey-cookers and down-on-their-luck-saddle tramps. But fill those same men with corn liquor and you might find men who are brave enough or foolish enough to walk into Hell. Pastor Windor and the group of men surrounding him stood waiting for their hearing to recover from the thunder of the stills detonating and watched horrified, as burned men floated on the surface of the creek water; some dead, and some badly injured and moaning piteously. After a while it finally quieted to the point that when Shepherd Sloan saw Lillie riding off towards the east some ways back in the woods across the creek and he told Pastor Windor about it he didn't need to shout to make himself heard.

When Pastor Windor heard the distant explosion of the dropped stick of dynamite on Sweetwater Road east of town, he looked at Shepherd Sloan and said, "Did I imagine that?"

"No sir, I'm afraid not." Sloan answered," shaking his head.

"Any chance it was thunder?" Toby asked.

The pastor shook his head unhappily, and said, "No, I wish it were; a nice hard rain would be a good thing. There are still fires smoldering over there that I'd love to see extinguished; fires that shouldn't have needed starting." He nodded across the creek. "Starting them was a terrible thing. Even though I wasn't the one who pulled the trigger; I was the one who planned it all, and put the plan into action. And after a while the end justifying the means doesn't make the means any easier to live with." He nodded toward the horror and the dead in the creek. "That's the worst thing I've ever done; and that's saying something." With some effort he shook his attention free. "I guess I better ride out to Sweetwater Road and see what's happening." Then he asked Sloan, "Shepherd, while I'm gone, will you and Doc please pull the injured men out of the water and do what you can for them?"

"Absolutely! Consider it done."

Toby said, "Hey, I want to ride along with you."

Concerned about what he might find on Sweetwater Road, the pastor began to shake his head and Toby said, "Please. If there's trouble, you might need me."

Doc Forrest spoke up, "You two can take my buggy if you'd like. It's out back. It would save you the walk to get your horses." Then he motioned toward the chaos of wounded Bleu men and said, "I think most of my patients will be within walking distance for at least the next few hours.

Pastor Windor said, "Yes Doc, that would be nice, and I thank you. I'm feeling more than a little tired; in both body and soul. Okay, Toby lets go. We can talk on the way."

After Pastor Windor and Toby rode away east through town the two doctors went to work. Both the one trained to treat humans, and the one taught as a healer of other ailing creatures, but who had, during his time as an Army medic, quite literally received his baptism under fire when it came to human patients.

They started by wading into the water and trying to identify who was alive and who was dead. In some cases distinguishing the difference wasn't easy. As the doctors were standing knee-deep in the water discussing how to proceed, Luke walked up to the creek bank, his feet spread wide to maintain his balance in the soft muddy soil. "What can I do to help?" he asked.

"You'd help my state of mind quite a bit if you'd sit yourself down in the chair up there on my porch," Doc Forrest answered. "By all rights a man who's been through what you've been through in the last two days ought to be in bed resting. But I know that's out of the question. So how about walking on down there to Dale Birmingham's house?" Doc nodded down the dirt street toward the home of the fisherman who had found Luke in the creek and pulled him from the cold water. "Take it nice and easy, and ask him to hustle on up here and give us a hand getting these injured men into my office. We've got to get them taken care of. You take it slow, but you tell him to hurry!"

Luke turned in the direction of Dale's house, but before beginning the walk said, "You know Doc, you should maybe practice what you preach just a little bit. That's awfully cold water you're sloshing around in. And trust me; I know a little bit about cold water. You're no spring chicken anymore. Don't you think maybe you should take a break for a cup of coffee and warm up? Just for a minute or two"

It was Shepherd Sloan that answered, "These men don't have a minute or two Luke."

So Luke said, "Understood. I'll go get Dale. I haven't had a chance to thank him properly anyway."

There were a hundred questions Toby had thought of to ask Pastor Windor in the time he'd known the man. But now that they were actually alone, riding along in the buggy and he had the opportunity to ask them, not a single one would come to mind.

After a minute or two of listening to the uncomfortable silence except for the clop-clop of the horses hooves and metallic whirring of the buggy's wheels spinning beneath them he decided to start with a recent question and said, "Pastor Windor can I ask you a question?"

"I believe you just did didn't you?" The pastor offered Toby a big smile.

Surprised by his response, Toby just sat and smiled back.

Pastor Windor said, "Well you seemed to be having a little trouble getting going. So what is it you wanted to ask me Toby?"

"Back there at the creek when you were talking about how terrible it was that you put the plan together and that it was the worst thing you've ever done, and then you said, "and that's saying something" Were you talking about during the war?"

"That was some of it Toby; the most of it, I suppose. Although sometimes it seems as though a person can spend their whole life trying to make sure that the scale they're balanced on is tipped more towards the positive than the negative. But when I stood there looking at all those men floating on top of Whiskey Creek I couldn't help but wonder."

"Wonder what?"

"Who's more to blame for them being dead, Napoleon Bleu for planting that row of stills in the woods across the creek; or me for planning how to blow them up?"

Toby said, "You only did it to keep them from taking over the whole town. And it's not like you had a lot of time to plan how to fight them off. Besides, isn't it better than if they'd made it across the creek and we would've had to fight them off right in the center of town?"

When Pastor Winder answered his voice sounded very sad, "a lot of them did make it across the creek Toby; but most of them were dead, and most of the ones that made it across dead would've died a lot easier if they'd died from a bullet than the way they did die.

But the one thing I want you to know Toby is that I planned for the fire to turn them back, not kill them. I hoped that when the stills blew up in front of them they'd stop their charge. I never dreamed they'd run right into the flames." Pastor Windor fell into one of his peculiar silences that always left Toby not knowing how to proceed. So he said no more, just waiting as they rode along, hoping the pastor would pick up the conversation when he was ready. The look in the man's eyes said he could be a lot of miles or a lot of years away, or both.

And Toby figured it would be best to let *him* decide when to come back to the here and now. It was probably best not to startle a man whose hand could draw a gun faster than a rattlesnake could strike.

Just a few minutes later they pulled in sight of Ben and Kate's store. Toby was reassured to see the men ringing the building, rifles in hand. Several of them raised a hand and waved at the oncoming buggy. One man yelled, "Hey Pastor, Toby what are you doing in Doc's buggy?"

Pastor Windor shouted back, "just taking it easy today."

When they'd passed the store Toby said, "Well, that's a good sign, everything looked good there."

Pastor Windor said, "Yes so far so good. But I still want to see what that sound was that we heard a little while ago. Plus Avey's still out there."

Toby said, "I think you're worrying for nothing. After how bad things went for them when they tried to cross the creek they probably gave up completely. And if Avey saw the way you out-drew Nappy I'll bet he's run clear to Texas by now."

"I hope you're right Toby. But I still want to take a look. And I've got a feeling he's still out there somewhere and somewhere a lot closer than Texas."

"What's his story anyway? Tell me about him. Is he really that fast?"

"Well, there's not that much to tell, or rather I don't know that much about him to tell you. I only got to see him draw that one time. I can tell you he's tall and lanky and has long red hair and a mustache that overhangs his upper lip like a bristle-brush. And, as far as his being fast; there are a few things different about him. For one, he's left handed, and he cross-draws; that means he wears his holster so when his gun's in it it's pointed where it would kill somebody walking to his right if it went off. Some men find it faster. I've never tried it. I never felt the need. Third, and most important; he uses a Buntline Special.

"What's that?"

"It's a Colt with the extra-long barrel. There aren't a lot of them around. Earp, the lawman down in Arizona uses one."

"Wyatt Earp?" Toby said. I thought he was Marshal in Dodge City, Kansas. That's what I read in a book back home before we left Pennsylvania."

Pastor Windor held back a smile. "Your book was right Toby, but people move; even lawmen. Earp's in Tombstone now. Anyway, like I was saying, the long barrel has its benefits and its drawbacks. Once it's out of the holster, the longer barrel makes it very accurate, but getting it out takes longer. It takes a really fast hand to be good with a Buntline. It takes a true natural to do it with no tricks." It took all the restraint the pastor could muster not to add, "Someone like you." But he didn't add it.

"Tricks? Like what kind of tricks?"

"Well, there's something a lot of gun hands do; men with all kinds of guns, not just the Buntline, but it's extra useful on the long barrel. And I'd bet a hundred to one Avey does it."

"Does Earp, the lawman you mentioned do it?" Toby asked.

"No, he doesn't have to. He's fast enough without it."

"What's the trick?"

"They'll rub a little bit of chicken grease on the inside of the holster. It makes the barrel slide out nice and smooth. Some men grease the barrel instead of the holster; but it comes to the same thing. What it boils down to is; if a man has time to get that long barrel out of the holster and aim, it's like he's holding a small rifle and he's an extremely dangerous man.

Also, I figure he was probably a cow-puncher at some time before he started hiring out his gun."

"Why do you say that?"

"Because in addition to cross drawing he uses an unusual holster called a drover's-clutch. It's a rig that looks simple enough; somewhat like a shoulder holster. Drovers use them because they normally carry the gun up high to keep it out of the trail dirt kicked up by the herd. But for some reason Avey wears his down low, not a lot higher than a regular gun belt. There's no telling why; men just do what feels best for them. Now you know as much about Avey as I do."

The pastor drew a deep breath, held it for a few moments before releasing it, and then added, "I only hope you're right, and he's a long way away from here. But people like Avey are like a bad cold; just when you think they're gone, they come back on you."

Just beyond the store they came within sight of the gauntlet of armed men lining both sides of the road; a half-dozen to each side. One of the men immediately snapped to attention and saluted. Toby looked at the pastor, attempting to gauge his response, then immediately realized he was attempting the impossible; something he should have known from past experience. Pastor Windor pulled the buggy to a halt in front of the first man they reached on the left side of the road and asked, "Fred what's been happening out here? Did I hear an explosion from out this way?"

Fred's response was immediate and enthusiastic. "Oh Pastor, you wouldn't believe everything that's been going on! I couldn't see everything real well from here. But I did see a couple riders come'n in Sweetwater Road side-by-side; both of e'm sittin' up high and lookin' around like hunters in the woods scannin' for game. 'Cept there wasn't nothing ahead of them but clear road clean into town except for us each side. But they were watching real close. Then a wagon came barreling down the road behind them. It was loaded with men, and they were loaded for bear. And they were firing off shots to beat all Hell; but not at us; not at anything, really. They were flinging lead everywhere; up in the air, off into the woods, down into the dirt road, Hell I was surprised they didn't shoot each other, pardon my French. It was easy to see every one of them was drunk as a skunk. And the man driving the wagon wasn't in much better shape, judging by the way he was driving those horses. The way he was pushing that team, he'd have driven those horses right into the ground and run them to death if Luther and Walter hadn't stopped them."

"What was that?" The Pastor Windor asked. Toby leaned forward in his seat beside the pastor with his hand cupped behind his ear with the rapt attention of a child listing to a bedtime story.

"Well, actually Luther only stopped the two horses riding in front. But he sure stopped 'em dead. They were both moving really good before he made them go down, so when they hit the ground they kicked up a lot of dirt, and made it hard for me to see what happened after that."

By the time Fred had gotten that far along with telling Toby and the pastor of the happenings on Sweetwater Road some of the other men had gathered around the buggy. A man who had been on the other side of the road stepped up and said, "I was a little farther down the road pastor, so I could see things little bit better."

"Okay, so what happened? Was there an explosion or not?"

"Not just then."

Pastor Windor looked around the group the men and said, "Is there anybody here that can please tell me if there was an explosion?"

"Yes there was. A stick of dynamite went off, and the fool that was holding it went up with it." Instead of the answer coming from any of the men clustered around the buggy in the middle of the road, it was delivered in Luther's typical bass rumble. He had stepped from the trees, unnoticed; not an easy accomplishment for man of his size, while Pastor Windor was quizzing the men.

He continued; "After I took down their two scout riders," he paused, then said, "I leg-broke one of their horses and had to shoot it. I hated that. Well, after I did that Walter drove his wagon across the road in front of their wagon like you planned. It was following behind those two lead riders just the way Luke told us to expect. But like Fred said, that driver was going hell-bent-for-leather, and all the men in the back acting just as crazy as Fred said; and we didn't expect that. The man driving it almost drove it right into Walter's rig. When he finally got stopped he just sat there, scared stiff I guess. Then one of the drunks in the back walloped him upside of the head with a bottle and pushed him off onto the road, and took the seat. When he tried to drive his rig toward town Walter dumped his load and it hit his wagon broadside and flipped it. All of the crazy-drunk men in the wagon got dumped in the road.

When I saw one of them pick up a stick of dynamite that one of Bleu's scout riders must have dropped and touch a flame to the wick,

I started swinging my chain. When he made to throw it, I let the chain fly at him. I got lucky.

He went down, and the dynamite went off. That's what you heard. It's that simple. Of course he didn't get back up, and neither did the five or six men that were close around him. The rest of them ran like scared rabbits."

Just then Walter walked up and said, "It all worked out just like you planned it Pastor; slick as a greased pig."

Toby stared at the pastor, stunned, then said, "You planned this, too?"

Pastor Windor shrugged.

Walter said, "Not bad for five hours, huh?" And then he added, "What do you mean, too?"

Toby said, "You think this's something, you should have been up in the center of town."

Pastor Windor climbed from the buggy and said, "Come on Toby, let's look around. There might be injured men who need help, hiding in the woods, watching us, afraid to come out."

In fact, they *were* being watched from the woods, but not by men who needed help.

After Toby climbed down from Doc's buggy, he followed the pastor to where he was bent over a man lying on the shoulder of the rutted dirt road. He was face-down with his knees pulled up nearly beneath him. His hands were spread open, and his fingers were dug into the dirt as though he'd been trying to drag himself off of the road. When Pastor Windor rolled him over his eyes were open. His eye rather; he had only one, the place the other should be was covered by a leather patch. Toby asked, "Is he alive?"

Pastor Windor pressed his fingers to the man's wrist. "No" But at a glance I don't see any bullet holes." Pastor Windor closed Wally's one eye. "I don't know what killed him; there's no telling. I imagine a lot of Napoleon Bleu's men drink themselves to death, and that's not always obvious to see. But I think this one may have been too close to that stick of dynamite when it went up." He nodded toward the small scorched-looking hole in the road six feet or so away. "It could have thrown him this far."

"It looks like he was crawling to get away," Toby said. "I think he was clawing at the dirt. He must have really been scared."

Pastor Windor said, "The middle of a war is a scary place to be."

Walter walked up behind them, and looking down at Wally said, "He's the one that was driving their wagon. After I cut my load loose and things got crazy I lost track of what happened to him. Didn't go too good for him, did it?"

"No, not at all," Pastor Windor answered. Then he said, "We'll have to round up some of the men from town for a burial detail."

"That's not going to be a lot of fun, is it?" Walter said.

"It never is."

Just off the edge of the road, on the south side, a little past where Walter drove his wagon from behind the grove of trees and blocked Wally's onrushing wagonload of drunken cowboy-outlaw-moonshiners, a woman and a man stood concealed behind a large oak tree and the thick foliage that surrounded it. The woman wore a calico dress and had her hair done up in pigtails. The man had long red hair and a mustache to match.

Lillie said, her voice just a whisper, "That's him; the preacher. That's the one Daddy hates so much; the one with the long black duster and buckskin hat. I don't know why. She pointed at Pastor Windor, who was just standing up from checking on Wally, his back turned toward them.

To which the red-haired man answered, "I don't care why. All I care about is that your old man's paying me very good money to kill him. He leaned against the tree, and bracing the long barrel of his revolver across his forearm, aimed it at Pastor Windor's back.

Lillie said, "You're going to back-shoot him?"

"Yep, that's the best way, that way he can't shoot back."

"Well I thought you were supposed to be so fast. And it turns out you're really just a coward."

"Lady, it's your old man that made this decision for me. When he offered me twice what I usually charge for killing a man I knew right then it was no ordinary man he wanted killed. And I'm not one to take any chances. It's just smart business."

Avey pulled back the hammer, sighted down the long barrel, and pulled the trigger.

Although she knew it was coming, the sound of the gunshot so startled Lillie that she nearly jumped out of her skin. As the echoes of the shot faded Avey laughed aloud and said, "It's just smart business lady." Then he turned and ran toward where they had tethered their horses. Lillie was dumbfounded at the realization that the vaunted fast gun she'd talked her father into hiring was nothing more than a gutless back-shooter. If she'd wanted the preacher killed that way, she could have gotten one of their moonshiners to do it, or done it herself. She also ran to her horse, knowing the citizens of the shabby little town wouldn't waste any time before they started looking for the killer of their precious God-pounder; probably with rope in hand.

In the middle of the road, Pastor Windor first crumpled to his knees and then slowly fell to the ground on his side before Walter, who was nearest to him, was able to get his arms under him, though he would have given nearly anything to keep the pastor from reaching the ground. After that that there was a long moment when everyone stood frozen in silent disbelief before anyone could move. All of the stunned men, with the exception of the teenager who felt as though the anchor-point of his world had just been torn away, looked in the direction the sound of the shot seemed to have come from, trying to spot the shooter. Toby's attention was focused on one thing and one thing only.

He was the first to reach Pastor Windor after Walter. The fallen pastor lay on his side in the center of a rapidly spreading patch of red wetness in the dirt surface of Sweetwater Road. Toby knelt beside him, his eyes instantly streaming tears, and picked the pastor's hand up from the ground, pressing his fingertips to his wrist. He had a basic idea what he was doing; he'd heard Doc Forrest explain what it meant to check for a pulse before, but he was doing it mainly mirroring what he'd seen the pastor do to the wrist of the one-eyed man only a few minutes before. He closed his eyes, concentrating fully on what he was hoping he would feel through his fingertips, but recalling something his father had often said; a simple cautionary statement meant to help him fend off disappointment as he grew older; "Hoping won't make it so." Now all he hoped for was that his father had been wrong, and that if he hoped hard enough he could hope it into being so. Then he felt a slight twitch, just under the skin. And just then he heard Walter say, "Look up yonder. Did you see that?"

"See what?" It was Luther who asked. Toby couldn't pull his eyes away from the rapidly growing circle of spongy red dirt around the pastor's body.

Without looking up from the pastor's still face he asked Walter, "What? What did you see?"

"Two people. They was on horseback; a man an' a woman. And they was goin' hell-bent for leather. They was really makin' tracks; goin' north toward the creek. They headed straight into the woods at a dead gallop like they were in a big hurry to get caught up to somebody, or get away from somebody. I only saw them for a minute or less, but I could tell they weren't interested in going cautiously; they definitely weren't tiptoeing along. They was puttin' the spurs to those horses.

Toby asked Walter, "Did you see what they looked like?" his voice was choked with tears. He lifted Pastor Windor's head from the dirt road, and unconsciously began rocking him in his arms like a child. The wet patch in the road grew larger, as blood poured from the hole between the pastor's shoulder blades

Walter shook his head. "No Toby, I'm sorry. They were really hauling it; like they wanted to be anywhere but here. And that didn't surprise me a bit, since hangin' around here would probably get them nothin' but an invite to a necktie party. I couldn't tell a thing of the woman, but that she had a woman's shape. I did catch a glimpse of the man's hair flying in the wind, though. He was riding so hard he was making his own wind. His hair was long and red, the reddest I've ever seen."

"Riding which way?"

"North, towards the creek, like I said. That's about all I could tell. They were in the woods in no time!"

Toby hissed through clenched teeth. He was looking down at the pastor, and when he spoke, there was no question to who he was speaking; "Avey…you said he was a back-shooter. He'll pay. Maybe not today, or tomorrow, but I'll make him pay."

"No Toby." Pastor Windor's voice was weak; actually no more than a whisper, and gurgled like he was speaking from under water. Blood poured from his mouth, and over his lips, then down his cheek and onto Toby's hands.

"No? How can you say no?" Through the sorrow, and the horror of watching the pastor fall, and seeing him so terribly wounded, Toby knew he should be thrilled that the man was even alive and speaking to him at all. But the emotion Toby most found himself feeling was anger. He was not just angry, but furious; the kind of fury that he'd never felt before. He was furious at Avey the back-shooter; of course. That was an emotion he felt on behalf of Pastor Windor, who he'd come to love like he'd loved no one since losing his parents. He felt the fury on the pastor's behalf because he wasn't sure the man had it in him to feel such anger even toward the man who had shot him in the back. And he was also angry at the notion he might be denied his opportunity for revenge. He knew that was a selfish anger. "How can you say no?" he asked the barely-breathing, dying man in his arms, praying for an answer, but not expecting one.

But one came; "I trained you so you could be close to your father through his gun, not to make you a killer." Pastor Windor's breaths were coming harder, each accompanied by more blood, both from his mouth and from the hole in his back. He whispered, "Do you remember when you asked me if I'd ever killed anyone?"

Toby thought hard for a moment then answered, "Yes, I do." His voice was hitching, choked with tears.

"Good." It was Pastor Windor's last word. His voice was choked with blood and hardly audible.

There were a few minutes after that when Toby could do nothing but continue to rock the pastor's lifeless body in his arms and sob. When he finally looked up Walter was standing over him. The big man stood with his hands folded before him and his head lowered respectfully, but with his eyes raised just enough to see when Toby had moved. He said, "Sorry Toby, I didn't mean to be hanging over you, or eavesdropping. Are you all right? I mean, will you be all right?" Walter knew it sounded stupid as soon as he said it, but he didn't know a better way to ask. And even though Toby was sixteen and far more grown up than many sixteen-year olds, Walter had a hard time not thinking of him as the boy that he had traveled across the country with in the wagon train back when Toby really was just a kid.

"That's okay Mister Denborough. I know you weren't listening in on purpose."

Walter said, "Still, saying goodbye to somebody is a personal thing, and it wasn't right of me to take that away from you Toby."

"Really, Mr. Denborough," Toby answered, his voice hitching; barely a hoarse whisper."It's all right; you're family."

"Thank you Toby", Walter said. He found himself scarcely able to speak. "And, you know you have a whole lot of family around here," he added.

Toby nodded, and said, "But I didn't have any to spare."

They stayed like that for a while, as though time had stopped; Toby rocked the pastor, and Walter stood by uneasily, wondering what he could do or say to comfort the boy.

Then Luther spoke up from the side of the road, where he'd walked up without either of them noticing, "Toby, why don't you let Walter and me take care of him? I'll go bring Doc's buggy up. We'll put him in there nice and gentle and take him back into town to Doc Forrest's office. He'll know the right thing to do. You can ride in with us if you want to or I'm sure one of the men who were on guard along the road would be happy to ride up to Grayson's Store and have Ben come back with a buck-board and pick you up and take you in to Doc's. Then you and Doc can talk things over and figure out how to do things just right for the pastor. I know how close you two were. And I know he would want you to be a part of things." Luther stopped speaking and sniffed. Then he added. " It would be your way of showing how much you cared about him, you helping to make the arrangements I mean; sort of a sign of respect."

Walter stood amazed; just as he'd been the night of the town meeting, when Luther, who usually didn't have two syllables to rub together, came out with something that said everything that needed saying, about as perfect as it could be said. And just like he had that night, Walter thought, 'He doesn't say much, but when he does say something, it's definitely something worth hearing.'

Finally Toby said, "Okay," and when Luther knelt beside him, he let the big man take Pastor Windor's body from him. But after he reluctantly relinquished his hold on the pastor's body Toby stood up and said, "Thank you, but as soon as I get my horse and my gun I know exactly how I'm going to show how much I cared about him."

Luther said, "You're going after Avey?"

Toby nodded. "You're damned right I'm going after Avey!"

Walter said, "Toby can I ask you one question before you do?"

"Yeah, what?"

"Pastor Windor asked if you remembered what he said when you asked him if he'd ever killed anybody and you told him you remembered. Were you telling him the truth, or were you just trying to ease his mind?"

"No, I remember. He told me he only killed to protect himself or someone else. That's what he did up in the middle of town. He didn't shoot Nappy till Nappy was about to draw on me. He killed Nappy to keep Nappy from killing me. And he didn't want all of those men to die when the stills exploded. He just wanted them to turn back."

"What, Nappy's dead?"

Toby had forgotten that Walter and Luther didn't know about all that had transpired along the creek bank in the center of town.

"Yeah," he said with more than a little pride in his voice; not pride in himself, but in the fallen pastor. "That fool thought he was fast, but Pastor Windor could have emptied his gun in him, then reloaded and emptied it in him again before Nappy hit the ground if he wanted to.

Toby pointed at the overturned wagon before continuing. "He only planned the traps here and up at the creek to keep Napoleon Bleu's men from coming across the creek and up Sweetwater Road to attack the town, and maybe kill a lot of our people."

Walter asked, "But do you think he would want you to do what you're about to do? Do you think he would believe in revenge?"

Toby said, "So I won't kill Avey unless he draws first. I'll be protecting myself."

"I'm not much with words, but that sounds like you're tryin' awful hard to make 'em fit what you want 'em to fit", Walter said.

Toby started to stalk away, in the direction of town.

Luther said, "Toby, what if Avey's faster? He is a professional gunman, you know. I don't know how Pastor Windor would feel about you going after Avey to kill him, but I do know how he would feel about you going after him and getting yourself killed."

Toby stopped and turned back to face them. "Maybe I'll back-shoot Avey. That's what he did."

"So, is that what you want then, to be like Avey?"

"No, I don't. But if I ever see him, he won't get the chance to back-shoot me." Toby dropped his arms to his sides and trudged toward town.

As soon as Toby was out of sight beyond the stand of trees that had hidden Walter's wagon from the onslaught of drunken cowboys as they came charging up Sweetwater Road, Luther brought Doc Forrest's buggy up and he and Walter carefully lifted Pastor Windor's body into the back and Walter took his own coat off and covered the pastor up for the ride to Doc's office.

Though the horse pulling the buggy was barely moving at a slow walk the two big men caught up to Toby before he'd covered a third of the distance to Doc Forrest's office. He'd barely come within sight of Ben and Kate's store when the buggy pulled up along-side of him.

When Walter, who had the reins, pulled the buggy nearly to a stop and opened his mouth, about to offer the boy a ride Luther elbowed him in the ribs and shook his head decisively. When Walter looked at him Luther whispered, "Give him time."

Walter whispered back, "Right."

But he did say to Toby, "See you in town."

Toby didn't answer; he only kept walking, head down and wondering when each of his feet had started weighing fifty pounds and when town had gotten to be a mile away. And as the weight of each foot grew so did the anger and the need for payback, and as the distance to town got greater so did the urgency to get started on his mission.

Upon finally reaching the store, Toby saw at least twenty people, more than a third of the population of Whiskey Branch, lined up across the long front porch of Grayson's General Store, all standing silently with their heads lowered. He figured they were some of the folks who had been holed-up in the store's cellar, and who by now would have heard about Pastor Windor. Walter and Luther would have stopped and given Ben and Kate a report on the results of the battle as they passed by on their way as they took the pastor's body to Doc's office. And they would, of course, have told them of his murder at Avey's hands. Whether Ben or Kate told the gathered townspeople of the pastor's death, or the news slipped out unintentionally, Toby didn't know, but it obviously got out. If not for the death of the man who was their spiritual leader and who had turned out to also be their military leader, they would probably be cheering at their victory over Napoleon Bleu and his gang of outlaws. But no one said a word, or even raised a hand in a wave. Toby kept walking; occasionally raising his headonly to be sure he was going in the right direction.

Finally, after walking for what seemed like an hour, but surely couldn't have been more than ten minutes Toby saw Doc's office. His only stop had been at his own home long enough to strap on his gun. Now he saw the doctor's buggy sitting right up along-side the back porch. Someone had swept or possibly just kicked the leaves away from the back of the buggy and dragged a boot through the dirt to clear a path so the few feet of ground separating the buggy and porch were clear. Walter and Luther clearly hadn't wanted to risk a misstep while handling the pastor's body. Toby rapped on the door and Doc Forrest opened it almost immediately. As Toby stepped inside Doc put his arm around the boy's shoulders and hugged him briefly. He said, "Walter and Luther told me what happened, and how it all came down." Toby looked around the room. Pastor Windor's lifeless body lay on the exam table that had held Luke's half-frozen but still breathing body less than twenty-four hours before. Now the blanket that had been pulled up only to Luke's throat was pulled up to cover the pastor's face.

"Where is everybody?" Toby asked Doc.

"I sent Dale Birmingham home after we finished pulling the men from the creek. He's worked his tail off the last couple of days.

Walter headed down to the store to check on Mildred and the kids and let them know he's all right. Luther went on back to his place. He desperately needed to get off his feet."

"Why?"

He didn't come out and say so, in fact he tried to hide it, but he'd been shot."

"Shot?" Toby exclaimed. "I don't believe it! He looked fine when I saw him a while ago."

Doc sighed, and said, "I guess he figured you had all the grief you could handle right now without worrying about him, too."

"Doc, are you sure? You're sure he was shot?"

"Yes, I've had too damned much experience at recognizing gunshot wounds to be wrong. There apparently was a lot of lead flying around at one point. I've seen bullet holes that were a lot worse, but there is no such thing as a good one. He got a deep graze along the outside of his left thigh. It didn't go in deep enough to hit bone and it probably didn't do any serious muscle damage, but it did bleed a lot before he stopped it."

"Stopped it how?" Toby asked.

Luther's a smart man," Doc answered. "He scooped up some of this morning's left-over frost from the grass and put it inside his pant leg around the wound. It froze the blood and stopped the bleeding. He said it's something his grandfather taught him. I suppose when you live most of your life as someone else's possession you learn any trick you can to get by. After he did that he slapped a little dirt around it on his pants to hide it from Walter. They were in the thick of the battle when it happened, and he didn't want it to get in the way. So I disinfected and bandaged the wound and made him go home. And, Luke is in my bedroom resting.

Jess stayed on the roof of the school until he could see that his help was needed more down here than his marksmanship skills were needed up there.

Now he and Shepherd are up in the field beside the cemetery burying the men who we pulled from the creek that didn't survive. There were ten of them. Of those ten, only four were carrying any kind of identification. Shepherd is making a list and a diagram. When Luke is well enough to go back to work he'll make crosses for the graves. The ones we have identification for will have names on their crosses; the others will have to be plain." Doc shook his head sadly.

"Plain crosses are plenty good enough. Did you save any of their men?" Toby asked.

"Only five. They've been moved to cots in the back room at the school, hopefully to recover. Burns are a horrible thing. I treated far too many during the war."

""Maybe that's five more than you should have saved," Toby said severely.

"Really?" Doc replied, just as severely.

"They're Napoleon Bleu's men, and it was one of Bleu's hired guns that killed Pastor Windor. And they're in the shape they're in because they tried to cross the creek and take over our town, you know. I think they deserve what they got. Don't you?"

"Toby, what I think doesn't mean a damn thing, and what you think means even less. When I became a doctor I took an oath; an oath written by a Greek physician so many years ago you wouldn't believe how many if I told you. And that oath says that it's my duty to treat the sick and injured to the best of my ability, period! And that's what I've always done and always will do!"

"I think you both need someone with a well-rested, level head to calm you down over a cup of coffee," Luke said from the doorway that led to Doc's bedroom. Then speaking to Doc, Luke said, "I think you should show him."

"Show me what?" Toby asked impatiently. "Then Toby realized , although a great deal had transpired in the middle of that one frigid Sunday he didn't even know what time it was. He could tell from the sun still shining outside Doc's south-facing window that evening hadn't begun to fall; but he knew that this time of year darkness came early and when the curtain of darkness began to fall it would fall rapidly. "What time is it?" he asked. "I want to hold Pastor Windor's service and bury him this evening."

Doc looked at his pocket watch. "It's three-twenty. But why on earth would you want to do that?"

Toby fought hard not to sound like a child on the verge of throwing a tantrum. At sixteen; and only four years from losing his parents, he was a long time from throwinghis last one, but suddenly he felt that both the need and talent could resurface. He hadn't felt so strongly about something in a long time. "Because I need to get started; I can't let him get a big head-start!" Toby was so anxious he could barely get his words straight. "Did you say Jess is with Doctor Sloan?"

"Yes," Doc Forrest answered, "He and Shepherd are on burial detail. "Why, Toby?"

"Cause Jess is the best tracker in town."

"Oh, and you want him to help you track Avey?"

"Damn right! And I want to start first thing tomorrow morning. I'd leave tonight, but it'll get dark too soon. That's why I want to have the pastor's funeral this evening, so we can go at dawn tomorrow. I'll ask Mister Walters to speak a service. I think he'll do it. He's a nice old man. He spoke a service for my sister when she died on the trip out here and he did a good job. He's not a preacher, but he'll have to do."

"Doc, you ought to tell him," Luke said.

"Right," Doc said. "Let's go in the kitchen and have a cup of coffee."

As they entered the kitchen Doc stopped and got a small wooden box that was secured with a padlock from a closet and sat it on the table. Then he poured them all coffee from the pot on the cook stove. Once they were seated he said, "Toby, you're practically wanting to run off like your pants are on fire and you're racing for the nearest water, to go after Avey. And I'm not going to debate the right or wrong of that. For what it's worth, you're not the only person in Whiskey Branch who would like to see Avey as dead as last year's grass. You do know that, I hope."

"Yeah, I know, but I want to personally kill the bastard."

Luke said. "Of course you do. So do I. And I'm sure most everybody else in town wants to. But are you in such a hurry that you don't want the pastor to have a proper funeral service and burial? Are those things that should be rushed? I mean, I don't know Mister Walters but I'm sure he's a fine man. But he's not a reverend."

"Avey killed our reverend, remember!" Toby shouted across the table at Luke.

Luke calmly said, "Toby if there's one thing I recall about Pastor Windor's Sunday messages it was how often he spoke on the subject of The Lord Will Provide."

"What does that mean?" Toby snarled, a little more quietly, but still angry.

While the exchange between Luke and Toby went on Doc unlocked the box and removed a formal looking certificate from it. He said, "This is what it means," and he laid the paper on the table before Toby. He tapped the paper with his finger. "I made Luke aware of this after you and Pastor Windor left for Sweetwater Road. Of course I had no idea then what would happen out there. I feel you should know about it now. As it turns out, on top of all the other talents Pastor Windor had, he probably could have made it as a Pinkerton detective. Do you recall him saying that he saw something more in Shepherd Sloan than meets the eye; something inside?"

"Yeah, I remember."

"Well, the pastor and I were talking one day and he mentioned that on several occasions Shepherd had shown a surprising amount of biblical knowledge and more than a little wisdom during their conversations, and it aroused his curiosity enough that over time he sent out a number of letters and telegrams, beginning with people from his own past. And that wasn't an easy task; with the nearest postal stop and telegraph office being in Sweetwater, it meant spending most of a day in the saddle every time he wanted to mail a letter or send a telegram. But apparently you can find out a lot if you ask the right questions of the right people."

Toby's impatience was nearly reaching the boiling point. "Okay, what are you getting at?"

"Well he found out that while Shepherd's father did win out when he insisted Shepherd go to veterinary school or he wouldn't pay for his schooling, you could still sort of say Shepherd won out in the end."

"Come on! What are you talking about? I want to get started hunting the man who left us without a pastor you know. So Shepherd Sloan's father paid for his vet school. What do I care about that?"

Luke put his hand on Toby's shoulder and said," calm down, or you're about to make an ass of yourself." Then he tapped the certificate on the table and said, "Continue Doc."

"Well, Toby, you may, or may not know that Shepherd used his medical skills to great advantage to treat wounded humans during the war. And trust me, someone who has had a limb blown off or a bullet pierce their gut doesn't care if it's a certified medical doctor or a veterinarian whose sewing them up to keep their guts from sliding out or keeping them from bleeding to death. Then sometime during the war, Shepherd received a letter from an attorney notifying him that his father had passed away, and that he'd inherited a substantial amount of money. By the way, I've discussed this with Shepherd, and he said he's fine with me talking about it; that it's okay to tell. He said if Pastor Windor thought I could be trusted, he thinks so, too. I'll try to finish the telling while he and Jess are still busy with the burying, and then maybe you'll understand why he's up there. I'm telling it to you now, the way he told it to me. Shepherd said that after the war, he did spend some time in New Orleans gambling, but not for long; it wasn't what he was looking for. He said that when he went there he went with the understanding that he was hiding out till he decided if he still wanted to be a Veterinarian. Then one day he woke up from a drunk and realized there was a difference between hiding out and just plain hiding. Like so many others, the war had changed him inside. He thought about the agony, the pain, the suffering, and the hate, and everything that went with it, and decided to take a leap of faith. That's the way he worded it; a leap of faith. So he used some of his inheritance to obtain a very different sort of education; he devoted nearly three years to it. That's what this is." Doc slid the certificate toward Toby and said, "Read." It wasn't said like a request. The certificate was printed on a heavy parchment paper, and much of the lettering was so old-fashioned and ornate that Toby had difficulty reading it; the letters featured a lot of lines of varying thickness, many of which were finished off with elaborate flourishes and whirls. He tilted the document back and forth to catch the light of the lamp from different angles to better see it, and finally said, "Am I reading this right? Does this mean what I think it means?"

Luke grinned and said, "Pretty amazing, huh?"

Doc said, "Yes, Toby. Pastor Windor was spot on when he said there was more than meets the eye to Shepherd Sloan. It turns out that not only is he Doctor Sloan, but he's also Reverend Sloan. After wandering around for a good while with no real aim, he spent just under three years in a seminary somewhere in the Colorado Mountains before deciding to move farther west, and ending up in Whiskey Branch purely by chance. That's why he was so quick to volunteer to go and help Jess bury the dead men from the creek. It gave him a chance to say some last words over them.

"How long have you known about this?" Toby asked; tapping a finger on the document.

"Pastor Windor told me about a week ago, when he gave me this certificate for safe-keeping," Doc answered. "He said since things were looking 'worrisome,' that was the word he used, like he was really concerned but didn't want to worry me; he wanted me to hang onto it. He also gave me another envelope that I haven't opened yet, though I'll have to soon."

"Why?" Toby asked.

"Because it says it's to be opened in the event of his death."

Luke said, "So Toby, you see, if you can rein your horses in till say… dawn tomorrow, there really is another pastor to give our pastor a proper send-off; someone we know Pastor Windor thought a lot of. And though what I'd like to have done if I'd had the time, is make him a casket with a fit and finish finer than any piece of furniture I've ever built, under the circumstances that won't be possible. There is a plain but serviceable coffin in my shop that will have to suffice, I'm afraid. There's no one who would have understood that more than Pastor Windor. Of course I'm not a stone-mason so I can't create a proper marker for him, but you can rest assured I will make him the best cross I am capable of making as soon as I can stand at my bench and then we can have a stone made in Denver and shipped in later, if you'd like.

Toby asked Doc, "So Doc, what's in the envelope, the one that said do not open till… you know?"

"I don't know for sure, but I would assume it's his will. I thought it would be proper to wait till after his service and burial to find out. That's what I intended, anyway. Does that sound all right to you two?"

""It sounds all right to me, "Luke said immediately, "What do you think Toby?"

"What say do I have in it?"

Doc said, "Well you're the only one chomping at the bit to charge out after his killer. You're certainly not the only one who thinks the man deserves to be punished, but no one else is personally out for revenge. I guess that means you should at least have an opinion, unless you just don't have the time.

Before Toby could respond the back door opened and Shepherd Sloan came in, accompanied by a swirling blast of cold wind-borne autumn colored leaves and a handful of snowflakes. As soon as he closed the door behind him he walked to the cook-stove and rubbed his hands together over its warmth. "Snow'll be heavy before tomorrow morning, I believe."

Doc said. Where's Jess?"

"Well," Shepherd answered. "When we finished up on the hill, Jess headed on home. He's pretty worn out. That ground's damn hard and he did more than his share of the digging while I was writing, drawing diagrams, and taking care of other things." He took several folded sheets of paper from an inside coat pocket and laid them on the table. Then he took off his coat and hung it on the back of the fourth kitchen chair before pulling it out and dropping heavily onto it like he was settling from his last legs. He let out a loud combination of a sigh and a groan as he did.

Luke said, "That was some sound, Shepherd."

Shepherd chuckled and said, "Yeah, I know, it's an old man sound, I inherited it from my father. But I didn't expect to be using it for at least another twenty or maybe thirty years yet. "

"Oh well," Doc said, "We all take the same amount of years to get old. It just shows more on some of us than others."

Shepherd nodded, and said, "Ain't it the truth?" Then he asked, "Do you have any more coffee Doc? I thought this day was never gonna' quit. An awful lot has happened since the sun came up this morning."

Luke said, "It wasn't a bad day for me, all things considered. If Dale hadn't gone fishing yesterday, I might be frozen solid now and on the way to being covered by snow. I think I'm getting an awful cold and I can't feel some of my toes at all, but it could have been a lot worse."

"How's that," Shepherd queried.

Luke coughed a raspy bark, and said, "There are only three toes I can't feel. From what I can see, they aren't turned black, so they ain't frostbit; at least not real serious; like I might lose them. And I've only got two fingers that are acting up. Losing a few toes would be bad. But losing a couple fingers or a thumb would be worse. So, like I said, it could have been a lot worse."

Luke smiled, and his smile looked to Shepherd like it might be more crooked than he ever remembered it being. And his lips still had a bluish cast to them. Shepherd hoped he was imagining it. Luke should be doing considerable warming up by then.

Shepherd nodded in agreement and said, "I think that's the very definition of looking on the bright side."

Doc said, "I think I can probably get one more cup out of the pot if I squeeze it hard enough, but it's liable to be a bit thick by now."

"That's okay, I've got good teeth," Shepherd told him.

"Good," Doc said, as soon as you get some warm caffeine in your gullet, I'll examine those toes and see how they look. If there's any skin splitting or blistering, I'll put some salve on them and wrap them. And we'll find you something suitable to wear on your feet till they heal up some. Some of the old Indian women who come down from the hills have some right nice moccasins they'd be willing to trade. They're woven of strips of squirrel or rabbit hide so they're warm, and they soak them with something to make them waterproof; I don't know what - but it works."

"That might cause a problem."

"How's that, Luke" Doc asked.

"Well, I haven't been doing any carpentry lately. I was busy being a spy; till I was discovered. Then I became a frozen treat for whatever large animal might have wanted to nibble on me. So while I was hanging around Napoleon's family-run liquor world, and thawing out in your exam room, I wasn't earning an income. So I have nothing to swap for these Indian foot-warmers of which you speak."

Doc offered a huge smile. "I think something can be arranged."

"How's that?" Luke asked cautiously.

"Lawanda, the Payaute woman who makes them always takes pity on tenderfoot palefaces like you."

Once Shepherd Sloan was seated, with a cup of hot, somewhat gritty coffee before him, Doc Forrest said, "Shepherd, I told Toby about your... here Doc paused, not knowing how to proceed, then added hesitantly, "Second profession?"

Shepherd said "Let's say my "calling", okay? And I told you if Pastor Windor trusted you I trust you. And I also said I trusted you to tell whomever you thought might need to know."

Doc said, "Well, I think Toby's at a place where his emotions might override his common sense. And I'd hate to see that happen, because

I've seen that turn out bad for good people too many more than a few times."

Shepherd wrapped his hands around his empty but still-warm coffee cup and said, "It's ironic that they use the term common sense when it's so dreadfully uncommon."

Luke said, "Shepherd, you sounded just like Pastor Windor right then."

"Thank You Luke, that's one of the nicest things anyone's ever said to me," Shepherd answered.

Then he turned to Toby, and said, "Toby, where might your emotions be in danger of leading you?"

Toby answered in a tone much less pleasant than the question was asked,

"I'm going to kill the cowardly bastard that shot Pastor Windor in the back! And nobody's going to stop me!" Toby was getting louder and more furious with every word.

Doc reached across the table and put his hand on Toby's and said, "That's not what he wanted."

What?" Toby asked, startled.

"When Walter and Luther dropped Pastor Windor off, Walter told me what the pastor said to you just before he passed when you told him that you would kill Avey for what he did."

"Why did he tell you that?" Toby shouted so vehemently that Doc jerked his hand back. Then he added, just as angrily, "I don't care!"

After taking a moment to compose himself Doc said, "You don't care that he told you not to kill Avey?"

Toby didn't answer, only shook his head.

Shepherd Sloan said, "Strange way to honor a man you claim to have loved so much; by defying his last request."

Toby said, "He was the one who taught me to shoot, and now I'm supposed to just sit on my hands while that killer goes free; the one that killed him. A god-damned hired gun. He could be anywhere by now. He's getting farther away by the minute. There's no telling how many people he's killed, or how many more he will kill. I'd be doing the world a favor if I killed him. And I need to get started. I'm wasting time." Toby trailed off, worn out, out of breath. He pushed back from the table and started toward the door, nearly at a run.

Then Shepherd said, in a surprisingly strict tone of voice, "Landon and I talked a lot, and it's really not what he would want, you know."

Toby stopped dead and turned. "What?"

"I said Landon and I talked a lot. Oh? You did know that men of the cloth have first names. Pastor Windor's was Landon. He was Landon Windor Junior in fact. He was named after his father."

"He never told me his first name." Toby said.

"Did you ever ask?"

Toby shook his head

"As I said, we talked a great deal. He spent a lot of time trying to help me get my head out of a bottle. And I'm slowly making it. He also unloaded a lot of deep hurt regarding his own old and painful relationship with his father. Apparently his father was so dead set against him becoming a pastor that he practically disowned him as a son. He once told me that by the time he left home as a young man the only thing he took with him without a bad memory to go along with it was his name, and that was only because he'd had it since he was born.

Another time he told me about the day he came up on you in the woods with your father's gun. And he told me he thought hard before he decided to teach you, and he only decided to teach you to use it in the hopes that it would help you feel closer to the father you'd lost because he remembered the loss he felt when his father quit caring about him, which was just as bad."

"He told you that?"

Shepherd nodded, "Yep, he told me that. You can take it to the bank. So, when he said he didn't want you to go after Avey and kill him because he didn't train you to be a killer he meant it. That's just the way he was."

"But I can't just sit and do nothing. It's killing me to know Avey's running around free while Pastor Windor's layin' in that room with a blanket over his face and a bullet hole in his back because of him. I 'gotta do something about it!"

"And you're so anxious to do it that you can't wait till tomorrow to give Pastor Windor a proper funeral?" Doc asked

"Well what more do we need to make it a proper funeral, now that we know we have a minister to perform the service?"

Doc answered his question with a question, "Toby, do you think the people of Whiskey Branch should be allowed the time to grieve the passing of someone who meant so much to each and every one of them?"

Shepherd said, "Toby, this could be your chance to do Pastor Windor proud by not displaying selfishness as a response to his death."

"Selfishness! What do you mean selfishness?" Toby slammed his fist on the table.

"You're not the only one who lost someone when Pastor Windor died today, you know," Luke told him. "So don't act like this pain is all your own."

Toby pushed away from the table and stood up so quickly his chair turned over backwards and clattered to the floor. "Well, okay, I'm going to find Jess and let him know that I'll be ready to go as soon as possible after sunup. Right after we have the pastor's funeral service. I'm getting out after Avey as soon as I can, and nothing else can stop me!"

Doc said, "You know Toby, you're taking one thing for granted that could be a real fly in the ointment for your plan."

"Yeah, what's that," Toby answered, fuming at again being challenged.

"You're just assuming Jess is willing to take off into the woods after an expert gun-hand. Just because Jess is the best tracker in Whiskey Branch doesn't mean he'll be interested in tracking a proven back-shooter.

Luke spoke up, "Unless of course, you're really interested in having him along because he's a crack shot with that Winchester of his," Luke said, playing on Toby's pride.

"Are you saying I'm afraid of Avey?"

"I'm not saying anything," Luke answered. "I'm just thinking out loud."

Then Luke said to Shepherd Sloan, "Well, it looks like the pastor's service will be at dawn tomorrow after all. Can we assume you'll be presiding at the farewell to Pastor Windor?"

"That you can," Shepherd said. "I imagine Miss Waters would be agreeable to using the schoolhouse for the service. I believe I'll go ask her as soon as I finish this cup of coffee."

Doc asked, "Shepherd, are you feeling sufficiently warmed up yet? I believe I have a part of a bottle of rye in the kitchen. A small dose might help brace you up before heading back out in the cold. Sometimes it's the inner man that needs doctoring."

"No thanks Doc. I don't have much in the way of will-power. I think I'll pass on your offer and just head over to see Miss Waters.

Miss Waters lived in a small, but perfectly cared for house adjacent to the schoolhouse property. Doc said, "I'll walk along with you and check on the injured men over there."

The sound Toby made reinforced his earlier-stated opinion of Doc's caring for Napoleon Bleu's men. He said, "I'm going home and clean my gun and get my gear ready. I'm going after Avey as soon as the pastor's buried tomorrow, with Jess or without him." He left Doc's office, slamming the door behind him.

Shepherd Sloan looked at Doc and Luke and said, "Vengeance is a poison for which there is no antidote. Once inside, it'll eat away at you till you're deader than Judas Iscariat."

Luke said, "There you go sounding like Pastor Windor again."

Shepherd said, "Well I think I'll quit on that positive note, and go see Miss Waters." He pulled his coat on and turned his collar up against the wind that could be heard outside, and then he and Doc left for Miss Waters' house

When asked, Not only was Miss Waters agreeable with the idea of holding the pastor's service in her schoolhouse; she stated that it was it an honor, and she would be hurt if the service were held elsewhere.

When Toby slammed out Doc Forrest's back door and began trudging through town toward his wagon-turned-house on the east end of Whiskey Branch he found the wind had picked up considerably and the little bit of snow that had been falling and had blown in the door when Shepherd Sloan entered Doc's office had gotten somewhat heavier and caused a small amount of accumulation that had left main street covered with a coating which was just deep enough to show his boot prints behind him as he walked. The pastor had been right that morning after all. It looked like the beginning of the real snowstorm Toby had feared would come during the night, or maybe not till the next day. The current snowfall would be only enough to both make the ladies of Whiskey Branch comment on how beautiful it was and to be a general nuisance in every other respect. He hadn't gone far before he came within sight of Luther's place, though it was really only the bright flames of the blazing fire under the forge which sat under the broad open roof of the shed of the blacksmith's shop adjacent to the livery stable part of Luther's business that was visible to Toby through the gauzy haze of the thickening snowfall. And as he got closer, he could see the smoke from the shed's smokestack rising against the few visible stars. When he got closer Luther hailed him, and Toby paused on his determined, purposeful walk toward home.

"Where you going, Toby?"

"I'm going after a killer."

"That's what I was afraid you'd say. Why don't you come in and talk about it?" Luther nodded toward his home, another example of Luke's handiwork, which sat behind his shop.

"No, I know you'll try to talk me out of it, and I've had enough of that. "Okay, step in here under the roof." They took a step closer to the forge.

One thing was certain; Luther was the one man in whiskey Branch who was never going to get cold on the job, no matter how frigid the weather turned.

Immediately, Toby said, "I'm going after Avey. I'm going to kill the bastard! Every minute I waste, he's getting further away."

"Okay Toby; let me ask you this. Do you have a plan? I mean something more than: I'm going to kill the bastard. I imagine more than one man has gone against him with that same plan and come out toes-up. I once told Pastor Windor that you were the smartest damn kid I ever saw. Now why don't you act like it?" You want him dead. So how can you do it without ending up dead yourself? And just why do you think Pastor Windor was so determined that he didn't want you to try to kill Avey? Have you given that any thought?" Luther fell silent, to give the young man time to study on the question.

"I don't know," Toby answered. "I guess cause of the 'Thou shalt not kill' thing in the Bible. "But I also remember him talking in one of his sermons about 'An eye for an eye. And for me, losing Pastor Windor was a lot worse than losing an eye would have been."Toby's voice hitched, and then he added, "Hell, I'd trade both my eyes to bring him back."

Luther held his hands out toward the fire blazing beneath the forge, warming them before shoving them deep in his pockets. "Well you know Toby," he said. "Pastor Windor was looking out for more than saving your soul when he told you not to kill Avey. He was also trying to save your skin."

"How do you figure?"

"Luther said, "Remember those dime-novels you told me you used to read about gunfighters before you and your folks came out from back east."

"Yeah, what about them?"

"Didn't those stories go that the man who was supposed to be the fastest always had men following him around wanting to be the one who killed him and took his reputation?"

Toby nodded.

Luther shrugged his huge shoulders. "Well let's suppose you do kill Avey? And don't you get me wrong now; that man needs killin'- there's no denyin' that. Well, then you'll be the man who killed the gunslinger that everybody was out to kill. So who is that goin' to paint a target on?"

Toby didn't have an answer. It was a concept he'd been totally blinded to in his all-encompassing fury. After a moment, he mumbled, "I never thought of that."

Luther put his hand on the boy's shoulder and said, "Toby, even as he was dying, the pastor was thinking of what was best for you.

Respect his wishes."

On the North Side of Whiskey Creek:

A loud pounding came at the door of the attractive yellow house that appeared so out-of-place sitting in the center of the clearing in the midst of a vast expanse of hundreds of acres of woods. It seemed even stranger than when Luke had first seen it, now that the grass all around the house was covered with the first skiff of fallen snow.

Millie answered the door; her head bowed, and her eyes downcast; as if expecting a blow." Oh it's you," she said, allowing herself only the amount of surprise she could safely get away with without receiving, at the very least, a severe chewing-out from Lillie, should her sister overhear, or at the worst, a sound cuff upside the head. She'd received so many of those over the years that her left ear didn't work properly anymore. To hear the thunder or wind of a distant storm, she had to stand or sit so her right ear faced the storm. And whether she was listening for something or not, there was an endless ringing; a damn unpleasant ringing in that ear. Covering the ear with her hand didn't stop it. Putting a pillow over it didn't stop it. It drove her so crazy that she had made up her mind to cut out the bell that was in there making the sound. She was lying on the floor in her room with her head on her arm curled under the ringing ear and wondering how deep she would have to push the knife into her ear to reach the bell that was making the constant sound. It was a scary thought. She knew it would hurt; she didn't like things that hurt. But then out of nowhere came a memory of Luke; and for just a little while the whistling went away. Or at least she didn't notice it. She remembered holding Luke's hand as they walked through the woods path and Luke's arm around her shoulder as they crossed the yard to Daddy's house. The sun was shining then; it was chilly, but sunny. And then the little while that they were alone on the porch in secret before Nappy ruined everything for her forever.

Millie was jogged from her reverie by the pounding that came again, slowly at first, and then more abruptly as the pounding became more demanding.

She stumbled to the door and pulled it open to find the tall mean-looking man with long red hair and mustache. She'd seen him before. She said, "Oh it's you."

"Damn right it's me, and I want my money. The job's done. The bible-thumper's dead; now I want paid." Then Avey bent and looked close at Millie. He smiled and said, "Oh, you're the nice one. It's the bitch I gotta' see. Where is she?"

Millie found herself responding in the strangest way. Coming out ahead in a comparison with Lillie even when it was a nasty monster like this man doing the comparing felt good, and she smiled at him, her freckled nose crinkling as she did.

Just then they heard Lillie's shriek from down the hall in the back of the house.

Avey looked at Millie, and said, "Never mind miss, I know the way. You have a good day." Then he pushed her roughly aside and rushed off down the hall.

Following the strident sound of Lillie's angry yelling, Avey had no trouble tracking her through the ground floor of the rambling old house to her father's room.

Through the closed door he could hear Napoleon Bleu gasping for breath in response to Lillie's yelling. Apparently the old man was every bit as bad off as she had pronounced him to be when they had gone out to the east road of Whiskey Branch together to take care of the preacher. When he heard Lillie shout his name he opened the door, burst in, and said sarcastically, "I hope I'm not the reason for all this uproar."

Napoleon Bleu lay in bed, a blanket pulled up under his chin, a whiskey jug close at hand on a bed-side table, with sweat streaming from his face in rivers. Lillie stood in the center of the room screaming at her father at the top of her lungs. To his credit; Napoleon was giving nearly as good as he got, though he had to pause to draw a ragged breath after each word.

"Lillie said "What the hell are you doing here you back-shooting bastard?"

"Have you forgotten, it's payday?" Avey said sweetly.

"I'll be damned." Lillie spat the words at him with a bitter smirk.

Then, wheezing as he struggled to manage the words, Napoleon Bleu said, "Pay the man."

Lillie turned again to her father, and was instantly again screaming, "You want to pay him all that money for back-shooting the preacher? We could have gotten any one of the still-tenders to do that for a hundred dollars and a jug. Or I'd have done it myself."

"You're the one who found him." The old man could barely gasp the words out.

"I heard he was the best; the fastest. I told him to take the preacher; to gun him like a man. Not to back shoot him!" Lillie was so furious she was near tears.

"Napoleon asked, "Is the preacher dead?"

"Lillie said, "He's dead"

"Pay the man."

Avey said to Napoleon Bleu, "I'd like to know why were you willing to pay so much to see him dead? You offered two thousand dollars. That's twice what I usually make for killing a man, and I didn't have to ask for it; you offered it up front, like you wanted to be damned sure you weren't turned down. What was it about him? What past did you have with him that made you want him dead so bad?"

"An ancient score, Mister Avey," Napoleon Bleu mumbled, the words barely intelligible. Both Avey and Lillie leaned closer to hear.

"Ancient; and also none of your business, and no longer important." Napoleon Bleu drew a long rattling breath that was followed by no more.

Lillie said, "Father!" It was said in the same shriek Avey had heard her using when she was arguing with her father about paying him. He was beginning to believe it was her normal speaking voice.

Vance Avey stepped up to Napoleon Bleu's still body and poked him in the chest with the barrel of his pistol, and getting no response, slid the pistol back in its holster.

Then Avey looked at Lillie and said, "Well, it looks like you're in charge of paying the bills around here now, so pay up. Two thousand dollars, I believe it was. I got the impression your old man was an evil bastard, but not someone who would try to back out on a debt. And you wouldn't advise that you do that either." Avey off-handedly tapped the revolver with the unusually long barrel hanging in the low-slung holster over his left shoulder. "Oh, and you have my condolences on your loss."

"Don't you threaten me, you smug bastard. I saw what you did, remember. I was there when you killed that preacher by shooting him in the back. A preacher!" Lillie had built up a head of steam till she was up to her regular shriek. "A preacher!" she repeated even more loudly.

"Oh, have you suddenly grown a conscience?" Avey asked.

No, I just wonder if you had to pay someone to carve the notches in your gun handle for you. I mean, how hard could it have been to outdraw a preacher? Why didn't you face him? Too scared? Was he that fast or maybe you're just that slow?"

"No, I'm not slow, just smart. If you'd take time to think once in a while you'd see it. And it might just benefit you.

"How do you figure that?" Lillie had quieted a bit, now she sounded nearly as interested as was angry.

"Well, Avey said, "I don't know what quarrel your old man had with the God-pounder and I really couldn't care less. They're both dead as stones, but one of them took the two thousand I was supposed to make for killing the other one with him. I know your old man had big plans for that little town on the other side of the creek that's going to be frozen solid before tomorrow morning. And I also know the kid that preacher was supposed to be training to shoot is going to be out for blood. Now, I don't know if he's really fast or not, but I don't plan on sticking around to find out." Avey walked from the room where Napoleon Bleu lay dead in bed into the hall.

Lillie panicked and followed him. Catching up to Avey, she grabbed him by the arms and rubbed up against his chest, turning on what she hoped was an attractive smile, and said, "You can't leave now. You're right; my father did have big plans for that grungy little hole in the wall. And there's no reason I can't still make them happen. But I'll need someone to help me make them happen."

In fact what had happened was that Avey's comments made Lillie realize Toby would be out for revenge, and Napoleon Bleu would be the most likely target for that revenge. But since he was dead, that put her next in line. Suddenly Avey seemed like a good person to have around. She wasn't foolish enough to think Avey would put himself in harm's way just to protect her. Even if she paid him; his back-shooting of Pastor Windor proved what a coward he was. He wasn't real bodyguard material. Still, if he was around Toby had someone other than her toward whom to direct his anger and need for retribution. After all, it was Avey who pulled the trigger, and the kid knew it. She'd looked into his horrified eyes as he watched Avey ride away. She knew the image of that red hair flying in the breeze must be frozen in the kid's memory as surely as the image of the kid's eyes was in hers.

Avey peeled Lillie's hands from his arms and said, "Look, I've gotta' make tracks. I want to get movin'. I'll just be takin' my two grand and leavin.' It's snowing out there, and there's ice underneath it. If I can outrun the worst of it I can be in Salt Lake City in a week. Now give me my money so I can say adios to your pretty sis and vamoose."

Lillie totally lost control. "Why do you call her pretty?" she shrieked. "We're identical. She looks just like me. Is it the damn freckles?"

Vance Avey laughed out loud and said, "Freckles, what freckles? She has freckles? No it's the smile. I only saw her smile once, but when she smiles it's a real smile; her face lights up. When you smile it makes me think of a snake that's spotted a small animal and is about to strike. There's nothing close to pleasant in it; it's scary."

"So will you stay or not?" Will you stay if I pay you two thousand to kill the kid? He could be planning to come after either one of us or both of us. It would only make good sense for you to be ready for him, and to make some money at the same time, wouldn't it? At least here you'll be close enough to keep an eye on him, and on what's happening over there. And I have a small army of men, and I'll make sure they're watching what's happening over there, too. You've already made two thousand dollars off my family. If you stay here and kill the kid I'll add another two thousand. Four thousand dollars is a lot better than two."

Avey snickered. "You're forgetting, I had a real good view of how much of your small army got blown up or burned up today. Plus, all the money in the world doesn't do a man any good if he's too far underground to spend it, lady. And there's a good chance that once the men in your small army find out that the man who was feeding them and giving them shelter is worm food they'll be gone."

"You're crazy as Hell!"

"Some of them might even decide life might be pretty good across the creek in that grungy little hole in the wall that your small army wasn't able to take on a Sunday when half the town was in church and the other half was asleep. Or at least that's the way I heard that moron brother of yours said it would be."

Lillie smiled her snake-smile. "Well, he's dead now."

Avey said, "You don't seem terribly broken up about it." Then he nodded back toward the room where Napoleon lay dead in bed and added, "That seems to be happening to a lot of the men in your family, doesn't it?"

"Don't you worry; the family business is in good hands."

"You do have a partner don't you; the one with the nice smile?"

Lillie laughed so hard she lost her breath. When she regained it she said, "Her? She can barely add four and four. She doesn't know how to spell business, let alone run one. She's an idiot."

"Well, speak of The Devil." Avey was looking over Lillie's head, down the hall toward the front of the house. Lillie turned and was nose to nose with Millie. She said, "How long have you been there?"

"A while. You're not very nice, you know. But your time is gonna' come."

Then Millie did something she'd never done in their lives; she pushed Lillie, hard. Lillie lost her balance, got her feet tangled and nearly fell. Then Millie turned and walked away.

Lillie said, "Where do you think you're going?"

"I'm going to talk to Daddy." She walked back toward her father's room.

Then Lillie once again began screaming at her, but Millie barely heard her. It was the first time she'd ever been happy for the ringing buried in her head. She was glad she'd been afraid to poke the knife in her ear and try to dig it out, because she could hardly hear Lillie at all over the ringing, and that was a good thing.

When Millie saw her Daddy, she knew right away he was dead. Just the same as she'd known right away that Nappy was dead. Except Nappy being dead was a good thing. This was different. At least Daddy didn't die with holes in his chest. And that was definitely a good thing.

A floor-board creaked behind her, making her jump like a child and squeal like a mouse. She turned quickly, expecting to see Lillie; she was already braced for the blow she was sure was coming. But instead Vance Avey stood behind her.

He said, "Sorry if I frightened you."

"Sokay."

"And I'm sorry about your father."

Millie looked at his gun where it hung in its holster. "Did you shoot him?"

"No, I didn't shoot him. I figure he had a heart attack; he was really old. I guess there are worse ways to die."

Millie surprised him by saying, "At least Mamma was wrong. She didn't like him moonshining. She said if he didn't stop he'd end up swinging from the gallows pole like her grandpa did back in the old country. But he died right there." Then she smiled at Avey and said, "Thank you for not shooting Daddy." And then she added, "But you can shoot Lillie if you want."

Unable to keep from returning her smile, Avey said, "Thanks, I'll keep that in mind." Avey looked at Lillie, who stood less than a dozen feet away just outside the doorway to the hall and winked.

Millie walked to her father's bedside, dropped to the floor, and taking his lifeless hand, began rocking forward and back and sobbing.

Lillie looked at Avey and said, "See, I told you she's an idiot, telling you to shoot me with me standing right here."

Avey stepped into the hall and said, "I don't know, if I were in her shoes I might say the same thing. I'd say you're just damned lucky she's never had a gun."

Lillie hauled off and slapped Avey across the face.

Avey did the last thing she expected; he slapped her back - hard, on the side of the head. Hard enough to make her bounce off the wall, barely keeping her feet under her. And for a brief moment she experienced, though she had no way of knowing it, the excruciating ringing in her ear that she'd doomed her sister to live with forever.

Lillie grabbed for Avey's gun but his skilled hand, trained by decades of repetition, had it unholstered and pressed to her midsection before her hand got close.

Lillie responded with the only weapon she had left, and one she was as quick with as he was with his six-gun; a scream. "Okay you bastard, four thousand to kill the kid!" Avey stood and smiled at her, relishing her mounting frustration.

"Five thousand!" She screamed, louder yet. Still Avey only looked at her, eyes wide, smiling and ignoring her increase in volume.

"Ten thousand!" Lillie screamed and then stomped her foot, causing a vase to fall from a nearby hall table to the floor and shatter. In the bedroom Millie cried out in surprise.

Lillie glared in the bedroom at her and screamed, "You shut up, right now!"

Avey told Lillie, "You really are a royal bitch, aren't you?"

Instead of screaming as he'd expected, a response to which he would have only laughed, she said, "You haven't had to deal with her thick-headedness from the time we shared a cradle. Ten thousand I said; take it or leave it! It's all I've got, if I've got that. Will you kill the kid for ten grand?" Lillie was fighting hard to keep the pleading tone from her voice, and she hated herself for the struggle. She'd always felt herself beyond such frustrations.

Avey said, "You're really afraid that kid's going to be out for blood, aren't you?"

"Aren't you?"

Avey looked at the floor and shuffled his feet like a little boy who had to pee; putting on a show, trying Lillie's patience to see just how desperate she really was; how far she could be pushed. "Well I don't know; from what I understand the preacher blew away that brother of yours like the punk had never touched a gun before. Now, I know that doesn't mean the kid is fast just because the man who taught him was fast. But it is food for thought; and the more I chew that food the more valuable I see myself being to you."

"I told you I don't have any more!" Lillie's voice had again become a grating screech.

"Why don't you talk to that small army of men you said you have. Maybe they'll be willing to take a pay cut if it makes the difference between keeping you healthy or not. Avey once more gave her a wink.

Lillie again stomped her foot.

Avey placed his finger to his lips and shushed her. When things fell silent they could hear Millie bawling uncontrollably from Napoleon Senior's bedroom. She was crying so hard she was having difficulty keeping her breath. Lillie looked in the door and said," Be quiet you fool."

"Millie gasped out, "Please wake up Daddy."

Avey said, "The King is dead; long-live the Queen."

The words had barely left his mouth when Millie stepped into the hall holding the Colt 45 she'd found in her father's night stand in both hands, and aiming it directly at Lillie's head, clicked the hammer back. Lillie glared at her sister, bared her teeth and hissed, "You…"

Vance Avey whispered, "I'd be very careful what you say right now Your-Majesty."

Then he bent so he was eye-to-eye with Lillie and said, "I suppose if I *were* your partner; your *equal* partner, I'd have a good reason to keep you alive."

Lillie sneered at him and growled, "I should kill you myself, you bastard."

Without bothering to rise again to his full height, Avey calmly reached out and took the gun from Millie's hand. She made no effort to resist. As soon as her hand was empty her arm dropped to her side and she returned to her dead father's bedside, where she again sat on the floor and began rocking and crying. Avey tucked the pistol he'd taken from Millie in his belt and said to Lillie, "Wow, I've already started earning that ten thousand, and I didn't have to take a step. On top of that, the person I saved your nasty ass from was your own sister. So if I've got to go up against that kid, especially not knowing how fast he is it ought to be worth more. And if you don't have more cash, that's your problem, not mine. If we can't come to some sort of agreement, I'm going to hit the road." Avey was speaking evenly and calmly, more like a businessman or banker than like a hired killer trying to make a deal to act as a bodyguard for a desperate criminal.

"Okay, you're my partner." Lillie said it as though the words tasted like vinegar crossing her lips.

"Your equal partner?"

"Yes, equal partner."

Avey nodded toward the room where her father's body still lay in his bed. "What about Sis? Is she a partner? It seems only fair. Will it be a three-way split?"

Lillie laughed a laugh that dripped venom but held no humor. "You must be joking. She's been an anchor around my neck my whole life. She's been worse than a kid sister 'cause she looks just like me. Except everybody says she's cuter, she's nicer, she's sweeter, she's more pleasant, she's built better, Once I even heard somebody say she looks younger."

"Is she?" Avey asked.

"Hell no! I'm actually younger, by more than two minutes!" Lillie shouted.

Avey squinted, looked close at her and said mockingly, "Of course, you're *obviously* younger. Anybody can see that; it's as plain as the nose on your face. And it's clear her nose is older; that's how it had time to grow those cute freckles." Again Avey winked at her.

"I hope that kid does kill you! I can't stand you!"

"I'm all broken up over that. But just remember; I'm the only thing standing between you and that kid from across the creek."

Then Avey added, "Honey I'm used to only looking out for myself. Partner or not you're just so much extra baggage I have to worry about. And at this point I don't know if you're a risk worth taking. There's a good chance that with your old man dead the money flow will dry up like a bad well during a drought. Things could change quick when word gets around that he's croaked. I think the best thing for me to do is leave you in the dust and ramble on."

"I've been running this business for years! My father was too old to know what was going on. Nappy didn't do anything but ride around to the stills and bully the drunks that feed the fires and steal our liquor. And my sister's been useless since the day she was born."

"Don't you mean the day *we* were born?" You were born at the same time weren't you? Oh wait. You said there were two minutes between you. That makes her your big sister, doesn't it? Shouldn't big sis be I charge of the business? Isn't that how royalty works?"

"You're through making fun of me!" Lillie made another grab. But that time she fooled him; she didn't grab for the gun in his holster, she grabbed for the gun he'd taken from Millie and tucked in his belt. And because she took him by surprise she got it. As soon as he realized she'd gotten the revolver free of his belt he shoved her hard against the wall. She fought to get turned around in the narrow confines of the hall and get the gun aimed at him. She'd totally forgotten that just a few minutes before she'd been trying to hire Avey as a bodyguard to protect her. Now the only thing her fury at being taunted by him could allow her to think of was putting a bullet in him. She was thrashing and stumbling around like a drunk in a broom closet; bouncing from wall to wall, and tripping over her own feet, she finally fell, landing on her ample ass with a thud that sent a slight tremor through the entire lower floor of the old house. As she fell she lost the gun. It bounced off the floor, and then a wall, then hit the floor once again. On its second contact with the floor, it struck the wood hammer-first. The gun went off, sounding like thunder in the close quarters, and throwing a muzzle flash that lit up the gloomy, narrow hallway like a photographer's flash-pan. The bullet smashed a fist-sized hole through the wall dividing the hall from the late Napoleon Bleu's bedroom, and judging by the sound that came from the doorway; the sound of shattering glass, it continued on through a window. But before penetrating the old plaster and wood, it purely by chance, tore a chunk of flesh from Vance Avey's left arm a few inches below his shoulder. A bright red spray fanned out across the wall behind him like a painter had waved a brush in a broad arc. Avey shouted, "You bitch!" and drew his six-gun with his thankfully uninjured right hand as lightning fast as ever. He shoved it against Lillie's forehead till the barrel pressed a dimple in the flesh. Instead of displaying the panic that someone would typically show under those circumstances she shrieked laughter. "What do you think of that, *Partner*?"

Avey pulled back the hammer. "I think if that bullet had hit my right arm, you'd be dead now. You'd be dead if I had to strangle you with my other hand, or if I had to put my boot on your throat and stand on it till you choked to death. Now give me the ten thousand, and I'm leaving! Forget about the partnership; I just want to be shed of you; and the sooner the better! I've got a kid to kill. And I want to be clear on this; I'm not doing it for the money, although money's the only thing keeping me from pulling the trigger right now. I'm *damned* sure not doing it to save your skin. I almost hope he does come after you, you crazy bitch. It wouldn't hurt my feelings to see you floating face-down in that creek. It'd be something I'd picture in my head every time my arm pains me. I'm going to kill him so he doesn't get a chance at me. I don't have any idea how fast he is. But he might decide to get me the same way I got his precious preacher, and I'm not about to give him that chance."

Lillie saw her chance at a parting shot and she took it. "Are you going to back-shoot him too?"

"No I'm going to call him out. It'll be a fair fight. And I plan on doing it right where everyone can see it, so there won't be any doubt. So when I kill him in a fair fight he won't be a martyr. It's bad enough knowing the kid's out to get me. I don't want any heroes from that little mud-hole of a town hounding me, trying to avenge another local legend. I'll kill him fair and square. That way they'll know I'm somebody best left alone."

Lillie followed him all the way to the front porch, where she stood and watched him unhitch his horse from the porch rail, looking up at her with that infuriating grin of his the whole time. Finally, furious, she said, "You!" the word coming out in one long snarl accompanied by a plume of breath in the frigid air. Then in a totally different, panicky voice she said, "Please stay; I'm afraid." Avey began to wonder if there wasn't a third sister; a triplet buried in Lillie's head, which only peeked out once in a while.

"Whoa, there it is," Avey said. "The mouth can speak the truth without bursting into flames. Who would have thought it possible? So, Miss Bleu; new head of the family business, just what are you afraid of? Is it just the kid, or is there more?"

"It's not just him; my father's dead, Nappy's dead, my sister *wants me* dead. I didn't give a damn for Nappy, but at least in his own stupid way, he did keep the still-tenders in line, and working. And it's clear the tenders hate me. I know it; I can see it in the way they look at me when I ride by the camps. What if they all pull out on me? Or what if they stay, but won't listen to me and get to dragging their feet, or start getting so drunk they can't be trusted to do their jobs without blowing themselves and my stills clear to Hell? And we've had enough of that, thanks to some marksman from across the creek." Up to that point Lillie's voice had sounded strained, but still focused on the business. Then it changed into something akin to what a mad dog or a wolf anxious to go on a killing spree might sound like if suddenly gifted with the power of speech. Her eyes narrowed and seemed to flare in failing evening light. Avey took an involuntary backward step. Her lip curled back and she snarled, "If I ever meet him; their marksman, I'll pay him back. I'll pay him in full! He's the one that killed my father."

Avey was confused, "I don't follow you?"

My old man has had one foot in the grave for a year. It was just a matter of time. Well when he heard those explosions going off one after another, along with all the yelling and screamin' he knew what was happening. He was old, but he could still put two and two together and get four. He didn't know exactly what was happening, but he knew a string of blasts like that probably spelled the end. And that's when his heart gave out; when he realized it all was gone. The last thing he said to me was he hoped the fire didn't make it up to the house he built for our mother." Lillie paused and looked thoughtfully up and down the length of the porch, then said, "What if the buyers really won't buy from me when they hear my father's dead?" The snarl had left her voice; now she just sounded tired and confused. "I'll be poor. I've never been poor. And what if the kid kills you? Then what? Then I'll be completely alone. I've never been alone."

"Oh so now you want me around not just for protection, but for company. A little while ago you tried to shoot me, now I've become very important to you. Isn't it funny how fast things can change?" Avey bent close to Lillie and laughed in her face; a loud, rude, braying laughter, devoid of humor, meant only to degrade and embarrass her. Then he turned his back on her, and without another word, walked toward his horse.

Trying for a forceful parting shot, Lillie yelled, "You better run!" and Avey heard the hammer click back on the revolver she still held behind him. Though she had screamed at him to run, Avey was in fact walking away in a slow purposeful manor intended to show how certain he was that she wouldn't pull the trigger; if for no other reason but that she would then be truly alone in a situation where all her bitching and bluster would count for exactly squat. His response to her scream, or more accurately, his lack of a response had an immediate effect; Lillie said, "Come back here right now, or I'll kill myself!"

Avey looked over his shoulder and saw that her desperate threat had been a hollow one. Instead of the gun pointing at him, it was dangling in her dropped hand, and she had lowered the hammer.

Avey said, "Not that I care, particularly, but "If you plan on doing that, I wish you would at least pay me first."

That got Lillie to screaming again. "You bastard!"She turned back toward the front door of the house, but was still screaming at him, even as she turned away. "Okay, you don't think I'll kill you, and you don't care if I kill myself. Maybe I'll go back in and put a bullet in my sister's empty head. She's useless anyway. What do you think of that, mister gunfighter?"

"I haven't known this family of crazy people for long," Avey answered. "But from what I've seen, I'd guess she has a lot more reasons to want you dead than the other way around." Avey paused, then went on, "Yeah, I think if your big sis wants you dead it's because you've given her cause. You, on the other hand are one of those people born with a hole inside. People like that have to fill that hole with something. In your case you filled it with hate. And your sister was the unlucky person who happened to be the handiest and easiest one for you to dump all that excess hate on when the hole in you got so full it couldn't hold any more. More's the pity."

"So, what makes her so special? I know what I look like, and I know what she looks like. I'm as pretty as she is. And I'm not as dumb as a stump like she is. So what's so special about her?" Lillie's voice was growing shriller, and she was getting more furious with every word. "What makes her different? Why is she better?"

Avey answered, "If for no other reason, I actually saw her smile once. I think if you even tried to smile your face would break."

Lillie again raised the gun, pointing it at his chest, and thumbing back the hammer.

Before she knew what was happening, Avey's gun was out of his holster and pointing at her face; practically touching her nose. He said, "I've enjoyed all of your company I can stand. I've got a pissed-off kid across the creek to deal with. And he could turn out to be a real concern, a real something dangerous, not just a colossal pain in the ass like you've gotten to be."

Avey holstered his gun and walked toward his horse.

From behind him Lillie moaned, "Please don't go." Her voice had taken on a wheedling tone. Her previous bossy attitude was totally absent. "If you stay, I'll pay you more; an extra five thousand!"

Avey turned and sneered at her. "I thought you said you were tapped out."

Lillie's shoulders dropped. "I don't have it now. But if you stay with me, I'll get it; I promise. You can trust me." She tried her best to sound believable, even offering a forced, clearly insincere smile.

Avey laughed aloud. Then he dropped her a wink. "Trust you? I wouldn't trust you if you were on your knees in church." He again began walking toward his horse.

When Avey had just reached his horse and was untying the reins from the porch rail, Lillie said, with a seemingly sincere tone of concern in her voice, "Will you be coming back? I mean do you really think you can take the kid?"

Avey asked her, "What do you care? Are you wanting a personal bodyguard, or are you just looking for a gun-toting heavy to take your brother's place as the thug in charge of keeping your lazy loafin' still-rats working?" Avey gave an exaggerated sigh, and spread his hands in an 'I can take it or leave it' gesture, but finished up saying, "I'll have to give it some thought, and you do the same. I'll do a little eyeballing at the situation across the creek and maybe see if I can even start up a few conversations over there. I don't expect to get any life-stories, but any little bit of info can often be quite valuable. As soon as your old man hired me to take on the preacher I started shadowing him. I always want to know my target. I was watching the preacher teaching the kid before that fool brother of yours was. When the preacher started training the kid, I started paying close attention to him too; and boy I'm glad I did." At first it was slow and methodical, but the preacher got that kid progressing more quickly. And within a couple weeks when the pastor and the kid were blank drawing against each other for practice, the difference between them got so close that I wouldn't have wanted to have to choose which of them to go up against. Of course in those situations you never have time to choose. You're lucky if you have a second or two. If you take longer than that, you're dead. I may make it back and I may not," Avey said with an intentional finality in his voice, and swung up into his saddle. As he reined his horse toward the direction of Whiskey Creek, Millie shouted from the front door of the house; her voice on the edge of dissolving into sobs, "Mister, before you ride away, will you help me bury my Daddy? Please? My Momma's buried under the shade tree out back. I'm sure Daddy would like to be with her." Millie's voice was disquieting; similar to Lillie's but without the strident, grating air to it. The voice only startled Lillie, but was both startling and briefly confusing to Avey. It was similar to Lillie's, and at the same time totally different. While almost the same in tone and timbre, the nuance was as different from Lillie's as the difference between night and day. While Lillie's voice tended to make him cringe, the new voice almost made him smile, even before he realized for sure who its owner was. He turned and found that Millie was standing in the doorway. She again said, "Mister, would you help me bury my daddy? Please?" She nodded toward the back of the house. "Mama's buried out back; Daddy'd like it if he was buried out there with her. I don't care what Nappy said. Daddy loved our mama better than he loved his. But Nappy's gone anyway." Millie finished that statement with a smile. Then she waked quickly back in the house, but returned almost immediately. She held something hidden behind her back and she grinned like a little girl; her freckled nose curling up cutely.

Then she said, "I'm glad the Preacher-man shot Nappy full'a holes.

"Nappy took Luke away. He threw him in the freezing water." She was sobbing and gasping for breath as she finished telling Avey what Nappy had done to Luke. "I hated Nappy!"

Lillie burst out laughing; the sound a harsh braying that instantly made Avey's head ache, and then shrieked at her sister, "You fool; he was sent to spy on us!."

Millie cried out, "I don't care; he was nice to me! Nobody's ever nice to me. I loved Luke!" Then her eyes grew big at a memory. "You're the one who told Nappy to kill Luke!" she snarled at her sister.

And then without another second's hesitation, Millie pulled the revolver from behind her; and holding it with both hands, shot Lillie in the head. And in the blink of an eye the life-long resemblance between the sisters was a thing of the past. As Lillie pitched forward toward the semi- frozen ground Avey saw a half dollar sized hole dead center in her forehead. Once she had landed face-down with a splat the fist-sized exit wound in the back of her head was clearly visible.

A few thoughts shot through Avey's mind in rapid succession; First, Little-sis sure can hit what she aims for. Second, she got rid of the nasty bitch that seemed to enjoy making her life miserable. Plus, she promoted herself to head of the family business at the same time.

Then he looked at Millie, standing, wobbling unsteadily back and forth from one foot to the other, with the spent revolver dangling from her hand, with the barrel pointed pretty much toward her own feet. She appeared dazed, as though she couldn't quite grasp what she'd done. Her eyes were glassy and full of unspilled tears.

Avey eased up to her and said softly, "Why don't I take care of this?" As he spoke he gently took hold of the revolver, and leaning close to her ear and speaking in a soothing near-whisper, he said, "Why don't you let me have it?" As he said it he slowly unpeeled her fingers from around the gun, working the index finger off the trigger first, as gently and cautiously as if it were a live snake waiting to bite him if he startled it as he untangled it from its resting place, wanting to separate it from the curved metallic sliver of death that was the trigger. When after a few slow moments the gun was actually more in his hand than hers he slid his other hand up her arm till his palm cupped her elbow. He paused and let it linger there to see how she would respond. When Millie didn't pull back, or look startled he gave a very gentle squeeze; just enough pressure to not be missed, but hopefully not enough to be misread, or to frighten her. He suspected that Millie's life had been so void of positive human interaction., and so totally controlled by Lillie's brow-beating that it could be awfully easy for her to mistake a simple show of kindness or concern for something more serious or even as something to be dreaded.

After a moment of only appearing confused Millie looked up at Avey and asked, "What are you going to do now, Mister?" At that point she sounded like nothing more than a lost, frightened child.

"Well," Avey answered. "First I'm going to find a shovel. I've got some burying to do. Then it's time to ramble on. Things got way more complicated here than I counted on. By now I expected to be over the hills and far away. And my business in the area isn't over yet. Just the money-making part of it is. There's a kid that's going to come looking for me if I don't go looking for him first. And I'd rather meet him on my terms than have him surprise me when I don't see it coming." Then he asked, "Do you know where there might be a shovel?"

Millie grinned. "There's one in the barn out back. Are you gonna' bury Daddy?"

"That I am, if you'll go get me the shovel. Will you do that?"

"Yes sir!" Millie turned and ran off toward the back of the house. As she trotted off Avey looked at the cavern Millie's bullet had left as it exited the back of Lillie's skull. He shook his own head and thought, 'I better bury her too before a possum or some other varmint moves into the back of her head.'

Before Millie came back around the house with the shovel, Avey said one more thing to Lillie, who was, of course, well beyond hearing, or being able to answer. He was fairly sure that if she could have answered, whatever she said would have been at best, unpleasant, if not just plain spiteful; as everything he'd heard come from her mouth when she was alive had been. Still, as he heard Millie's feet slapping on the cold-stiffened grass as she hurried back around the house, he looked down at Lillie's lifeless corpse and said, "It's a damn shame you didn't pay me off before Little-Sis became sole-owner of the family business."

And the back-shooting murderer felt the corners of his mouth curl up in a smile as he spoke to the evil twin on the semi-frozen ground in the yard of the out-of place house in the center of the clearing in the woods.

As unhappy as he was at missing out on his payday, he couldn't help but feel a bit pleased at Lillie getting what he felt she deserved. And though he was fully aware he was every bit as deserving of what she'd received as she had been, he wasn't a person who would let something like guilt color his way of thinking; not right then. He couldn't allow himself to be distracted, not with so much at stake. Fault was useless and time consuming, not to mention unprofitable.

"Were you talkin' to Lillie?" Millie, the freckle-faced sister asked as she walked up, dragging a rusty spade behind her.

"Just saying goodbye," Avey answered, fighting the urge to laugh aloud. "Don't you want to tell her goodbye?" he asked.

Millie wrinkled her nose like she'd smelled something foul and said, "I don't have anything to say to her. I just want to get away from her and never ever have to look at her again."

"Nor am I a bit surprised," Avey said. "Can you ride a horse?"

"Sure can," Millie answered proudly. "Daddy taught me, long time ago. Back 'fore he got sick."

"Do you have a horse?"

Millie nodded eagerly.
"Lillie's horse is hitched to the rail out back by the barn. It's still saddled and everything."

"Avey looked at the sun, moving westerly toward the horizon.

"I've got to leave, once I get done with the burying." Avey bent and grabbed Lillie's lifeless body by her feet and dragged her off the porch, her head thumping down the several steps. He glanced at Millie, curious to see if she would show any reaction, and saw only a small smile. Once Lillie was on the ground at the foot of the steps Avey walked around the area probing the ground with the spade for a spot soft enough to offer easy digging. Finally finding a spot that would do, he turned over a rectangle of cold earth and slid Lillie's corpse into the hole. When he'd shoveled dirt over her, he asked Millie, "Do you want to put any kind of marker on her grave? A cross or anything?"

Again Millie wrinkled her nose as if smelling a sour odor and shook her head.

Avey nodded toward the house and said, "Okay, I'll go bury your Daddy with your Mama now."

Millie nodded. "You can put a cross 'atoppa' him."

His sense of good will about exhausted, Avey shrugged and walked into the house. He pulled the old man's body from the bed onto a blanket, and grabbing the blanket's corners, dragged him through the hall and out the house's back door. Once outside he glanced around, looking for a likely spot to dig another grave. But before he had a chance to give the area a real look Millie spoke up from behind him, "Mama's buried right over yonder, at t'end o' the porch." She pointed toward the corner of the house.

Avey shrugged, thinking, 'at least the old man's withered away to damn near nothing, and I don't have far to drag him.'

As always, his only concern was for himself. Feeble-minded though she was, the freckle faced sister also was the only remaining member of the family who ran a big moon-shining business. Whether the no-goods that worked for the old man and the other sister would pay any attention to this woman or not, he didn't know. But, he did know that she was his only remaining shot at a piece of the Bleu family's cash. So if digging a grave and throwing dirt on the old man would make her happy, he could bite the bullet; for now. If the situation didn't show signs of a quick pay-off he'd be as gone as yesterday's sunrise. Avey walked to the end of the back porch and found an old cross sticking from the ground that was so weather-beaten and sun-faded the name painted on the crooked cross-slat was unreadable and he plunged the spade into the cold earth next to it. As he did, he thought he felt a rain drop hit his hat, then a second. He tried to tell himself it wouldn't turn into anything.

It was already going to be more difficult than burying the bitch out front had been; the sun had been on the front of the house, so the ground out there hadn't been as cold or hard. Behind the house, where he was now; shaded from the sun, the ground was frozen and digging was that much harder. And the fact that he was cold himself didn't make it any more enjoyable. Now because he'd stuck around trying to chase a lost cause he wasn't just a fool, he was a fool in the rain.

After he'd scooped a half-dozen shovels full of dirt from the cold rocky ground; barely making a dent in the hard soil, he paused. Propping the shovel against the lop-sided cross that leaned crookedly next to where he was working, he pressed his fists to his back and stretched, trying to work out the kinks brought on by the manual labor to which he was so unaccustomed.

While he was thus distracted, he was startled to hear a sound from behind him. Totally unprepared, he spun around too fast, nearly falling when his boots slipped on the frost-slicked grass. He fully expected to find the kid from the town across the creek; the preacher's protégé, drawing a bead on him. But instead he found that the source of the sound was Millie, the surviving Bleu sister, who stood on the porch leaning on the railing and peering at him. She asked, her voice a frightened whisper, "Are you going to bury Daddy deep so the animals won't get at him?"

His patience at an end, Avey kicked the shovel aside, knocking the old cross over in the process and stalked around the house toward his horse.

"Aren't you going to bury Daddy?" Millie cried out as he disappeared around the corner of the house, her voice hitching.

"He can lie where he is, as far as I'm concerned!" Avey shouted without looking back. "He's so pickled from all the rot-gut he's swilled, he'll probably look the same in ten years as he does right now; not that that's a good thing."

Then Avey paused just long enough to give Millie a finger wave over his shoulder, like you would give a child, and said, "I'm outa' here freckle-face. If I were you, I'd get on that horse your bitch of a sister left behind and put this mess far behind you. That's what I'm aimin' to do. I've enjoyed all of this damned place I can stand."

The last thing Millie heard of Vance Avey was the sound of his horse's hooves fading away in the distance. She stood and looked down at her father's ancient, wasted body lying on the cold ground for a short while before picking up the shovel and beginning to scrape at the hard soil, tears streaming down her face till they dripped from her chin as she struggled in the icy air. Before two minutes had passed, her bare hands had coated the rough hickory handle of the shovel with blood that froze almost instantly, gluing her hands to the wood, making it nearly almost impossible for her to drop the tool when she quickly became too fatigued to continue with the fruitless attempt to produce a person-sized hole in the ground.

Finally she dropped exhausted to her knees, clutching the spade with both hands, with the point of the blade jabbed into the ground to keep herself from falling headlong into the barely-there depression she had been trying to deepen into a grave for her beloved father.

Looking at his sickly, withered old body, and knowing she would be unable to dig him a proper grave, all she could manage was to say,

"I'm so sorry, Daddy. If I'd had two bullets Id'a pointed the gun at Lillie and made her bury you; and *do it right*, Id'a Made Lillie Bury you right next to Mama. Even if I had to shoot her in the foot to make her know I wasn't *foolin.*' And once you were in the ground, good and proper; *then* Id'a shot her." Millie paused for a breath, and to backhand tears from her face. Then she went on as if her father was sure to carry on his side of the conversation; hopefully to tell her that she had done well and he was proud of the way she had handled things. She said, "With Lillie and Nappy gone, it's just you and me now Daddy. But you don't have to worry; I'll never leave you."

When Napoleon didn't answer, Millie rolled him up in the rug Avey had used to drag him on, and started to collect sizable stones to cover him with, in lieu of a real burial. At the first sign of a warm day, she would turn over enough soil from under the porch to fill in around the stones and make it more of a proper job.

As she worked she talked to her father; the last talk she would have with him. Unless they really would meet again someday in The Great Beyond like Mama told her about when she was a little girl. Even then Lillie had been mean to her, and a kernel of hatred for Lillie had begun to grow inside of Millie. As they grew older Lillie had continually made Millie's life more unbearable. The reasons were few but clear;

Lillie *was* smarter, and felt obligated to lord it over Millie.

Though they appeared identical in nearly every respect, Millie did develop an attractive sprinkle of freckles across her nose and cheeks.

In addition to the freckles, Millie had a slightly darker complexion and hair that was just a tad more auburn than Lillie's mousy brown tresses. Those features combined to make Millie look somewhat younger. All those small things were finished off with a pretty mouth filled with teeth as perfect as keys on a Steinway. And that youthful look faded not a lick as the sisters grew into middle-age. At the same time, nature wasn't as kind to Lillie. It was something that, though Lillie would never say it out loud, was nearly enough to make her bite through nails. And on the occasions when she was depressed enough to dip into the family product, she might have chewed through a railroad spike, imagining it to be her sister's throat.

And the thing that had always made Lillie most despise her sister was that Millie really had always been their father's favorite.

When Millie had collected a fair-sized pile of stones, she dragged her father's body into the slight depression in the earth that Avey had managed to make and commenced to covering him up, talking to him as she worked.

"I thought the red-haired man was going to bury you proper Daddy, like he said. But he lied. He wasn't nice at all. I hope the boy from the town 'cross the creek kills him. Hope he kills him just like the preacher-man killed Nappy."

Then, in the midst of her grief and anger, a quick smile came to her face, as she remembered walking with Luke, and she told her father, "Nobody's been nice to me but you since Mama died, 'cept for Luke." Then just as quickly her smile faded. "Then Lillie told Nappy to kill Luke," she added.

Then she recalled watching Nappy flop on his back when the preacher-man plugged him. And the way the hole appeared in Lillie's head when the bullet finally made her shut her pie-hole. And

Millie's smile returned, lighting up her face like a sunrise. "But now Nappy's dead, and so is Lillie; and that's just fine with me," she said to her father somewhat conspiratorially; as if sharing a secret.

When Millie had finished covering up her father she went in the house to the kitchen and started a fire in the cook-stove. It was evening, and she was getting hungry. Soup sounded good for a cold night like the one that was falling. She felt sure she could find vegetables in the root cellar and there was venison hanging out in the smoke house. She might even sip a glass of the squeezins. She'd never been really crazy about it, even though Daddy loved the awful stuff, and Lillie constantly preached about how important the nasty stuff was to the family. In Millie's opinion, although it did make her feel warm inside on cold nights, it also made her miserable the next morning. And the way it had made Nappy act (just as mean as a snake) made her decide she could do fine without it. If she felt the need for something to warm her insides tonight, she'd make due with a pot of coffee. It would warm her up without giving her an all-day headache tomorrow. With the soup and coffee, she'd be fine. And tomorrow, she'd begin figuring out what she would do from now on. Lillie had called her stupid for so long, Millie wasn't sure she hadn't been right. But starting tomorrow, she'd have to try to figure it out. Maybe without Lillie around telling her she was stupid all the time she might not feel so stupid. Millie knew her memory had never been very good, but once in a while when someone said something that really seemed important it would stick in her head; especially if it was her Daddy that said it. She recalled her daddy once giving Lillie holy-hell for ragging on Millie and calling her stupid, and calling her a fool, and calling her worthless. When it happened Daddy was younger and still getting around better, and he sounded so angry that Millie thought he might snatch ahold of Lillie and fetch her a good sound lick to shut her up. But he'd just spoken to Lillie in a tone of voice that made his meaning very clear. He said, "Given the proper chance, people will live up to your expectations of them. If not given the proper chance, people will live *down* to your expectations for them.

There had been a few times back in their daddy's younger-healthier days that Millie had seen him get furious at Nappy over something especially foolishhe'd done regarding the family business and cuff him soundly up-side the head. Nappy did show that he was made of stronger stuff than Millie would have expected. The first time Daddy delivered him one of those blows, he saw it coming and got his feet set shoulder-width apart and managed to keep to his feet, though he was forced to take a double step back. Another time Daddy was waiting behind the front door when Nappy entered the house. He caught Nappy on the left ear with no warning.

Nappy fell against the wall, preventing himself from sagging to his knees in the long narrow hall. Millie remembered the streak of blood Nappy had left down the hall at ear-level as he slid down the hall toward the living room, feeling the definite need of the wall to stay upright.

One thing she'd noticed already, in just the few hours Lillie had been dead, was that since Lillie wasn't constantly harping at her, the incessant ringing in her ear had faded to the point of being almost gone. She wondered if the whistling wasn't something her mind had produced to blot out the nonstop bitching and complaining that she had been deluged with for years at the whims of her horrid sister. As Millie went about cutting cubes of venison and chopping vegetables for soup, she began to cry, the tears came unbidden as her thoughts of her deceased father arose in her mind, along with thoughts of Luke; the stranger she'd found herself very attracted to despite knowing practically nothing about him. But even in her not-very-quick-mind Millie bore an awareness that her slowness had a way of helping her to block out and ignore the unpleasant happenings that were always going on around her like the thunder that came with a storm had a way of helping her block out and ignore the ordinary noises and distractions; especially the incessantly unpleasant noise that came with having a nasty twin sister.

A hundred times over her growing-up years Millie had been told by her Mama that God had a reason for everything, and that she shouldn't be ashamed of the way she was; no matter what Lillie said. When Millie was small, Mama had said over and over, "Your Daddy and I love you enough for the whole world. To us, You. Are. Perfect! And don't you forget it. And don't go worryin' 'bout tryin' to change a thing about your sweet-self." Mama always smiled 'bout fit to split' when she praised Millie. It made up for all the hurt Millie got dumped on her by her foul-tempered sister, and later on by her cruel ass of a half-brother.

These were the memories and thoughts that churned through Millie Bleu's mind as she went through the motions of making a hot supper; intentionally preparing enough for extra guests, just in case some should show up. She knew that there were a couple families who lived nearby; no more than a couple miles away; off through the woods; or at least, there used to be. They had come to visit once in a while way back before Mama died. Millie recalled them showing up on Sunday afternoons most times. And when they left Daddy would always make sure they had a jug to take along. And sometimes, if the visiting neighbor was one of Daddy's hunting and drinking buddies, and they'd been pullin' hard on the squeezins while there, Daddy would make Nappy ride along with the neighbor for a ways so he could pick the neighbor up and put him back in the saddle if he was too drunk to stay on his horse.

Now, as forgotten memories came rolling back Millie found her fear at being alone was beginning to be mixed with a trickle of excitement. On her first time alone as the lady of the house; she didn't know what to expect. She'd felt alone the biggest part of her life; then all of a sudden Luke, the newstill-tender showed up and was nice to her, right from the git-go. It just proved that anything was possible. But then when Nappy dragged Luke away behind his horse, Millie had felt a miserable clenching in her chest, that could only have been a broken heart, like she used to hear some of the mountain girls who picked corn for them sing about as they worked. Maybe things wouldn't get a speck better now that she was on her own, but by-damned, she was going to hope for the best, but be ready for the worst. Though she felt crushed when she thought about how much she'd miss her Daddy, it was all she could do not to giggle at the knowledge that she'd seen the last of both Nappy and Lillie.

She'd fix up a good meal, and get Daddy and Mama's house cleaned up nice; in the hopes of things turning out well. But, she'd also keep the gun she'd used to kill Lillie around handy in case things turned bad. Yep, although the word philosophy was way beyond Millie's understanding, that's what she had hit upon; a new philosophy - "Hope for the best, but be ready for the worst."

On the South Side of Whiskey Creek:

9:00 am Monday - The day after Vance Avey assassinated Pastor Windor:

Every resident of Whiskey Branch, Nevada, from the eldest senior citizen to the youngest baby in arms was gathered in the one-room schoolhouse, once again pressed into service as a church; this time for a funeral service that each of the town's residents would have done anything in their powerto prevent. But now that it happened, there was nothing that would stop them from showing their respect and love for their departed spiritual leader and friend.

The sun had risen on a surprisingly mild morning. But before the first rooster crowed anywhere in the small town Walter Denborough and Luther Wilson had arrived at the town's little cemetery with pick and shovel in hand, and, working by lantern light, begun to prepare a grave for Pastor Windor. They talked as they worked. As Luther raised a pick-axe over his head in preparation for bringing it down into the semi-frozen ground, he paused to look to the east where the sun was just peeking over the horizon, casting shadows through the trees that lined the cemetery on that side. He said, "You know what, Walter? I believe it actually got a little warmer overnight." His breath sent out plumes of steam in the early morning air.

Walter snickered, "I don't thing spring's on us yet. Fall's barely over.

We got a whole winter to deal with yet."

"Yep, but when I went out to feed the horses this morning the trough was hardly iced over at all. It's a long way from warm, but there could be a whole lot worse day for a funeral," Luther said.

"This is gonna' be a baddn' for Whiskey Branch, no matter what the weather is," Walter said.

Luther nodded. "Ain't no good day for a funeral. Especially one that's gonna' hurt like this one."

Walter nodded. "Truer words were never spoken. But this time of year I'll welcome a warm day anytime one shows up. I suppose God decided Pastor Windor deserves good weather for his send-off." Then he said, "Yesterday I wouldn't have bet one of *your* dollars that Toby could have been talked outa' takin' off after Avey. Even after he found out about Shepherd Sloan being a reverend, he wanted to hit the trail right then instead of waiting to have a proper funeral. He wants to kill that man in the worst kinda' way."

Luther said, "Can't say as I blame him. Wouldn't grieve me none to put a bullet in him my own self."

"Pastor Windor didn't want him to do it. You know that. You were there when he died. And I heard him tell Toby not to kill Avey myself," Walter said.

Luther drove the business end of the pick deep in the earth, then paused and said, "Yeah, I know. Toby stopped at my shop yesterday right after he walked away from seeing the pastor's body at Doc's. He was hurtin' bad. Hurtin' mor'n a boy his age has any right to be hurtin'. All he was looking for was somebody to tell him it was okay to ignore what the pastor said so he could go kill Avey with a clear conscience."

"So what did you tell him?" Walter asked.

"I told him that I figured the pastor wasn't looking out for Avey when he told him that. That it was Toby he was looking out for."

"How so"

"I learned enough on the road from Virginia to here to know that every gunfighter has a row of other gunfighters wanting to kill him to take his reputation. If Toby killed Avey, he'd be the one on everybody's list. You can bet Pastor Windor knew that."

"So he told Toby not to kill Avey to protect Toby?"

Luther nodded

Walter asked, "Do you have any idea how good Toby is?"

"I talked to Luke after everybody left Doc's the other night, before the pain killer put him out. He said that after he saw Nappy watching Pastor Windor and Toby practicing he decided to sneak up there and take a look for himself. He said after a few Saturdays it looked like Toby was more than holding his own with the pastor. And you saw the pastor when Nappy pulled on him. He was greased-lightning."

"Yep," Luther said somewhat sadly. Then he looked toward the eastern horizon and pulled his pocket watch from his jeans. "I think we're done here. We best be getting cleaned up for the service." He kicked the dirt from the head of the pick and propped it over his huge shoulder.

Walter said, "Yeah. I sure ain't lookin' forward to it, but I sure ain't gonna' miss it." He banged the shovel blade on the ground to dislodge the clods of soil.

Their sad duty complete, the two friends began the walk towards their homes to prepare for the funeral of one of the best friends either of them had ever known.

They hadn't a clue that behind them, hidden just back far enough in the trees to be sure the bright early dawn light didn't cast a perceptible shine through his red hair, Vance Avey had stood and listened as they talked while they worked.

Once the noise of the two big men had faded in the distance toward the buildings of the crummy little town, Avey made his way toward his horse. As he mounted up, he mused about the latest turn of events. He hadn't gotten paid, and the dumb twin killed the crazy twin, pretty well destroying any shot he had of taking over the moonshining operation. There was at least one good thing he'd overheard. At least he now knew that the bible-thumper had for some ridiculous reason told the kid not to kill him. And from what he'd heard the one grave-digger saying the kid was fast; which was something he hadn't known before. But now it didn't make any difference. It made no sense to him why the preacher told the kid what he told him, but foolish or not, it meant the kid wasn't a threat, so he couldn't care less why.

But Avey had shown up at the cemetery and started eves-dropping in time to hear only that Pastor Windor had told Toby not to kill him, not to hear Luther explain *why* he felt Pastor Windor had told him so. But he thought he knew why. The pastor didn't want the kid to carry a reputation.

Instead of mounting up and immediately riding away from the town, and forgetting the whole mess had happened, as he'd intended before overhearing the conversation at the cemetery, Avey led his horse away as quietly as possible till he was far enough away from town to be out of earshot before climbing in the saddle. Then he started riding slowly east toward the creek crossing that would lead him in the direction of Sweetwater. As he rode his mind was churning, turning over possible ways to salvage this whole fiasco, and put some money in his pockets. From what he'd seen of this pitiful excuse for a town, nobody in the place was rolling in money. But if it was common knowledge that the bible-thumper had told the kid not to kill him; something he'd kill to find out, or at least threaten to kill to find out if the chance arose, there could still be a jackpot here. If the kid was as popular as the preacher had been, maybe the yokels that lived in these shacks would pool what they had hidden in their mattresses to pay him off to not put a bullet in the kid. It wouldn't be as much as he'd come to these God-forsaken boondocks expecting to come away with, but anything's better than nothing. Plus, he could still gun the kid down, even if he took the pay-off from the sod-busters. It wouldn't be the first time he'd gone back on a deal. Then he wouldn't have to worry about the kid getting over his promise and shooting him in the back some day. Avey knew from past experience that over time anger eats a person away from the inside out. He wasn't interested in waiting for the kid to sneak up on him a year or two from now. It doesn't take a fast gun to put a bullet in somebody's back from an alley or from behind a tree. The idea might actually appeal to the kid, since it was how the preacher got it. Avey rode off mulling over his options.

As Vance Avey crossed Whiskey Creek at the Sweetwater Crossing the pastor's funeral service was getting underway.

The plain pine coffin sat on two saw-horses at the front of the school building. It was the one that had been in the back of Luke's shop when Pastor Windor was killed. As Luke had said in Doc's office when first discussing the pastor's funeral; he would have preferred to build the finest coffin ever. But sometimes, things don't work out the way you would prefer them to.

But though the box was plain on the outside; inside, Pastor Windor lay on a quilt that Mildred Denborough spent an entire winter hand stitching the year before. And he would go to meet his maker with his head resting on a silk pillow given to Miss Agnes Waters by her children on her sixtieth birthday.

By the time Shepherd Sloan had concluded his first duties as the town's new pastor by welcoming everyone to such an unhappy but important occasion, virtually every one of the town's ladies and more than a few of the men were sobbing.

Shepherd first spoke briefly of how he felt incredibly honored, but also unworthy of presiding over a service in honor of a man as decent and devout as Pastor Windor. A man who; more than any he'd ever known didn't just preach religion, but preached, and lived Christianity.

He spoke of the personal conversations they had about their very different pasts; and the roundabout paths that led them to the same calling in the same place. And he spoke of the part Pastor Windor had played in helping him in his struggle with the bottle. Then he paused for a moment before saying, "I would like to ask that you folks would call me Pastor Sloan, rather than Reverend Sloan. Pastor Windor once said to me that he preferred pastor to reverend because it felt less pious, and more family-like. It made him feel more approachable. If it was good enough for him it's okay by me.

Now, I'd like to open the floor up to anyone who would like to say a few words.

Miss Agnes Waters timidly raised her hand.

"Yes Miss Waters?" Shepherd said.

"Do I need to stand? She asked shyly.

No ma'am," Shepherd said. "Not if you feel more comfortable sitting."

With a relieved look, the lady drew a deep breath and said, "Well, I'd just like to say that sharing the schoolhouse with Pastor Windor for his church services made me so proud, I can hardly put it into words." Her voice hitched as she fought to hold back tears. "And that's all I think I can say," her voice cracked and faded. She'd lost the battle with trying to contain her tears, and their tracks shone on her cheeks. She sniffed a few times, and Katelin Grayson handed her a handkerchief with which she dabbed her eyes.

There were a few moments of awkward silence broken only by a couple of coughs, then Walter Denborough spoke up, "Pastor Sloan, may I please say a few words?"

"Of course, Walter. Please do."

As the big man stood up, his hard-working frame creaked like a thick sapling being bent, and with a resounding pop from an occasional joint; possibly a knee, hip, or ankle that sounded like a pine knot exploding in the fire place. Shepherd Sloan thought back to how just a matter of hours before, Walter had made it clear how little he thought of Sloan's worth as a part of the community. It always amazed him how quickly loss could either drive people apart or draw them together. He was just thankful that under these extremely difficult circumstances the people seemed to be coming closer.

Walter cleared his throat nervously, and Mildred stood up and took her husband's hand, which nearly dwarfed hers like the hand of a child.

She gave his hand a squeeze and whispered in his ear, "Go ahead, dear. Say how you feel. You can't say the wrong thing if you speak from your heart."

Walter cleared his throat and said, "Not long before the twins were born Pastor Windor and I were talking, and he explained to me, in that way he had of making things seem so simple that even someone like me can understand. He explained to me why my girls think their mother can just about walk on water." He paused and looked down at his wife. "That was something I shouldn't have needed to have explained to me." He paused to swallow the lump in his throat. "Then he told me about a writer he thought I would enjoy reading. I came clean and told him I couldn't read. He didn't laugh, or even act like he thought ill of me for it, or that I must be slow or just plain dumb. What he did was talk to Miss Waters about giving me reading lessons in the evenings. So in a little more'n a month, with Miss Waters' help and with my girls helping me with homework I could read good enough to start in doing some of my own paperwork at the mill. And if I keep practicing, someday I'll be able to help my kids with *their* homework.

Pastor Windor was always doing special things that probably didn't seem very special to him, but were really special to the people he did them for. Like helping me get knowledge that will let me learn about the world in ways I never would have otherwise. And giving me the smarts to even take some of the load off Mildred by doing my part with the saw mill's bookkeeping. That will give us both more time to spend with the youngin's and with each other. Pastor Windor was more than a preacher," Walter said emphatically. "He was a real friend to everybody." Then Walter nodded to the room in general and sat down slowly and carefully, as though a little shaky.

Shepherd Sloan said, "Would anybody else like to say anything?"

Kate asked softly, "Pastor, would it be all right if I said the prayer that the vicar said over my brother after he was killed while he was plowing a field back in Dublin way when I was a little girl?" She sniffed back her own tears.

Shepherd Sloan nodded and said, "I'm sure Pastor Windor would've been honored by that Katelin."

She stood, and Ben stood by her side, with his arm around her.

Kate closed her eyes, bowed her head and said softly, "May the road rise up to meet you. May the wind be always at your back. May the sun shine warm upon your face; the rain fall soft upon your fields, and until we meet again, may God hold you in the palm of His hand." Then in a low reverent tone, she added, "Amen." as did everyone else in the school building.

Shepherd Sloan said, "The Lord has seen fit to bless us with a surprisingly beautiful day for this solemn occasion. The sunshine and warmth lends a bit of pleasantness to an unpleasant necessity of life. It's a fine day to say farewell to our good friend. Is there anything else anybody would like to say?"

Unexpectedly, Doc Forrest spoke up, his voice calm but firm, and said something totally out of character for him, "I hope the soul of the back-shooting bastard that killed Pastor Windor wanders in loneliness and torment forever."

The stunned silence that followed his proclamation lasted only a second before Toby said, "Not till I'm done with him!"

A low murmur passed through the group of mourners, stunned by the shocking turn of events that had taken place during the funeral service. As it would have in any small town, news of Toby's reaction to Pastor Windor's death and the way it happened had spread quickly, so his response to Doc Forrest's startling statement wasn't nearly as surprising as Doc's statement had been in itself.

Uncertain how to proceed, Shepherd Sloan said, "I suppose at this time those of us who wish to join at the cemetery for the graveside service should line up at the front door. And would those who have volunteered to serve as pallbearers please come forward?"

As the majority of the townspeople formed a line at the front door of the school building, the pallbearers took up their places. Walter, Luther, Jess, Doc Forrest, Ben Grayson, and Luke, who wasn't able to contribute much from a physical standpoint, but insisted on participating while leaning on a cane, lifted the coffin and carried it out the building's side door to Doc's buggy; now pressed into service as a hearse. Shepherd Sloan took the reins and the buggy led the procession up the trail to the cemetery.

As they walked, Luke asked Doc Forrest, "What caused your change of heart, Doc?"

"What do you mean?"

"The night after Napoleon Bleu's men attacked across the creek and so many of them got burned. I overheard you and Toby. When you told Toby you had been working to save them; he said maybe you should've let them die. You told him something about taking an oath to save people. You sounded pretty serious about it. You sure sounded different in the church a little while ago."

"Luke, I took an oath to heal the sick and save lives. If Vance Avey broke his leg, I'd splint it. And if he had pneumonia, I'd try to help him breathe. But he murdered a close friend of mine. When Avey dies, like we all eventually will, I hope he burns in Hell."

Luther, who was walking behind Doc and Luke, carrying the coffin by one of the makeshift rope handles, said, "Doc, what you said surprised me, but I understood it. What worries me is that it sounds like Toby may not be able to make himself follow Pastor Windor's last request of him."

Luke said, "Teenaged boys aren't known for self-control."

Luther answered," I hope he keeps his anger in check. If he goes up against Vance Avey, there can't be any good end to it."

"What do you mean?" Walter asked. "You think Avey's that good?"

"Luther shrugged his huge shoulders. " If Avey's faster than Toby, Toby's dead. If Toby's faster, Avey's dead, and then Toby will be a mark for every yahoo who wants to be fastest gun in the west. After that Toby'll spend every day looking over his shoulder. And eventually somebody faster will push him too far. Either way it turns out bad; real bad."

Luke, who held a rope-handle in one hand, and leaned on the cane with the other, said, "I hope you're wrong about him not being able to hold his temper."

"You and me, both," Luther answered. "But it's hard to predict what a teenaged boy who is hurting bad will do. I remember telling Pastor Windor one time that Toby was the smartest damn kid I ever saw. I only hope he can be smart when it matters most. He's in a no-win situation. I'm not sure even Pastor Windor could have come up with a good answer for this problem."

After the final portion of the funeral was complete; the pastor was laid to rest, and people were beginning to go their own way and begin drifting toward their homes, Ben caught sight of Luther and waved him over to where he stood by the gate at the entrance to the small cemetery.

Luther said, "I hope we never have to go through anything that hard again."

Ben said, "I agree. What I wanted to talk to you about, though, is that last evening, when it was getting dark enough that it would be easy to walk into a tree, I heard somebody shooting down by the creek. I walked down that way and took a look. If someone was lookin' to plug a beaver or muskrat down in the bottoms where the waters are movin' slow below the twist, it would be easy to accidently pick off somebody's pet dog in the gloom and evening mist. The mist was right thick with it bein' warmed up and all. I wouldn't have been able to tell anything 'bout who it was, except the moon was full and the clouds blew over for a minute. And there was Toby, drawing and firing at a row of bottles a good thirty feet away from him. But what was most amazing was that he wasn't just shattering them, he was shooting the necks off of them. I swear if they'd still had the corks in them, I think he could've blown the corks clean out of them.

I don't know if he's as fast as Pastor Windor was; those bottles weren't shooting back, like Nappy was preparing to, but the necks of those bottles made a smaller target than Nappy's chest. And Toby didn't have any problem at all hitting them. So he can sure hit what he's aiming for."

Luther said," That must've been not long after he stopped at my shop on his way home. We had a talk about why I thought Pastor Windor told him not to go after Avey. I was hoping it might calm him down."

"Well," Ben said. "That was only six or seven hours after he saw Pastor Windor gunned down. He was still wound up by then."

Luther said, "It sure sounds like he's getting ready for Avey, no matter what the pastor told him; if he didn't even wait till after the funeral to start practicing, he's right impatient."

Ben nodded. "Yep. But, at least, for what it's worth, now I know he's a hell of a shot. So if it comes down to that, there's a good chance he'll come out of it upright and breathing."

As the cluster of folks walked from the cemetery toward the body of the town of Whiskey Branch, most broke apart into family groups going in their different directions. Then again there were the occasional bachelors; like Jess and Luke, who debated heading alone to their own places. But Ben waved them down and they joined the conversation he and Luther had been having. When Luke heard about Toby's late evening quick-draw practicing he gave it a moment's thought and then said, "You know something? It seems like forever since our war with the Bleus happened, with Pastor Windor getting killed and the battle across the creek and on East road and all; but all of that was just yesterday. And the actual fact is we don't know a damn thing about what's happening on the other side of the creek. All we know for sure is that Nappy is dead as a can of corned beef. Pastor Windor took care of that. And old Napoleon's not likely to take kindly to that."

Jess said, "I saw a lot of Bleu's men go down when those stills blew. I was watching with the pastor's spyglass from a' top the school, remember."

"But I was over there playing spy, remember," Luke answered. There were a lot more men than that working for the Bleus. That doesn't mean that any of them will give enough of a damn to come after us. It's more than likely they all headed for the hills when the first still went up. They probably figured that their jobs went up in smoke with the stills."

"And they also lost more than a few men on East Road," Luther added. "Hopefully they don't have enough men left to move on us again."

Ben suggested, "Why don't you all come up to the store and we'll talk it over; try to figure out what we should do. We should probably do more than just keep our fingers crossed, don't you think?"

Luther nodded and said, "I'll ride by the saw mill and tell Walter to come up."

Just then Kate walked up and took Ben's hand and asked, "You about ready to go, hon?"

Ben said, "Yes, let's head to the store and put some coffee on."

"Why? It's going on noon. You don't usually drink coffee with lunch"

"I'll tell you on the way." Ben took Kate's hand and walked her to their wagon.

In less than thirty minutes Luther Wilson, Walter Denborough, Luke Parker, Jess Ivy, and of course Ben and Kate were gathered around the pot-bellied stove in the store's stock room. They each had a cup of coffee from the pot Kate had simmering atop the stove. Doc had caught wind of the impromptu meeting and laid the whip to his horse to get his buggy through town to the store quickly. When he rapped at the door and saw the surprised look on Kate's face at seeing him, he said, "If your husband and his friends are figuring out a way to make work for me patching them up, don't you think I should at least know what's going on?"

Swinging the door wide, she said, "Come on in Doc. They're downstairs, go on down. There's coffee on the stove, if you'd like some. "

As soon as the doctor reached the bottom of the stairs, Ben said, "Howdy Doc. Why am I not surprised to see you here?"

Walter said, "Not much misses that old coot."

Doc said, "Walter Denborough, I'll have you know, I'm younger than you are. Remember, I'm your physician. I have seen your birth certificate. And I'm not sure it wasn't written with a quill, like the Bible."

He paused and looked around the room, where they had not so

long before had their planning session regarding how to address the problem of the Bleu family. The most obvious, as well as the most disturbing difference was that at the previous meeting Pastor Windor had been not only present, but in charge. His absence made a big hole in the group.

"Okay, so what's going on?" Doc asked.

Ben started off by bringing Doc up to speed with regard to Toby's quick-draw practice session.

Doc's response was, "I can't say I'm surprised. He's hurting really bad. At his age he hasn't had much experience at learning how to blow off steam, as they say in the factory towns. I guess blasting away at bottles is his way to do that. He looked at Walter, "The way you might go out to your lumber yard and swing an axe into a log a hundred times." Then to Jess, "Or the way you might go out in the woods and shoot pine cones out of the tree-tops."

Jess said, "But Walter's log or my pine cones don't shoot back. Napoleon Bleu's men might. And Vance Avey damn sure would. If he hasn't hit the trail, that is. That's what we're worried about; the not knowing. And I'm not just concerned that Toby's getting ready because they could start trouble, because that's not really a bad thing, but that he might go looking for trouble."

"Kate, who had come downstairs and was in the process of refilling coffee cups said, "Didn't Pastor Windor tell Toby not to kill Avey before he died?"

Doc said, "Yes, but a teenager can go from sad to mad right quick, especially when he's hurting."

"Then there's another problem." Ben said. "If Toby goes looking for Vance Avey on the North side of the creek, he may walk into a hornet's nest of Bleu's men. We have no idea what's happened over there in the last twenty-four hours."

"So? Luther said. "What's our next move? Or do we have one?"

"It would be real nice to know what's happening over there," Ben said.

"Yeah," Doc agreed. "But things turned out bad for Luke when he went spying."

"Jess spoke up, "How about something more out in the open."

"What do you have in mind?"

"Well, since it warmed up a little, I think it' d be a good time for Walter and me to go across the creek and do some hunting. What do you think Walter?"

Walter grinned. "Sounds like a plan. You take your Winchester and I'll take my scatter-gun: maybe bring home a deer and a pheasant or two."

"And get a look-around at the same time," Luke added.

"It'd be a shame not to while we're over there, wouldn't it," Jess said.

"Only thing is; since it did warm up, practically overnight, you'll have to go out East road to Sweetwater crossing to go across the creek.

"Why's that?' Kate asked.

"Well, even though we only had a little bit of snow and frost, when it melts off it'll bring up the level in the creek pretty quick," Ben answered.

"And that means the twist will get to swirlin' right quick too," Luther said. "And you know how wicked that can be."

Walter said, "It's not up much yet. I got no trouble wadin' across. And the water will be warmer than it would've been just a couple days ago. I've been wet before. Besides, I could stand a little shrinkin.' And I'm too damn heavy to float away."

"I'll keep an eye on him," Jess said. "We'll cross upstream from the twist where it's calm. We'll be okay. We'll go maybe mid-afternoon? Whadda' ya think, Walter?"

Walter gave him a thumbs-up.

"All right, But please, you two try to act like you've got some sense," Doc scolded. "I don't like it; I don't like it a bit."

He nodded toward Luke. "I just brought this one back from the dead. You think I enjoy dealing with that kind of thing?"

"It wasn't a lot of laughs for me either, Doc," Luke said.

"I know. I just get a little particular about the way people treat the bodies I try so hard to keep functioning in this little slice of wilderness."

Surprisingly, it was Katelin who put an end to the debate.

Her brogue coming through loud and clear she said, "Doc, I don't want to see anybody go across that creek any more than you do. And I'm pretty damn positive they're not going because they want to, but because the only thing that could turn out to be more dangerous than doing the wrong thing is doing nothing. There may be nothing to fear over there; I'm prayin' it's that way. But if there is something, shouldn't we know about it?" She stopped talking and locked her blue eyes on him.

Ben snickered and said, "Give it up, Doc. She's tough any time; but when she's right, you don't have a prayer.

Doc dropped his head and said, All right. I know when I'm outvoted. It's just that I remember how helpless I felt when you went over there, Luke. I didn't like that idea, and I don't like this one. Sometimes I feel like I'm the only one not doing anything to help."

"Don't you believe it, Doc," Luke said. I'd have a lot less toes and maybe fingers too, if not for you. You do plenty! Don't you ever doubt it!"

Doc finally gave up and said, "Okay, just don't do anything stupid."

"Jess said, "You must be talking to him." and pointed at Walter.

"I was talking to both of you," Doc said; more severely than he had intended. "I'm getting a little too long-in-the-tooth to start making new friends. So I can't afford to lose any of my old ones. Do you understand?"

"I understand Doc", Jess answered.

"Walter said, "Same here."

"Doc nodded and told them, "When I leave here I'm going back to the school and check the back room. I should have done it after the funeral. At first light this morning I had lost all but two of Napoleon Bleu's men who got burned nearly to death trying to charge across the creek. I doubt they're still alive, but I've got to check"

"Ben said, "I'll walk over with you Doc. I'll give you a hand with the burying."

Luther said, "I'll come along, too Doc. I'm right good with a pick and shovel."

After draining the last of the coffee pot, they climbed the steps and everyone but Kate left the store. On the porch Walter asked Jess, "Hey, do you still have Pastor Windor's spyglass?"

"Yeah, back at my place. Why?"

"I just thought it might come in handy when we're checking things out across the creek."

"Okay," Jess answered, and gave a small salute. "I'll pick it and my rifle up and meet you a hundred yards upstream from Doc's place in what, an hour?"

Walter nodded. "And wear your high boots. With it warmin' up like it has it's gonna be real damn muddy."

"Yes, mom; see you in an hour."

Only six minutes past the hour Walter and Jess had agreed upon, Doc waved at them from his front porch as they loped their horses up the creek road slowly along the relatively calm buy slightly higher than normal water,

The mud in the street was deeper, noticeably so, but not enough to cause the horses any difficulty. The men spoke as they rode, with Walter saying; "This isn't hard ridin', but I'd hate to have to get down fast. If you didn't land right you could sink in up to your knees and then you'd play hell getting out; If the mud didn't suck the boots right offin' your feet."

Jess answered, "Yes' sir. You better damn sure hang onto that scatter-gun. You drop that cannon and get the barrels plugged with mud and you'll be carrying a double-barrel bomb."

Doc waved them over to the porch and told them to tie up for a couple minutes. Then he waved them to two chairs on the porch, and saying he'd be right back, walked inside the house. A few moments later he returned with two cups of coffee he set on the arms of their chairs. Then he went in again and immediately came out with a small metal bucket with smelly steam rising from it. A paint brush stuck up from the bucket. Doc proceeded to use the brush to spread what turned out to be melted pine sap over the two men's boots, and also up roughly the bottom foot or two of their pant legs. He did it without a word of explanation, and without asking permission.

When he'd finished Walter said, "Mildred ain't gonna' like havin' to get that stuff outa' my jeans." He snickered as he said it. He knew why Doc had done it, and didn't want to say thanks out loud. It was a game between them; like the earlier quibbling over who was older.

"Quit complaining. Gettin' it outta' my pants and off of my boots won't be any easier than yours. But it will be nice to stay a little dryer inside of them," Jess told him.

Doc said, "It's true, it has gotten a little warmer. Two days ago it was cold enough to freeze the clapper off the Liberty Bell. So you're lucky you're wading the creek today, if you're determined to do it at all. But even though it's gotten some warmer, it's still plenty cold enough to give you a death chill if you get drenched to the skinand walk around in wet clothes for any length of time. So the more water you can keep off of you the better.

"I know Doc, thanks." Walter said. Then to Jess, he asked, "You ready? We ought to get going while the sun's still high. It's only going to get colder."

"Yeah, let's hit the road." Jess climbed down the steps from Doc's porch, holding tightly to the railing. Walter followed him.

Doc asked, "Leg aching you, Jess?"

"Some."

"Want something for the pain 'fore you go?"

"No, I wanna' stay on top of my game. Don't know what we might run into." He swung up into his saddle. Walter did likewise.

Walter took a look at the fairly-still water of Whiskey Creek, and then said, "Looks pretty mild. What do you think, Jess? You want to ride upstream a little further, maybe put a little more distance between us and the twist?"

Jess nodded and they both waved to Doc and rode slowly west along the creek bank to look for a suitable place to wade across the creek and check out what, if anything, was happening in what had been the Bleu family's territory only a day before.

After about ten minute's riding they paused and Walter asked, "What do you think?"

Jess pulled Pastor Windor's spyglass from a pocket and scanned the far bank. "Judging by the saplings growing outta' the water on that side, I'd say it looks like the ground doesn't fall off into the water too fast, so when we get to that side we shouldn't have any trouble getting up on the bank. We can poke around ahead of us before we wade in here so we don't get surprised by stepping in a hole.Doc's right about it still being too damn cold to walk around soaked."

"Not to mention keeping our iron dry," Walter said, patting his double-barreled shotgun like a pet dog.

Jess took another look through the glass and pointed across the creek. "I believe if we cross here and go up through there a hundred yards or so beyond the trees we should come up on the place where the stills were before they went up in flames. 'Course there won't be 'nuthin' left of them there now 'cept a big damn scorched spot in the ground."

"Okay, time's a 'wastin." Walter said, and climbed to the ground. He propped his shotgun across his shoulders and turned toward the creek.

"Right behind you" Jess got down, laid his Winchester across his shoulders and fell in alongside Walter.

They tied off their horses to a sapling and slogged down through the ankle-deep mud to the water and out into the creek water; which was only knee deep on Walter but rose almost to crotch-level on Jess. Jess said, "Damn, that's colder than I thought it'd be!"

"Just remember the next time you're laughing at me for being as big as a house, how handy my size was at keeping my important parts outa' the water."

"I'll try to remember that," Jess said, fighting to keep the shivering from causing his voice to tremble; knowing it would give Walter an opportunity to rib him. "So are we going, or not?"

"Sure, come on. " Walter waded into the creek, with Jess following close behind, being cautious about his footing on the slippery bottom, with his bad leg, as always, throwing him slightly off balance. He lifted his rifle from his shoulders and held it at arm's length over his head, in case he should lose his footing and go down. When Walter glanced over his shoulder and saw what he was doing he was a little surprised, but not totally shocked that Jess was showing more concern for his Winchester than for himself.

They moved cautiously, but steadily, wanting to reach the far bank and get on dry ground before the afternoon turned to evening and the temperature began to fall.

Just as Jess felt the creek bottom firm up beneath his feet, Walter raised his hand in a hold-on gesture. When Jess stopped and shrugged, Walter cupped a hand behind one ear and pointed up toward the woods on the creek bank they were approaching.

After a moment of waiting in silence, Jess said, "What?" in a soft whisper.

"Heard a horse up there," Walter answered, nodding in the direction of what might be a clearing some ways off through the trees in the distance.

"How far off?"

"Couldn't tell," Walter answered. "Not too far, I think." Sounded like it was on dirt, not leaves or grass, so there must be a path or trail in there."

"Good. Maybe we can track whoever it was," Jess said.

"Yeah, with the ground bein' soft, maybe so. Just as long as there ain't been a lot of other riders around."

"Okay, let's move on." Jess eased around Walter and took the lead. "I'll take point for a while. We don't know who was on the horse you heard. Maybe we should go in quiet-like. And I make a lot less commotion in the woods than you do."

"Okay, just don't snap that leg of yours. I wouldn't like that a bit and Doc would like it even less."

"I'd like it a lot less than either of you," Jess replied.

They moved on up the creek-bank, guns held over their heads, keeping them well out of the water. When they had moved away from the slow moving water about twenty yards or so Jess reached in his pocket and removed Pastor Windor's spyglass. He shook it briskly to throw off the creek water that clung to its brass body and lenses. He put it to his eye and turned from side to side, scanning the area, both upstream and down, looking for anything out of the norm. After a moment he pointed towards the woods a little ways upstream from where they stood and said, "The stills were over that way" Then he held the glass out to Walter and said, "Take a look.

Walter scanned the area along the edge of the woods and said, "Right there." He pointed. "If you look close at that stand of pines running along there, you can see where there's definitely a path beat down through the woods between the trees. Goes right up yonder towards where those stills were explodin' yesterday."

Jess nodded. "Yep, that's right about where a pile of Napoleon Bleu's men came a runnin' from when the fire was scorchin' their asses."

"Okay, let's stroll on up there and take a look around."

Jess said, I'll make you a deal; you stroll, I'll keep looking around. I'll be right with you, but while you're watching ahead, I'm gonna' watch the woods around us and behind us so we don't get flanked."

"Sounds good to me; I'm not in the mood for surprises. I've had my fill of surprises lately." Walter shook his head.

"You and me both. Let's head up the trail, and look for tracks." Jess started toward the opening in the trees.

They didn't have to go far into the shade of the trees that overhung the partially overgrown path before they came across the clear signs of a horse that had recently followed the trail in the direction of the creek, and then turned back on itself toward the deeper woods and again moved away from the creek.

Jess, who had bent to examine the tracks, said, "Looks like the rider couldn't make up his mind."

"Or maybe changed it," Walter said. "Things didn't go so well for the people from this side of the creek ya' know. Whoever the rider is might have had a change of heart; or maybe grew a yellow streak up his back. If he remembers what happened over here after your Winchester went off over there." Walter pointed across the creek toward town. "He may have decided it was safer back the way he came."

Jess said, "Well, time's a wastin'"

They started up the path following the horse's trail. It was easy trailing in the soft ground.

About ten minutes later Jess; who was in the lead, held up his hand in a signal to stop. Walter immediately stood still, and after a moment softly whispered, "What?"

"I heard a horse whinny."

"Where."

Jess pointed ahead and to the left.

Walter nodded in the direction Jess had pointed and they started slowly on up the trail, listening intently and peering through the trees.

They were so intent on listening for the sounds of a horse, and so focused on the woods to the left of the trail that Walter practically walked into a man leaning against a tree on their right. The man startled them by saying, "You're as big as an ox, aren't you? And judging by how careless you are, just about as dumb as one, too." The man began laughing.

Despite being taken by surprise, Walter reacted with remarkable quickness.

In barely the amount of time it took to think about it, his double-barreled shotgun had gone from held overhead to resting in the crook of one elbow with the other hand wrapped around the stock and his finger resting on the dual triggers. The twin bores of the big ten-gauge barrels were leveled on the chest of the man who stood before them, who was snickering loudly, seemingly unfazed by the gun aimed at him. Walter looked down at the shotgun to confirm that both hammers were pulled back, something else he'd done with smooth practiced ease. He moved his feet slightly to see that he had a firm footing on the soft ground. Even a man of his size could be thrown off balance by the kick of the big shotgun if he was forced to fire both barrels at the same time.

For a moment nobody moved and everything was quiet. Then a horse whinnied a little way off and the man stopped laughing and said, "Do you know who I am?"

Walter looked at him through narrowed eyes. "Yeah; I know who you are. You're Avey. I saw you ridin' off after you shot our pastor in the back. I recognize the hair. I saw men ride off that fast during the war. They were always the cowards; the ones that were slapping their horses so hard you could see the blood flying from the animal's flanks. Those were the men that didn't have the guts for a real face to face fight."

Avey spoke, his voice the snarl of a mad dog, "If you knew how fast I am, you wouldn't talk to me like that."

Walter said, "I know one thing for damn sure; I see your hand make one twitch toward that fancy holster I'm gonna' pull both of these triggers, and somebody's gonna' be gathering you up with a rake."

Jess laughed. "Why would anybody bother raking up the likes of him?"

Walter said, "Would you want the next rain storm washing his leavins' into the creek where we get our water?"

"Good point," Jess answered. Then he said to Avey, "Well, Mister fast-gun. You don't have a snowball's chance in Hell of clearing leather before he can pull those triggers. And it wouldn't even matter if he missed one trigger. It wouldn't take but one of the loads of buckshot from that scatter-gun to cut you in half.

Then Jess patted his rifle and added, "It wouldn't much matter if he did miss you. You'd be dead before you went six feet. I'd blow you out of your boots just for the pure enjoyment. So there's about a hundred percent chance of you dying of lead poisoning today. The only thing that's not for sure yet is when, and whose lead will do the poisoning."

"You two sure are brave when both of you have got the drop on me," Avey said defiantly.

"We've seen how you operate." Walter answered. "I always figured there's nothing much lower than a back-shooter. But now I think different. There's got to be a special place in Hell reserved for someone who back-shoots a preacher from a hiding spot in the trees. Is that what you call brave?"

Walter was growing madder by the second, and Avey could tell it.

His bravado deserting him, he started to say something, but stumbled over his words, becoming tongue-tied; obviously embarrassed by his fear being so clearly on display. Finally he managed, "So, is this how you plan to protect the punk kid that that crazy bitch was so scared of?" As he said it he nodded off to the North, past where the row of now destroyed stills had been.

"Jess said." What makes you think Toby needs our protection?"

Avey sneered. He spoke directly to Walter, "I was doing a little listening this morning. I overheard you and the big nigger talking while you were digging the ditch to plant the God-pounder. I heard you say the preacher told the kid not to kill me."

Jess ratcheted the lever of his Winchester down and back up and pressed its muzzle against Avey's chest. "You better watch your mouth; and watch it close. That big man is a good friend of ours."

Avey grinned. "It doesn't matter to me. It won't be the first time I shot a big black dog."

Walter said, "And that wasn't a ditch, it was a grave."

Avey swelled up his chest and mustered up enough guts to say, "The only difference between a grave and a ditch is the shape."

Walter spit in Avey's face and answered, "Good; we don't have to be particular when we make the hole to throw you in."

"So you do plan on killing me? I guess you have to, since the preacher didn't give the kid permission."

Recalling what Doc had said earlier, Walter said, "A teenager can go from sad to mad pretty fast. And he just might forget what the pastor told him if he's facing you. I can't speak for Jess, but I might just let you slink on outta' here, so'long as you're slinking away from our town. And down the line if Toby decides to put a bullet between your eyes someday; it wouldn't break my heart a bit."

"Wouldn't make me shed a tear, that's for sure," Jess added.

"So I'm supposed to believe I can just walk away and you won't shoot me in the back," Avey said skeptically.

"Don't judge everybody by how low you are." Walter told him. "If I was going to kill you, you'd already be dead. I'm not about to wait till you're walking away and back-shoot you. Now, this is your only warning; get gone, and stay gone."

Jess pointed up the trail with the barrel of his rifle. "Start walking, and don't look back. If you do, I'm going to dot both your eyes."

Walter said, "He can do it, too. Don't you doubt it for a second. Now go, before I change my mind!" Walter prodded Avey hard in the chest with the barrels of his shotgun to make sure his point was perfectly clear.

Vance Avey flashed a snakelike grin and turned his back on the men.

As he began to walk away he laughed and then delivered an infuriating parting shot, "Tell that kid I'll see him later."

Walter jammed his shotgun's butt plate against his shoulder and sighted down the barrels toward Avey's back.

Jess put a hand on the shotgun and gently pushing it down, said, "No, you said you wouldn't back-shoot him. That's not who you are. That's him. He'll get his. People like him always do."

Walter said, "Yeah, I just hope I'm around to see him get it."

They stood where they were till Avey had gone far enough to be out of sight behind the trees around a gentle bend in the trail. A minute or so later they heard a horse whinny in the direction he'd gone, then the sound of hoof-beats receding fast in the distance.

After waiting another ten minutes to be certain Avey hadn't back-tracked to surprise them, Walter asked Jess, "What do you think? Should we go on a ways and see if there's any sign of other people stirring over here? If Avey's hanging around, who knows what other trouble makers might be hiding up in these woods?"

Jess said, "Yeah, why don't we at least go on as far as where the stills used to be. It's almost impossible that the Bleus have got any stills up and running already.

"Unless," Walter said, "They already had stills built but not operating. They could have had them fired up and running in no time."

"If they have anybody left to run them. Why don't we go take a look?" Jess said.

Walter nodded, and then said, "I can't help but wonder what Avey was doing prowling around here."

Jess said, "Maybe he was doing the same thing we're doing; looking around, keeping an eye out for trouble."

Walter patted the stock of his shotgun and said, "If I get him in front of this again he's going to find more trouble than he ever thought there was in the world. Pastor Windor never told *me* not to kill the bastard."

They went up the trail toward the former site of the Bleu stills, constantly looking around for signs of activity in the area.

Vance Avey rode away from his accidental confrontation with the two men from the crummy little town across the creek disappointed and angry.

His discussion, such as it was, with the men proved two things;

One; that they weren't afraid of him; also that they were at least somewhat confident that the kid could take him, if it did come to a showdown.

That meant that his plan to milk the town for cash for leaving the kid alone was out the window. If the kid was really fast enough to give him a fight, and mad enough to forget what the preacher told him and the hicks in the town knew it, they had no reason to pay him off.

Two; There may be more gun-toting townsmen like the two he met who would make sure he'd never get close enough to the kid to take him on.

Either way the facts he found out on his little fact-finding mission didn't make him at all happy.

The only thing he had discovered before running into the men on the trail that gave him any hope at all was that there were still some of Napoleon Bleu's men hanging around. He'd seen signs of them first; hoof prints and boot prints in aimless circles all over each other in the muddy, scorched ground where the stills had been just a day before. Not the slightest sign that an organized search of any kind had been run. No two straight lines of tracks in the whole mess.

The very senselessness of the mess of tracks showed him that the remaining men had no plan or organization. So what they needed was someone to lead them; and he was just the man for the job. But first things first; first the kid. Without that damnable nuisance hanging over his head, he could get down to business. He had seen the piles of cash that crazy bitch Lillie brought back from Sweetwater, so there had to be real money to be made here. Now, he wondered if with the kid out of the way, and his time fully focused on getting the stragglers of Bleu's men back to work, and could he make it pay off for him? Now he had to plan his next step.

As the day wore on, and Avey rode away, Jess and Walter heard the repeated firing of single regular shots back across the creek from the direction of town. Walter said, "Sounds like Toby's practicing."

Jess just nodded. Let's get moving." They started up the trail and found the hoof prints of Avey's horse, where he had tied it off to a low branch while he walked the trail. Then they went farther up to where they soon came upon the same purposeless jumble of tracks that Avey had found.

"Well," Walter said. "At least we know somebody's been messing around here."

Jess pointed back toward the creek. "See the burnt trees? That's where the stills were."

"That makes sense." Walter pointed. "See the flat patches in the ground, and those holes are from tent stakes. There were tents set up here. This must be where the still-tenders stayed."

"Jess laughed. " Didn't exactly live in the lap of luxury, did they?"

"Food and moonshine are all some people need, I guess."

"Let's get back to town and let everybody know what we found."

Walter nodded in the direction of the creek

"Which wasn't really much," Jess said.

"The one thing we did learn didn't make me happy at all; that Avey's still alive, and still hanging around."

Jess nodded. "Yeah, that bastard can't be up to anything good. Come on, let's head back."

They went back down the trail the way they had come, and waded across the creek, and then hurried to their horses, anxious to beat the temperature drop that would accompany sundown.

As they mounted up Walter slapped the leg of his jeans to shake off as much of the water clinging to the material as possible. The tree sap Doc brushed over the cloth had prevented a lot of moisture from soaking through, but the breeze was kicking up and a little wet would soon feel like a lot.

Walter asked Jess, "Wanna' stop by Docs, and let him know what we saw?"

"Let's at least let him know we made it back across okay, Jess answered. "He might even put some coffee on for us. He was right about being lucky it's warmer than a few days ago, but it's plenty cold enough. If it was as cold as when Nappy dumped Luke in the creek, we'd never have been able to wade across. We'd have had no choice but to ride out East road to the crossing. Then there'd have been no chance of doing any serious looking around without being seen."

"Yeah, it's a good thing we did it the way we did. I wasn't really expecting to find anything. But somebody's definitely been up to something over there. And I'm glad we know it's going on, even if we don't know what it is."

"Yeah, so after we go to Doc's place, then, what do you think? You want to stop by Toby's?"

"No, I think the morning will be soon enough. I'm afraid that when he hears Avey's still around he might want to take off after him again. That might turn out bad. Let's see how Doc, Shepherd and Ben feel about it before we hit Toby with that news."

Walter nodded; the nod barely discernable from his shivering. "Makes sense to me, let's go." They rode on to Doc's. After a brief talk Doc climbed in his buggy and followed them to Ben and Kate's store. They stopped along the way to round up the people who had been present when Walter and Jess had planned their trip across the creek.

Again gathered around the stove, and sipping coffee, they discussed the situation;

Kate summed it up very succinctly, "Seems like no more than a few days ago, the worse thing Whiskey Branch had to deal with was winter coming on. I mean, we figured the Bleus were up to no good on the other side of the creek. But that seemed almost far-off. Then Luke almost died because of them. Pastor Windor warned us that they were real bad news. And almost like they needed to prove him right he got shot in the back by one of their hired guns. Now Toby's ready to run off hell-bent-for-leather after the gunman. And if he does we could lose him. It's hard to believe how much bad has happened in what seems like no time at all. I don't know if this town can stand much more."

"So, does anybody have a suggestion about what we should do, if anything?" Luke asked.

Doc said, "I think we have to let Toby know Avey's still hanging around. He ought to be on his guard. We don't know why Avey's still here, but Toby should be aware of it. All we can do is try to convince him that chasing off after Avey would be a mistake. But he deserves to know the killer is around."

Walter said, "We should have killed the bastard when we had the chance."

"I've thought the same thing a hundred times since we came back to town," Jess answered.

"You two aren't the murdering types," Doc said, matter-of-factly. "Even when somebody deserves murdering as much as Avey."

Ben said, "To tell you the truth, after seeing Toby practicing the other evening, I'd almost like to see him face off with Avey. I've never seen Avey draw. But if he didn't have the guts to face off with Pastor Windor, he might not be as fast as we've been assuming he is. And Toby's damn fast, at least from what I've seen."

Kate shook her head and said, "Don't even say that. What if Toby goes up against Avey and Avey is faster?"

"Don't forget," Doc added, "Pastor Windor told him not to kill Avey."

"You really think he'd just stand there and let Avey gun him down because of that?" Luke asked.

"I hope we never have to find out."

"So" Ben said, "We'll let Toby know Avey's still around, but try to keep him from going off half-cocked, right?"

Everyone nodded agreement. As they prepared to split up Luther said, "We gotta' let Toby know Avey's still in the area so the boy can keep lookin' over his shoulder. How he chooses to handle the situation if he ever comes up against Avey is something only Toby can decide. But we've seen what Avey will do to somebody when they've got their back turned to him. We can't leave Toby in the dark."

"Okay," Luther said. "Toby and I have already talked about Avey. He might be willing to pay attention to me. I'll tell him tomorrow; about mid-morning. I don't want to hit him with news like that before his eyes are full open. Nobody's thinking their best when they're half asleep. I'll try to keep him calm. I think maybe he'll do all right. I remember telling Pastor Windor that Toby's the smartest damn kid I ever saw."

The next morning broke clear and chilly, but not bitter cold.

After giving it further thought, Vance Avey had decided it was time to confront the kid in the town, and get it over with so he could hit the road. But he also decided that, given the confrontation he'd had with the two men who clearly weren't afraid of him; he shouldn't ride into town by the main road.

He'd considered doing what he'd done to the preacher. But that would make the kid a martyr. He'd already made that mistake once. He already had the kid out for his blood. He didn't need a whole damn town full of idiot sodbusters taking potshots at him.

He'd face-off with the kid. But he'd do it from across the creek. That way everybody in town could see him take the kid out. Shooting across the width of the creek would be no problem. He wasn't stupid enough to stand up on that big rock cliff like the fool Bleu punk did when he called out the preacher. Being twenty feet up there was as good as painting a target on your chest. The preacher didn't shoot him off the cliff; but he should have. The idiot was asking for it. And though nobody in the town knew it, Avey had been watching from the woods. It was seeing the preacher shoot the chump's hat off that made Avey decide that shooting the preacher from the trees was a safer bet than calling him out. Avey had still been watching when the preacher put three slugs in the Bleu idiot's chest.

Avey decided he would call the kid out from across the creek; but at his same level. And he would be rid of the nuisance for good. There was no way a teenaged kid could be as fast as the preacher that taught him. As that thought went through his head, it was followed by two more words that came unbidden; 'I hope.' He'd never been scared before, at least not that he had ever admitted to himself, but now he found himself; anxious. It was a self-serving word; one that, at least in his own mind, allowed him to deny the fact that he was a coward.

If he hadn't overheard the men at the cemetery say that the preacher told the kid not to kill him he'd have already headed for the hills.

The next morning Vance Avey decided he needed a good breakfast. After giving it some thought he could think of only one place where he might find one.

The last thing that Millie Bleu expected on a clear chilly morning before the sun was hardly up and while the birds were still singing their good-morning songs was to hear a pounding at the front door. She'd seen or spoken to nobody since the foul-tempered red-haired man had ridden off and left her on her own to finish burying her daddy.

The pounding scared her. But it also excited her. It didn't take her long to get lonely there in the pretty house in the clearing. She'd hated her sister; but she now knew that even bad company was better than no company at all. Millie knew she wasn't smart. She'd always known it. And it wasn't likely she'd have ever gotten the chance to forget it. Not with Lillie calling her stupid at least twenty times a day. Lillie had called her stupid more often in her life than she had called her by her name.

Millie dropped the dish towel she'd picked up to dry a pitcher before the pounding came and hurried to the door, still clutching the pitcher in one hand.

Suddenly frightened, she pulled the curtain aside and peeked out the door glass.

The nasty red-haired man stood on the porch, bent over with his nose nearly touching the glass, staring in at her. Millie yelped and dropped the pitcher, which shattered at her feet.

Avey pounded on the door again, hard enough for the glass to rattle in the frame. He yelled, "Come on! Open the damn door!"

Squeaking like a frightened mouse, Millie pulled the bolt back and opened the door. "What do you want?" she cried.

"Food; I don't want a thing but food. I didn't think you'd still be here. I thought you might have been smart enough to do what I told you to do and hit the road. But I'm glad you didn't. Fix me something to eat. You have food don't you?"

"Some. Not much. I should have a few eggs in the coop and there's some bacon out back in the smoke house. There's coffee on the stove."

Avey pushed past her and walked toward the kitchen. "Get to it! I've got things to do!"

Millie started sobbing "Yes sir." She went out the back door to get the bacon and a few eggs. When she came back in the nasty red-haired man was sitting in her daddy's chair at the head of the table with his muddy boots up on the table, sipping coffee. Crying, Millie set about preparing breakfast for him.

Thankfully, when he had his fill of coffee and had eaten the last of her bacon and two of the last three eggs, he stomped out. She was happier to have him gone than she was sad about being alone again.

When she heard the sound of his horse receding in the distance she wiped the frost from the window glass and peered out to be certain he was gone. Once she felt certain he had really gone away, she began searching for something to have for her own breakfast. Finally she came upon some bread that was only a little moldy. She fried the one remaining egg and washed the sad meal down with coffee. Then she went out and sat by her daddy's grave and listened to the birds for a while, till the sun was all the way up.

Showdown

With his belly full of food, and a good night's sleep behind him, Vance Avey had nothing on his mind but getting far away from the mess that had come down on him and hung over him like a cloud since the day he'd received the wire from the crazy Bleu sister telling him that her father was looking for a gunfighter. He'd needed the work at the time, and sent a wire back arranging to come and talk about the job. When he heard how much the old man was willing to pay to see the preacher dead he couldn't figure it out. But why look a gift horse in the mouth? Then the day he saw how fast the preacher was when that stupid Bleu kid called him out, Avey had started wondering if maybe the money was actually too low. But now the preacher was dead; and he'd gotten paid exactly nothing for the job. At least before he died the bible-thumper had left Avey a gift; orders to the kid that he was not to kill him. That was another thing he didn't understand. Just one more gift horse he wouldn't look in the mouth.

But now it was time to put this nightmare behind him.

After he left the slow-witted Bleu sister at the house in the clearing Avey stopped at the head-end of the trail leading to the creek before starting down to confront the kid who had become such a nuisance. Without dismounting from his horse he emptied his gun and reloaded with fresh cartridges. He then dipped his fingers into a small leather pouch that hung on his saddle horn before wiping his fingers over the length of the barrel, and then settled the gun in his holster.

And then, without giving a glance toward, or a second thought to the scorched muddy sight of the Bleu's moonshining encampment Vance Avey rode down the trail toward Whiskey Creek. He did wonder as he rode if the old man had been pleased by the fact that the creek had gotten its name from his family crime business being built along its bank. Or if the old man's brain had been too pickled to realize that the grimy little town across the creek got its name the same way.

Just a little more than a hundred yards past where he'd run into the two gun-wielding townsmen the trail Avey was following broke from the woods into the open nearly across the creek from Doc Forrest's place. He tied his horse to a sapling and began walking along the bank toward where the stupid Bleu kid had been when he'd called out the preacher. After giving it some thought, Avey had decided it would be the proper place to do away with the preacher's protégé. Right out where the whole town had a clear view; right where the preacher had taken out Bleu. He walked down the creek bank till he was across from what passed for the main part of the town. Just as he'd expected, the muddy street was practically empty; the lousy town dead. There was so little sound coming from the far side of the creek that he could hardly hear it over the churning noise of the swirling water that separated him from it.

Avey prided himself on being resourceful when the need arose. Recalling how the far bank of the creek had suddenly been lousy with gawkers when Napoleon Bleu Junior decided to commit suicide by calling out the preacher, Avey decided to call some attention to himself. Pointing his gun toward the sky, he fired three shots in rapid succession. Then, as loudly as he could, he bellowed, "Hey, where's that punk kid that's supposed to be such a fast draw?" Then, in a show of his practiced technique, Avey ejected the spent cartridges and instantly replaced them.

Then he yelled, "Hey, anybody awake over there?" Or is that pitiful excuse for a town so boring that you all fell asleep?

Well, once I blow that kid you are all so fond of out of his shirt, you'll damn sure be awake!" Avey fired one more shot into the air.

By that time doors had started banging open up and down Creek Street and faces were appearing in windows.

Within a few moments a small crowd of men had gathered on the far side of the creek from where he stood. The murmuring of the group was now loud enough to be heard clearly over the sound of the whirlpool spinning in the center of the creek. Among the crowd Avey recognized the two men who had confronted him on the trail in the woods. He also spotted the huge black man who had been one of the two he'd overheard while they were digging the grave. He hoped he didn't have to kill him; that might take a lot of bullets. He even recognized the guy that Napoleon Junior was supposed to have killed for being a spy. So; just one more thing that idiot couldn't do right.

Then the murmuring of the group across the creek grew so loud that it nearly drowned out the churning sound of the rushing whirlpool before him.

Holding his right hand; his non-shooting hand above his eyes to shield them from the morning sun Avey peered across the creek. Then, almost as though his motion had been a signal, the group on the far side of the creek fell eerily quiet. Confused, and more than a little concerned, Avey scanned the group.

His concern turned to outright fear. Though he'd never seen him before; he had absolutely no doubt the teenaged boy who stepped forward from the front of the group of people was the one he'd heard so much about.

Showing no hesitation, the boy walked forward, closer to the creek bank on the town side of the creek. He reached up and casually lifted the front of his hat as he came, giving him a clear view of the man across the creek from him. Watching closely, Avey saw immediately that, if nothing else, the preacher had taught the kid the right way to strap on a gun. His belt hung at a slight angle; with the gun-hand side higher than the other making it one smooth motion to draw the gun as he brought his hand up. Avey also saw that someone had cut the leather away from the front edge of his holster, making it easier and faster to get the barrel aimed forward. No doubt something the preacher was responsible for. It wasn't something a rookie kid would know how to do on his own. The more Avey saw of the kid, the less confident he felt.

When the boy reached the edge of the bank on the far side of the swirling whirlpool; nearly to the point that the toes of his boots would be wet, he stopped. And then he did something that really unnerved Vance Avey; he reached up and tipped his hat slightly. The movement was slow and careful, so as not to be mistaken for a move to draw.

Infuriated, Avey growled, "Do you know who I am?"

Sensing that things were coming to a head, the crowd behind Toby discretely fanned out to be more out of the range of fire, but still close enough to see and hear what was happening.

Toby answered, "Yeah, I know who you are. You're Vance Avey; the chicken-shit coward that shot Pastor Windor in the back.

Avey yelled so loud his voice cracked, "Boy, you wouldn't talk like that if you knew how many notches I have on my gun!"

Toby shouted back, "No, how many?"

"Fourteen. And I've killed more than that, but I didn't want to weaken my grips any more so I quit notching at fourteen." Avey was yelling louder as he went.

"Really!" Toby yelled back more loudly to match Avey's volume Were any of them face to face or were all of them back-shot?"

"You're a real smart-ass, aren't you kid?"

"No, I just know a coward when I see one."

Toby took a step forward into the creek; the swirling water rising to his ankles and said, "Hey Avey, since you're not really good enough to try someone straight-up without sneaking up from behind, maybe you better move closer so you'll have a better chance. I'd hate to take advantage of an old guy like you." Toby took another step into the whirlpool. The water reached to the middle of his shins.

Avey screamed, "You little son-of-a bitch," and took two quick steps into the creek. He immediately stopped yelling and looked down, surprised either by the temperature, or the force of the churning water.

"What's the matter Avey?" Toby yelled. "A little water won't hurt you. "There's no soap in it! You don't have to worry about it washing the coward-stink off of you!" Toby laughed loudly and took another step into the swirling water.

In the group behind him, Shepherd Sloan leaned over to Luke and whispered, "What in the hell is Toby doing?"

"Luke whispered back, "He's baiting him."

"Why?"

"Your guess is as good as mine."

Jess said, "Toby better not take another step."

Walter asked," Why?"

Jess said," That old Colt of his uses paper-patch bullets; if they get wet, they're useless."

"What about Avey's gun?" Walter asked.

"Nope; his 45 won't have a problem unless it's in the water for a long time and the cartridges get really soaked."

"You sure?" Luther asked.

Walter was he one that answered, "Jess's the lead slug expert. If he says so it's true. If it doesn't have two barrels and sling buckshot, I'm lost.

Doc asked, "So why does Toby keep walking in deeper?"

Luther spoke up from behind him, "Toby's been around this whirlpool since the day it appeared. He knows where the ledges are under the water. He knows how far he can walk in without stepping in a hole where his gun would go under."

So, you think Toby wants Avey closer 'cause he's spoiling for a fight, or do you think he has another reason for trying to get Avey deeper in the twist?"

Doc said, "I don't have much, but I'd give it all to have the answer to that."

Luke said, "I don't believe I've missed Pastor Windor as much as I do right now. He'd know what to do."

Shepherd Sloan said. "If there's one thing I've learned; it's that it's never too late to pray."

Luther said," I'm in," and closed his eyes and lowered his head.

Almost immediately his attention snapped back to the confrontation happening across the breadth of the whirlpool.

Toby was again taunting Avey, "Boy, you really are a first-class coward; afraid to go up against a pastor, and afraid to get a little bit wet. Or is it me you're afraid of?" Then Toby laughed a loud mocking laugh.

Avey yelled again, his words unintelligible.

"What was that?" Toby called back calmly. Did you say you don't think you can hit me from there? Well maybe you should come a little closer. Unless you *are* afraid of me, that is!"

"This time Avey's response didn't even resemble words; it was just a furious scream. But Toby's taunts had the desired effect. Vance Avey took a step forward, right into a hole in the creek bottom. The hole wasn't really very deep, but he immediately was up to his waist in cold, swirling creek water.

His mouth opened in a large O, but nothing came out. His expression was that of a man too startled to make a sound. After a moment he took a step backward and caught his balance, and again started yelling obscenities at Toby, who just stood looking at him coolly for a long moment, then laughed.

Vance Avey gave a maniacal shriek and went for his gun. When he began to draw the gun his shock was far more severe than even when he'd taken his surprise step in the hole in the creek bottom.

The men across the creek could see the alarm on his face clearly. Before the long barrel of the pistol was fully out of the holster Avey actually looked over his shoulder for an instant as though considering fleeing toward the woods.

Then, realizing that quickly escaping the water of the creek wasn't possible he finished pulling the gun and aimed it at Toby.

Toby had his gun out and the hammer back in less time than it would take to blink an eye. He fired once.

Vance Avey screamed; not with anger, but with pain. The Colt Buntline Special went pin-wheeling through the air; the morning light flashing off its long barrel. A fan of Avey's blood accompanied it. Avey dropped to his knees in the shallow water. His mouth hung open; producing a sound that consisted of a mashed-up blur of moaning, screaming, and cursing, but peppered throughout with copious amounts of crying. Even with the fast-moving whirling nature of the water in the twist the townsmen could see small plumes rising in tiny crown shapes when the fat tears streaming from his eyes connected with the churning water. Avey had sunk to his knees; a combination of the hole he had unexpectedly stepped into and the weakness that must be coming over him from the cold water that was now not just up over his holster, but well above his gun belt and had turned the calico of his shirt dark with the color of the muddy water. There was also a steady drip of blood falling from his injured left hand, turning the water around him a pasty pink color.

By the time the sound of Avey's scream had faded, Toby's gun was back in his holster.

The men on the town side of the creek stood watching, wondering exactly what had just happened, and what would happen next.

What they saw next was Vance Avey struggling to his feet. He half waded, half stumbled up the far bank of the creek. Once he got his footing he ran as fast as he could to where they could see his horse tethered to a small tree. Grabbing the saddle horn, he clumsily hauled himself into the saddle, nearly falling as he did, and rode off up the trail into the woods at a gallop.

The men gathered closer around Toby. Everybody wanted to say something to him, but nobody knew what the right thing to say was.

Finally Shepherd Sloan stepped into the shallow water and put his hand on Toby's shoulder and said, "Well, in the end you didn't kill him. That must have been a hard decision."

Toby gave him a smile that made him look wise beyond his years and shrugged.

Shepherd said, "You take as long as you need." He turned and walked back to join the other men on the bank.

Doc said to Jess, "Hey Jess, do you have Pastor Windor's spyglass on you?"

"Yeah Doc, I don't hardly feel right without it anymore." He took it from his hip pocket and handed it to Doc.

Doc slid it to its full length and scanned the bank in the area where Avey had stood across from Toby when he drew his gun. He laughed and said, "I thought so."

Walter said, "What's funny?"

Doc handed him the glass and said, "Look on that big flat rock about ten feet to the left and behind where Avey was standing in the water when Toby fired at him.

Walter looked where Doc pointed and said, "Is that what I think it is?"

Doc nodded.

"Can't be," Walter said, shaking his head.

What?" It was Luke who asked. Doc handed him the glass and told him where to look. He too was stunned nearly to disbelief.

Doc told Shepherd, "You were half right; Toby did kill Avey, just not yet.

"What?"

Doc said, "Do you remember when Ben said Toby was so good when he saw him practicing that he could have been shooting corks out of the bottles?"

Shepherd nodded. "I remember."

Doc handed Shepherd the glass and pointed out the flat rock across the creek.

Shepherd looked through the glass and whistled softly.

Doc said. "Toby didn't kill Avey *yet*. But what's going to happen the next time some gunslinger that's after Avey's reputation draws on him and Avey goes for his gun with no thumb on his gun hand?"

"Avey's a dead man," Shepherd answered.

Luther said, "I told you Toby's the smartest damn kid I ever saw. Pardon my French."

"When I saw the blood fly, I thought it was just because Toby shot the gun out of Avey's hand," Luke said, "And did some damage in the process."

Luther said, "I suppose he could have done that. But Avey would have just gotten another gun. He can't get another thumb."

Jess said, "That's why Avey almost fell when he tried to mount his horse. He grabbed for the saddle-horn with no thumb on his left hand. It's a wonder he didn't fall on his face."

"That woulda' just about broke my heart," Walter said, snorting, and shaking his head.

All the while, as they'd been discussing what had happened, Toby had been standing in the shallow water of the twist, looking toward the woods where Avey had ridden away.

As if he knew they had run out of questions with no answers, Toby turned and walked up to them, saying nothing.

Walter asked, "You okay Toby?"

"Yeah, don't I look okay?"

Shepherd said, "You stood there in the creek for a long time. We were a little worried about you; that's all"

"No, I'm good. I was just thinking about Pastor Windor, and something he told me that really came in handy; that might even have saved my life."

"What's that?" Luther asked.

"It was the reason I kept trying to draw Avey deeper into the twist."

"Were you trying to get him in deep enough for the water to knock him off his feet?"

Toby flashed his boyish grin. "No; just deep enough to wash the chicken fat out of his holster."

Then Toby told them about the trick that Pastor Windor had clued him in to; the trick used by gun-fighters who carried the long barreled weapons.

When he'd finished, Toby added, "I don't know how much it slowed him down, but I figured I'd take any edge I could get."

Luther nodded and again told the others, "See, I told you; the smartest damn kid I ever saw."

Luke said, "And nobody ever doubted you for a minute,"

After a few more minutes' discussion, the group decided the most logical thing to do was to head for Grayson's store, and bring Ben and Kate up to speed on what had happened at the twist.

Luke commented that he was surprised that Ben, *and* possibly Kate, hadn't shown up to see what was going on when the shooting started.

Doc; always the sensible one said, "Ben showing up wouldn't have surprised me, but he's awfully protective of Kate. He'd have hog-tied her to keep her out of harm's way. She's probably still in the storage cellar, with a couple men sitting on top of the door with guns. For that matter, there might still be quite a few of the other women and children holed up there. It hasn't been that long since we had a small war happen here. Ben's no doubt watching over that group with the other guards."

"Right, Doc." It was Jess that agreed with his analysis. "So let's go catch him up, and decide what to do, if we should do anything."

They again headed to the store; the place that had become the town's unofficial headquarters.

After some discussion Shepherd Sloan pointed out a fact so obvious that everyone in the group was both amazed and embarrassed at not having thought of it before.

He said, "You know, as soon as we began having trouble with

the Bleus we should have sent a wire from Sweetwater to the U. S. Marshals in Carson City."

"And most definitely after Vance Avey murdered Pastor Windor," Doc said. Even if the Bleus hadn't done anything illegal before that, there's no way Avey could get away with that."

Luther said, "That red hair would look good spread out over a noose, wouldn't it?"

Kate took Ben's hand and said, "I think it's about time for a trip to Sweetwater to pick up some stock isn't it, hon?"

Ben nodded. "You're reading my mind, like always. I'll go tomorrow. Anybody want to ride along?"

Shepherd Sloan raised his hand. "I'll go, if it's all right. "That's fine by me. We'll roll out about seven in the morning; we should get there around nine thirty. The telegraph office is in the post office"

"

By half-past noon the following day Ben and Shepherd Sloan were back. Ben reported that he had sent a telegram to the US Marshals' headquarters in the state capital explaining all the recent events in the area of Whiskey Branch. He included the details of the attacks on the town by the men working for Napoleon Bleu and his family, and everything leading up to the murder of Pastor Landon Windor by Vance Avey.

He also said that before they'd left Sweetwater to return to town, Mister Williams; the telegrapher who sent the telegram for him promised to send someone to Whiskey Branch with a message as soon as he received a response from the marshals.

So all that was left to do was to wait, and try to return to as normal a life as possible. The day after Ben sent the telegram Doc likened the town trying to go on as normal without Pastor Windor to a body trying to go on living after its heart had been cut out.

That statement brought what was nearly an angry reply from Shepherd Sloan, "I think it would sadden Landon Windor if the town didn't at least try to go on as normal as possible."

"How do you figure?" Doc asked.

"Do you think he would want the town to die just because he did?"

Doc said only, "No, I suppose he wouldn't."

A little after ten am three days later a young man walked into Grayson's General Store and introduced himself to Kate.

He said, "Hello, I'm Robert Williams. My father operates the telegraph office in Sweetwater. He sent me over with a message for Ben Grayson. It came in during the night. I didn't read it, but the heading says it's from the U.S. Marshal's office in Carson City." He held it out to Kate, who took it, and told him, "Ben's my husband. He's out back feeding the horses. I'll go call him right now. He's been expecting this. Thank you so much."

"You're welcome. Should I wait for a reply?"

"Do you mind? I'll tell him to hurry."

"Not a problem. My dad said he could tell it was important when your husband and the other man came in to send the wire."

"Okay!" Kate hurried out the back of the store, with the telegram in hand. She was back in less than two minutes. Ben came behind her, winded, and barely able to speak, his tongue getting tangled up, he was so excited.

He stuck his hand out toward the young man. "I'm Ben Grayson. You're the one who brought the telegram?"

"Yes sir, I am. I'm Robert Williams. My father told me to stay and see if you wanted to send a reply."

Ben shook Robert's hand till the young man nearly lost his balance.

Then he said to Kate, "Darlin' get this young fellow a cup of coffee while I write a message for him to take to his father."

Then he pulled up a chair for Robert and one for himself. Kate brought him a pencil and a sheet of paper. After carefully rereading the telegram Robert Williams had delivered he wrote his reply. He then laid both the telegram and his reply before Kate and asked, "Do you think everybody will be okay with me replying without checking with them first?"

"Kate said, "I believe everybody will think you did exactly right."

Ben took five dollars from the cash box, handed it to Robert along with the message he'd written, and said, "Please take this to your father and ask him to get it off as soon as possible. I'll stop in the next time I'm in Sweetwater and make good on any extra I owe him if the five dollars doesn't cover the cost. Do you think that would be okay with him?"

"More than likely; he's pretty reasonable, most of the time."

Ben said, "Good. Robert, it was nice meeting you. We'll walk out with you.

Ben and Kate walked Robert Williams out to where his horse was hitched to the rail in front of the store. As he rode off, Ben said, let's walk up through town and pass this telegram around." He patted his pocket. Kate went back in the store long enough to put a note on the door saying that they would be back in a half hour, then she locked the door and they left.

The half-hour time limit Kate's note on the door had placed on Ben and Kate gave them more than enough time to walk up Creek Street, enjoying the mid-day sunshine, and stop where they needed to stop.

Before Ben and Kate returned to the store Shepherd Sloan, Luther

Wilson, Walter and Mildred Denborough, Luke Parker, Jess Ivy, Doc Forrest, and Toby had been made aware that U.S. Marshal Raymond Clark would be visiting Whiskey Branch the following Saturday afternoon. Ben had taken the liberty of telling the marshal in his wire to come to the store. When he said he hoped that was all right with everyone, he heard not a single complaint.

The Marshal's story

On Saturday, the mid-day sun was still so close to being perfectly overhead that the posts holding up the porch roof in front of Grayson's store covered their own shadows.

Ben and Kate sat side by side on the porch in cane rockers enjoying the sunshine. Ben took out his pocket watch and, for the tenth time, at least, checked the time.

Kate said, "You're going to wear the numbers off the face of your watch from looking at it, if you keep it up."

Ben said, "I hope he didn't get held up."

"Who would try to hold up a US Marshal?"

"I don't mean like that. I mean I hope something didn't come up."

Kate grinned at him. "I know. What time is it?"

Ben checked his watch. "Ten after twelve."

"The man's wire said he'd be here this afternoon. It's only been afternoon for ten minutes. And we're not even sure where he's coming from, or how far he has to travel. Try to be patient."

Then Kate said, "How about if I get us coffee to warm us up with while we wait?"

Before Ben could answer, they heard hoof-beats coming from Creek Street. Only a moment later a very large man on a big bay horse rode up to the store. Before he had reigned his horse to a stop Ben and Kate saw the badge pinned to his vest. When he slid down from the saddle it was clear that he stood six foot-six easy. Even the badge he wore seemed oversized to match the man's stature. He took off his hat and slapped it against his leg to knock off the trail dirt. Ben stood and walked to the porch rail and asked, "Are you Marshal Clark?"

"That I am," he answered amiably. "And would you be Ben Grayson?"

"That's me. And this is my wife Katelin."

"Kate said, "Kate will be fine."

"Kate it is, then," the marshal said.

"Climb on down," Ben told him. "We've been looking forward to talking to you."

The marshal slid off of his horse and climbed the few steps to the porch.

Then he said, "I've got some information that might be interesting to you folks. It might take a little bit of time to do the tellin' if that's all right."

"That's okay with me," Ben answered. "I've got nothing special to do today, and all day to do it. But if you don't mind, it would be nice if we could round up about a half-dozen other folks who've been real involved in what's been happening around here lately, so they could hear what you have to say, too."

Marshal Clark nodded. "Fine by me; I've been told my voice carries like a train whistle, so talking to a half-dozen people won't strain it any more than talking to a couple."

Kate said, "I'll put on coffee, then go let the people know. It won't be taking long for them to arrive. I'll be betting they'll be here like the little people are holdin' a lit twig to their britches." Kate went into the kitchen.

Ben smiled at the marshal's puzzled expression, and said, "I'll explain while she's gone."

After Kate brought Ben and Marshal Clark coffee, she went out the back door to the corral to get her horse so she could ride through town and tell a handful of people to hurry to the store.

As soon as she left, Ben explained Kate's affection for what she referred to as 'the little people.'

Marshal Clark said, "I can understand that. In my business, there's not a day that goes by that I couldn't use some extra good luck."

"I think that's true of any business."

Ben and the marshal had no more than finished their coffee than Kate rode up to the front of the store, moving fast. She dismounted quickly, trotted up the steps and said, "I've gotta' put on more coffee!" Then she pushed through the door into the store, letting it slam behind her.

Ben stood up and told the marshal, "I believe company's coming."

The dust of Kate's arrival had barely settled from the air before Doc's buggy pulled in from Creek Street, followed by the Denborough's wagon with both Walter and Mildred aboard. Riders on horseback began coming after that. Soon the hitching rail was filled up; from Marshal Clark's big bay at one end to Doc's buggy horse at the other.

Once again Ben and Kate's store room was being used as an improvised meeting room; this time on a very informal basis. The group was small. The room seemed especially large without Pastor Windor there.

In addition to Ben and Kate, Walter and Mildred Denborough, Luther, Doc, Luke, Jess, and Toby were there, as well as Shepherd Sloan.

After Marshal Clark met everyone, the big man started out by saying that he'd taken the stage in to Sweetwater where he'd rented the horse at the livery stable.

Then he said, "Mister Grayson's telegram explained in some detail what you folks have gone through dealing with the Bleu family. I know it doesn't do anything to take away from the hurt you've had to deal with because of them. But for what it's worth, they have a long history of causing trouble for people who didn't deserve it."

Luther asked, "Have you ever had any run-ins with them?"

"Not lately. They've been dodging the law for a long time. Sadly they've gotten smarter since they came into the states."

"What do you mean, since they came into the states?" Walter asked.

The Bleus have made as many enemies among Canadian law enforcement ranks as they have among us here in the United States.

The fact is, that's where your Pastor Windor first crossed paths with

the Bleus; in Canada. But he wasn't a pastor then, he was just Landon Windor. He wasn't always a pastor."

Toby snickered, and most everybody else smiled at the marshal's words.

Marshal Clark asked, "Did I say something funny?"

"No," Luke answered. "You just said something that the pastor said about himself more than once. It's kinda' strange to hear somebody else say it about him, that's all."

Luther said, "If I may ask, what was the pastor doing in Canada when he crossed paths with the Bleus, back before he was a pastor?"

Marshal Clark drew a deep breath, and said, "At one time, years before he became a pastor, Landon Windor was a bounty hunter."

After a full five minutes of silence that was so thick it felt like you could almost touch it, Kate stood up and said, "I don't believe that! I won't believe that!

"I'm afraid it's true, young lady, though he wasn't a typical bounty hunter; not in any way."

Kate crossed her arms and stomped her foot. "It's not possible!"

Marshal Clark asked, "Can I explain? You might understand better."

Kate glared at him.

Ben touched her arm. "Let's hear the man out, darlin."

"Okay, but I'll never be believin' it!" Kate's eyes flared.

The marshal began, "Landon Windor was a bounty hunter; but not like most other bounty hunters I've ever known of. He didn't just pull a poster off the wall and ride off with the intention of shooting a man down to make the bounty.

The thing that was most different thing about him was he didn't go after someone unless he was asked to by the law. After a while it got so the authorities would contact him and ask him to go after the especially bad ones. It was that way the two or three years he lived in Canada *and* when he moved back to the states."

Doc said, "I do recall him once mentioning living in Canada."

Luther added, "Yep."

"Well," the marshal continued. "When word got around about his skills, the law in the states started calling on him to track down the particularly dangerous, especially brutal ones, just like up north. That's how he and Napoleon Bleu originally butted heads."

"How's that?" Luke asked. Then he added, "now that you mention it, it did seem that Pastor Windor knew a hell of a lot about the Bleus."

"And Napoleon Bleu did hire a gunfighter to kill him," Doc said. "So there had to be some history there."

Marshal Clark said, "I told you Landon Windor wasn't a typical bounty hunter. That was true in several ways. The biggest difference between him and other bounty hunters was that he'd do everything possible not to kill someone. He only killed as a last resort; to avoid being killed, or keep someone else from being killed. As far as I know; in the years he was a bounty-man he only killed three men. It just happened that one of those was Nathanial Bleu, Napoleon Bleu's younger brother."

"Good God!" Shepherd Sloan said. "That explains a lot. Now we know why Napoleon Senior hated Pastor Windor with such a passion."

Marshal Clark said, "Trust me, Nathanial Bleu needed killing if anyone ever did, but I'm sure Napoleon Bleu doesn't see it that way.

Landon Windor began trailing the Bleus in Canada at the request of the Northwest Mounted Police. It was just Napoleon and Nathanial then; Napoleon hadn't married and didn't have any children yet. Nathanial was nearly twenty years younger than Napoleon, but a hundred years meaner.

The two of them decided to rob a trading post about twenty five miles north of the U.S/ Canadian border. While Napoleon sat outside drinking moonshine and letting Nathaniel take all the chances, Landon Windor crept up to the rear of the building and slipped in the back door.

He gave Nathaniel Bleu a chance to surrender, but in the end he was forced to put a bullet in the man's forehead as the outlaw held a Bowie-knife against the throat of the fifteen-year-old daughter of the trading post's owner. The girl said Windor told Bleu to drop the knife four times, but he kept pressing it tighter against her neck till he drew blood and she felt sure she was going to die.

She also said that as soon as Landon Windor fired, she heard a horse gallop off before Nathanial Bleu even hit the floor. So apparently Napoleon didn't stick around to check on his brother before he headed for the hills."

"Not much for brotherly love, huh?" Shepherd said.

"No, not much," Marshal Clark answered. "But the man sure can hold onto a grudge."

"Kate said, "I hope he chokes to death on it; nice and slow."

"Well, once your pastor made Napoleon Bleu an only child, Bleu decided to head south. Maybe he thought that by crossing the border into the United States he would be immune from prosecution. That wasn't true. On top of that, once the U.S Marshal's Service received a wire from the Mounted Police headquarters in Canada The Marshals also requested Windor's services. After that Landon Windor made it his mission to track down Napoleon Bleu. That's how he ended up here in your town; he was tracking Bleu. It took him a long time to find him; but your pastor wasn't one to give up once he started something. Of course, tracking Napoleon Bleu wasn't the only thing he was doing during all that time."

"Really, what else was he doing?" Toby asked.

"Well, it's possible he kept busy doing things we're not aware of; but the things we are aware of were really interesting."

Ben said, "Such as?"

"Well he was still chasing bounties. And still bringing them in alive. The interesting thing was what happened after he'd catch them."

"What do you mean after?"

Marshal Clark laughed. "Once, after he got paid a five thousand-dollar bounty for bringing in a bank robber in Oregon the local Baptist church got a donation to pay for their new sanctuary. And a school in western Utah found a bag of cash on their doorstep after the local paper ran a story about their need for funds for books for the school library. Just the day before, Landon Windor had brought in a gambler-turned-killer for a thousand-dollar bounty.

Such things seemed to happen real often.

And of course, he also found time to go to seminary and become a pastor. He really was a man of many talents."

Luke said, "I have a question."

"What's that?" The marshal asked.

"Where do you go from here? I don't mean literally; I mean what's the plan as far as going after the Bleus and Vance Avey? And how do we fit in?"

"Well, you folks know the situation around here a lot better than I do. What can you tell me that will be helpful in putting together a plan for going after the Bleus?"

Walter spoke up, "When Jess and I went across the creek we saw that the area where the stills used to sit was deserted. At least there's no sign that anybody's been living or working there, like when the stills were up and running. The area was pretty well trampled up, like there's been a lot of activity, but no signs that anybody's started up moonshining again; at least not yet."

Jess said," "But there's no telling what Napoleon has in mind; especially with Nappy dead."

"Nappy?" Marshal Clark said.

"That's what everybody called Napoleon Junior."

"What happened to him?"

Shepherd Sloan answered, "He's as dead as Judas Iscariot."

"How did he die?"

Jess explained, "He got brave. He wanted to show what a big, bad gunfighter he was. He picked the wrong man to go up against. He called out Pastor Windor. And when he drew on the pastor, instead of putting a pullet through Nappy's heart Pastor Windor put one through his hat. That made Nappy mad as a wet hen. It proved he didn't have a prayer of taking the pastor. So Nappy drew on Toby. That's when Pastor Windor put three holes in Nappy's chest."

Toby said, "I asked the pastor once if he'd ever killed anyone. He said only to protect himself or someone else. That's what he did that day; he killed Nappy to protect me."

"Like he killed Napoleon Bleu's brother to save the girl in the trading post," the marshal said. "I talked to a lot of people about Landon Windor, and what I always heard was; "The two things he respected most; were life and the law. He brought in a lot of bounties. Every one that he brought in sitting up in the saddle would have been as easy or easier for him to bring in across the saddle; but a dead man can't stand trial. He didn't want to be the judge *or* jury. He wanted to bring them in, plain and simple; and get them away from people they might harm. "

Marshal Clark asked Kate, "Do you think I could bother you for another cup of coffee, young lady? Then we'll talk some more about what to do."

"More coffee coming up," Kate answered, the fire gone from her voice.

She poured more coffee all around.

When she finished, Marshal Clark said, "What I'll do is arrange to have a half-dozen deputy-marshals come into Sweetwater in four or five days, and with what you can tell me to go on, we'll blanket the area on the north side of Whiskey Creek and find out if any of Bleu's men are still in the area, and round them up if they are."

Doc said, "Well between the two skirmishes they mounted against the town on that one Sunday they lost sixteen men that I counted. So there are less to round up than there once would have been."

"How many men did you lose?" The marshal asked.

"None."

"Impressive." The marshal nodded.

"Thanks again to Pastor Windor."

Luke spoke up, "There were a couple things I discovered while I was over there scouting."

"What's that?"

First, the Bleus live in a little house that sits in the center of a field in the middle of the woods. You get to it by following a path that twists and winds along through the woods in mostly a northern direction. And Old Man Bleu has twin daughters. One's named Lillie. If she has a heart, it's as cold as a snake's heart in a snow drift. She's the one that found out I was spying on them. She told Nappy to kill me on the spot. Millie, the other twin, talked him out of it. She kept saying she'd "*tell daddy.*

I got the feeling that she has Napoleon wrapped around her little finger and also that she's kind of slow; like maybe she never really grew up. But if it wasn't for her I'd have caught a bullet instead of pneumonia, so I'd hate to see her end up behind bars just for being related to animals."

"Understood; I'll try to see to it she doesn't suffer for the sins of the father," Marshal Clark said.

"Oh," Luke went on. "They're almost identical. Other than their personalities, the only difference is that Millie, the one without fangs and horns, has some freckles across her nose."

"Got it." Marshal Clark reached in his saddle bag that hung on the back of his chair, and pulled out a large rolled-up card. Before unrolling it he said, "You'll find this interesting." He unrolled it and held it up;

WANTED DEAD OR ALIVE

VANCE AVEY

For the Crime of Murder

Reward $1000

Before anyone could respond to the poster, Marshal Clark said, "I know the reward should be ten times that much, but because of *where* Avey killed your pastor, the Governor of Nevada set the amount, and he acts like the money is coming out of his own pocket.

Also the same poster will be going up all over western Canada. The only difference will be that up there it will be in English and French.

So as a result of doing Napoleon Bleu's dirty work Vance Avey will have bounty hunters in two countries chasing him in addition to all the lawmen that will be looking for him."

"Do you think he'll hang?" Luther asked.

"It might be the luckiest thing for him," Marshal Clark answered.

"What?" Shepherd asked, disbelievingly.

"I've never been hanged, but supposedly, if done right it's so quick that it's almost painless. And at least it will come after a trial. In his situation, he could end up dying in worse ways."

"Like what?" Surprisingly, it was Kate who asked.

"There's always a bounty-hunter shooting him. A lot of them prefer taking their shots from a long way off. And all bounty-hunters aren't crack-shots. A man can die really slow from being gut-shot."

"Amen," Doc said.

"And," the marshal went on, "Not all lawmen see things the same way."

Toby asked, "What do you mean by that?"

"It could lead to a few different things. Since lawmen aren't eligible to collect rewards, it's not unheard of for some small-town sheriff who makes half what he feels he deserves to pass along information he might get on a wanted man to a brother-in law or the like. Then to make sure that the fact never comes to light, when the wanted man is captured and the bounty is paid the prisoner conveniently gets shot 'trying to escape'. That way there's no trial.

Then there's another possibility that's just as illegal, but in the case of Vance Avey, almost understandable."

Luther asked, "What would that be?"

"As I said, Landon Windor was very highly thought of among lawmen in both the United States *and* Canada. And even law-enforcement folks know that through the wrangling of fast-talking lawyers, people who deserve to hang sometimes get off. There could be some sheriff or deputy out there who's dealt with Avey or someone just as bad as him who wouldn't think twice about putting a bullet in him before taking a chance on him getting off.

It could be even worse if he's turned in to the Mounted Police in Canada."

"How do you figure?" Walter asked.

"If Vance Avey got turned in to a Mounty who happened to be an old friend of Landon Windor's, a knife in the gut could look pretty good by comparison to what other things they could come up with."

"What in the Hell; in comparison to what?"

"Those men are creative when it comes to their horses. Avey could end up with each wrist and ankle tied to a different horse. Then someone fires a shot in the air to start them running."

Kate let out a small yelp, and then said, "That's *too* awful! Even for someone like Avey."

Jess said, "After hearing all of that, maybe it would be best if Avey stays loose till some really fast gun-toting hotshot calls him out. Then he'll get what he really deserves thanks to him calling out Toby, even if he doesn't see a rope."

"Doc added, "I saw, and performed, way too many amputations during the war, but none that were as unexpected, and definitely none that were done faster than the thumb amputation Toby performed on Vance Avey's gun hand."

Marshal Clark said, "I gotta' say, I'm kinda' sorry I missed that."

He downed the last of his coffee, then slung his saddle bag over his shoulder and said, "I'm going to be heading back to Sweetwater now. I'll send a wire to headquarters as soon as I get there, and request some deputies to help me search on the north side of the creek." He checked his pocket watch. "I probably won't get a reply till tomorrow morning, at the soonest. I'll stay over in Sweetwater tonight. And you can be sure I'll keep you up on anything that happens."He shook hands all around, then tipped his hat and left the store.

Ten Days later:

Around 2: pm on the second Tuesday after Marshal Clark's visit, Robert Williams, the son of the telegrapher in Sweetwater once again came in Grayson's store with a telegram from the marshal. It was addressed to Ben, and the message was simple; I have quite a bit of information to share. Please send me a wire as soon as possible and let me know when I could meet with you folks again.

Sincerely, Marshal Clark.

Again, Ben wrote a reply message for Robert to take to his father, and sent Kate on the rounds of the town to let everyone know.

As Kate headed for the door Ben said, "I hope what I suggested works for him."

"Me too," Kate answered as the door swung closed behind her.

Ben's reply suited Marshal Clark, and four days later, another Saturday found them once again gathered in the store room of Grayson's store.

Always the consummate hostess, Kate made sure everyone who wanted coffee had a fresh cup.

Marshal Clark took a paper from his pocket, and peering at it, began by saying, "I'm glad everyone is sitting down." As he said it, he flashed a smile so big it barely fit on his face. "If you'll recall, when I was here the last time I showed you a wanted poster on Vance Avey. I also said that the thousand-dollar bounty should be at least ten times as much for murdering Landon Windor. Well, as it turns out, I'm not the only one who felt that way. I think I told you about some of the good things he did with the bounty money he earned in different places during the time between him killing Nathanial Bleu and tracking Napoleon Bleu to this area. I also said that in all of those years there was a lot of time that we don't know what he'd been doing.

It turns out that once those posters started going up, and word got out that Avey is wanted for killing Landon Windor; we started hearing more about what he'd been doing over those years. The governors of both Utah and Oregon posted bounties that were so high they shamed Nevada's governor into tripling his bounty. Then a wire came in from the governor of California. Washington was next; both were states we never knew he'd worked in. Then; Arizona. And not surprisingly; Canada pitched in, in a big way."

The marshal had to pause and ask Kate for more coffee.

Kate was shaking almost too much to pour it. "You're not making this up, are you?"

"No ma'am I'm not. At this moment, with everything totaled up, Vance Avey's no-good carcass is worth twenty-thousand dollars; dead or alive."

Shepherd Sloan, who was the first one able to speak said, "The Lord certainly does work in mysterious ways."

Walter, who had once expressed the opinion that Shepherd was nothing more than a worthless drunk slapped him on the back and said, "You sure said a mouthful there, Pastor Sloan!"

"Also," Marshal Clark continued, "I wanted to let you know what we found when we checked things out across the creek."

"Did you have any trouble with Napoleon Bleu?" Doc asked.

"Nobody's ever going to ever have any trouble with Napoleon Bleu again."

"How's that?"

"Well, when the deputies and I found the house you told us about," he said, nodding toward Luke, "Millie, the twin you mentioned was there. She was alone. She seemed thrilled to see us, even though she had no idea who we were. She said she'd been alone since Lillie and daddy died. That's all she could say for a while, for crying. Then she made us some tea. After a little bit she calmed down and I got some information from her. You're right, she's not very clear on things.

After a little while I got out of her that Lillie and Napoleon were buried out back of the house.I asked how they died. She said her daddy just stopped breathing while he was arguing with Lillie after they found out Nappy was dead. Millie seemed really proud that she had gotten to tell them Nappy was dead. I asked her how Lillie died. Millie grinned really big and said, "I shot her in the head." Then she said, "The mean man with long red hair was here then. He said he'd help bury daddy, but after I shot Lillie he rode off and I had to finish doing it myself."

Luke said, "Well, for what it's worth, from what I saw of how Lillie treated Millie, Lillie deserved whatever she got.

Marshal Clark said, "Oh yeah Luke, when Millie found out I knew you she was real concerned about you. She was real pleased when she found out that Nappy didn't kill you."

"If you see her again, tell her I was worried about her too", Luke said.

"Why don't you ride over yourself and tell her before she leaves?"

"Leaves for where? Are you jailing her?"

Marshal Clark shook his head. "Not if I have anything to do with it. And under these circumstances I can't imagine anybody pushing to prosecute her for a crime we don't absolutely know she committed. All we know after a quick examination of the shallow grave her sister's body was in is that somebody did indeed put a bullet dead center in her forehead. But Millie also said in the breath after she said that she shot her sister in the head that the mean man with the long red hair had been there. I don't know a lot about Millie Bleu, but I know a lot about Vance Avey. If I had to bet on who put a bullet in somebody's head, my money would be on Avey.

"So where's Millie going?" Luke asked.

There's a very nice older couple who live about a half-day's ride north of Sweetwater; a doctor and Mrs. Grant. They have a big home around ten miles past the stage way-station. There are eight people with Millie's sort of problem who live with them. They're mostly kids and teenagers. I know Millie doesn't fit that description at all. But I rode up and told them all about her situation, and told them that she'd been living alone and kept the house neat and spotless despite having no help at all.

The Grants are getting up in years. They've offered to let Millie come live with them as a housekeeper for room and board, if she'd like. They could use the help. She'd handle the cleaning and cooking, and take care of the garden. It seems like a good situation for everybody."

Luke asked, "And Millie's okay with the idea?"

"She's a little nervous. I get the impression she's hardly ever been more than a mile from that house."

"That's very possible."

"But she can't live there alone," the marshal said. "Even if the loneliness didn't kill her, the house will eventually get to be too much for her." He looked at Luke evenly. "A little reassurance from someone she trusts couldn't hurt."

Kate said, "That makes a lot of sense, doesn't it Luke?"

Doc added, "Sure does."

Luke said, "You all can quit now. I'll ride over and see her in the morning." Then he told Marshal Clark, "I'll send you a wire after I talk with her. Then if she decides she likes the idea and wants to meet those folks I'll borrow a wagon and I'll take her up there when the time comes."

Kate gave him a smile. "Whenever she's ready to go we'll use our wagon. I can help her pack up whatever belongin's she wants to take with her, and I'll ride along. It might make her feel a bit more comfortable havin' another woman along."

"Good idea, darlin', as always,'" Ben said.

The following morning about an hour after sunrise Luke rapped on the front door of the oddly out-of place little house that he'd first been led to by Millie Bleu before so many things had changed for everyone. He kept reminding himself that nothing had changed as much for anyone as had changed for Millie. She'd lost absolutely all the family she had. And though losing Lillie and Nappy was no great loss; for someone with Millie's limited understanding of life outside of the little house; she probably felt completely lost.

Millie opened the door and looked blankly at Luke, no sign of recognition showing on her face. She said, "Did you knock?"

"Yes I did. Hi, Millie, how are you?"

Still, she looked only puzzled.

He said, "It's me; Luke. I've missed you."

Millie rose up on her toes, putting her eye to eye with him. Then after a brief moment; recognition lit up her eyes like someone lighting the wicks on two lamps behind dark windows at the same instant.

She let out a childlike squeal and said, "Luke, I'm so happy you're alive!" She threw her arms around his neck.

"Luke said, "I'm happy I'm alive, too."

Millie said, "I thought for a long time that Nappy killed you. Then a big man with a badge came and told me you weren't dead. I'm glad to see you. I don't like being here by myself. I'm awful lonesome. I don't miss Lillie or Nappy at all, but I miss daddy somethin' awful. Will you stay with me forever Luke?" Millie pleaded. She squeezed him more tightly. "I don't think I can stand to be alone any more Luke!"

Luke gently took her arms from around his neck and said, "Millie, let's sit in your kitchen for a spell and talk. I think I know a way that you don't have to be alone."

"You'll stay with me?"

"No Millie, I can't do that."

"Why? Is it because I'm stupid? Lillie told me I was stupid as far back as I can remember."

"No Millie, It's not because you're stupid. Don't say that; because you're not stupid! And you've got to stop thinking you are. Lillie called you that because she was a mean person who was jealous of you."

"Jealous of me?" Millie asked disbelievingly.

"Yes, jealous of you; because you didn't have to be mean to be happy. Lillie wasn't happy so she didn't want you to be happy. Spending your whole life being mean to people isn't a very enjoyable way to live. Lillie had to scare the men who worked for your daddy to get them to do what she wanted, didn't she?"

Millie nodded.

"Okay, can we sit and talk?"

Millie nodded and said, "I'll fix tea."

They went to the kitchen. Millie fixed the tea. Luke told her about the Grants, and their invitation for her to come and visit; with the possibility of later moving in. She was at first disappointed that Luke wouldn't consider moving into her daddy's house with her. But then he explained that he had friends in Whiskey Branch who would miss him, and that he was the town's only carpenter. The people of the town needed him to fix things for them. And once he explained to her how much her help would mean to the Grants, she became interested in the idea; as long as he promised to come and visit.

It was a promise Luke was happy to make.

Before riding back to Whiskey Branch, Luke went to Sweetwater and sent Marshal Clark a wire letting him know that his visit with Millie Bleu regarding the Grants looked like it would turn out positive.

Prescott, Arizona

Vance Avey stumbled out through the bat-wing doors of a dimly-lit saloon. He clutched the neck of a three-quarter-empty whiskey bottle in his right hand; the one that was still capable of clutching anything. His new mission in life was learning to draw right handed so he could go back to that crummy little town by the whirlpool and kill the punk kid that took away his gun hand. Actually; that was his long term mission. His short term mission was to stay on his feet long enough to make it to the outhouse and then to his hotel room. The sawbones he'd found to sew up his hand after the kid shot off his thumb had done a lousy job, and he'd drained the bottle of laudanum the man gave him for pain before that night was over. That was weeks ago. His hand still throbbed constantly.

Whiskey was a poor substitute for the pain killer; but any bartender would sell him all of it he wanted.

At least finding a belt and holster for a good right handed rig was easy. Learning to use it wasn't. He stepped off the boardwalk to the dirt street and turned toward the corner of the building to go to the little two-hole outhouse around back.

He'd taken two steps when a no-nonsense voice behind him said, "Vance Avey; stop right there, and put your hands behind your head! Do exactly what I say or I'll kill you." It definitely didn't come across like a request.

Avey stopped dead, his boots kicking up puffs of dirt from the bone- dry street. He put his hands behind his head as he'd been told.

The voice from behind him said, "Lace your fingers together."

"Why?"

"Because you'll be extremely sorry if you don't." The man behind Avey sounded impatient. "I've ridden a long way to find you, and I'm not in the mood to be understanding."

Avey felt a gun barrel prod him in the back. He laced his fingers together.

The man behind him said, "Missing a thumb, huh?"

"Lucky for you," Avey shot back.

"Oh yeah, why's that?"

"Because if my gun hand was whole you'd be dead now," Avey growled.

"I guess we'll never know, will we?"

The gun prodded Avey in the back harder. "Walk."

Avey sounded as scared as mad now, "Walk where?"

"Not far, just down the street to the sheriff's office."

Avey tried to snap his head around and was clouted on the side of the head by what was either a long, strangely heavy pistol or an unusually short rifle. His eyes rolled back and he went to his knees, and then to his back. After a few moments water splashed over his head, and when Avey opened his eyes, spitting and sputtering water, the man who had come up behind him was holding a canteen, and pointing a gun at him. He said, "On your feet; we're going to see the sheriff."

Though Avey hadn't seen his face before, there was no doubt in his mind that he recognized the voice of the man who had stopped him on the street, made him put his hands behind his head, and then knocked him out.

"I don't think I can walk; I'm too drunk, and you gave me a hell of a thump," Avey moaned.

"Get up. The sheriff's office is a good twenty yards away, and I'm too tired to drag you."

Avey hung his head, nearly bawling. "I really can't."

"You better find the strength. I may be tired, but my horse is as fresh as a daisy.

The rapidity with which the prospect of being dragged behind a horse down twenty yards of dirt street sobered Avey up was remarkable. He climbed first to his knees, then to his feet. With some gun-barrel-in-the-back encouragement, Vance Avey shuffled down the street and was soon a resident at the Prescott, Arizona city jail.

Kate was at the front counter, filling a box with canned goods and a bolt of calico cloth for Jenny Jones so the lady could get started making dresses for her twin girls for the upcoming school year. Ben was in the back making a list for his next trip to Sweetwater to pick up stock. The shelves weren't bare, but were getting enough empty spots that it wouldn't be long before he'd have to make the trip. He occasionally grumbled about having to go, but Kate knew that he actually enjoyed the opportunity to see something beyond the inside of the store and the same dirt streets and hills he looked at daily.

Ben frequently asked her to ride along; but she always pointed out that someone had to mind the store; not just for their wellbeing, but for that of the town.

Kate wasn't surprised when the door swung open, setting the little brass bell that hung from it tinkling; but she was surprised when Marshal Raymond Clark walked in, practically needing to turn sideways to squeeze his broad shoulders through the width of the opening.

"Well lookie here!" Kate said. What might be bringin' you here, unannounced, marshal, if you don't mind my askin'?"

The marshal laughed and answered, "I don't mind you asking at all young lady; because I came with good news. Actually a couple pieces of good news; if you think you could round up your usual gang of accomplices."

"That I can! You come on in the back and make yourself to home." Once the marshal was seated in the back room with Ben, Kate poured them both coffee, and excused herself to go gather up the people who had become the marshal's regular audience.

As she headed for the door, Marshal Clark said, "Be sure to bring Toby."

"I surely will!"

Fifteen minutes later Marshal Clark was sitting with Ben, sipping his fourth cup of coffee when Doc Forrest pushed through the door from the front of the store. Luther was behind him. A moment later the bell rang in the front of the store announcing that someone had come in. Ben said, "I wonder who that is."

His question was answered when Walter bellowed, "Where is everybody!" from out front.

"We're back here, you moose!" Doc shouted.

Walter pushed the door open, but before coming in, he looked over his shoulder and said, "Well come on." Then he stepped aside enough to let Luke and Jess squeeze past. Luther came next, then Shepherd Sloan.

Ben said, "Where's Katie?"

"She's right behind me," Shepherd answered. "Her and Toby."

Marshal Clark said, "Good; I've got news for everybody, but especially for Toby."

Doc shook the marshal's hand and said, "Well marshal, what brings you to Whiskey Branch? It's a little unusual; you showing up unannounced.

Not that you aren't always welcome," he was quick to add. "But we've gotten used to you sending a wire to let us know you're coming."

Luther asked, "Isn't that the bay out front that you were riding last time; the big one?

"That's very observant of you."

"I'm a blacksmith and I run a livery stable; horses are my business."

The marshal nodded. "I had a feeling I'd be back, so I bought the horse the last time and the livery man in Sweetwater boarded it for me. It's a lot better than hoping he has one that's big enough for me when I get off the stage."

"So what's the news?" Toby asked.

"Everybody should sit down."

Is it that bad?" Kate asked."

"No, just the opposite, in fact.

First; Vance Avey is in the city jail in Prescott Arizona."

Shepherd said, "Praise the Lord."

"Second; he was captured by a bounty-man named Randall. He and Landon Windor were old friends; so he has no love for Vance Avey. He told the Prescott sheriff that deciding to bring Avey in alive was a tough choice, but just like your pastor did it when he was hunting bounties, that's the way Randall does it. He brings them in alive unless they give him no choice.

Also, this Randall is, like Landon Windor, a rare good-hearted bounty hunter. Toby, when Randall heard about how close you and Landon Windor were, and then found out that you shot the thumb off Avey's gun-hand because the pastor told you not to kill him, he made a decision. He said since you made taking Avey in so easy he is going to split the bounty with you fifty-fifty. The funny thing is; he thought the bounty on Avey was still a thousand dollars. He had no idea that so many people had piled on money and run the bounty up. But he also told the sheriff down there he'd have gone after Avey for nothing just because he killed Landon Windor.

Also, within a week from now all of the states that committed to contributing to the bounty on Avey, as well as Canada will have sent their contributions to the Federal Marshall's headquarters in Carson City. Within a week after that, Robert; the young man you've met from the telegraph and post office in Sweetwater should be bringing you a wire notifying you that a bank draft for ten thousand dollars is waiting for you at the Sweetwater Post office. I'll also receive a wire when it's there. Once I know it's there I'll catch the next stage to Sweetwater and deliver the bank draft to you personally, if that's all right."

Toby was speechless.

As usual, Walter wasn't, "What do you think, Toby?"

Toby shrugged, "I don't know what I think. Should I be happy that I'm getting a lot of money because somebody killed Pastor Windor?"

Shepherd Sloan said, "You're not getting the money because somebody killed Pastor Windor; you're getting it because somebody feels you deserve it. The man who put away Pastor Windor's murderer feels you deserve it."

Toby asked Marshal Clark, "Do you think Avey will hang?"

"I'd say it's more than likely, unless he draws a jury of total idiots."

Kate spoke up, "I hope he hangs."

Then she said to Toby, "You should accept the money, Toby. It would make Pastor Windor happy. He always wanted the best for you."

Toby nodded. "Okay, I guess."

Walter asked, "Does that make you the richest young man in town, or the youngest rich man in town?"

Jess said, "Is there a difference?"

Walter shrugged. "Ya' got me."

Luther, as always the voice of reason said, "Toby, now I guess what you'll have to do is figure out something worthwhile to do with all that money."

"I already have an idea," Toby answered.

Shepherd said, "I have faith in you. You'll choose wisely."

A little more than two weeks after Marshal Clark's visit with the good news of Vance Avey's capture, Luke and Kate took the short wagon ride to the unusual little Bleu house and Kate helped Millie gather up the clothing and other possessions she cared enough about to take with her. They included a few well-worn dolls and a couple dresses so small that they must have been hanging in the closet since she was in her teens. But Kate made no effort to dissuade her from taking them along; figuring that anything that might help Millie feel comfortable in her new surroundings couldn't hurt. Before climbing on the wagon for the ride to Sweetwater and then on to the Grant's home, Millie led Luke and Kate out back. Luke let Millie clutch his hand as she said her tearful goodbyes to her mother and father. Then he was saddened but not surprised when she spit on Lillie's grave. He supposed Lillie had it coming; small payback for a lot of years of abuse. Millie waved goodbye to the house as they drove the wagon away.

One month to the day from his capture in Prescott, Arizona at the capable hands of the bounty hunter; Randall, Vance Avey was transported, under guard, by stagecoach to the town of Sweetwater, Nevada where his trial was held before the Honorable Judge James Lockard; a judge in good standing in the state of Nevada. At the recommendation of his lawyer Avey pleaded not guilty. During the trial Avey's lawyer claimed that he had been railroaded by Napoleon Bleu and his daughter Lillie, who led him to believe that Landon Windor was a hired gun who had been paid to kill them; and so Avey was only acting in good faith as a bodyguard to protect the lives of a loving father and his devoted child and as such deserved to be found innocent.

After hearing the testimonies of Toby Dove, Walter Denborough, and Luke Parker the jury took only twenty minutes to return a verdict of guilty on the charge of murder. The judge took even less time to pronounce the sentence; that Vance Avey would be hung by the neck until dead.

He was to be transported by stagecoach, under guard, to the territorial penitentiary in Virginia City to await execution.

Five days after the trial Kate was again surprised by an unexpected visit from Marshal Raymond Clark.

This time the instant she saw him walk in the store she could tell things were different.

She said, "I've got a feeling you're not bringin' good news this time. I can see it in your face."

"I'm sorry to say you're right, young lady. I was hoping I wouldn't be bothering you folks again till I brought Toby his reward money. But unfortunately that's not why I'm here."

Kate asked, "Should I go get the others?"

The marshal nodded, "I'm afraid so; and as soon as possible!" And please tell them to bring their guns."

"Okay, Ben's down in the cellar. Yell down and let him know you're here, please!"

"Will do! You hurry on."

Kate ran to the door, looking over her shoulder as she did. "No sooner said than done!" she promised as she went out.

Toby was first in the door.

Marshal Clark was leaning on the counter waiting when he came charging in.

"What is it?" Toby demanded. "What's wrong?"

"Toby, where's your gun?"

Toby pointed toward the front of the store. "It's out there, hanging on my saddle-horn. Why, what's going on?"

"From now on I don't want you leaving home without it strapped on and fully loaded, unless you hear differently from me," the marshal said firmly, without more explanation.

Toby was getting angrier by the second. "I want to know what's going on!"

"Vance Avey escaped!" Marshal Clark said. "And he nearly killed a guard doing it. That's what's going on! Toby, you showed a lot of guts and more than a little smarts before; but it's time to pay attention, and listen up! You're a brave kid, but I've been a marshal for a long time and dealing with animals like Vance Avey is my specialty and it's what I get paid for."

"We're no slouches at putting lead where it needs to go, either," Jess spoke up from just inside the door of the store. Walter stood behind him, like an oversized shadow. They each held their respective killing irons; Jess' Winchester was propped against his shoulder, Walter carried his double barreled scatter-gun with the stock clenched under one arm and the barrels lying in the crooked elbow of his other arm.

Both men looked prepared for whatever awaited them.

Luther pushed past the two armed men; followed by Doc and Shepherd Sloan, "So how did Avey get away? Wasn't he supposed to be under guard?" Luther demanded.

"He *was* under guard; and he was shackled; both feet *and* hands.

"So what happened?"

"The stage stopped at a way station about seventy miles after they left Sweetwater to change horses. They were using a guard from the prison instead of one of our deputies. The man is young and never dealt with the likes of Vance Avey; and it cost him. Not that I'm sure that anyone with any amount of experience would have thought of what Avey did."

"What did he do?" Toby asked.

"As the stage was pulling up to the way station, Avey started yanking on his left hand in the steel cuff, till he had blood pouring from the wound where his thumb used to be. When his hand was good and soaked he yanked on it so hard that his hand pulled through; with no thumb to stop it. Then he slung the chain on the other cuff across the guard's face and blinded him."

Shepherd said, "Good Lord."

"It's my fault," Toby moaned. "If I hadn't blown his thumb off, he couldn't have pulled his hand out. And the guard wouldn't be blind."

"If you hadn't blown his thumb off, you'd be under a cross beside Pastor Windor now," Luther said.

"Did Avey kill the guard?" Walter asked."

"No, he had a lot of blood running down his face, but he's alive, and he's not permanently blinded. He was able to see within an hour. Things will look fuzzy for him for a while."

""Thank God for that."

Marshal Clark added, "But while he couldn't see, Avey took the man's gun, pistol-whipped him with it, and then used it to shoot the chain off his leg-irons. We found pieces of the chain on the ground. Then he stole a saddle horse from the way station and took off. The man who works the station said Avey shot the other two saddle horses in the corral so nobody could follow him. The guard also said Avey laughed at him while he beat him with his own gun. And he said as Avey rode away he yelled, I'd love to stay and chat, but I've got a score to settle!

So it's a sure bet he's going to show up here," Marshal Clark said.

He looked steadily at Toby. "That's why I said I don't want you going out without your gun; Avey's not far away. And now he knows that you're fast, and you're smart. You were fast and smart enough to ruin his gun hand the last time he faced you. He's sure as hell not going to give you a fair fight. I figure he'll try to get you the same way he got your pastor."

Tipping his head toward Walter, who stood next to him, Jess said, "Avey's not going to have such an easy time sneaking up on Toby's back as he did Pastor Windor's. There'll be two of us seeing to that."

Marshal Clark patted the holster that held the Colt Peacemaker on his hip and said, "Three."

Vance Avey stood behind the tree he'd chosen to shoot from. The choice was actually easy; in fact almost a sentimental one. It was the tree from behind which he'd killed the preacher. By now the word that he'd escaped had surely reached the shabby little excuse for a town; so it wouldn't take much of a ruckus to draw everybody out here. He didn't care who else showed up, as long as the kid who'd taken his thumb did. He intended to kill the kid; one way or another; the how didn't matter, not even a little bit.

Once Avey was squeezed in behind the big birch tree, he bent and pulled piles of dead leaves in around his feet to prevent any chance of his boots being spotted by someone riding in East Road from the direction of Sweetwater. He expected the kid that would be his target to come from town, but it would be a hell of a thing for some sod-buster to come up the road and catch sight of him. That damn kid was as good as dead; of that Vance Avey was sure and certain. He hadn't forgotten that the whole mess started because he took what looked like a piece-of-cake job killing the preacher for a big payday that he never got. All he did end up with was a gun hand that was as good as useless; and the chance that he'd never see another payday; big or small.

There were no Bleus left to pay, so the preacher's kid would pay; and pay with his life. Avey downed half a bottle of rye in one swig and leaned against the tree to wait.

When the rye had begun to spread its warmth from his gut, and helped to somewhat ease the throbbing in what remained of his left hand, he decided he'd waited long enough. He flexed the fingers of his left hand. It was a reflex action. His brain knew his thumb was gone, but his hand seemed to have a mind of its own. As soon as he thought of a gun, his hand started getting ready.

The right-handed belt and holster rig he'd picked up a couple weeks after the kid ruined his left hand was gone. He'd lost it when the bounty hunter blind-sided him in Arizona and he ended up in the town jail. After all the time he spent practicing with it, and getting pretty damn good; now it was probably on the hip of some twelve-dollar-a-month deputy sheriff in Prescott, or lost in a poker game.

So the one he now wore would have to do. It still had the blood from the stage coach guard's face on it; but that wouldn't keep a bullet from coming out of the barrel. If he had to draw down on somebody, his instincts would see him through. His reflexes were lightning fast, no matter which hand. You could take away a thumb, but you can't take away instinct.

And he'd learned the first time around that the damned kid wasn't somebody to be taken lightly. He wouldn't give the punk a chance this time.

Avey stood stone still and waited for near silence from town, and when it was so quiet he could hear birds chirping in the distance he fired three shots in the air. Then he did his best to melt into the trunk of the tree and become invisible. He hadn't forgotten the two men who'd confronted him on the other side of the creek. There was a chance they would arrive first. He would have to play it by ear when the time came; decide whether to try to hide from them if they did get there first and wait for the kid to show his face or try to deal with them first.

It didn't take long for his shots to get a response. In no more than half a minute he heard multiple hoof-beats in the distance growing close; fast.

It sounded like at least two or three riders coming his way; and wasting no time getting there. Avey turned sideways, trying hard to put the broad tree trunk between him and whoever was charging down the road toward him.

When the riders were close enough that the road dust they were kicking up was coming into sight Avey stuck his head out far enough to take a quick look; but hopefully not far enough to be a target. He could see at least four horses coming as well as one wagon.

While Avey's reflexes may have been quick in many respects, his jump- back-and- hide reflexes weren't nearly on a par with Jess Ivey's eagle-sharp hunter's eye. A roar crashed the still air and part of Vance Avey's red hair was painted a deep crimson color as the lower tip of his right earlobe disappeared.

Walter pulled his wagon to a stop beside where Jess had just reined his horse to a halt and said, "Not bad; you did that before you even stopped."

Several more horses pulled up to dirt-flinging stops behind Walter's big lumber wagon, mostly hidden from Avey's sight.

Knowing that hiding was now out of the question; Vance Avey stepped from behind the tree and defiantly bellowed, "All right, it's the damned kid I want! But I'll take on anybody that tries to get between me and him! I'll leave a whole row of you stupid yokels here in the dirt if that's the way you want it."

"Okay, how about me first; If you think you're man enough."

Vance Avey didn't recognize the voice, but when he got a look at the man who'd spoken he knew who it was, though he'd only seen him at a distance before.

Shepherd Sloan stepped from behind Walter's wagon into the open and faced Avey. He had his gun strapped on. When Avey just stared at him Shepherd said, "I said, how about me first? Or maybe I should move around to your left side so you can hear me. I t doesn't look like your right ear's in any too good'a shape."

Avey laughed. "I know you. I saw you when I was watching the town after old man Bleu hired me. You're the drunk. I saw you puking between your feet every morning. The kid sent *you* out to protect him from me?"

"Nobody sent me anywhere. I'm here because this town has had all of you we can stomach."

"And you're going to stop me?" Avey pointed in the direction of Shepherd's gun belt. "With that?"

Shepherd shrugged and said, "Stranger things have happened."

Avey sneered and said, "Not in this life."

"And in what life would you have thought a teenaged boy would blow your thumb off?"

Avey sounded shaken, "So; town drunk, do you think I'm scared of you? You're probably seeing three of me right now."

 Shepherd said, "That's okay; I'm really a very good shot. I'll aim at the one in the middle. If that's you, you're a dead man.

Avey laughed "This town doesn't have much to offer up against a real man.

First, a kid that's too soft to kill a man because he promised he wouldn't; and now a god-damned drunk!"

Then another man stepped from behind the wagon; the biggest man Vance Avey had ever seen. Not big in a way that didn't concern Avey; but big in an imposing way. Tall and broad shouldered; he strode forward in a very self-assured manor. He said, "How about me? I never made anybody any promises, and I'm not drunk. I haven't had a drink in days.

When the big man was twenty feet away Avey spotted the badge he wore.

 "Marshal, huh?"

The big man nodded. "Sure enough."

Avey stuttered for a moment, his throat choked with fear, and then he said, "I thought Marshals were supposed to be something special.

You expect me to draw against you with my off-hand after just a few weeks of practice, against you drawing with your regular gun hand? Is that the kind of fight U'S. Marshals call fair?"

Marshal Clark slowly, carefully reached across and took his gun from his holster with two fingers and stuck it in his belt on his left side.

Then he looked at Vance Avey and said, "Okay, all fair and square now; your off-hand against mine." Then he asked, "You going to draw Avey, or talk me to death?"

Avey froze, saying nothing.

The Marshal said, "This town, and the world in general has had enough of you. We're going to have this out here and now. My friend here," he added, shifting his eyes for just an instant to Shepherd Sloan; "will count to three. You can draw on two. I won't draw till three."

"I don't like it," Avey sputtered. "How do I know I can trust you?"

"You don't have a choice. It's the best deal you're going to get.

Count Shepherd!" the marshal ordered.

Shepherd Sloan shouted loud and clear; "One! Two!"

Vance Avey drew the Colt 45 that he'd taken from the injured stagecoach guard and fired off a shot that went wild; doing nothing but burying itself in the scarred side of Walter's lumber wagon. Avey thumbed back the hammer, preparing to fire again.

But, before the echo of Avey's shot had faded from the air; Shepherd Sloan shouted, "Three!"

Marshal Clark had his Colt out of his belt before Avey had a prayer of being ready to fire.

The Marshal's gun spoke only once; but once was all it took.

Vance Avey got a stunned expression on his face. His eyes grew almost impossibly wide, and his mouth dropped open in a big yawning O.

He gasped out one word, "No!" He then dropped the gun, and reaching up, stuck his index finger in the gaping hole in his chest as if needing to prove it was real. Then, shaking his head in utter disbelief Avey simply fell over; his head making a resounding thump against the tree on his way to the ground. Some of his long red hair stayed on the trunk, stuck in the bark, moving gently in the breeze; like a flag marking the tree where he had hidden to murder Landon Windor. Toby walked up to where Marshal Clark stood. He said, "I stayed back there out of sight, like you told me to."

The marshal put a ham-sized hand on Toby's shoulder and said, "I know you wanted to face Avey yourself, but take it from someone who's had to kill; it's a terrible thing. Even though it's part of my job, and even though men like Vance Avey need killin' in the worst kinda' way, it's still a terrible thing. When you know that the last breath a man drew before you put a bullet in him was the last breath he'll ever draw it kills a little bit of you too. Pastor Windor didn't want to see that part of you die.

"But you're the law."

"I've always looked at the law like I look at my gun. It's necessary, but I hope I don't have to use it."

Toby looked puzzled.

"I hope that people knowing that the law is there will make them think twice before doing something illegal. Vance Avey ignored the law more than once; and he ended up dying by the gun."

Walter asked, "Weren't you taking a hell of a chance, letting him fire on two, and you waiting till three. I mean even with him firing with his off hand, as you call it, that gave him a big jump on you."

"I knew Avey was a coward; and a scared man tends to get careless;

Avey got careless, and all he hit was your wagon."

Shepherd said, "That was a hell of a draw for your left hand."

Marshal Clark smiled and said, "I've always been ambidextrous."

Toby asked, "What's that mean?"

"It means I can write with either hand."

Shepherd snickered. "More than just write, I'd say."

"Just doing my job."

Walter gave Avey's body a shove with his foot and said, "What do we do with this?" He looked at Shepherd Sloan "What do you say, Pastor?"

"Can we haul him in your wagon?" Shepherd asked Walter.

"Yeah."

"Okay, it's really cold out. Wrap him in canvas and put him in the trees behind the cemetery. Cover him with rocks to keep the varmints off of him. We'll bury him when the ground thaws some.

"You gonna' say some words over him then?"

"I'll have to think on that," Shepherd said. "Just get him out of my sight."

Just as Walter and Jess were throwing Vance Avey's corpse on the back of Walter's wagon, Doc Forrest's buggy rolled up. Doc had the reins. Both Ben and Kate were on the bench seat next to him.

Kate said, "We heard the shooting from the store. I rode up to Doc's as fast as I could and told him."

Doc said, "I'd ask what's been happening, but I can see the only thing I really care about. He pointed to the pool of blood running from under the tailgate of Walter's wagon, warm enough to steam in the frigid air; where Vance Avey's hair could be seen moving in the breeze. Doc said, "Shepherd, as a man of God, I don't know if you believe in curses or not, but personally I believe that our town has had a curse lifted; we're rid of the Bleus and of Vance Avey."

Shepherd Sloan said, "Doctor, I concur with your conclusion."

Toby looked up at Marshal Clark and asked, "Just how tall are you??"

The marshal said, "Toby, somebody once asked President Lincoln how tall a man should be.

President Lincoln's answer was; tall enough for his feet to reach the ground.

What Mister Lincoln meant was; a man shouldn't be judged by his size."

Kate wrapped her arms around herself and shivered. "My God, it's getting cold."

Marshal Clark blew breath into his hands to warm them and started to walk toward his horse. I've got to go. I need to get to Sweetwater and send a wire to notify Carson City of Vance Avey's demise. I'll see you folks when I get the word about Toby's reward money.

Kate said, "It's a shame you can't stay the night."

"Why's that?"

"There'll be a full moon tonight. And it's hard to believe, but there's nothing much prettier to look at than the Whiskey Twist when it's frozen over and the moonlight's shining on it. Even a monster like that can be beautiful.

"They say beauty's in the eye of the beholder. I'll have to take your word for it for now. My visits here have made a lot of paperwork I've got to catch up on. But I'll come back soon, I promise."

After the Curse was Lifted

Marshal Clark visited again three weeks later and delivered Toby's bank draft for ten thousand dollars; his half of the bounty on Vance Avey, as requested by Randall, the kind-hearted bounty hunter who had captured Avey in Prescott, Arizona.

Being in the middle of winter by that time, he decided he couldn't refuse Kate's invitation to stay the night and get a look at the Whiskey Twist in the moonlight when it was frozen over.

Later; at the first sign of spring thaw Vance Avey's corpse was dragged, literally, to a hastily dug ditch behind the cemetery, a hundred yards away from the area where the town's residents were or would be, interred. He was buried in the same canvas he'd spent most of the winter wrapped in. Doc Forrest signed his death certificate, stating he would almost have been willing to pay the state for the pleasure of doing so. After a great deal of soul-searching Shepherd Sloan did say a few words over Avey's grave.

Three years to the day from the awful day Vance Avey murdered Pastor Windor, Shepherd Sloan had the honor of presiding over the dedication of the Pastor Landon Windor Memorial Chapel.

Everyone in town was in attendance. Even Marshal Clark was there.

The building sat beneath a canopy of tall shade trees next to Miss Agnes Water's schoolhouse.

The small chapel was beautifully designed by Luke Parker, who also served as foreman of the project; although still walking with a limp as a result of three toes lost to frostbite from his trip into the freezing water of Whiskey Creek at the hands of Napoleon Bleu Jr.

There was no shortage of volunteer labor for the project. People were standing in line to help.

The lumber for the project was provided by Walter and Mildred Denborough. When the congregation attended services, they would also be sitting on pews crafted by Luke out of lumber from the Denborough's sawmill.

Ben and Katelin Grayson made certain that nobody went hungry while working on the building. Thanks to Jess' unfailing Winchester the crew had plenty of meat to go with the vegetables and other foods that Ben and Kate provided.

The crowning moment of the building project was when Walter pulled his wagon up with the item special-ordered from Virginia City.

It took both Walter and Luther; the two biggest men in the town to muscle the crated-up object off the back of the wagon.

Walter said, "Wow, you sure this won't be too heavy?"

He was speaking to both Luke and Luther.

Luke shook his head. "No, there's no way I'd take a chance with this; it's too important. It'll be fine."

"Luther said, "Same here."

So they uncrated the big bell; ordered from Virginia City; shipped by rail and wagon; and most suitably of all; paid for by Toby Dove with the bounty money he received as a result of the capture of Vance Avey.

The two big men managed to get the heavy bell attached to the thick rope and with considerable effort pulled it up into the short bell-tower; only thirty feet tall; all that could fit beneath the trees. And as they promised, the tower Luke designed never creaked, and the pulley Luther created never squeaked.

The first ringing of the bell came at the conclusion of the ceremony.

A lot of prayers were said and a lot of tears were shed in honor of Pastor Windor.

Shepherd Sloan said, "What are you thinking about, Toby?

"I wonder what my parents would say if they were here."

"I don't know it all, but I'm sure it would start with, "We're proud of you."

After the ceremony everyone went home feeling like the town now seemed complete.

The end